W9-BEM-442

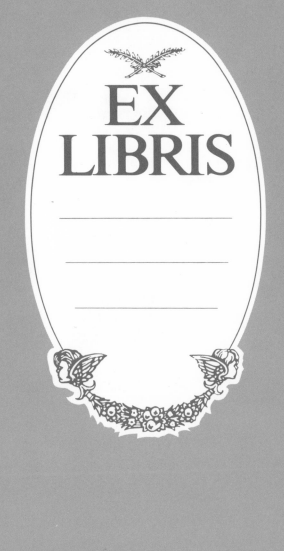

EX
LIBRIS

Romance Treasury

THE ROMANCE TREASURY ASSOCIATION

NEW YORK · TORONTO · LONDON

These stories were originally published as follows:

LAIRD OF GAELA
Copyright © 1973 by Mary Wibberley
First published by Mills & Boon Limited in 1973

GOLDEN HARVEST
Copyright © 1973 by Stella Frances Nel
First published by Mills & Boon Limited in 1973

ROCKS UNDER SHINING WATER
Copyright © 1973 by Jane Donnelly
First published by Mills & Boon Limited in 1973

ROMANCE TREASURY is published by
The Romance Treasury Association, Stratford, Ontario, Canada

Editorial Board: A. W. Boon, Judith Burgess, Alice E. Johnson
and Ilene Burgess

Dust Jacket Art by Will Davies
Story Illustrations by Muriel Hughes
Book Design by Charles Kadin
Printed by Alger Press, Oshawa, Ontario and
bound by T. H. Best Printing Co. Ltd., Don Mills, Ontario

ISBN 0-373-04038-5

Printed in Canada   A038

CONTENTS

Laird
of
Gaela
Mary Wibberley

The scars caused by the crash had gradually disappeared—except one. The one inside, that was a constant reminder of her rejection by the man she loved.

On Gaela, the Hebridean island where her cousin, who requested her help, wrote mysteries, Tara felt she would be safe from taunting eyes and speculation. But en route she met Jago Black, who showed little sympathy for her self-pity.

Who was this domineering, secret man, who had loomed suddenly out of the dark misty night, taking more than a passing interest in her? He frightened her and stirred within her a sensation of being overwhelmed by a force she could not control.

CHAPTER ONE

TARA DIDN'T SEE THE MAN. It was difficult to see anything, for the mist had descended suddenly, and this, combined with the darkness, made an effective blanket to deaden both sight and sound. A boat horn blared distantly, and she shivered. There had been a lost lonely tone about it that echoed her own mood.

She shrugged irritably and turned to look out from the quay. But there was nothing to see, only gray swirling ribbons of mist that swerved and curled down to the black oily water only feet away. If she should trip or stumble. . . . Tara took a step back, and the sudden movement jarred her leg so that she winced. She immediately recalled the incident on the train from Inverness when she had stumbled against a suitcase jutting out into the center aisle. Two youths had sniggered, and a man had been watching and seen what had happened. That had upset Tara more than the youths' muffled guffaws—for they were somewhat drunk and didn't really count. But the man . . . he had such an odd expression in his eyes, almost as if he *knew*. Tara had reddened and turned quickly away to find her seat. But the man's face had remained in her mind for a while afterward, despite her attempts to read the magazines she had bought.

The slap of water on stone brought her back to the dank and dismal present. There would surely be no ferry to Gaela that night, and the sooner she booked a room at the hotel the better. Even on a damp January night there could be other travelers, and there was no other inn for several miles. She turned; a figure loomed up out of the mist, as she felt her treacherous left leg let her down, felt the shoe slither helplessly on greasy stone. Then a man's hands were on her arms pulling her to safety, and a man's voice—almost amused—was saying, "I don't think you'd enjoy a swim in that—not tonight anyway." And Tara knew who he was even before she looked up.

She had never heard him speak before—there had been no need for words on the train—but the voice matched the face, and as she looked up into the man's eyes, she instinctively tried to pull herself free, her hand going to her cheek in a defensive gesture of protection lest he see the scar.

"I was all right. I wasn't going t-to . . . ." To her horror she found herself beginning to stammer.

"Looked like it to me, and I didn't fancy waiting until I had to jump in, you see?" No doubt about it, he was amused.

Tara felt her temper flare, but manners fought a brief battle with it, enabling her to murmur, "Thank you."

"You're welcome. The ferry to Gaela stopped running a couple of hours ago, by the way."

They were on the stone road now to the inn. Tara stopped. "How did you know . . . ?" she began, puzzled.

"Why else would you be looking out at this time? It is the only ferry to leave from here, isn't it? I want to get on it myself, but no go. Where are your cases?"

"I left them in the station waiting room while I went to see—"

"All right, I'll get them. You want to wait here or in the pub?"

"Just a minute, Mr., er . . . ."

"Black. Jago Black, Miss . . . ?" There was an inquiring, polite tilt to the head she couldn't quite see clearly—also that air of suppressed amusement she found quite intolerable.

"Mr. Black, I'm quite capable of getting my own cases." She had no intention of telling him her name.

But if he thought she was a cripple . . . . One thing she could not abide was pity.

"I'm sure you are. But I'd hurry if I were you. There are only three bedrooms at the pub. I've got one, and there was an American couple asking about showers when I booked, so . . . ." He shrugged. Tara softened slightly. Maybe he was only trying to be polite. It was just that it was difficult to accept that a man, any man, could want to help her simply out of good manners and not from some misguided effort at gallantry.

Swallowing her pride, which was an effort, she said, "Thanks for telling me. I'll be there in a moment. Goodbye." She turned and left him outside the mist-shrouded inn and walked on toward the station around the corner. She was aware that he remained standing there watching her before the mist swallowed him and the building, and Tara made an intense effort not to let the limp show. She was very conscious of it, which didn't help, and she felt an unreasonable surge of resentment that he should have been witness to her humiliation on the train. To a man like him it had meant nothing. He spoke in a completely assured manner; he walked casually and confidently. What could he know of her agonies and doubts? Of the effort it had cost her to come alone so far to stay with her mother's cousin, Lalla Baxter, the one person who didn't feel sorry for her, who treated her as normal, not some freak who had not only been badly hurt in a crash but had been jilted as a result of that accident—just before the wedding.

Tara picked up her two heavy cases from the waiting room. Gaslight hissed softly, casting a soothing green yellow light all around her as she went back to the door, and heartbreak, like a tangible pain, halted her step so that she stood there for a few moments before going on. It had been eight months ago almost to the day, but the awful nagging hurt was as real as ever, and she wondered what David was doing now. Her parents had said she was better off without him if he could do what he had done . . . but they didn't understand. They tried, but they really didn't know. Lalla did, however, and she had made one of her rare visits to England from her Hebridean home for the sole purpose of cheering her niece up after the crash. And now Tara was going to stay with her for a couple of months, because Lalla needed assistance with a book—Tara could type well—and because Tara's mother, in desperation, had asked for her cousin's help. This last fact was unknown to Tara. Out of the blue had come Lalla's letter, begging her to come and visit and take pity on a poor middle-aged writer who couldn't cope.

It seemed like the ideal solution. The doctor had been pleased that she wanted to go away; Tara's mother, too, had been pleased—apparently surprised as well—and had even fooled her daughter, who perhaps because of her new bitterness had a sharp awareness of other people's intentions and was not easily deceived.

And now she was here. But not quite. Gaela was only six miles away, but it might have been the other side of the world, because of all the mist that effectively sealed it off from the mainland. And Lalla would be waiting and would guess that Tara would put up at the inn. It was no use phoning, she knew. The island's only telephone was in a booth outside the village post office, and whoever answered it would have to walk three miles to Lalla's house with the message.

Tara smiled reluctantly as she opened the waiting-room door. Her mother had been horrified when Lalla had first told her of the telephone situation. "But, my dear," she had protested, "what on earth do you do when you want to call anyone?"

"Walk to the village with a pile of pennies clutched in my hot little hand," had been Lalla's descriptive reply.

"And don't you see, it means I can't be pestered by my agent. If he gets angry, at least I can get on with my writing in peace."

She was near the hotel now. The cases were too heavy. She should have accepted the man's offer to .... *No,* she told herself fiercely. *Be independent. You'll have to learn some time. It might as well be now.* But she had to put them down on the smooth mist-dampened cobblestones for a few moments. The doctors had said it would be a year before her strength fully returned. They hadn't said anything about the limp, except vague murmurings of, "It'll go in time." *They* didn't know how it felt to be just that much slower than everyone else, so that it was necessary to try harder. Tara gritted her teeth and picked up the cases again. She pushed open the door of the inn and was met by a blast of hot air. There was no sign of the man, for which she was profoundly thankful. There was no sign of anybody. . . .

She caught a glimpse of the pale ghost of a girl and moved slightly, startled, then realized it was a mirror, and that thin blond creature in the dark coat was herself. Curious, she moved nearer to the glass, leaving the cases by the door. The shadows danced around her, the light from an oil lamp standing in the thick wooden bar wavery and yellow. What had he thought, her reluctant rescuer? Had he noticed the scar as well? But she hadn't seen that flash of pity in his eyes that she had grown so used to looking for. She reached up her hand and ran a forefinger down it, a thin silver thread around the curve of her jaw. It was all that was left after the plastic surgeon had done his work, but it was enough to remind her, every single time she saw her face, that it had been enough to drive David from her—David the perfectionist, who had tried to hide the mingled pity and horror on his face every time he came to visit her in that quiet hospital room. And in the end she had sent him away.

He wouldn't take the ring—the price of his conscience, perhaps—so Tara had given it to the Oxfam shop, to do someone some good. . . .

"Good evening. Can I help you?"

She heard the voice and turned to see a small thin man, presumably the innkeeper, standing by a door with a look of polite inquiry on his face.

"Oh, yes. Do you have a room, please?"

He nodded slightly. "There is just one. You have come from the train?" His accent was the soft familiar one she knew well from previous visits, so long, long ago . . . .

"Yes. The ferry to Gaela isn't running, is it?" She had to hear it again, even if she already knew the answer.

"Ach no, it is stopped these few hours past. But no doubt the morning will be fine again. Eh . . . these will be your cases?"

"Yes. Thank you." He picked them up, and Tara followed him, up the twisting stairs that led off from the side of the bar and along a narrow passage. He stopped and pushed open a creaky door, which revealed a small, bleakly furnished room. The bed looked warm though, and almost as if reading her mind, the man said, "My wife will put the bottles in for you. Eh, you'll be wishing to eat, no doubt?"

"Please." She was starving. *It must be the air*, she thought. She hadn't felt so hungry for months.

"Aye well, there will be dinner in the dining room. I will away now." And he was gone, melting away like a shadow and pulling the door shut after him. It creaked again, and she winced.

From nearby came the sound of running water and a man whistling, quietly but clearly, some pop tune that was annoyingly elusive. On a sudden impulse, Tara went to the wall and pressed her ear to it. The sounds were instantly magnified, so the washbowl must be on the other side of that thin partition. She wondered if it was the American or the man who called himself . . . what was his name? Jango? She frowned. No, that wasn't it. Jago, yes. What a weird name—Jago Black. A weird name for a strange, unnerving man. She shivered. He would probably be eating, too, sitting near her in what was probably only a small dining room—watching her—seeing her face. She fought down the feeling of sickness that rose in her throat. It didn't matter. It mustn't matter. He was a stranger, and she would not see him again after tomorrow. But there she was wrong.

Nearly twenty minutes passed before Tara pulled herself together sufficiently to go downstairs. During that time she had unpacked her nightie, being careful not to disturb the other contents of her suitcase, and had brushed her silky blond hair in such a fashion that if she held her head a certain way the ends hid the scar. Then after a quick dab of lipstick she had gone to the stairwell and had paused for a moment, hearing the quiet sounds of the small hotel—a faint creak as a board moved in a floor somewhere, the distant clatter of crockery, and, more distant still, a dog's deep-throated bark.

Gripping the curving handrail tightly, Tara made her way down. She wore the gray pantsuit in which she had traveled from home. Her hair was fine and silky, and the red satin scarf at her neck contrasted vividly with its soft gold. And her face, though slightly pale with the fatigue of the journey, was as beautiful as it had ever been, if only she knew it—delicately molded, her fine high cheekbones and widely set brown eyes softly feminine as was the rich full mouth beneath the small straight nose. Once her eyes had been full of laughter, but now they were clouded with the bitterness she felt. Bitterness of rejection by the man she had loved, the man she thought had loved her. It had been a long time she'd spent in the hospital, five months in all, and David had not been there to see her when she finally came out, with all scars healed, except one. And she had another deep hurt, but that was inside, and couldn't be seen by anybody.

There were some locals in the bar, talking among themselves, and the voices became hushed as she paused again at the foot of the stairs, wondering which way to go.

"Would it be the dining room you are looking for?" one red-cheeked fisherman took his pipe from his mouth to ask her. You didn't often see beauty like that in Kirkgarron, and it would be interesting to see if the voice matched the face.

"Yes, please." She could still smile, and did. The fisherman saw that faint strip of white on her chin and wondered . . . . "Aye, well. 'Tis that door away to your left, miss." He nodded as she thanked him and began to walk in the direction his pipe was pointing.

The dining room was as small as she had feared, with one large table to seat eight, in the center. Four places were set, but only one man sat there—her reluctant rescuer, as Tara had dubbed him. He was concentrating on his soup and didn't see her at first. She touched the chair across from him, ready to pull it out, and he looked up. Their eyes met briefly, and Tara received a distinct shock. She had not seen him properly before, either on the train or outside in the mist. But now she did. Her first absurd thought was, *I don't like him!* But it was not because of the way he looked or acted, it was an intangible sensation of being overwhelmed by some force stronger than she had ever met before.

He stood up politely, then sat down again as she did, giving a brief nod toward the other chairs and saying, "The Americans have gone out to take photos."

His words were so unbelievable that Tara managed to

forget the awful self-consciousness his presence aroused in her. "D-did you say photos . . . in *this*?"

There was no doubt about it, he seemed vastly amused by something. His smile transformed that strong attractive face so that she took a deep breath, dismayed. She didn't like him, but she had to admit that he was a fascinating-looking man.

"Yes. Maybe I looked as surprised too, when they told me, because the man explained. They've got a camera that does everything except take X-ray photos, as far as I can make out. I saw it. Come to think of it I wouldn't be surprised if it took those, too. It's got flash attachments, infrared lights, an extension lens—just about everything. Must weigh a ton. They think this li'l ole weather's got such a fantastic atmosphere about it"—his voice had slid effortlessly into such an American twang at the last few words that Tara smiled reluctantly—"that they decided to go for a walk and take some pictures." He broke a crusty roll in half thoughtfully, while a plump red-cheeked woman walked in with Tara's soup. After she had gone he added, "That might prove interesting when they get home and have them developed."

She looked up from her soup, puzzled. "Why?"

A crooked grin flashed briefly. "They might see things they didn't see when they took the photos."

"Oh!" She bent quickly to her plate again, feeling a warm tide of color rise from her throat. She was a fool to have asked! Tara closed her eyes, wishing she were anywhere but there—with him. Her spoon felt enormous, and she wondered if he were watching her drink her soup. Her appetite had suddenly gone. How would she manage the next half hour or so? She wished that the Americans would come in from wherever they were, and take away some of the intolerable strain she felt just being in the presence of this man.

Then, mercifully, a diversion came. The plump woman came in again carrying a tray full of dishes. In the following minutes, while plates and cutlery were being exchanged, Tara was able to gulp down her soup. She was also able to watch the man Jago unobserved. He was looking up at the landlady, asking her something about how late the bar would be open. . . .

He was very dark, his hair long enough to touch the collar of the tartan shirt he wore under a chunky gray sweater. His mouth was wide with that smile, the lower lip slightly thicker, slightly jutting above a strong square chin. His eyes were dark brown and thickly lashed, imperceptibly slanted under thick brows that met in the middle above a nose that at one time looked as though it had lost an argument with a door, for there was an elusive, faintly battered look about it. Tara dragged her eyes quickly away as he half turned again. The whole effect was undeniably attractive in a strong virile way, and yet—no, she was mistaken—his hands were not those of a fighter. They were clean and tanned, the fingers long and well shaped, with short straight nails, speaking of a sedentary job. Not a man who lived by his hands. . . .

Tara realized that the woman was speaking to her and looked up. "I'm sorry?" she said, flustered.

The woman smiled reassuringly. "Will I take your plate, miss?"

"Oh, thank you."

A few minutes later the door from the bar opened, and the two Americans, young, energetic, and tanned, came in exuding instant friendliness and noise.

Soon afterward Tara was able to make her escape, leaving them talking to Jago Black about the state of American roads compared to British ones. In her room she leaned against the door and heaved a sigh of relief. At last she could relax. Jago had made a determined effort to draw Tara into the conversation, but she had politely avoided being involved. She didn't want to talk to anyone, didn't want to meet strangers who frightened her because they looked like they were afraid of nothing. She moved restlessly away from the door and sat on the bed. It was eight o'clock. She should phone her mother soon, and then go to bed, for it had been a long tiring journey from her home in Cheshire. She was feeling more tired than she usually did because of what had happened, and the strain of having to talk to him. . . .

There was a sharp rap on the door, and Tara swung her feet to the floor before calling, "Come in." She thought, *It must be the landlady with a lovely hot water bottle to warm the bed.* But then her hand touched a warm patch at roughly the place where her feet would go; the door opened, and the subject of her thoughts came in.

"Oh!" Tara gasped in astonishment and dismay.

Jago Black smiled, gave a brief incisive glance around, taking everything in, and said, "Sorry if I disturbed you. I wondered if you'd like to come for a drink in the bar?"

"For a drink?" She could only repeat it foolishly.

"Yes. With the Americans and me."

"I . . . no . . . thank you." Her fingers clutched the tartan coverlet convulsively. "I'm going to bed soon."

He cocked one thick, black, disbelieving eyebrow. "At eight? It's a bit early, isn't it?"

Tara swallowed. What did one have to do to get rid of a man like him? And why had he asked her to go for a drink? Was he feeling sorry for her? Quickly she answered. "I've been traveling for hours, and I'm really tired." She wanted to get up, to make him leave the room, but was unable to move. It was as though something held her back, as if she didn't want to walk closer to him, to let him see. . . .

"Aren't we all?" He shrugged. "However, if you're really decided . . . ." He looked around, and his expression clearly conveyed what he thought of people who preferred poky hotel rooms to warmth and drinks. "I won't push it. I don't stay where I'm not wanted." Then he added softly, "As we're going to be neighbors, it seemed the neighborly thing to do."

Something in the way he said it stung Tara. Almost insolent, his tone implied that he hadn't really expected her to accept. She retorted, "Don't you mean you were doing your good deed for the day? Well, you've done it, you asked. Now you can go and enjoy your drink with a clear conscience." She didn't know what had made her say the sarcastic bitter words, only that he looked like such an assured, supremely confident man that nothing could ever touch him, and she had had the absurd urge to try.

There was a brief silence, then he looked at her slowly, his glance traveling from head to toe and back. Hard brown eyes held hers in a glance of pure steel.

"Tell me," he asked softly, "are you always so sorry for yourself?"

She stood up and went toward him, demanding angrily, "How dare you!" She stopped then, because he showed no sign of retreating. "Please go . . . now." Tears sprang to her eyes—tears of tiredness and the weakness she still felt.

"I'm going, don't worry." He turned on his heel, and paused with his hand on the door. "Good night, sleep well." Then he was gone, and the door shut firmly behind him. Horribly shaken, Tara collapsed on the bed again. What an awful man! She remembered something he had said, "as we're going to be neighbors . . . ." *What an odd thing*, she thought. As if staying in the same hotel in adjoining rooms had any significance! She was to remember his words again soon afterward, and know their true meaning—and she would be even more puzzled.

Wearily she lay back, and saw his face again, as it had been just before he left. She shivered. Strangely enough, she had been almost frightened, almost scared of a perfect stranger who meant nothing to her. But deep down she knew her reaction was because of what had happened, first on the train, then at the slippery quayside, and Tara turned her head from side to side in despair. Would she, she wondered, ever forget the humiliation?

TARA STOOD on the quayside again. It was nearly eight-thirty, and the night had gone, taking the damp fog with it and leaving a fine drizzling rain that was rapidly soaking into her warm dark coat. There was nobody else in sight except a boy on a bike, whistling tunelessly as he delivered papers. Overhead a gull wheeled, shrieking, and Tara shivered with the cold. What a way to begin her stay! There was one consolation. She hadn't seen Jago Black at all, and the boat was coming nearer over calm rain-spattered water, with black smoke rising from its brave red funnel.

In a few more minutes she would be aboard. The prospect was infinitely attractive. There was a tiny cabin on the boat providing shelter, and Tara would sit in it, safe and warm. She would watch Kirkgarron recede, and feel a sense of freedom. . . .

Nearer and nearer the ferry came, and now she saw the pilot, a huge Scot resplendent in shiny oilskin and sou'wester, standing at the wheel. She looked around for one last reassuring sight of the hotel, and everything was silent. Then she saw the front door open, saw a tall dark figure step out, heard shouted farewells. She turned away, closing her eyes in sudden despair. "Oh, no!" she whispered. It was him—who else would it be? He seemed to be following her, almost like a shadow. Resignedly she looked out over the water, the fine rain beading her face and making it damp and cold. Another half hour at least they would have to spend together in the tiny cabin, with nowhere to look except out of the windows or at each other. With a quick movement, Tara felt in her purse for the magazine she had put there at the end of her train journey. She would have to hide behind that. It would be better than nothing, and yet he would guess what she was doing, and there would be that half amused look again.

"Good morning." The voice came from behind her, and she had to turn to answer him.

"Good morning." He wore a hooded anorak of dark blue, and black trousers. The only luggage he carried was a blue carryall which looked precariously full. *Good!* Although it seemed incredible, he must have come only for the day. Tara's face must have showed some slight expression of relief, for she heard a soft laugh and looked sharply at the man. But his face was innocent of anything except a pleasant, studied blankness.

"Boat's nearly here," he remarked. "You missed a good time in the bar last night."

"Really?" She half turned away, to let him know she had no intention of continuing the conversation. "I'm glad you enjoyed it." It was an effort to speak to him, and she watched the boat bump against the old car tires that lined the jetty, then bump again. The pilot came out and fastened his rope almost immediately.

"Ye'll away on board," he called, "and I'll be back the moment." He stumped off toward the post office, which nestled against the hotel.

He had grinned at Jago Black—Tara had seen it—as if he knew him. She bit her lip, and then, as a hand came on her arm, stiffened.

"What—" she began.

"I'm getting wet. Do you want to get on board or not?"

"Yes, but—"

"Go on. I'll throw your cases on after you." To Tara's horror, she was swung up and over the side and onto the slippery deck of the boat. Before she had time to think about it, her cases followed her, skidding slightly on the wet deck and coming to rest against the cabin steps. Jago Black landed lightly beside her, and Tara quickly bent to pick up her cases before he offered again. She took them down the three steps and stowed them beside the door.

The rain had grown heavier. It drummed on the cabin roof, and the windows were salt-encrusted and translucent as she had remembered them. The seat that ran all the way around in a horseshoe shape was shiny and hard, but the trip wouldn't be long.

Tara glanced discreetly at the man who was settling himself down, unzipping his anorak, pulling a paper from his pocket. A gentle sigh escaped her. So he didn't feel like talking either. Perhaps he'd got the message at last. Tara sat facing him, wondering if anyone else would come. She lifted the magazine from her bag and began to read. At least she tried to, but something was disturbing her concentration, and she found her eyes going over the same advertisement again and again. At last she looked up briefly—to see Jago Black's eyes on her.

She took a deep breath and felt herself blush. Quickly she looked down again, but the words on the page danced crazily to the rhythm of her heartbeats. She swallowed hard.

"Sorry. Did you think I was staring?" He had an uncanny ability to read thoughts!

"Yes. Weren't you?" she answered shortly, only

stopping herself by an effort from adding, "I wish you'd go away!"

She had to look up at him, and somehow the most maddening thing about him was his expression. He shook his head. Those brown eyes were even darker in the shadowy confines of the small cabin, and his face was stronger. He smiled slowly, and his teeth were very white against the darkness of his features.

"I was trying to do the crossword," he tapped his newspaper carelessly. "Yesterday's, but it's still annoying me. Are you any good at them?"

She was torn between a blunt refusal and the honest curiosity roused in her by the question. She had done a lot of crossword puzzles while she was in the hospital, and the habit had stuck, so that now she usually managed to finish the daily paper crossword in ten minutes.

Weakly, knowing she shouldn't, she said, "What are you stuck on?" He looked down, and she wasn't sure if she had imagined the slight grin before his face vanished.

"Here . . . I wish they had a light in this darned boat . . . 'Stringy feline's bed.' It's two words of four and—"

"Cat's cradle?"

"What?" he looked down at the paper, then accusingly at Tara. "You've already done it!" he said.

"No," she shook her head. "Honestly I haven't. Sometimes they just come like that."

He shook his head wonderingly. "Amazing! You know, I've been looking at that for ages." He handed her the paper. "Just take a look at two down, will you? I'm damned if I can see what it is."

Too late she realized what was happening. Even as she lifted the paper to see the clue in what little light came from the windows, he moved across the cabin and sat beside her. Tara froze instantly, her face showing her feelings. He didn't seem to notice, but fumbled in his anorak pocket. "Ah, that's it." He produced a pen, and just then they heard the deep rumble of engines. A light flickered overhead once or twice, then came on fully, making her blink after the dimness. The cabin lurched and jerked as the boat swung around. Tara felt herself sliding sideways helplessly with the sudden movement, and put her arm out in an attempt to steady herself. Jago Black's hand came across her waist, pulling her back toward him as the boat lurched again, then settled itself, so that the only sensation of motion was the deep throbbing of the motors behind them.

With an abrupt, jerky movement, she put her hand to her waist and took hold of his fingers. "Take . . . take your hands off me!" she breathed. Immediately he did so and moved slightly away. Then he looked at her.

"Did you think I was going to try and seduce you? I'd have a job in here, wouldn't I?" He gave a short laugh. "I thought you were going to slide off on to the floor, and with—" he stopped, too suddenly. Tara knew what he had been about to say.

"With my bad leg, you mean—the one that lets me down? You don't need to be so tactful, Mr. Black. It would be difficult for you not to have noticed, wouldn't it?" She felt as if she were choking, and her hands tightened helplessly.

He said softly, "Why are you so bitter about it? It's not very noticeable—"

"Please!" She turned sideways so that she was facing him. "Please spare me the platitudes. What do *you* know? What does it have to do with you?" She swept the soft blond hair back from her face and pointed to the scar, which was whiter now, she knew, because of the anger making her cheeks pink. "Take a good look here as well while you're at it, then you won't need to pretend about that."

Instead of looking away, he did just as she told him, leaning nearer and looking closely at the thin silver line traced along her jawline. Angrily she let her hair fall back, nearly choking again. "Satisfied?" she managed to say with great effort.

"It'll fade in time," he answered.

"Will it? I suppose you're an expert on these things. That's what they said . . . but they don't have to live with it, do they? Nor do you."

"You make it worse for yourself, you know," he remarked. "Is that why you wouldn't come down to the bar last night?"

The helpless anger refused to go away. If only she didn't feel so weak, she would be better able to defend herself against this subtle attack, this cunning wearing away of all her shreds of confidence. She answered sharply, "Can't you just take 'no' for an answer? Do I h-have to h-have a reason?" She held her hands tightly together on her lap. The newspaper lay on the seat between them. She wanted to hand it to him, to tell him to take it and leave her alone. If only she didn't feel so completely helpless. If only. . . .

"No, of course not. But you're fighting all the time, aren't you? No one's fighting you, so why don't you relax and—"

"Shut up! Leave me alone!" Tears glinted in her eyes as she swung on him. Tension pulsated in the air of the tiny compartment, and he looked at her, his strong face full of a gentle concern that filled her with sudden overwhelming anger. Tara's breast heaved. Who was he? She hated him, she knew that. Hated him for seeing through her disguise and for daring to speak about it. That was the worst thing, hearing the words and not being able to fight them.

And then he did something very surprising. He reached out his hand and touched the scar.

"Just listen to me a minute," he said. Tara knocked his hand away with a sudden desperate movement and stood up.

"Don't ever t-touch me again," she whispered. "How dare you!"

He stood up too and they faced each other, the cabin bristling with electricity as if a live current was between them. His eyes held hers, lit by a black flame that threatened to consume her. She was frightened by what she saw. A muscle tightened in his cheek, his chin jutted dangerously. "Let's see," he said softly, and taking her completely by surprise, pulled her into his arms and kissed her.

Too stunned to pull away for a few moments, Tara found herself relaxing against a strong hard body. Then realizing what was happening she pulled herself free with a desperate effort and gave him a stinging slap on his face. She turned, hand to mouth, and stumbled up the steps to the slippery deck.

She clutched the rail, and the rain washed away the taste of that kiss. She found she was trembling as she saw Gaela loom darkly out of the rainy mist, and a sob rose in her throat. Why had he done it? What madness had possessed him? She had seen his face in that instant before he had held her, and in it had been a strange and puzzling look. Not of pity, or anything like it, but of something she could not—did not want to recognize.

Gray dots resolved themselves into houses, and the pilot, thinking no doubt that the crazy English passenger had come on deck to see the sights, obliged with, "Yonder is Gaela, miss. Eh, you'll be staying there awhile?"

"Yes, for awhile." She would have to go down for her purse and suitcases, but she didn't want to go yet. *Let him come up first.* She hoped, childishly, that she had hurt him. She had put all her strength into that slap, but he had scarcely moved. It was almost as if he had expected the blow.

She saw a small lone figure swathed in raincoat and sou'wester, and a laugh struggled with a sob. She waved and the figure waved back, and a faint cry came floating over the water. She was nearly there, and then she would be able to forget him.

Minutes later the boat bumped against the wooden jetty and the pilot lassooed a post with the skill born of years at sea.

"I'll get my cases," Tara shouted, and turned back, bumping right into the man who had silently come up behind her. Then something terrible happened. As she moved past him, she heard Lalla cry with astonishment, "Jago! Why didn't you tell me?" Tara turned again, not believing her ears.

Jago Black was leaning over the side shaking her aunt's hand and saying, "I wasn't sure if I could get away. It's nice to see you again."

The next few minutes Tara spent paying her fare, transferring her luggage over the side, being assisted ashore by the helpful pilot, and greeting her aunt, who had Jago standing at her other side. Lalla looked at Tara, her face beaming. "You've already met. Isn't it lovely! Tara, this is Jago Black. Jago, my cousin's daughter, Tara Blaine . . . . "

And Jago, his face showing nothing except polite blankness, held out his right hand and said, "How d'you do?" But his left hand went to his cheek to stroke it momentarily, and Tara could barely look at him. Uppermost in her mind was the thought, *They're like old friends!*

There was worse to come. But she didn't find out until she reached Lalla's house.

CHAPTER TWO

LALLA PAID Hamish, the driver, after he carried Tara's cases into the large, comfortable living room. She shut the door after him, and they heard the rumble of the ancient taxi—the island's one and only—as he started up and went back along the road to the village. They both knew he would be whistling, for he rarely stopped, and Lalla smiled. "I've had more comfortable rides, but at least he's always there when you want him." She patted the couch. "Sit down, Tara. I'll put the kettle on for coffee. I've pulled this up close to the fire for you—what a perfect pig of a day, isn't it?—and then you must tell me all about your journey, and meeting Jago."

She was halfway along the passage that led to the kitchen before she finished talking, and Tara smiled. She didn't obey her aunt's instructions, but followed her out to the kitchen, and watched her fill the kettle and lift down the cookie box. Lalla would never change. She looked the same now as she always had, small and wiry, and dressed in a blue pantsuit, with her hair a little grayer but still swept back because it had a natural curl she hated. She had a beaky nose and a strong chin, and would be the first to admit that she was not a beauty. But she had attributes infinitely more important: a kind and generous nature, devastating wit, and a realistic approach to life that was very reassuring. Tara shook her head now, bemused as ever that from the pen of this small, middle-aged woman tripped fast-moving thrillers that had kept thousands on the edges of their seats for the past ten years or more. The name Damien Corbett stayed comfortably in the center of the best-seller lists, and none of the readers knew that the adventures of the full-blooded, sexy heroes had actually come from the imagination of a woman. "It's lovely to be here again," Tara said, leaning in the doorway, and beginning to relax after the strain and tension of the last few days.

"Lovely to have you, but you know that already. And I have so much work for you to do . . . . You might change your mind in a day or so when I get you at it."

Tara laughed. "I doubt it. I'll be glad to get started again . . . and you know, I'd love to be able to actually read a Damien Corbett without buying or borrowing it."

"Idiot!" Lalla turned from the cupboards where she was setting out cups and plates. "You'll be disappointed. It's not half as interesting in handwriting. Anyway," she pursed her mouth, "never mind work! What about you meeting Jago? What a surprise to see you both getting off that old boat! You could have knocked me down with a feather."

Tara moved uneasily. What on earth could she say about him? "Yes," she admitted slowly, "you did look astonished." *And so was I*, she added inwardly, *stunned would be more like it*. But Lalla's next words were even more of a blow.

Oblivious of Tara's strained expression, she went on, "It's even more of a surprise to me because I'm putting him in this new book. He doesn't know, of course—that would be fatal—but with him living next door, I'll be able to—" she stopped at Tara's gasp of sheer horror. "What on earth is it? Are you ill?"

"D-did you say next door?" Her mouth could barely frame the question.

"Why, yes! He's not here often, of course. Comes, oh, I would say every three or four months for a few weeks and then vanishes. Oddly enough, he was here just before Christmas . . . . Tara, what is it?"

Tara shook her head. "It's terrible. I didn't think I'd see him after today . . . oh dear! Oh, Lalla, he's awful . . . when I . . . we . . . saw you . . . I'd just slapped his face!" She blurted the words out, unable to keep the dreadful truth in any longer, and she wasn't prepared for Lalla's reaction. The older woman dropped the cookie jar lid with a clatter and whirled around, her face lit with an impish smile. "How priceless! What on earth had he done? Tell me, I'm all agog!"

HALF AN HOUR LATER they were both sitting by the fire. Empty coffee cups and a plate with just one cookie rested on the hearth as Tara wriggled her toes and stretched again. The story had been told, and now she felt much better.

"I thought you'd have known he lived near here at any rate when I offered him a lift in the taxi," Lalla remarked as she lit another cigarette and threw the match into the heart of the flames.

"I suppose it didn't register. I was still getting over the first shock," Tara admitted ruefully. "Lalla, what is he exactly? I'm a bit . . . well, you know, frightened of him. I can't explain it, but he makes me . . . w-worse in a way, I suppose."

"Mmm, yes? Do you know, I haven't a clue myself," Lalla confessed. "All I know is that he appeared about three years ago, right out of the blue, moved in next door, and asked me if I knew of a cleaning woman. So I told him about Morag, and she's looked after him ever since, when he comes. That's why I was so surprised to see him. He usually writes to her a few days before he comes so that she can clean and air the place . . . and she tells me, of course. In fact," she added thoughtfully, "if anyone knows anything about him, it'll be her. She's a dear woman, but the most incredibly nosy creature I've ever met!"

They both laughed, but Tara's laughter was tinged with dismay. There was something else she had to ask.

"He . . . when he's here, what does he do? Er . . . do you see a lot of him?"

Lalla gave Tara her shrewd look. "You don't fool me with that innocent air, my girl. What you mean is, will you see much of him when he's here?"

"I suppose I do," admitted Tara ruefully. "You're too clever!"

"Well, actually, I hate to say it, but it's virtually open house when he's here. Of course he knows I write every morning without fail, and he wouldn't dream of coming in then, but . . . well," she chuckled, "he fascinates me, and I encourage him like crazy. He's a most interesting talker, and we often go on for hours, arguing about this and that, and putting the world to rights . . . you know."

Tara's heart sank. "But how come you've never found out about him? I mean, people do talk about themselves, don't they? And as you know him so well . . . ." she bit her lip.

"He just said once that he had a very demanding job, and that when he comes here, it's to relax completely. I took the hint. You would have, wouldn't you?"

Tara nodded. "Yes." She gave a little shiver. "There's something very . . . mysterious about a man like him, though."

"I know, my dear. Why do you think I've got him as the main character in this new book? It's something completely new for me. Not a thriller, I'm having a rest from those . . . . It's going to be a family saga, spanning several generations, with dozens of characters and lots of things happening. I'm itching to get on with it, and seeing him here again unexpectedly . . . well, that's a bonus, I can tell you."

Tara was silent. Dismay filled her at the thought of Lalla using him as a character in a book. She didn't understand why, but she resented the idea very much. Jago Black had refused Lalla's offer of a lift in the taxi.

He had said that he had some shopping to do, and that he had to see Morag, the woman who cleaned for him, but Tara knew that part of his reason for refusing was connected with her. A sudden lost sensation encompassed her. She had come up here to escape . . . but from what? Would she ever be able to escape from herself?

She looked down at her hands, clasped tightly together on her lap. She had begun to relax before, but since they had started talking about Jago, some of the tension had come back. She must try, she knew, to relax here, and become normal—or as normal as she would ever be again—for if she didn't manage to, what was there in the future?

"Oh, Lalla," she said softly, "help me." The words were a soft murmur, a plea from the heart, but Lalla heard and put a hand around Tara's shoulder.

"I will, my dear. Truly I will . . . you'll see." But her kind eyes were troubled.

TARA'S BEDROOM was at the back of the large cottage and looked toward the higher ground leading up to the center of the island. The landscape was bleak, lonely, wild, and heart-stirringly beautiful. Tara didn't know what it was about the place that always affected her so much. She had been to visit only twice before, the most recent being four years ago when she was sixteen. But the memories had stayed vividly with her throughout the time between, and she knew instinctively why her aunt was able to write there better than anywhere else. She sat on the deep window embrasure and looked out. Lunch was over, her clothes were almost all unpacked, and she was having a rest for a few minutes, for she tired easily.

Tara ran her hand along the window frame. The window was open, and the bright yellow curtains stirred slightly at her side. The rain had stopped at last, and a wintry sun struggled through the clouds. There was always the sound of water from the spring that spilled down the mountain and grew in strength as it neared the house and the shed, where the dynamo whirred permanently, supplying Lalla with the electricity she needed. She had had the machinery installed when she had bought the house, more than ten years previously. She had made other improvements, too, having central heating put in as well as the open fireplace in the living room; even in the coldest, bleakest winter, there was warmth and hot water. One of the four bedrooms was her writing room, with desk, chair, typewriter and the piles of exercise books that she used at fantastic speed. The house was furnished well and comfortably, and as Tara looked around her she suddenly remembered the house next door, separated only by a thin walkway. She had been in there on her last visit, when it had been empty, and had been stunned by the contrast between it and Lalla's. The walls had been crudely plastered, discolored by years of peat smoke, the rooms dank and gloomy.

Tara looked over at Jago Black's back garden, and wondered if he had done much to the cottage since buying it—how long?—four years ago. It had had no electricity either, and someone had left an oil lamp on a rickety table by the window. That, and a chair, had been the only items of furniture left.

Later Tara asked her aunt about it. "Has he had electricity put in next door?"

Lalla shook her head as she pushed her chair slightly back from the table. "No. I did ask him when he first came, but he said he preferred to use the lamps. I must say I thought it a bit odd myself. I mean, it would be the first thing I'd think of, how about you?"

Tara nodded thoughtfully. "Yes. What's it like inside? His house, I mean?"

Lalla smiled. "He'll show you around if you ask him . . . no, I was only joking, child, don't look so dismayed. Quite pleasant, actually. A bit bare for my taste, but then men aren't so bothered about those little touches we find essential. He's got a fitted carpet—red, I think—good furniture, some quite old, and lots of books. There are books all over the place. It's a wonder they don't get damp in winter when he's not here. In fact I told him as much, and ever since he's had Morag light a fire every few days when she comes here. And that's all. He seems like a man of simple tastes, I would think, but very interesting all the same."

"Mmm." Tara wasn't committing herself to an opinion. "He must have bought it through the lawyers you dealt with in Inverness."

Lalla lifted her eyebrows. "You know, I suppose he must have! I never thought about that. He just arrived one day, introduced himself, and spent the next couple of weeks supervising the arrival of his things from the mainland. Both these houses, and a few others in the village, originally belonged to Angus Cameron, the old laird, who died just before I moved here. I suppose the lawyers must have advertised Jago's cottage and he bought it." She sighed. "You know, you've got me curious again. I must ask him in and try some discreet pumping!"

"Don't you dare!" Yet Tara was only slightly reassured by the gleam in her aunt's eye as she spoke. She knew her too well, and tried to change the subject. She wasn't sure anyway why she should be so curious about Jago Black. The less she had to do with him the better. "You mentioned the old laird who died. Was he the one who lived in the Big House?"

"That's the one." Lalla sighed. "That would make a story all right!" She filled her cup from the coffee pot and pointed to Tara's, who shook her head. "That beautiful old house just moldering away . . . it's painful to think of it."

"I know. I walked up there when I came last time," Tara said. "There was something ghostly and sort of pathetic about the place. It's enormous, isn't it?"

"Yes. About fifteen bedrooms, as well as the usual entertaining rooms downstairs. And a portait gallery round the landing . . . ."

Portraits? Something, an elusively faint memory, was stirring in Tara's brain, and then was gone as her aunt continued, "And a conservatory that's overgrown with weeds."

"It's a wonder the windows haven't all been broken," said Tara, "or have they by now?"

Lalla shook her head. "No. There are no vandals on Gaela, thank the Lord! It'll stay like that until it's sold, or molders away from age."

Tara shivered, suddenly sad. Inside her was born the determination to go again to the old Big House before her visit ended, for something, buried deep inside her mind, was puzzling her, but she couldn't for the life of her think what it was.

THE NEXT DAY was Sunday, and Tara was woken by her aunt drawing back the curtains with a flourish to let in clear, watery sunlight.

"Good morning! Did you sleep well?" she asked brightly.

Tara groaned and tried to sit up. " 'Morning, Lalla. Oh! I must have slept like a log. I feel as if I've been unconscious for *hours*."

Lalla laughed. "That's the Gaela air. It has that effect at first. You'll soon get used to it, and it's good for you anyway."

"I'm sure it is." Tara saw the cup of tea steaming gently on her bedside chair. "Oh, you're an angel!"

"I know, dear. It's just to wake you up. We're going to church."

"Oh! But . . . I . . . ." Tara began, that old familiar panicky feeling rising inside her at the thought of meeting people.

"No buts, you'll enjoy it, honestly! We have a traveling preacher, name of MacMurdo, from the mainland once every three weeks, and he's a darling! A bit of the old hellfire and brimstone school, but everybody goes when he's there. They call him the missionary, by the way, so don't go getting confused and thinking you're in darkest Africa!"

She went out, leaving Tara to drink her tea in peace.

Tara knew what Lalla was doing and, strangely, she didn't mind. With her mother, and other well meaning relatives and friends, attempts to 'bring her out of herself' had tended to make Tara retreat more into her shell, but about Lalla there was something so irrepressibly right that she found herself looking forward, almost, to listening to the missionary.

An hour later they were dressed and ready to walk to the church, which was about two miles down the road toward the village. Tara looked ruefully down at her feet, clad in a pair of Wellingtons. There was no such thing as dressing up for church on Sunday on Gaela. The road was too rough for shoes, and, as there was always the possibility of rain, both wore old mackintoshes over their coats and sou'westers on their heads. Tara smiled at her aunt. "And I brought all my nice clothes," she said in mock dismay.

Lalla laughed. "There'll be time to wear them later. You'd ruin decent shoes on this road, and it'll likely rain before long. Right? All ready? Good. Let's go," and she closed the door firmly behind them. They walked past Jago Black's cottage, still and silent as if he was sleeping, and past the thick clumps of pines that bordered the road on either side.

"Now tell me if I go too fast for you," Lalla said, "and I'll slow down." There were no tactful hints with Lalla, no embarrassed sidelong glances at Tara's weaker leg. Tara didn't mind at all.

"I will," she assured her. "But I can walk okay without getting tired. It's just sometimes, if I turn suddenly. . . ."

"I know," Lalla nodded. "I think you'll find walking is good exercise. I find it so, anyway. I wouldn't have a car if you *paid* me. Of course, I can't drive . . . ." and her laugh was so infectious that Tara had to join in.

They had both sobered before reaching the small corrugated iron building that was Gaela's only church. It was ugly on the outside, and not much better on the inside, with plain benches set in rows on either side of a center aisle, and a dark painted table at the front. Tara glanced curiously around as the islanders filed in, their faces rapt and pious. It was hard to believe what Lalla had told her on the way, that it was for them one of the biggest social occasions of the month, that a lot of surreptitious gossiping was done before, during, and after the service, and that it was the practice of the congregation to pass around "sweeties," usually mints, to suck during the duller parts of the service.

So fascinated was she that she wasn't aware of the man sitting down on the bench in front of her aunt or of their whispered voices until she felt a slight nudge in her ribs from Lalla. Then she looked, and stiffened in shock. Jago Black was sitting there as large as life, dressed in his blue parka, with Wellingtons pulled up over his black trousers. She froze as he looked around, perhaps sensing her eyes on him, and was barely able to answer his brief greeting. Then she saw her aunt's apologetic grimace as if to say: "I didn't know, honestly." Tara looked around, wondering why he had sat in front of them. But there was no other room, so he had had no choice. Lalla waited until his attention was claimed by an elderly islander in front of him and whispered, "I've never seen him here before."

"No?" Tara whispered. She hadn't expected to see him either, and if she had known . . . . Her thoughts were interrupted by shuffling and coughing, and the entire congregation stood up at the entry of the missionary, a tall gaunt man with burning eyes and a wild shock of gray hair. He started off the service by thumping the table loudly and asking if any of them had seen the devil that week. Tara felt an approving murmur run around the people gathered.

Lalla nudged her. "He's in good form today," she whispered. "You'll see."

And indeed he was. Coughing and whispering ceased as if by magic, and only the faint scents of drying macs and peppermints arose as sixty or more jaws sucked silently and raptly on their "sweeties." But Tara didn't concentrate on the missionary as much as she should have. Instead her eyes seemed to be on Jago. Of course he was in direct line between her and Mr. MacMurdo, but even so, she was slightly annoyed with herself for finding that she was looking so frequently at him. She didn't want to, and yet. . . . The hood of his anorak was down, and his hair grew very thick and straight and almost black. She could see his profile clearly—a strong outline that showed strength and character, especially in that stubborn cleft chin. And he had kissed her. . . . Tara turned warm, then cold, because she knew he hadn't done it for the normal reasons that a man kisses a woman. It had been almost as if he had been conducting a cold-blooded experiment. Her lips tightened angrily at the thought. The utter arrogance of the man! She was glad now she had hit him, although earlier she had regretted her impulsive act. *He deserved it, didn't he?* she asked herself, but there was no answer, only her quickened heartbeat and breathing as she relived those few startling moments.

And there came another memory, perhaps even more startling. He had said something in her hotel room about them being neighbors. She hadn't understood it then, but now, looking back, it seemed to have been astonishingly prophetic. Had he known who she was? But how could he have?

Tara stole a quick glance at Lalla as the preacher's words thundered around them. The older woman's face was rapt, intent, as everyone else's was except possibly Tara's, who had more urgent thoughts churning inside her. Had Lalla known he would be coming? No, she had been genuinely surprised and pleased when she had seen him beside Tara on the ferry from the mainland. What then? Tara looked down at her lap, trying desperately to concentrate on the missionary's words. He was now on the evils of drink and dancing, and one or two feet were being shuffled a little uneasily. And Jago . . . what did he think about all this? Had he come because he had heard it was good entertainment? Tara couldn't see him as a man who would attend church, but she did not know him, not at all. And it was at that moment, with sinking heart, that she realized that in all probability they would have him as company on the journey home.

THE RAIN STARTED when they were a few hundred yards from home, not gently, but with a sudden roar and bucketing fury that was as strong as it was unexpected. After the first gasping surprise they all started to run, and the already muddy road had become a brown quagmire in seconds. Huge drops bounced upward from the slippery brown mud beneath their feet. Tara felt herself skidding, then with a gasp righted herself. Lalla was slightly ahead, laughing, and hadn't seen her. But Jago must have, for he slowed down and reached back to grab Tara's hand with his own. For a second she resisted. Then helplessly, unable to thwart that firm grip, she let her fingers curl around those stronger brown ones. She was caught up in his flight—her own legs surer now—and not afraid of falling. The pain was there, but she ignored it, and out of the sheets of water surrounding them in almost solid walls, she saw the houses emerge. Lalla had taken one swift look back, called out something that the rain had drowned out, and had gone on.

A stone was hidden in the mud of the road, and Tara trod on it. New pain shot up her left leg immediately so that she cried out.

Jago slowed, turned, saw the icy whiteness of her face and said "What is it? We're nearly there . . . just a few yards more."

"Then go on . . . I c-can't. . . ." Tara tried to pull her hand free. Let him go, if he didn't like to get wet. Lalla was already nearly home.

"Don't be an idiot." Without slackening his hold, he exchanged hands, so that his left one was free to go behind her back, around her waist, holding her, supporting her. . . .

"I said let me go!" The pain made her voice ragged, and the tears that had come with it mingled with the heavy raindrops.

But he didn't let her go. The sharp spear of agony moved up the center of her leg, which gave way beneath her. Tara felt herself going down. She would have fallen, but instead she was lifted and held in a pair of strong hard arms. He had to slow his flight and walk, and she turned in her struggle to be free, saw his face, and cried, "Why?"

"You little fool! Did you think I'd leave you there in the middle of the road?"

"Yes," she panted. He pushed open the gate with an impatient foot, and they saw the wide open porch door. Lalla had vanished.

"Thanks," his tone was dry, but Tara didn't care. "You deserve to be dropped, right now, in the nearest puddle." And he laughed. Tara hated him, and she didn't know why, except that he made her feel so weak and helpless that it was unnerving.

The porch was wide and dark and full of old mackintoshes and Wellingtons and brooms. He put her down and wiped his hand across his wet face. As Tara involuntarily backed up, he said softly, "Don't worry, I'm not going to kiss you again. Once was enough."

"Oh!" she turned away, but couldn't walk. She had to stand there, as if glued to the cold damp floor. She saw him move and said, "Leave me, please."

"What is it? Your leg? Give me your arm—" he began.

"I don't need . . . I don't need. . . ." She shook her head helplessly, and the tears of pain ran freely down her cheeks, no longer hidden by rain.

"Help? I think you do," he said quietly. "But you have a remarkably stubborn streak for one so young."

Lalla would come out in a moment. She *must* come. Tara bent to rub her knee, and heard the door open. She thought it was Lalla, but as she looked up she realized Jago had gone. Then, miraculously, the locked muscles were free, and she went slowly in, relief making her face glow.

Jago stood in the passage doorway, and was calling something to an invisible Lalla, for Tara heard her murmured reply. He stopped abruptly at Tara's entrance, turned to face her, and nodded.

"I see you made it at last," he remarked. "Good."

Then he turned again. "Look, I won't stay for a cup of—"

"Yes, you will!" was the other's faint but indignant answer. "Good gracious, of course. You can have lunch if you like."

Tara waited and listened to them, wondering as she watched Jago if she was imagining things. No, she wasn't, she decided suddenly, seeing the darkly amused expression on his face. Just then, when he turned toward her, it was as though he had been laughing at something. Laughing at her. He had found the fact that she had been unable to move extremely amusing. His next actions confirmed it. He came back into the living room, unzipped his anorak and hung it neatly by the door on one of the pegs. He looked at Tara's sodden mac as she struggled out of it, then at her face; and he grinned just before he turned away to go back to the kitchen. There had been nothing nice about the grin; it had expressed his thoughts quite clearly: *Don't expect an offer of help from me.* Tara gritted her teeth and managed to pull her arm out of its sleeve. Damn his arrogance! She would show him. She would!

But that was easier said than done. He stayed, of course. Tara had known he would, and he was pleasant and charming. And yet . . . and yet there was that indefinable something in his manner when he spoke to Tara, something she couldn't place or explain, a quality almost of cool secret amusement that made her uneasy. Whether Lalla noticed or not, she said nothing, but it seemed to Tara that she occasionally looked at him oddly as if wondering what there was that was different about him.

It put Tara on edge. She exerted herself to appear completely confident, managing almost to forget that silver thread-like scar that had helped to change her life.

After lunch was over Lalla pushed her chair away

from the table, surveying the remains of the roast chicken and a few lonely potatoes. "Ugh! Washing dishes should be abolished," she said. "We'll do it later. . . ." as Jago stood and began to stack plates. "No, Jago, leave them. Come and sit by the fire and tell us what you're doing here again so soon. Not that I'm complaining," she added hastily, as she eased herself into the comfortable armchair beside the roaring fire. "I'm delighted, of course. But I didn't expect you for several weeks at the very least."

He sat down on the couch, and after a moment's hesitation, Tara followed. It was either that or remain at the table, and that, she imagined, would delight him. It meant she was between him and Lalla, and she wondered fleetingly if he had deliberately placed himself so that she had to sit on his left, and he had to look across her at her aunt. She could feel his nearness quite strongly. The couch was technically a three-seater, but he sat nearer the center than the end, and was only inches away from her. He made her feel small, and she moved uncomfortably as he answered Lalla in his deep pleasant voice. He was a soft-spoken man, but his voice carried as if he were used to talking and being listened to. He wore a different sweater, a thinner dark gray one with a white shirt underneath, and his long legs were stretched out indolently, almost as if he were used to being there. He had taken off his Wellingtons and had left them on the porch, and there was a small hole in the toe of one of his socks. Tara smiled inwardly at this evidence of imperfection. His voice intruded into her pleasant reverie: "I might not be able to be here as long this time, but I needed to get away."

Because he had annoyed her so much that she couldn't resist, Tara asked, "From what?" She looked at him as she spoke, and smiled to let him see that the question was an innocent one.

Those brown eyes turned to her in sudden challenge. "From my work," he answered.

"Yes, but what is it?" she persisted.

He shrugged. "A lot of things. You could call me a . . . " he seemed to hesitate, but it was so momentary that it might have been her imagination, " . . . a teacher."

"Oh." It wasn't what she had expected.

Lalla broke in, "Jago, how interesting. Why didn't you tell me before?"

He grinned at her aunt, and Tara noticed his teeth. They were strong and white, and one had a very small chip missing.

"It's something I like to forget about when I'm here. Not because I don't enjoy my work, but because I'm under such intense pressure that I can only relax when I put it out of my mind." He turned to smile at Tara, and quite suddenly she knew he was lying. It might have been something in his eyes, a sudden darkening of that sherry brown. They dared her to ask more, but Tara didn't accept the challenge. She couldn't. Jago was too near, much too near, for comfort. She looked toward her aunt for rescue, and Lalla rose to the occasion, quite literally. She stood up.

"You know, I forgot about the coffee, she said. "I'll go and make it now." And she walked out, leaving Tara wishing, quite absurdly, that she were anywhere else but where she was.

Jago said softly, "Set your mind at rest, did I?"

"I . . . what do you mean?" She had to turn to answer him, but it wasn't easy.

"That I'm not a convict on the run."

She tried a casual laugh. It didn't quite succeed. "Heavens! How silly! As if I would think. . . . " She faltered, for his eyes really were quite fascinating. Such long lashes—not too long, of course, but thick as well, and the whites of his eyes were very clear. She could see tiny flecks of black in the brown of the irises. She swallowed hard. For a moment she had felt as if he were about to hypnotize her.

Pulling her scattered wits together, she managed to look away, saw his feet, and blurted out, "You've got a hole in your sock!"

They might have been talking about footwear for hours, so little surprise did he show. He wriggled the offending foot. "Yes, I know. When they get too bad I throw them away."

"That's wasteful."

"Isn't it? But it's my one extravagance. What's yours?"

Tara stiffened and moved away a few inches, the limit of her freedom. Just who did he think he was anyway? He was insufferable, impertinent, and without any finesse at all. She had never met anyone like him. She clasped her hands, and he looked at them and said, "Why don't you relax? Or don't you like being asked personal questions?" And, without waiting for her answer, he went on, "Because if you don't, you should try and remember not to ask them." And now he was openly laughing at her.

"Oh! You . . . you. . . ." Tara turned on him angrily. "I could . . . c-could. . . ."

"Hit me?" His mouth quirked. "You already did. Once." And he smiled slowly. "But I really wouldn't advise you to try it again. You'll just have to learn to control your temper."

"I don't need lecturing by you, even if you are a teacher." She said it in a way that implied her doubts. "And I had a right—you shouldn't have kissed me!"

"True." He shook his head slowly. "It was a sudden impulse." His voice dropped into a cockney whine. "I just don't know what came over me." He had the accent dead on, as he had had with the Americans, but Tara was in no mood to be amused.

She said sharply, "You ought to get your impulses under control if that's where they lead you. Men who go around kissing strange women can get themselves into a lot of trouble. And you should know that, *if* you're a teacher."

Jago scratched his ear thoughtfully. "Do I detect a certain tone of disbelief in your voice? Are you trying to tell me something?"

Now was the moment when she should tread carefully, but Tara was too mad to care. "Yes. I don't think you're a teacher at all!"

She felt almost lightheaded, but she didn't like the look on his face—a hard, shrewd glance that seemed to bore into her as he asked quietly, "Then what do you think I am?"

"I don't know. I just think you're not prepared to tell anyone, for reasons of your own."

"But you asked. You wanted to know."

"It . . . it was just for something to say." But she faltered. Damn the man! He smiled a crooked smile.

"No," he said softly. "I don't think it was. You thought it would get me angry if you asked. Why? Had your aunt told you I wouldn't talk about my work?"

Where was Lalla? Coffee didn't take this long, surely? Tara started to get up, but it took her several moments, her leg being as it was, and she was pulled down quite firmly as Jago, with one hand still at her waist, said, "Now, let's not run away. I just asked you something."

"I was going to see about the—"

"Coffee? Yes, I'm sure," he finished for her. "But I'm also sure Lalla can manage admirably without you, and why should you want to get me mad?"

"Because . . . because you're an arrogant beast!" she burst out, and pushed his hand away from her waist.

Such a strong hand, long-fingered, firm . . . and as impudent as the rest of him. "And keep your hands off me!"

"You didn't say that when you nearly fell in the water at Kirkgarron," he commented.

"I wouldn't have nearly fallen in if you hadn't loomed up out of the darkness like some Jack the Ripper," she shot back. It was odd, really, that their exchange was having an almost exhilarating effect on her. Her cheeks tingled with warmth, a fire lit by that inscrutable glow in his brown eyes. She felt alive, vibrant— something that had not happened for many long months. She would not, she positively would not let him have the last word, and she wondered if he ever lost his air of cool amusement. *It would*, reflected Tara, *be almost interesting to see. Almost, for I don't really care.*

He began to laugh, genuinely delighted. "That's quite descriptive—Jack the Ripper. I must remember that. I thought it was your leg that let you down. What have you done to it?"

Shocked, she met his eyes. "W-why d-do. . . ." She stammered helplessly, stunned at his bluntness.

But he wasn't finished. "You've been in an accident, haven't you? Is that why you're always trying to hide the scar?"

With a wordless cry of anguish, Tara tried to struggle to her feet, but he held her again and said quickly, "Tell me. Talk about it. It will help."

Eyes blazing, she turned on him. "It won't. You know nothing. Don't tell me. . . ." her breast heaved with emotion; and she felt as if she had gone white, drained of all color with the shock of his crude, violent, unforgiveable words. But he had not finished, not even now, seeing her and knowing the effect of what he said. In a low urgent voice he went on, "I *am* telling you now. You've allowed yourself to sink into a condition of self-pity because of what you think are outstanding deformities.

But they're not. That's scar's nearly invisible. You could cover it with special make-up and I guarantee not even your closest friend would be able to tell. And your leg—"

"Stop it. Stop it!" she breathed, and her hands went up to fight him away. He anticipated her move, and two steel bands closed around her wrists as they reached his face. Desperately she struggled to free herself, but she was no match for him. Even if she had been fully well, she would have been as weak as a kitten compared to that hard muscular strength. But she had to try.

"Don't, please don't, Tara," he said, and he wasn't laughing any more.

"Let me go!"

"If you promise not to hit me." Those brown eyes gleamed.

"No, I won't . . . I hate you!"

The struggle was very one-sided. With him, it was almost as if—Tara couldn't even put it into words, but it was as if he were a spectator, watching what was going on. There was something terribly impersonal about him as he effortlessly held her, not only with those steely fingers, but with his eyes . . . those eyes . . . such a color . . . so. . . .

Tara realized that she was no longer struggling. Quite suddenly she was still. Her breathing was shallow and ragged, and gently, very gently, he eased her hands down so that they rested in her lap. Then he released her.

"All right?"

"No. You're awful," she whispered. The fire had gone, but she didn't know why.

A distant clatter of cups broke the spell. The door opened and Lalla came in with a tray. Jago went over to take the tray from her, and the waters closed over that small but significant incident. The ripples vanished as Lalla proceeded with the age-old ritual of dispensing coffee. Tara watched Jago as he knelt on the fireside rug, holding a cup steady. His profile was sharply etched against the background of glowing coals. Tara wondered at her temerity, but she could not, would not, let him speak to her as he had. Who did he think he was? She no longer knew. She was getting more puzzled and frightened every time she saw him. Some deeply feminine instinct warned her that he was a man of great power. She didn't like him, and wanted as little as possible to do with him, but that, she knew, was a vain hope, for Lalla liked him and he was her welcome guest whenever he chose to come. Suddenly Tara had a tingle of anticipation. What would he be like, this character based on Jago in Lalla's book? She knew that it would be interesting to see, very interesting. The thought was puzzling to her, and vaguely disturbing.

CHAPTER THREE

THE NEXT COUPLE of days were spent settling in. On Tuesday morning Morag was due to come, but before she arrived Lalla and Tara spent an hour preparing the second living room at the front of the house for Tara to type in.

They moved a table over to the window, and Lalla brought the typewriter down from her own study. "There," she said. "I won't be needing that for awhile. I tend to spread myself out a bit when I'm doing the first draft of a novel, you know." Tara smiled, remembering the shock her first sight of Lalla's study years before had given her. Pens, pencils, erasers and sheets of paper had been spread out in apparent disorder, but Lalla, oddly enough, knew where everything was.

"Can I just get everything straight?" Tara asked her now. "I type a good copy of this," she tapped the bulging loose-leaf folder on the table, "and you want two carbons. What if I have any queries?"

"Mmm, yes. I mustn't be disturbed, dear. I suggest you have a quick look through the manuscript before I start my morning's work. You should have a good idea from that whether it'll be straightforward. And don't forget, Tara love, I'm not expecting you to race through, you know. If you type ten pages today, I'll be satisfied."

"I'll start now." Tara sat down and opened the book carefully. Half a dozen sheets fluttered to the carpet, and she looked up. They both burst out laughing together.

"Oh dear," Lalla admitted, "I'm afraid I couldn't get them all in. Still, I'm sure. . . ." her voice tailed away.

"I'll manage. Of course I will." Tara smiled. "I can't wait really . . . honestly. Go on. I'll skim through the first twenty pages or so, and let you know of any problems before you're too engrossed in your other epic."

"And I'll make coffee!" Lalla clapped her hands as if she had just had a brilliant idea, then she went out. For a moment Tara gazed in front of her, unseeing. With her aunt's departure, the memories of Sunday came back to haunt her. She wondered, not for the first time, if Lalla had known that she and Jago were arguing, and if she had deliberately kept out of the way. It seemed probable. She had been gone a long time, and there had been an odd expression in her eyes when she returned. Tara bit her lip and bent to look at Lalla's sprawling handwriting. What did it matter? He had kept out of the way since Sunday. *At least he has some decency*, she thought wryly. Tara had seen him only once. The previous night when she had opened her window she had seen him come striding down the hill, a dark shape nimbly moving over stones and clumps of heather as if he knew every inch of the way. Tara, hiding behind the curtains, had watched him. He could have been coming from the direction of the Big House, which she thought was odd, for she could think of no reason for him to be there. Short of asking him, she would never know; and she had no intention of doing *that!* She smiled reluctantly to herself and began to read the manuscript at last.

Morag arrived before Lalla went upstairs to begin her new book. Tara heard voices from the other room as she read the first pages of the manuscript, and it seemed to her that something was wrong. Something in Lalla's voice gave that impression, and Tara put the bulky papers down and listened. A minute later Lalla came in, closing the door quietly behind her. She gave Tara a little smile. "Slight hitch," she whispered. "Morag's had to bring her granddaughter Fiona with her. Her daughter-in-law, the girl's mother, is ill or something . . . and I . . .

we wondered if you could possibly keep an eye on her while Morag does upstairs."

As Tara stood up and said, "Of course I will! I can read in there . . . ." Lalla added,

"She's not quite normal. I mean, you really have to watch her. She's a beautiful little girl . . . a terrible tragedy, but . . . well, you'll see what I mean. Come and meet them."

Curious and not a little disturbed, Tara followed her out of the quiet warm room and into the main living room. A thin wiry woman with gray hair stood there holding the hand of a girl about seven. The girl was small, with bright blue eyes and beautiful features, sadly marred by an expression of blank defiance—and something else.

The woman spoke. "Mr. Black said you had a visitor when I was there just." She smiled at Tara shyly, showing strong yellow teeth, and Tara went forward to shake her hand.

Morag turned to Lalla, "I am sorry indeed to have to bring Fiona today, miss, but my son's wife is ill with the one she is expecting, and cannot do with her." She turned to Tara. "She is not all here, you see, miss, and flies into terrible tempers. It is the Lord's will, we know, but it is more than her mother can manage at a time like this."

Tara heard the words, but they scarcely registered, so shocked was she at the way Morag spoke. It was almost as if the girl were not there. Fiona, however, showed no response. Her eyes were fixed on the carpet and she stood passively. Tara's heart went out to her with a surge of emotion she knew she would never be able to put into words. She forced a cheerful smile.

"I'll look after her, of course, Mrs. . . . ?"

"McWhirter, but I would be obliged to be called Morag, for no one here on Gaela calls me by the other."

"All right, Morag. Thank you."

Lalla appeared greatly relieved. "There now, you can do the bedrooms first, Morag. Tara, bring the papers in. You might be able to skim through while you and Fiona are in here." She turned and went toward the stairs with Morag in tow, and Tara was left with Fiona. The girl hadn't moved from where her grandmother had left her, but her eyes flickered upward as Tara went to get the manuscript. Tara caught the look and faltered in her step. *What had been there? Suffering?* She closed her eyes for a second, then she went quickly out and came back with the papers, which she put on the table. She went over to the girl and gently touched her arm.

"Would you like to sit down, Fiona?" she said slowly and clearly.

Fiona's arm was thin under the blue sweater she wore, and she flinched at Tara's touch. Very slowly she looked up, and Tara got the full force of her painful expression. She drew her breath in sharply at the sudden anger she saw there, and for a second felt sorrow. She had never met a child like this before, and mingled with her instinctive sympathy was a feeling of utter helplessness.

She did not know what so soon was going to happen. She could not foresee the shock that in a strange way would be instrumental in changing both her and Fiona's lives. All Tara knew was that she was in that bright, warm, normal living room, with a little girl who could not speak and who appeared to have a smoldering temper.

From upstairs the faint whirr of a vacuum cleaner somehow intensified the atmosphere in that room. Tara went to the table and picked up the manuscript. She looked at Fiona, who was now watching her, and smiled. "I'm going to sit down," she said. "Why don't you? See . . . on the couch beside me." Tara sat down and with studied carelessness opened the book and began to read. It was difficult to concentrate, however, and the words didn't make sense. She persevered. Perhaps it was best to ignore the girl, but Tara knew, even as she thought it, that she couldn't.

With a sigh she patted the cushion beside her, and said, "Come on, Fiona, it's warmer here." At the same moment there was a sharp knock on the outer door, and Jago walked in.

What happened next had a dreamlike quality, and afterward Tara couldn't remember the exact sequence of events. Certain incidents in life are, in a way, timeless. You can suddenly think about them years afterward, and it is as though they just happened, because they have an immediacy that can dispel the time barrier. Thus it would be for Tara with what happened next. She would always feel again the same sense of horrified amazement and the urge to cry out. . . .

Jago came in, looked at Tara and Fiona, and said without preamble, "I know you've got work to do. I'll mind Fiona at my house if you like."

"Oh, but I don't think. . . ." strangely surprised, she got to her feet, and saw Fiona's hands go up to her face as the girl began to cry softly in a horrible, strangled way. Tara looked quickly at Jago. He was watching the girl with that same abstract expression she had noticed before.

Quickly she said, "Can't we do—"

He interrupted her. "No. Leave her to me. Don't—"

Then Fiona turned around, and before either of them could guess what was in her mind, she reached out and swept several of the small glass ornaments off the mantelpiece. They shattered on the stone hearth and lay there twinkling in the light, while Fiona looked up with an expression of satisfaction on her face.

Before Tara could move, Jago strode forward, picked

the girl up and shook her. With a shocked exclamation, Tara moved forward to stop him, but Jago, without turning around, said, "Leave it. Stay *there*."

She froze in her tracks. There had been something in his voice that she could not, dared not disobey even though she didn't know why. She watched in horrified fascination as Jago put Fiona down and knelt in front of her, holding the thin arms tightly as he began to speak. The little girl's face had turned white with shock. Tara, freed from the fear that held her, started to move until she heard his words which were strangely familiar.

Jago spoke loudly and clearly, and each word was emphatic. "Fiona, I can help you. *I can help you.*" He touched his chest and then the girl's very gently. Tara could only see his profile, and she watched with fascination. There was *something*—some intensity—that was communicating itself to the girl, who now stood very still as if listening. A strange sensation began to fill Tara; she could not have moved if she had wanted to.

Her eyes saw Fiona's face lose some of its pinched sullen look as she very slowly nodded. Jago stood up, still holding her, and turned to face Tara. Perspiration ran down his forehead, as if it were very hot or as if he had been running.

"I'm glad you didn't interrupt," he said. "I had to know something, and now I think I do. I want you to help me. Will you?"

Tara nodded. "Yes."

"Good. Then listen carefully. I met Fiona for the first time about an hour ago. Morag says she's simple . . . a 'daftie' was her way of putting it . . . but I don't agree. I saw a glimmer of something. I think she's suffering from deafness, and I'm going to try to prove it. Is there a bell here, or something that will make a loud noise?"

Tara thought rapidly. "No, not a bell. I can't think of anything. . . ."

"Then will you do something?" He was not looking at Fiona as he spoke, but continued to hold her gently.

"I want you, in a few minutes when I give you a signal, to go behind Fiona and clap your hands as loudly as possible. Twice. That's all. First though, will you bring her a drink from the kitchen? Anything will do—water, milk, orange juice."

"Yes." She went straight out, too dazed by what had happened to think straight, let alone argue.

When she came back with a cup half full of milk, Jago was sitting on the couch and Fiona was standing in front of him. He took the cup from Tara and handed it to the girl. "Drink that," he said, and smiled. She took it obediently and began to drink, and with his face turned so that Fiona couldn't see his lips he said very quietly "Now, Tara."

She went behind Fiona, and, close to the child's head, clapped her hands loudly. The report echoed around the room like a gunshot, but Fiona never even blinked. Jago stood up and looked at Tara. "Well?" he said.

She swallowed. "It's possible. But it doesn't. . . ."

"It doesn't prove anything, or even if that's all that's wrong with her, but it could be. I'm going to see Morag. Where is she?"

"Upstairs doing the bedrooms. Shall I go . . . ?"

"No, stay here with Fiona." He went out quietly and shut the door behind him. Tara, her legs suddenly very weak, sat down. The atmosphere in the room was completely different now. Something, some strange quality brought by the girl, had gone, and with sudden recognition Tara realized that it had been fear. Fiona had been frightened before and now she wasn't. She sat down in Lalla's easy chair, finished her milk and put the empty cup on the hearth. One of the slivers of broken glass was dislodged by the movement; Tara looked up quickly. Her eyes met Fiona's, and she was astonished to see the

girl's eyes fill with tears. While Fiona slowly bent and
picked up the fragment, Tara moved quickly, fearful in
case the little girl should cut herself. She knelt down and
gently reached out for the piece of glass.

"That's all right, Fiona, it's all right," Tara reassured
her. She turned and swept all the pieces together with
the hearthbrush and looked around for something to
put the pieces in. She knew she didn't want to go out to
the kitchen in case Fiona hurt herself.

The door to the hall opened, and Jago came in. His
face gave nothing away, but Fiona stood up nervously,
as if she knew where he had been. Tara's mind was one
whirling mass of confusion, and she put her hand to her
forehead. Had it all really happened? She too stood up
and asked, "Well?"

"Nothing . . . yet. I can't talk now. Fiona," he went
over to the girl who stood by the fireplace. He tilted
Fiona's face up, and she didn't resist him. *She trusts
him*, thought Tara in wonder. *She met him only hours
ago, yet she trusts him.* Tara was strangely disturbed by
the knowledge, and her heart beat faster as she remembered her own instinctive dislike of him which, even
after what had happened, was just as strong.

She suddenly didn't want to stay in the room. "I-I'll
make coffee," she blurted out, and fled to the kitchen.
Safely there, she leaned against the cupboard and tried
to collect her scattered thoughts. Everything had happened so quickly. Shaking her head as if that might
clear it, Tara went over to the sink to fill the kettle. Even
if Jago didn't need a hot drink, she did.

When she went back to the living room with the tray
of coffee and a paper bag for the fragments of glass,
Jago and Fiona were sitting on the couch looking at the
sketch pad he had on his knee. Tara put the tray down
quietly on the table, curious to know what they were doing yet loath to disturb them. She quickly swept the bro-

ken glass into the bag and carried it out to the kitchen. When she went back, she poured two cups of coffee, and, leaving his on the tray, took her own to the chair, where she sat down. She could see now that he was sketching something, and that Fiona was watching intently. Impelled by a force stronger than she knew, Tara stood up and gently crossed behind the couch. The sketch pad was covered, in swift bold lines, with pictures of animals and trees and people. Tara stood motionless, now knowing what Jago would do next. She imagined that he would try and teach Fiona to say words, but she was wrong. With a swift movement he ripped the piece of paper from the pad, put the sketch block on Fiona's lap and pressed the pen into her hand. He put his own hand on the girl's cheek and turned her to face him. Tara saw again a certain intensity in his eyes that made her tremble, but Fiona caught and held that glance hungrily as if she needed it.

"Copy these pictures, Fiona," he told her, speaking, as he always did with the girl, slowly and clearly. To demonstrate his meaning, he took her fingers on the pen and began to guide them over the paper. Suddenly Fiona nodded.

Tara realized that she had been holding her breath only when she at last released it. Watching the girl's thin and frail hand covered by the firm strong fingers of the man beside her, Tara could not move or speak, not even to save her life.

TARA WASN'T ABLE to tell Lalla about everything that had happened until much later in the day, when their work was over and they were sitting by the fire drinking coffee. Lalla was a good listener—more so, Tara suspected, because she was hungrily lapping up facts to help her with her character in the book. They were at the part where Fiona had tentatively begun to copy the simple animals drawn by Jago when Lalla burst out, "It's incredible! I wouldn't have believed it! What patience that man must have!"

Tara nodded, reluctant to admit anything good about him but nevertheless affected in a way she didn't begin to understand. "I know. He . . . doesn't look like a man who'd bother. But, Lalla, he did. And she drew those pictures, copied every one. They were quite good. He . . . he put her pictures in his pocket afterward and gave her the ones he'd done to keep."

"Mm, interesting." Lalla looked suddenly thoughtful. "I wonder. . . ."

"What?"

"Oh, nothing," she shrugged. "Then what?"

Tara clasped her hands over her knees and cast her mind back, seeing everything as clearly as if it had just happened. "Well, then he seemed to . . . to lose interest. It's difficult to explain what I mean, but it was as though he'd done something he set out to do, and it was over." She gave a little shudder. "Oh, Lalla, I can't explain it, but there's something awfully cold-blooded about him at times. He's like a . . . a scientist in a laboratory doing . . . experiments. . . ."

Lalla burst out laughing. "What an imagination! You should be a writer."

Tara bit her lip, then smiled reluctantly. "Yes, I know it sounds silly, but I was there. He sort of switched off. He drank his coffee, said goodbye to Fiona and went. She changed after he'd gone too . . . went back to what she'd been before. It's almost frightening. He . . . he's like a hypnotist!" She shivered.

This time Lalla didn't laugh. She gave Tara a strange look and nodded slowly. "Yes, I think I know what you mean. Did he tell you what Morag had said?"

"No. I didn't ask. He didn't look very pleased. Oh, Lalla, do you know something? He frightens me."

The older woman patted Tara's knee. "My dear, he does the same to me at times. He's a very complex character, our Jago, a very deep person. And you know something? For all that calm exterior I can sense smoldering fires inside. Yes, I know I've got a vivid imagination! I wouldn't be writing if I hadn't . . . but there's something, some one thing I can't explain. I'll bet he's got the very devil of a temper if the right thing triggers it off. I'll tell you something—I'd like to be a safe distance away if he ever loses it."

Tara was silent and thoughtful. Deep inside her she knew the truth of Lalla's words, and at the same time she pictured Jago kneeling in front of Fiona and telling her he could help her. The scene was unforgettable, deeply etched in her memory and, in a way, very moving. Tara stirred uneasily. What was he, this Jago? Would she ever know? And why did she *want* to know? They were questions she dared not even ask herself, let alone someone else.

GRADUALLY, AS THE DAYS passed, Tara began to feel more at home. The weather was bad, with rain and sleet turning the road outside into a quagmire. Morag was unable to travel, so Tara and Lalla had to look after the house themselves. It didn't matter. Tara was calmer than she had been since before the accident. Even the intense hurt of rejection was beginning to fade, and sometimes when Tara thought about David, she had difficulty remembering what he looked like. His image blurred and the once intolerable ache lessened with each day. Occasionally to her surprise, Tara found herself thinking of their next-door neighbor, Jago. She had no difficulty picturing that mocking, amused face. He had kept out of the way, as if knowing that Tara didn't like him.

But one day, exactly a week after his last disturbing

visit, he arrived quite unexpectedly. It was mid-morning, so Lalla was busy writing upstairs and Tara was typing. A thin fine mist was dispersing slowly, and Tara got up from typing a particularly complicated chapter to flex her fingers and to stretch her aching back. As she stood by the window for a moment she saw Jago coming up the path towards the house. He looked up at the same instant and their eyes met. He looked cold and wet, and Tara's heart skipped a beat. He held up a bundle wrapped in newspaper and pointed toward the front door. Tara's lips tightened, but she had no choice. For some reason he wanted to come in.

Her hand went instinctively to her face. She had almost managed to forget about the scar, but seeing him brought back her self-consciousness. Even as she went to open the door, she wondered why it should be true. Why did this stranger, this awkward, smiling man, manage to make her feel clumsy and embarrassed? She didn't like it one bit.

"Hello," he greeted her. He had every intention of coming in, that was clear. Tara moved back quickly, feeling as if she might be trampled.

"Do come in," she said.

The sarcasm wasn't lost on him. He grinned quickly, disarmingly. "Thanks."

For a moment he stood there, just looking at her, and Tara wanted to move away. Instinct fought with reason, and she managed to stand her ground. He was so disconcertingly tall and broad-shouldered. She had noticed it before, of course, but somehow with just the two of them there, it was more obvious. The fact that she wore flat-heeled slippers didn't help either, and it was with great annoyance that she looked up at him and said, in a voice that was a little distant, "I'm afraid my aunt's working. If I can give a message for later. . . ."

"I know she's working. It's you I've come to see." He

held out the small newspaper-covered packet and Tara took it, feeling the warmth of it from his hand.

"Letters," he explained. "It won't bite. And the paper's there to cover them from the rain."

Tara felt the flush creep slowly upward from her neck. "Oh, I see," she said faintly. She swallowed hard, knowing how ungracious she must sound. "Thank you. Will you . . . er . . . sit down for a moment?"

"How nice of you to ask." He had automatically taken off his muddy Wellingtons on the porch, and now with deft easy movements he peeled off the soaking anorak and hung it up. Tara watched him, wondering not for the first time how he could manage to make her feel small and helpless in just a few gentle words. What a terrible man! But he had taken the trouble to bring some letters and the least she could do would be to offer him a drink.

"Would you like a cup of tea or coffee?" she asked as he sat down by the roaring fire and began to rub his hands. He looked around and gave a mock shudder.

"Coffee, please. It's freezing out." Funny, his hair was all wet and glistening in the light from the fire. Dark and shiny, black . . . blacker than night, and straight. . . . Tara's heart skipped a crazy beat. His eyebrows met in the middle, and she remembered Lalla's words about him probably having a fiery temper. Well, that was supposed to be a sure sign, wasn't it?

"Where is it?"

She gave a little jump. "What?"

"The smut. Is it on my nose?"

"Oh!" she turned away abruptly. How dare he! "I was just t-trying to remember if you take sugar," she lied quickly.

"Ah, yes," but he didn't believe her. "None, thanks." He smiled before turning away.

Tara went out to the kitchen and made coffee. When

she returned he was leaning back in the chair with his eyes closed as if tired.

"Here you are. No sugar."

After handing it to him she looked, not too ostentatiously but not discreetly either, at her watch. "Gracious, almost twelve. The time does go quickly when you're working, doesn't it?"

"It's all right, I'm going after I've drunk this. I want to ask you a favor first."

"W-what is it?"

"I've been to see Fiona's parents—Morag's son and daughter-in-law."

"About Fiona?" She leaned forward in her chair. "What did they say?"

"About my theory of her being deaf? Exactly what I thought. They don't think much of it. In fact I'll lay odds that they think I'm a big, daft Sassenach."

"Oh!" There wasn't much Tara could say, and she didn't try. A slight smile touched Jago's mouth, as if he guessed.

"But because they're possibly sorry for me . . . and think I should be humored—and also, I suspect, because I employ Morag and pay her twice as much as I should—they agreed to let me talk to Fiona and try to help her when Morag brings her."

"But . . . I don't see . . . " Tara began. She was puzzled.

"I want her at *my* house. I want to have her for an hour or two when Morag comes here. And I need a woman there with us. She's never been alone without a female relative of some sort around—which is fair enough—so I need a chaperone. You, if you will. Will you?"

Tara froze with shock. "I don't . . ." she began.

He swallowed his coffee in one gulp and stood up. "Don't say a word now. Think it over. I don't want you to do anything, just be there. It'll only be for a few hours a week, and I'll pay you."

Anger flared briefly. "I don't want *money*," she cried, with scorn. "It's not that. It's . . . are you sure . . . you can help?" She faced him. "What are you?" she cried. "Tell me!"

Those brown hypnotic eyes met and challenged her own lighter ones, and she faltered under that deep steady gaze. "I've told you already," he said slowly. "I'm a teacher."

"No . . . no, you're not! I don't. . . ." She hesitated, courage nearly deserting her in the face of that strength. "I don't believe you."

He smiled, but it wasn't his usual grin. There was a deadly quality to it, a cold, frightening quality that unnerved Tara and made her move uneasily. "Tell me," he said softly, "what does a teacher look like? A bit stooping? Elderly . . . spectacles. . . ?"

"No," she cried. "No, its not that. It's just . . . I think you're something else but I don't know what!" He didn't look like her idea of a teacher anyway. Maybe he was a rugby coach or an athlete, but the thought of him sitting at a desk and lecturing on physics was ridiculous. There was something else, too, that had made her say what she had. She didn't understand it but deeply buried inside her was the knowledge that, when she discovered the truth about him, she would understand a lot of other things that had puzzled and intrigued her about him ever since they had met.

He nodded, and Tara was aware again of that distant quality in him. It made her want to shake him, and at the thought her fingers tingled. The idea of actually touching him was both shocking and exciting. Suddenly weak, Tara began to turn away. "I'm sorry," she began hesitantly, "I shouldn't have. . . ." She found herself being gripped firmly, and was forced to look at him.

"Yes, you have a right, in a way," he said. "Of course you have. Suppose I did more harm than good to Fiona? That's what you're thinking, isn't it?"

But Tara couldn't be sure any more what she really did mean. She shook her head faintly. "I don't know," she admitted. "Let me go."

"In a minute. I'll tell you something first. I'm not a bungling amateur. I promise you I can help Fiona. Not as much as I would like to . . . yet, but I swear I won't harm her. Does that set your mind at rest?"

"Yes," she answered. "Yes, it does. And I'll help." She hadn't intended to commit herself so soon, but something made her.

He released her abruptly, as if, having heard the words he wanted, he had no further use for her. "Right," he said. "I'll go and let you get back to your typing. The weather's improving rapidly. Morag should be able to come in a day or so. Now that I know, I've got some things to get ready. I'll be seeing you." He went to where his coat was hanging, and Tara remained where she was. She was shaking inwardly. This man had the power to frighten her in a very primitive, emotional way. She didn't like or understand it, and she wished she had the courage to fight it. She had never met anyone like Jago before, and very gradually she was coming to understand why Lalla found him so essential to the book she was writing. There *was* something fascinating about him. And much, much more—but what, she didn't know.

LALLA WAS INTERESTED in Jago's request. She looked shrewdly at Tara that evening as they both prepared supper in the kitchen.

"You know," she remarked, as she busily grated cheese for the spaghetti bolognaise that Tara was watching in the pan, "isn't it strange how things seem to work out? I mean, you arrive . . . then next thing Fiona comes. He seems keen to help her . . . and you're here to help her, too."

"It is strange," Tara agreed, and looked at her aunt. "And *he's* strange too . . . oh, I don't mean crazy, or anything like that. But, well," she shrugged helplessly, "he's so impersonal sometimes, like a . . . computer." She shook her head at Lalla's startled burst of laughter. "No, I know it sounds ridiculous, but he is, and I don't know why. He frightens me!"

"Yet he wants to help a little girl whom he thinks is deaf," said Lalla gently. "He can't be all that impersonal to want to do that. A lot of people wouldn't bother. They'd just accept Morag's definition of her as a "daftie," feel sorry and leave it at that. But he didn't . . . ." As she spoke, Tara remembered the scene in the living room the day that Fiona had deliberately broken the ornaments, and Jago had picked her up and shaken her. There had, in those unforgettable moments, been nothing impersonal about him then. On the contrary, a crackling, vibrant energy had filled the room, a brief irresistible strength of will that neither she nor the girl had been able to resist, and which had made her heart beat faster. No, it was only occasionally that she saw the remoteness and wondered about it. There was nothing to tell her then, in that kitchen, that all too soon she would discover the reason and that nothing would ever be quite the same again.

THE WEATHER had improved vastly the next day, and Tara woke to see a pale sky with a sun trying to shine through watery clouds. She stretched and got out of bed, fingers itching to begin typing again. She was near a particularly interesting part of the Damien Corbett thriller, with the hero tied hand and foot in the cabin of a cruiser loaded with explosives. It seemed impossible that he could survive.

Tara dressed quickly, wondering whether Morag

would turn up. She found her heart beating faster at the thought of going next door to watch Jago work with Fiona. She wondered what he would do and was annoyed with herself for her curiosity. Of course she would love to see the girl improve. It would be a miracle if Jago could prove that she was deaf, and not mentally retarded. But could he? Who was he to think he could, alone, find out? Tara, as she washed her face, found her thoughts wandering back to that dreadful scene on the ferry from the mainland, when he had referred to her leg and her scar so blatantly. Would he be as hard with Fiona? As Tara pulled on a warm Aran sweater, her mouth tightened rebelliously. She would not, she positively would not just stand by and let him. She would speak up and to hell with him! She fastened the belt on her gray pants, pulled the chunky sweater over her slim hips, and went downstairs for breakfast. It seemed to her, as she went into the living room, that Mr. Jago Black was the kind of man who was used to getting his own way in everything. Well, the time had come for a change, and she, Tara Blaine, might give some shocks to that confident man. Blissfully unaware of the shocks she herself was to receive before the day was over, Tara went into the kitchen to make a pot of coffee.

AT TWO O'CLOCK, Tara had had enough typing for one day. She pushed the last sheet of the most exciting chapter so far into the wire tray and got up from her chair to go to the window. Her eyes, back, and fingers ached. Outside a cold breeze teased the bare trees, and a few puddles shivered in the muddy road. But the air was fresh, and the sun, admittedly weak, shone down bravely. Tara decided to go for a walk. She needed some exercise, having been cooped up in the house for several days. She knew Lalla would still be busy upstairs, and didn't dream of disturbing her. As she went out to the kitchen, an idea took hold and strengthened, and she decided to visit the Big House—the ancestral home of the old laird. Tara looked around the kitchen, and decided to take sandwiches and a thermos. She would leave a note, and if she set off immediately, would be back before dark, for it was only three miles uphill. The views would be breathtaking on such a clear day as this.

Tara almost laughed as she bent to the cupboard that held the thermos. It was like playing hooky. She felt young and almost happy as she put on the kettle for coffee and began to butter crispbread, the winter standby when fresh bread was not available. She would wrap up well, and take an extra scarf to protect her face from the wind. The walk would give her an appetite for the coffee and food at the top of the hill. It would do her good. Her fingers ached to get on with typing, but she knew she shouldn't for she was tired enough to start making mistakes. She would come back refreshed from the walk, and maybe do more typing that evening, for the desire to find out what happened to the hero was overwhelming. She hesitated a moment as she put the crispbread in a plastic bag. Should she take the rest of the manuscript with her? No, better to leave it completely for an hour or two. It would be all the more stimulating and interesting to return to.

Tara filled the thermos, put both sandwiches and coffee in a shopping bag, and, as an afterthought, dropped in a magazine, a half empty packet of Lalla's cigarettes and a box of matches. Tara smoked occasionally only when she was working, but felt as if she might enjoy a cigarette at the top of the hill. Something at the back of her mind was bothering her. She couldn't grasp clearly what it was, and sometimes a cigarette helped. . . .

She wrote a note, put it in a prominent place on the living room table, and went out on the porch. The Wellingtons were cold at first, but after a few minutes began to feel more comfortable. She had passed Jago's house, hoping that he wasn't looking but walking carefully, so that her limp was lessened, just in case. It didn't matter, but Tara felt it was important that he should see it was nothing at all to her.

She struck upward along the familiar track that was hardly even a path, just an occasional lessening of the thick grass and springy heather. It all squelched underfoot anyway, track or no track, and the best guide was your eyes. As long as you knew what rocks and trees to look for, you would find your way. The air was salty, sea-laden, with that tangy freshness peculiar to the Western Isles. Tara found she was breathing deeply, like a thirsty child drinking fresh water. Her leg ached only when she paused, so she kept on steadily, not looking back. There would be time for that when she reached the plateau and the whole panorama unrolled before her. She would know again the ache in her heart that such beauty always brought, because to her beauty could be sad in a way. She couldn't explain it, she only knew that sometimes, seeing the gray sweep of a mountain or a gull etched against a pale sky, she wanted to weep.

She had to stop after awhile to get her breath, and she turned, leaning slightly backwards for balance. Everything was far away. Two tiny roofs were visible, like children's toys, and the smoke curled out of two chimneys, straight upward. So the wind had dropped, Tara realized. That was a bit odd, but it didn't strike her. She looked at the two dolls' houses set by a winding yellow ribbon of road with the dark, cruel sea just a stone's throw away for several minutes. Then, breath regained, she began to walk upward again.

The air was cold, and it stung color into her cheeks and made them tingle. The prospect of a cup of hot coffee and a cigarette was too wonderful to contemplate, so she thought of other things—of the letter she had received from her mother the previous day, giving her news, but not mentioning David. She had asked if Lalla was all right to work for. Tara smiled a little to herself at the thought. If they only knew it, the typing she was now doing was probably the best thing that could have happened to her. She would write back tomorrow, and Morag would take the letter, as she always did, to the village. It was Lalla's suspicion that Morag steamed the letters open before she took them to the post office, but Tara didn't mind. She wouldn't write anything personal . . . there was no one to write *private* letters to . . . . At that thought her breath caught in her throat and she had to cough.

The next minute the Big House came into view. Tara stood still to look at it properly before she got too close. It was tragic to see it so neglected and forlorn-looking, a large building with its many miraculously intact windows staring blindly out toward the sea. The stone walls of the house were strong enough to last another thousand years, but slate shingles were missing from the roof and moss grew in the gutters. The front door was large, and the paint, once a rich brown, was weathered and flat. For just a few moments Tara had a vision of the house as it had been and could be again, and the sensation was disturbing.

She looked around her, trying to picture the gardens as they once must have been, with rolling lawns and tough, hardy trees and shrubs that would survive the bitter winds from the sea. There would have been a certain elegance even so, and that, with the distant background of water and islands, would have been more than enough beauty for anyone living there. Tara sighed a little and moved on.

The front door was unlocked, or had been the last time she was there. There was no reason to suppose anyone would have locked it since, for no one was interested in the place now. The old laird had been dead almost twenty years, and the house had been gradually dying ever since. Tara knew little of the story, only that there had been family feuds and much unhappiness. Maybe that too was preserved between the ancient solid walls, for she always experienced a slight feeling of sadness on seeing the place, as if things were regretted but were too late to change. It was eerie because there was nothing frightening there and Tara did not consider herself psychic, but it was as if someone were trying to tell her something.

Shaking off the fancy, she went to the door and pushed. It creaked open slowly, and a musty smell came out to meet her. In the distance there was a quick scutter of tiny feet. Tara paused, smiling slightly, to let her eyes adjust to the gloom. She had no fear of mice. They were in for a treat with her crumbs of food. She had also seen several sheep on the hillside on her way up. If there was a back door open several of them would be sheltering in comparative warmth from the bleak January weather.

The hall was vast, and the stairs led up to a huge square landing, which once must have echoed to the sound of laughing voices. There was nothing there now except the moldering carpet and the pictures lining the four walls of the landing. These were the portraits that had been bothering Tara ever since she had come to Gaela.

She looked at her watch. Nearly three, and there was time to look around before sitting down for the small picnic she had brought. And then, after a cigarette, it would be time to return home. Maybe Lalla would still be busy with her writing and wouldn't even know Tara had been away. She was walking up the stairs as these thoughts crossed her mind, holding on to the banister which creaked with age. From the distance there came a faint sound that might have been a sigh. Tara started momentarily, then went on. She had no fear of ghosts. She carried her own phantoms, far more painful ones, with her. Her scar and her leg both were reminders of that day when her dreams had crumbled into dust as fine as that which lay on the banister. Tara ran her fingers along the old wood. She was at the top of the stairs now, looking along the picture-lined walls, and the fine dust stuck to her fingers. She looked at the nearest portrait. Suddenly, she knew what had been nagging so firmly at the back of her mind. The picture was of Jago Black.

CHAPTER FOUR

TARA STOOD QUITE STILL for several moments to absorb the shock. This had been in the back of her mind ever since she had first met Jago, but she had not consciously recognized him as the man in a picture. She went closer to look properly and to read the faded brown letters on the gold label at the bottom of the frame. "Angus Stuart Cameron, 1784-1863," it said. Her eyes traveled slowly upward to the face of the man standing there resplendent in full dress tartan, with one hand on a dog's head. Those eyes, those hypnotic eyes, were the same as Jago's and it almost seemed as if they were looking at her with subtle mockery, even from over a hundred years ago. This man's nose was straighter, but the mouth, that mouth that had . . . . Tara's hand went instinctively to her own lips at the memory of that unfortunate kiss . . . that was the same, well shaped, sensual, with full lower lip jutting slightly.

She took a deep breath and shook her head slightly. She knew that people had doubles, but this was too much of a coincidence. The painter had caught an expression so fleeting that if you looked too long it vanished. But it was there, in a first glance, and Tara had seen that same look on Jago's face several times when he was unaware of her watching. It was an arrogant, powerful, almost noble look. She walked along slowly, curious to see if there were any more pictures similar to that one. Several were of women, and their names were gently redolent of the past: Catriona Ishbeal Cameron, Flora Barbac Cameron. There were some men, more recent, but none like that startling first one. Tara reached the end, and was almost back in the spot where she had begun. She stopped in front of the last picture and went almost dizzy for a few seconds, holding onto the rail for support. For just a moment it had seemed as if she had been looking at a mirror. The girl in the picture looked down at her, and the faint smile on her face seemed for an instant to grow . . . . But it was all imagination, of course, and as Tara stepped nearer she knew that it had been a trick of the light. Even so she was intrigued to read the name at the bottom of the frame: Helen Stuart Cameron. 1791-1880.

How odd, she thought, *because Helen's my second name.* It was coincidence, of course; Helen was a very common Scots name. But even so, something lingered after Tara had gone downstairs, picked up the shopping bag and stood for a moment in that huge cold hall, wondering where she should eat. Then she remembered that there had been chairs in the huge dining room to the left of the hall. How nice it would be to sit by a window, drink coffee, and imagine living there, seeing that view every day if you wanted to.

She opened the door gently, and dust rose for a moment from the carpet. Tara crossed the room, and a chandelier winked and gleamed faintly in the light from the window as it moved in the disturbed air. There was the faintest tinkling sound as the glass fragments shivered. She moved a chair and dusted it before she sat down. The windows hadn't been cleaned for years, but there was no real dirt to cling to the glass, only the fine powdery dust that was everywhere. The view was clear and sharply defined, and breathtakingly beautiful from this angle. Tara poured out some coffee and lit a cigarette, for she wasn't hungry yet. The coffee steamed gently in the huge cold room, and she curved her fingers around the plastic cup gratefully. It was hot and sweet, and even the cigarette was perfect. For several minutes Tara sat there relaxing, contentment filling her as she looked out, and carefully avoided thinking about the pictures. Before she went home she intended to look at them again. Until then, better just admire the view . . . the view, which oddly enough was not quite as clear as it had been. For one moment Tara wondered if it was the coffee steaming the window, then laughed at the thought. How ridiculous! But even as she watched, the distant sea vanished. It quite simply dissolved in a sudden curtain of white. She stood up, not alarmed as much as curious, and went to the window and rubbed it. Nothing happened. There was no sudden clearing, because it wasn't the glass that was clouded. The mist was outside. Thick, white, and sudden, it blanketed everything in the distance and rolled nearer every moment.

It was then that Tara had her first twinge of alarm. Without further thought she put her cup down on the chair, hurried out to the front door and flung it open. Thick white vapour swirled in; she couldn't even see the gardens. With the suddenness characteristic of Scottish mists, the house was surrounded by a thick white wall. Now suddenly frightened, Tara slammed the door shut and ran back into the room where she gulped down her coffee as if it might give her strength. She drew deeply on the cigarette. What should she do now? Try and get home quickly? Even as that idea crossed her mind, she rejected it. She would be lost within minutes in a thick wet cotton mass that could disguise and distort even the most familiar landmarks. Instinct told Tara that she was safe here, in the house. But for how long? How long would she have to stay a prisoner? Soon darkness would fall, and what then? An old house in daylight was one thing—quite another when it grew dark with no light or heat.

The cigarette burned down and she flung it into the fireplace, turned toward the window. The white, clinging curtain mocked her and she turned quickly back again. That settled it. The fog could last for hours, maybe all night. Trying not to shudder, Tara looked around, deciding what would make good fuel for a fire. She breathed a sigh of relief for the impulse that had made her throw matches and cigarettes in the bag. The magazine, too, because if there was wood, the paper would start it burning. And now was the time to work before it got too dark to see. She went quickly along the narrow passage to the kitchen. It was as good a place as any to look, and there might even be coal there. With a hopeful heart, Tara opened the door to the kitchen and went in.

MORE THAN AN HOUR later she was sitting in front of a crackling fire in the huge room. Smoke curled upward and hot sparks danced crazily before vanishing up the black chimney, while outside the day grew darker and colder. She gave a little shiver as she looked toward the window. She had been looking every few minutes, but she knew it was useless even as she did it. The mist was here to stay, certainly for a few hours and possibly until morning. Tara looked at the pile of fuel stacked neatly by the fire. It had been hard work, but there was enough to keep her from freezing until morning came. A fire was always good company, even if it wasn't a roaring one like Lalla's. Tara bit her lip worriedly. What would Lalla be doing? She wasn't the type to panic, but she would be anxious even so. Would she realize that she would have the sense to stay put? Tara hoped so, and worrying about it wouldn't help. Determinedly she knelt and piled a few more twigs on the flames. Then, looking at her watch, she poured her second cup of coffee and lit her second cigarette from a twig on the fire. Every match was precious now, and nothing must be wasted. The coffee was still hot, and there were two cups still left in the thermos, and all the food. She would eat supper at nine, then try to sleep on two chairs. Tara had seen a mattress upstairs, but it had looked heavy and cold, and she knew she wasn't strong enough to drag it down.

She sighed, took a deep satisfying swallow of coffee, and looked down at the yellow crackling flames. Warmth crept out slowly from the hearth, and she regretted not bringing the manuscript. There would have been sufficient light to read by, crouched in front of the fire, and it would have taken away some of the dreadful lonely feeling that was reaching out toward her from the darkened corners of the room.

"Stop it!" she told herself firmly. "It's your own fault, and the time will soon pass." It helped, talking out loud. She wondered what would happen if she sang . . . .

And then she heard it. Unmistakably, unbelievably, heard Jago's voice calling her name. For one frightening, hair-tingling moment she thought of the pictures upstairs, and wondered . . . .

Then it came again, louder, nearer. She heard his footsteps in the hall and ran to the door, nearly spilling her coffee in her haste.

"I'm here!" She forgot for a few moments that she didn't like him. It was such a relief to know she wasn't after all the last person on earth. But when she saw him walking toward her, the fear and self-consciousness all came back. She faltered and said absurdly, "What are you doing here?"

"Well, that's a lovely warm welcome!" He stopped in front of her. He was laughing again, and she didn't like that, either. He was very tall, and dressed in denim jeans with matching jacket, unzipped to reveal a thick black polo-necked sweater, and a leather belt with a solid square buckle. It was so dark and he was so dark that Tara was obscurely frightened again and turned back quickly into her safe room. He followed her in, and she saw him swing a rucksack off his back onto the floor. She looked from him to it, and back again. "I don't understand," she said.

He ran his fingers through his soaking wet hair. "No, you wouldn't." He said it lightly, tolerantly, as if she were slow-witted. "You idiot," he went on, "I've come for *you*."

"But . . . in this? I don't. . . ." she stopped because she was beginning to stammer.

"Lalla came to me in great alarm waving your note," he pulled up another chair as he spoke and sat down in it with a huge sigh. "Ah, that's better. What's that? Coffee? Got any for me?"

"Yes, of course." She poured some from the thermos into her cup and handed it to him. Belatedly, feeling rude and childish, she said, "I'm sorry, but I was so startled—"

"Don't, please." He lifted his free hand. "I have had warmer welcomes in my time from young women, but don't force it." He fumbled in the pocket of his denim jacket. "Want a cigarette?"

"No thanks. But this . . . you found your way in *this*?"

"I know it like the back of my hand, or thought I did. Had a few tricky moments about a quarter of a mile back. It's like a quagmire; I went up to my knees in it." He lit a cigarette and inhaled deeply. "But I promised Lalla I'd find you and I have."

"You think we'll find our way down in the dark?" She looked doubtfully at the gray wall outside, which was growing darker with every minute that passed.

He shook his head. "I had some slight hopes, but no, I don't think so. Not now. Not after what happened."

"Then why have you come?"

"I've told you,'" he looked at her. His dark eyes were glinting in the firelight, but whether with amusement or annoyance she couldn't tell. "Because I promised Lalla I would. She didn't like the thought of you being here alone all night, although she hoped you'd have the sense to stay here."

"As you can see I have." Tara got up from the adjoining chair and walked nervously to the window. "I'm not frightened of the dark, or ghosts or anything." As she spoke, she fleetingly remembered the portraits. Now was not the time to mention them, however; there was something far more worrying on her mind.

He lifted a disbelieving eyebrow. "No? Not a little bit nervous?"

"No." She said it very firmly.

He shook his head. "Then I've wasted my journey."

"I didn't mean that! But you can't . . . you can't . . . ." she floundered, seeing his mocking expression.

"Ah! I get it. I can't stay? Is that what you mean?"

"Well, yes. I mean . . . well! Look, couldn't w-we try and m-make it back?"

He stood up decisively, putting his empty cup down on the mantelpiece and striding over to her at the window. Taking Tara's arm, he swung her around. "Look!" he pointed outside. "Look at that. I've just struggled up here, because if I hadn't offered, Lalla would have come herself and I know damn well she wouldn't have made it . . . and all I get from you is frightened bleating about 'shouldn't we try and get back?' Now what the hell is it? Do you think everyone's out to seduce you or something?"

"Oh!" Tara took hold of the fingers on her arm and tried to pry them off. "Really! I—"

"Really. Yes! Come on, out with it. Is that what you're so goddamned nervous of? Because if it is, tell me and let's stop beating around the bush."

It was fortunate that the darkness hid the heightened color in her face. "How dare you!" she managed at last. "W-why do you always say such awful things to me?"

"Because, my sweet child, you ask for them! Look, I

came up here because I had no choice. I didn't expect to be welcomed by you with open arms, but I didn't imagine that you'd think I was some old lecher. . . ."

"I didn't!" she gasped. "I just . . . it's . . . well, it took me by surprise, that's all." Damn him! He made her feel so young and stupid, somehow. Taking a deep breath, she said more calmly, "I'm very grateful you've come. Of course. And I appreciate it. And of course I d-didn't think anything of the kind. . . ." She nearly faltered at his disbelieving snort but swallowed and went on, "I've got some f-food. Are you hungry?"

"No, not yet. Save it. I've brought some anyway. We'll need it later when it gets really cold. Why don't you build up that fire?" He went over and began piling on logs, leaving Tara to rub her arms where his hard fingers had dug into her.

"Oh, please, don't waste them. . . ." she began, and was silenced with his steady look.

"Keep a good fire going. I'll find some more fuel after. You'd have frozen with that tiny glimmer, so it's a good thing I came. Right, I'll unpack first, then get some more wood." And as if sensing that she was about to argue, he added, "I know where there's plenty. You didn't look in the cellar, did you?" Tara shook her head. "No, I thought not. There's piles of peat and wood there. I'll get my flashlight out first. Come and help me."

Tara followed Jago wordlessly, wondering if he always took charge like that. Being a teacher would explain it, but she still didn't believe him. He knelt and unstrapped the rucksack and pulled out one blanket, then another. He looked up as Tara put them on a chair. "Two," he said, grinning. "One for you. One for me."

She took a deep breath but held her tongue. He handed her a thermos. "Soup," he explained. "And I've got some cake and sandwiches . . . ah yes, here. Careful, put the parcel on the mantel. There's a flashlight . . . here we are. . . ." A yellow path of light shot across the room. "That'll do for now. Right, I'll go and get some fuel. I've got a groundsheet in the rucksack. There's a bed upstairs with a mattress on it . . . I'll bring it down afterwards. Stay there."

With those disturbing words he took the flashlight and went out of the room. Tara was left standing by the chairs, wondering if she had heard right. She licked her suddenly dry lips. This was far worse than she had imagined, but she knew better than to say anything.

Belatedly she realized that she should have offered to go down to the cellar to hold the flashlight while Jago collected the wood. Quickly she went to the door and felt her way along the corridor toward the kitchen. The cellar door was open. From down below came noises, and a wavering light showed faintly.

She called out, "Can I help?"

The sounds stopped, then Jago's voice called, "Yes, but watch the stairs. Hold on, I'll bring the light." She heard his steps, saw the beam slanting up from the cellar, and heard his voice again, "Slowly now."

Holding onto the wooden rail, Tara descended between whitewashed walls and waited for Jago to guide the way. He held the beam downward and she followed him. Her private thoughts at that moment were little short of chaotic, but whatever she thought about him, she had to admire his directness of purpose. He had found a large wooden box and had been stacking peat and wood in it. It was nearly full. He handed Tara the flashlight and their hands met in a brief accidental touch that made her want to jerk away. She didn't, however, because she feared his mocking scorn more than that sudden disquieting tingle.

"Fine." His voice was impersonal. "Let me finish filling this, and then we'll go. That should do for the night, and we know where to come if we need more, don't we?"

Quite suddenly the words she hadn't intended to say came out. She didn't know what made her say them, yet she couldn't have resisted if she had tried. "You know this house very well, don't you?"

He turned around from stacking the last few pieces of wood and his eyes glinted darkly in the light. She saw his grin too, and her lips tightened.

"That seems like a loaded question. What exactly do you mean?"

"Just that I . . . I saw a picture. . . ."

He didn't let her finish. "Ah! So you did, did you? Hmm, and tell me, Miss Tara Blaine, what did you make of it, eh?"

He had finished stacking the wood, and stood up straight and tall before her, and cocked his head inquiringly.

"It . . . it could be you," she said, because there was nothing else to say.

"Yes, so it could." He picked up the box and nodded. "Right, lead the way. We can't talk down here."

She had no choice, and he followed, guided by the flashlight beam that somehow wasn't as steady as when he had been holding it. Once upstairs in the room again, he put the box down near her small pile of twigs and turned to her.

"All right. It could be me. It isn't, obviously, but it was a relative of mine, my great-great-grandfather, give or take a 'great' or two. I can't honestly remember. The point is, if you've seen it and recognized it, someone else might. I think I'll take it down."

"Oh!" Tara was startled. "No, don't." Then she had a sudden afterthought. "Why . . . and how . . . I mean. . . ." She stopped with the sudden feeling that she was treading on dangerously thin ice.

"Please *do* go on." His voice was smooth and polite, with the merest glimmer of humor in it.

He's enjoying this, she thought wildly. It made her say angrily, "You're a sadistic beast! No, I won't go on. I don't care who you are, do you hear me?" She moved to the mantelpiece and put the flashlight down on it with a bang.

The faint beam was diffused. The light in the room was vague and shadowy, although the fire spread a certain amount of warmth and illumination. Tara saw the slight, careless shrug.

"Right, so we'll drop the subject. Now, the fire's safe. I'm going to bring the mattress down, if it's not too damp. Are you going to bring the flashlight or not?"

His tone quite clearly implied that he didn't give a damn either way, so she nodded reluctantly. "Of course I'll bring it. Now?"

"Yes." He waited for her to go first, then, when she hesitated again as a very startling thought came into her mind, he took the light himself and began to walk out, leaving Tara with no choice but to follow quickly. As they went up the stairs, she didn't care about his scorn, amusement, or anything else. She was going to say what was on her mind. She would do it here and now, the sooner the better, because if she didn't. . . .

"Look, just a moment." They were on the landing, near the picture, but it had to be said. "*One* mattress we're taking down?" She couldn't help the slightly high note of her voice.

He stopped abruptly and stood looking down at her, but there was no light on his face, and she had to imagine the expression on his features. It wasn't difficult.

"Yes."

"F-for whom?" she swallowed hard.

"Ah!" There was a wealth of meaning in his voice. "I have no intention of sleeping on a floor if I can help it.

So it's for us both. It gets damned near freezing here at night, even with that fire, and if you're concerned about the proprieties I assure you you have no need to worry at all. I'll treat you like a sister."

"No," said Tara. "I'm sorry, but really, it's a bit much. You have your mattress . . . I'll take a chair."

"Please yourself." He paused, then added softly, "Is that all? May I go now?"

"Oh!" She struggled for words and heard him laugh. Then he was striding along the wide landing, and she followed. Her heart beat rapidly at having her fears confirmed. He actually expected her to sleep next to him on a mattress! She gritted her teeth. The man was utterly impossible.

He shone the flashlight briefly into a room, and the beam came to rest on a huge double bed with a mattress lying on top. "Here," he thrust the flashlight back at her. "Hold it steady while I feel . . . ." Then he was leaning over, pushing and prodding at the lumpy blue mattress. "Hm, better than I thought. Almost like home. Amazing really, I imagined it would be damp. Right, I'll roll it up and you can lead the way back." Silently seething, Tara held the beam steady as he bent and rolled it up. Then he heaved it into his arms and his voice was muffled, "Off you go."

Bossy beast! she thought, leading the way and being careful to direct the beam so that they could both see. *Do this, do that, and he expects to be obeyed. Serve him right if I switched the light off and let him struggle.* The temptation was so overwhelming that her finger actually trembled on the switch. But she knew she didn't dare. It was quite absurd, but his personality was so strong that she couldn't defy him.

HALF AN HOUR LATER they were sitting by a good fire drinking hot soup and eating sandwiches. Everything would have been perfect, Tara reflected, as she gazed into crackling yellow flames, if only it hadn't been him with her. She couldn't relax, and he knew it and seemed amused by the fact. Everything was colored by the brittle atmosphere that surrounded them. Every word was charged, so that she wondered fleetingly exactly what everything he said *did* mean, and had to hesitate before answering. He was perfectly relaxed, which was obvious by the way he sat with one elbow crooked over the back of his chair, his long legs crossed, and his head occasionally turning to look out at the ghostly gray night.

"Cigarette?" His voice broke into her chaotic thoughts.

"What? Oh, thanks." She took one from the proffered box and waited for him to flick his lighter. Their eyes met briefly, darkly, across the flame and her heart lurched. There had been just for an instant something so sensual about that look, so charged, that her hand trembled on the cigarette and she gave a little gasp as she drew in the first mouthful of smoke.

"Not too strong?"

"No. I . . . I don't smoke a lot," she said quickly.

"I don't either. But there are times, like this," the casually waved hand expressed everything, "when I feel like one. What time do you make it?"

Tara peered down at her watch, holding it to catch the lively firelight. They had switched the flashlight off to save the battery.

"Almost nine. Oh!"

"What is it?"

"I was just thinking about Lalla." She had to bite back a faint sob. "She'll be awfully worried—"

"Stop it. It doesn't do you any good and it certainly can't help her. Of course she'll be worried. But I made her a promise and I don't break my promises. I said I'd find you and either bring you home or stay with you.

She knows I know the route like the back of my hand."
He gave an indolent shrug and drew deeply on the cigarette. "So relax and make the best of it. I suggest we settle down to sleep soon. This mist might clear away
about six, and if it does we can start back down right
away."

Alarm flared within her, and she wished she hadn't
spoken. Of course they would have to sleep some time.
Of course she knew she was safe . . . didn't she? Tara
looked quickly into the dancing flames as if seeking an
answer. *Do I?* she wondered. *I don't know him, not
really. I certainly don't like him, but that's no guarantee of
protection.* She trembled slightly as the irrational fear
swept through her. She moved uneasily, heartbeats erratic. His next words seemed to confirm her fears.

"We'll have a drink of whisky. Lalla made me bring
a flask, and it'll help us to sleep. . . ." and then, as
she turned her wide, horror-stricken eyes on him, he
stopped. "What on earth have I said?"

Too alarmed to care, Tara stood up and walked to
the window, praying desperately for the miracle to happen and the mist to clear.

Then, hearing his footsteps behind her, she whirled
around.

"Don't touch me! Go away . . . leave me. . . ." and
then she was being shaken roughly so that the next
words were shattered into fragments, shaken so hard
that her teeth chattered.

"You stupid little idiot!" he said each word clearly
and concisely, as if he needed to impress them on her.
"Are you actually frightened of *me*?"

"Y-yes." She shrank away from the touch of those
strong brown hands, and impatiently he released her
and ran his fingers through his hair.

"You really are the most exasperating woman!" He
spread his arms wide in a helpless gesture. "What do I

have to do to prove I'm not a sex maniac? Tell me!"
Then he began to laugh, and Tara's temper flared.

"Stop it!" she gasped. "Stop it! You're hateful! Always l-laughing at me. I hate it, do you hear?" She put her hands to her ears, tears of tiredness and weakness filling her eyes and spilling out over her cheeks. Her soft golden hair tumbled about her face as she shook her head helplessly. Jago stopped laughing and looked at her, but she didn't see that look.

She didn't see the softening of that hard brown face, or the way his jaw muscles tightened, but she felt his hands on hers, pulling hers away from her ears, and heard him say in an oddly gentle tone, "I'm sorry, Tara. You're tired, and I'm an unfeeling swine to laugh at you. Don't cry . . . please." Then, as she looked up, very slowly, to face him, he added, "I only asked you to have a drink because I thought it would relax you. You're all tense. I understand your feelings, but I assure you I'm not going to make a pass at you."

She gave a shuddering sigh and flicked the hair from her face. In those few words he had made her feel ridiculously childish. "I-I'm sorry," she said. "And I will have a drink. Just a drop. B-but I'm still going to sleep on the chair."

"All right. If I were noble, or a gentleman, I'd offer to let you have the mattress, but I'm too damn tired. And I've tried to sleep on chairs before. You haven't, I'll bet. I'll leave room for you when you change your mind."

That was one thing Tara knew she wouldn't do.

SHE HADN'T really slept, and a slight sound, a distant scamper of tiny feet, roused her to full awareness. Tara shivered as the full impact of her position came to her, and she tried to move but couldn't. She was too cold and too stiff, and the chair seemed to be digging in all over her body. Biting her lip and stifling a groan, she tried to sit up, and looked over to where Jago lay on the mattress only feet away. She could barely see the black huddled shape of him; his heavy regular breathing told her that he was fast asleep. He had kept his word, and the other half of the mattress stretched invitingly empty. Tara looked at her watch in the last glimmers of the dying fire. Eleven-thirty. He had been asleep for two hours during which she had sat wrapped in a blanket, growing gradually colder and more uncomfortable, and during which all sorts of frightening images had come to plague her. Tara's head was heavy, her leg ached, and she knew, quite suddenly, that she could not spend another minute on that chair. Teeth chattering with cold, she carefully moved from the hardest chair in the world and very silently and carefully lay down on the mattress beside the sleeping man. The softness was unbelievable, but she was still freezing. She lay rigid, not daring to move, as stiff as a board and about as cold until a gruff, sleep-filled voice said in her ear, "For God's sake lie properly, woman!" She felt blankets being pulled and moved, and his was over her, and hers was over him. She was too frightened to speak or utter a sound until he added, "Move up . . . there." His arm was pulling her roughly toward him, then she was somehow curled up in front of him.

The warmth was immediate and comforting. Faintly she heard, "And if I hear one more peep out of you . . . about *anything* . . . so help me, I'll thump you, understand?"

The last words were blurred, but the meaning was quite plain.

"Yes," she murmured, trying not to shake. She really was warmer—it was almost miraculous. "Yes, I understand." But he was asleep again, she knew by his breathing. Slowly, very slowly, Tara relaxed, too, and fell asleep.

TARA WOKE SUDDENLY, and the room was freezing. Her face was so cold she couldn't feel it. For a moment she lay there puzzled, not knowing where she was. Then she remembered, and turned slightly, unable to move much because of the heavy arm across her body. She saw Jago's face dimly, his eyes dark and shadowed, and knew by his breathing that he was still deeply asleep. Her body was warm, and she wanted to snuggle down against him, but dared not. She had woken up because she was thirsty, and she looked up and saw the thermos on the mantelpiece. If she moved ever so slowly, and lifted his arm ever so gently . . . .

It took a full five minutes, but it was bliss to stand up and stretch and look out of the window. The mist was lessening slightly. She drank half a cup of the lukewarm coffee and flicked on the flashlight for a few seconds to see the time. Nearly five. Her heart lifted. Perhaps in an hour or two . . . . But first she had to get back without disturbing Jago. She almost slid onto the mattress, edging nearer so that the blankets were over her. She had never imagined it could be as cold as this and thought soberly that, if she had been alone, she could have frozen. She turned toward him carefully, and lifted the blankets to her chin, suppressing one small shiver.

Then quite suddenly she knew he wasn't so deeply asleep. Something had changed, the quality of his breathing maybe, but it wasn't the same, and there was a sudden tension. She was aware of it and tried to force her breathing to slow down, but it was difficult. She closed her eyes, willing herself to feel sleepy, and felt his arm come over her, around her waist. She heard the mumbled voice, still full of sleep, say, "Oh darling. . . ." and she gave a murmured exclamation and tried to move. But his arm pinned her down, and then Jago kissed her. It was a sleep-warmed kiss, his face and lips still relaxed with drowsiness but awake enough to have found her mouth. Until, horrified yet filled with a strange frightening excitement, Tara found the strength to push him away, and he woke up.

Their eyes met across the shadowy inches between them, and she saw the gradual awareness come into his. Then he looked across the room, puzzled. Tara sat up, and so did Jago.

"You said . . . you *said*. . . ." she began, trembling.

"I'm sorry." He ran his hand over his face, rubbing his jaw. "I was dreaming. I'm sorry, Tara."

Her breast heaved, and she put her hand to her mouth. "Go away!"

"No, let me explain first. It wasn't—"

"I don't want to hear!" She still trembled, but lacked the will to move away. Who had he thought was lying beside him? Who was he so used to sleeping with that it was normal to wake up and kiss? The chaotic, disturbing questions tormented Tara as she sat there huddled in the blankets, and she was strongly, tinglingly aware of him being so near. If she reached out one hand. . . . She closed her eyes. It didn't matter. He had been asleep, and the minute she had resisted, he had stopped. But there was one thing more disturbing to Tara than the kiss itself, and that was her own reaction to it.

She had enjoyed it, had wanted it to go on. Shakily she got to her feet. He followed her, touched her arm, took hold of her and turned her around.

"Tara, I didn't know. . . ." he began. She stayed still. She didn't know why it happened, but the tingling on her arms where his hands touched wasn't her imagination, it was real. And the desire to fight him was gone. Subconsciously she imagined it was because it was five in the morning, the weakest time, when mind and body are at the lowest ebb, but she didn't care any more. She was cold and sleepy.

With her tousled hair tumbling about her cheeks and

her face pale with fatigue, she looked up and watched him with a kind of hungry intensity, just as Fiona, too, had regarded him. He stood still— tall, dark and shadowy. But there was no mistaking his broad shoulders, the proud tilt of his head, the animal magnetism he positively radiated. Tara shivered, but whether with excitement or cold, she didn't know.

"It's all right," she said softly, and looked down at his hands on her arms, feeling that she might fall if he wasn't holding her. "It's all right. I know you thought I was s-someone else." Her head drooped, it was so heavy. "I'll sit in the chair . . . ." she began. Then her legs buckled beneath her, and her shivering became obvious.

She heard his indrawn breath, heard him say "You're frozen! You'll get sick! Lie down, Tara, I'll keep you warm . . . and don't worry."

She allowed him to lead her back to the mattress because she was too weak to resist. She felt strangely comforted, almost like a child being looked after by a mother as she obeyed wordlessly his soft commands. Then he was lying beside her, his long length was against her and his arms were around her. The blankets were tucked tightly around them both, but now he had changed. He was so near, so intimately close, yet he had become distant and impersonal again.

As she closed her eyes she said, because she had guessed it, "You act like a doctor or something." Her words were softly blurred, because the warmth of him was stealing through, comforting her whole being. She barely heard the reply she had known he would give.

"I *am* a doctor, Tara," he murmured.

WHEN SHE WOKE again it was lighter, but now she knew where she was; there was no puzzling, half frightened awareness. Tara opened her eyes and lay quite still, fully relaxed, very warm and comfortable. Jago still slept beside her, and his arms were around her. He stirred faintly and murmured, "Two pints," and Tara smiled to herself. Beer or blood? She should have known he was a doctor. It had nagged at the back of her mind whenever he had been with Fiona. In part it explained that impersonal look of his . . . partly but not entirely. Tara felt that she had to learn more about him to set all the pieces of the jigsaw tumbling into place.

Something else he had told her the previous night came back to her. He was related to the old Laird and he wanted to keep it a secret. If she hadn't been so stupidly contrary he would have told her more. She passed her tongue over her dry lips. She was more refreshed now, after just a short sleep, and she knew why. Before she had felt tension because of the bizarre circumstances, but the second time she had been too tired to fight him. More than that, she had trusted him. She had known she was warm and utterly safe for as long as she stayed there. She turned her head slightly to look at him, wanting to see his face without him being aware of it.

She faced him now, and she looked at him as if wanting to imprint the image of his features in her mind. His hair fell over his forehead, almost down to his dark thick eyebrows. His strong face was relaxed in sleep, and there was something very gentle about him. Tara's lips curved in an involuntary smile. If he knew she was watching him! It was strange that he had admitted being a doctor. Perhaps he had been too tired to realize that he was giving himself away. She knew now, and it was somehow pleasant to be in his confidence about something. She had an almost irresistible urge to stroke his face and wake him, to tell him it was time to be getting ready to go. She had to clench her hand tightly to stop herself from doing it. *This is ridiculous*, she thought faintly. *I can't stand the man, and yet here I am . . . .* She closed her eyes for a moment. *Ridiculous, of course. It's only because of what's happened.*

Of course it was. She was simply grateful to him for turning up out of that awful mist as he had, and taking charge, in a most satisfactory way, relieving what would have been the intolerable loneliness of a night alone in a freezing mansion with only mice and ghosts for company. . . .

"Hello," he opened his eyes suddenly and grinned. Tara smiled back.

"Hello," she answered.

"Tell me," he said, "do you come here often?"

"Well," she pretended to think about it, "not often . . . only in fog."

"Ah!" he gave a slight nod, as if satisfied. "That explains it."

"Explains what?"

"Why I don't often see you on this mattress. It is comfy, isn't it?"

"As good as any in the Ritz. Not that I've ever been," she added hastily.

"No," he frowned. "Me neither. Well, I suppose it's time we got up. I mean, it's very pleasant here, but we can't really stay here all day. Or can we?" He cocked a hopeful eyebrow at her.

She considered that thoughtfully. "Not really. Not *all* day." It was odd. They were playing a harmless little game that she was enjoying more than she had enjoyed anything for a long time. . . .

"Mmm, yes. What time do you make it?"

"Haven't you got a watch?" she asked severely.

"Yes, but I think you're lying on it at the moment and I can't be bothered moving."

"Oh well, it's . . . er . . . ." she squinted hopefully. "Um . . . nearly eight."

He groaned. "And I'm starving. What food do we have?"

"Do you want me to go and look?"

She shifted imperceptibly, and he said "No, not yet. In a few minutes. I don't really want to move yet, I'm too darn lazy. Besides, I think both arms are paralyzed. I'm not really sure if I can move them."

She gave a huge mock sigh. "That's a relief! I'm safe for awhile." She didn't know why she said it. It was getting pretty close to forbidden ground, but he didn't seem to notice.

"Thanks for the sympathy! The least you could have done was to offer to massage them back to life. After all, you've been lying on them for hours."

"At least three, and not both arms," she rejoined sweetly. "Are you implying I'm heavy? Because—"

"Heaven forbid! You're a mere feather, nay, gossamer weight, but," he made a face, "one needs to move occasionally, doesn't one?" And he smiled.

It was a nice smile, the sort he gave to Fiona or Lalla, and Tara's heart lurched uncomfortably. To cover up, she said quickly, "How did you chip your tooth?"

"What? Oh!" he grinned. "In a rugger scrum . . . and before you ask, that's also where I broke my nose. Or hadn't you noticed?"

"Er . . . yes, I did wonder. Rugger . . . ." she shuddered. "Ugh! Rough game."

"Rough?" he pondered that for a few moments. "Yes, you have a point. It is a mite ungenteel. I don't play any more. Got some sense now."

Then Tara did something ridiculous and startling. She didn't even know she was going to do it until it actually happened.

She reached up with her free hand and very gently touched his nose, feeling the slight crookedness—that most attractive crookedness—midway. "You poor thing," she said, and meant it. Then, realizing what she'd done, she added, "Oh! Sorry! I didn't—"

"Don't stop now! And don't apologize either," he grinned, but it wasn't quite a grin. His face was near, so near and warm, and somehow . . . . She couldn't remember afterwards how it happened, but they must have both moved forward just a little, and their lips met in a long, lingering, warm, tender, magical kiss that went on and on. . . .

Tara spoke first. "Mmm, that was nice, but we shouldn't. . . ."

"Isn't it nice to do things we shouldn't?" And he kissed her again, longer and even nicer, if that was possible.

"You promised," she said, after an eternity when they managed to part their lips for a few brief seconds to catch their breath, "You *promised* not to make a pass at me."

"I'm not making a pass, I'm kissing you."

"Ah!" The logic was wrong somewhere, but he said it so convincingly that it sounded right. She didn't care anyway. This was right, too.

"Oh, I see." She put her hand up to stroke his face, and his arms, which weren't paralysed at all, tightened around her. "Your face is rough," she said after a moment, "and it hurts."

"It usually is first thing in the morning. You didn't bring a razor, did you?"

"Forgot it! Silly me!"

"Then," he said decisively, "you'll just have to put up with it, won't you?" And he kissed her again.

Then suddenly it wasn't a lighthearted joke any more. Quite suddenly it changed. They drew apart, and their eyes met in that deep unspoken message that is as old as time. Tara felt the throb of his heart and his deep unsteady breathing, and saw what was in his eyes. She closed her own. Before it went any further, she knew she must move away, must move. . . .

"Tara?" First it was a question, then he said it again, "Oh, Tara." There was something in it the second time that melted her bones and turned her blood to fire. She didn't dare open her eyes, because of what she knew he would see in them. Jago's hand moved across her back, and around. . . .

"No," she said with a painful effort.

There was silence, and he was still. Then he spoke, and his voice was ragged, almost harsh. "No?"

Tara shook her head imperceptibly.

He took a deep shaky breath. "All right," he said. "We'd better get up, shouldn't we?" There was a blank hurt in his voice that made Tara long to comfort and re-assure him, but she didn't dare to. The situation was so explosive, the air in the room sparking and crackling with such invisible tension, that she didn't dare even to touch him.

He moved away without looking at her and got to his feet, and, zipping up his jacket, went out of the room.

Tara swallowed hard, and her face burned like fire. Slowly, stiffly, she got to her feet and brushed down her crumpled sweater and pants.

She went to the window and looked out. The mist had not cleared, but it was thinner and the sun was trying to get through. It would soon be safe for them to leave.

She didn't want to think about what had happened. Her nerves were one jangling mass of taut sharp pain, and she wanted to cry, but she wasn't going to. Not now, not here.

She heard his footsteps coming along the hall and she hugged herself nervously, pressing her fingers into her arms and not looking around.

Jago came in. "There's a spring near the back door," he said, and she turned slowly. She had expected anger, but he wasn't angry. He looked very much like he normally did, and she relaxed slightly. He had rinsed his face in the water, and it was still wet, as was the front of his hair. "I'll tidy up and then we'll go. It's light enough to see our way down, or will be in half an hour."

"I'll go now." She moved quickly past him and went out, along the hall and down the steps to the kitchen. When she returned everything was packed away, and he was waiting for her.

Tara wanted to say something, but she didn't know what, only that she felt utterly wretched. She picked up her shopping bag and he said, "Give it to me. It'll fit in the rucksack." Silently she handed it to him, and he added, "Cheer up. It didn't happen."

She looked at him then, and he gave her a faint crooked smile. "If it makes you feel any better, I'll apologize," he said.

She took a deep breath. "No, don't," she answered. "It wouldn't anyway."

"I've got to say something before we go," he went on. "Just this. I honestly didn't intend. . . ." he stopped briefly. "Put it down to body chemistry." He shrugged. "Oh, what the hell! I thought I was clever, but I wasn't as clever as I thought, and I am sorry, because I'd promised you you were safe and—"

"Please stop," Tara breathed. "It was as much my fault as yours. It was so lovely and warm there . . . ." she gave a small laugh. "And it was nice just talking . . . well, joking really. I . . . I didn't know it w-would turn out like that." And she watched his face, and bit her lips in distress.

The faint smudges under her eyes accentuated her early morning beauty, and bright unshed tears glistened on her lashes. She saw the softening in his own brown eyes and wondered how she had ever disliked him. It didn't seem possible. He was everything that a man should be, strong yet gentle. He could have been nasty with her for apparently leading him on, but he wasn't. He took everything in his stride, and never faltered. *Oh, Jago!* she thought. *I've been wrong about you. So wrong.* One day she would tell him.

HALF AN HOUR LATER they were well on their way home. At a particularly rough spot, Tara's leg hurt her and she faltered. Jago turned around, saw her face and took her hand. "I'll help you," he said quietly. The mist was patchy now, thick in parts and thin and swirling in others. Their hair was damp because the mist was as wet as any rain. Tara was glad of his hand, warm and strong, and they half scrambled, half walked in a silence that was companionable and relaxing. Suddenly the white swirling curtain lifted, and seeing the two houses standing side by side, she squeezed his gentle, comforting hand.

"Home," she said. "Isn't it marvelous to be home again?" And she saw him smile.

Then, almost as if it had been planned, a small wiry figure came out of the back door of Jago's house and stood watching them. It was Morag. The expression on her face spoke volumes and would have been almost comical at any other time. Tara froze, and without thinking why, slipped her hand out of Jago's.

She heard his muttered oath; then he said, "Well, Tara, it looks as though it'll be all over the island within a few hours that we've just spent the night together."

CHAPTER FIVE

TARA SHIVERED, suddenly cold at Jago's words. "Oh, no!"

"Oh yes. You can bet she's seen that my bed hasn't been slept in, and she'll have been over at Lalla's. It's just bad luck that we didn't get home before her. An hour ago. . . ." he shrugged. They were on the road now, and Lalla came to the door and ran down the path towards them.

"Oh, my dears," she began. "You don't know how glad I am to see you." Then, seeing Tara's expression, she asked, "What—"

"Morag just saw us," Jago explained. "And her expression was quite plain."

"Oh dear! Well, come in," she led the way up the path. "I'll have the tea made in a jiffy. You must be frozen. I've had the kettle simmering for hours. It's a wonder it's not boiled dry."

It was wonderful to be in a warm, comfortable room again. Tara looked around and caught Jago's eye, and she smiled, just a little.

"Do you mind?" he asked. They were alone. Lalla had gone off into the kitchen to make tea and toast.

"There's nothing we can do about it," she answered. "And if we tried to explain, it would make it worse, I suppose."

"Yes, it would," he agreed. "I couldn't care less for myself, but for you it's different, I know." He scratched his cheek thoughtfully. "I could strangle the woman sometimes. She knows everything about everybody on Gaela."

"But not everything about you," Tara said quietly. "I . . . I won't say anything about the picture if you don't want me to."

"Oh, that." He shrugged. "Thanks. It's not a dark secret or anything. I just prefer some things to be kept private at the moment." He had swung the rucksack to the floor, and bent now to take out Tara's folded bag and thermos. He put them on the chair and straightened up. "Look, tell Lalla I won't stay. I need a shave and a wash, and I hope Fiona's at my house."

"Do you want me to come?" Tara asked.

He narrowed his eyes. "This morning? Aren't you too tired?"

"No. I want to come, honestly. I want to help."

He nodded. "Then thanks. I'll away now. If she's not there I'll let you know straight away. And, in any case, don't hurry. You must have some food and a hot drink first. I'll see you."

She went to the door with him, and as he was about to open the porch door she said, "Jago?"

He turned slowly. "Yes?"

"I . . . thank you for everything."

He smiled lightly. "It was a pleasure." His eyes met hers, and his look was steady and disconcerting. "I mean it . . . all of it." Then he turned away and the door shut behind him.

Tara stood there for a few moments before going into the house again. She felt curiously lightheaded, almost dizzy, and she knew it was only partly caused by hunger.

SHE HAD TIME to think when she was sitting in Jago's home later. There was so much that had happened, so very much to think about. It was the first time she had been in his house. She sat quietly in a corner of the living room with an open magazine on her knees, but she wasn't reading. The room was warm and comfortable in a different way from Lalla's. The furniture was older, and had been skilfully chosen to blend with the old house. The warm red carpet underfoot provided a perfect background to rich mahogany and rosewood. Books, hundreds of them, were all around, and a fire burned brightly in the fireplace. Jago was on the other side of the room with Fiona, playing with colored cardboard shapes. Tara knew it wasn't just a game at all, it was deadly serious. Morag had told Jago that Fiona always had a woman with her wherever she went, and that was why he had asked her to be there, just sitting quietly but available if needed. She was glad to help him, more glad than he would ever know.

Tara thought about his being related to the old laird and about his being a doctor. She thought about other, more private things and wondered if she was beginning to find herself falling in love with this big, strong, utterly marvelous man. She knew now why Fiona trusted him instinctively. Tara had seen a look almost of hope and love on the little girl's face, and her heart had skipped a beat.

He was infinitely patient, but firm. Fiona had tantrums when something went wrong, but he was always in control. Tara allowed herself the luxury of watching him, because he was too busy to look up.

He had changed out of his mist-dampened sweater into a white pullover. The sleeves were rolled up to his elbows, and his arms were strong and muscular, darkly covered with hair. The gold watch on his left wrist made his arm look more tanned, and at that moment he was picking up a square of cardboard to hand to Fiona.

As always the girl watched his face with a hungry intensity, as if trying to understand him. If she was deaf, as he thought, she lived in a completely enclosed world of her own with no way of communicating. Maybe he was right. Tara fervently prayed so, clenching her hands tightly until the knuckles showed white. There was so much that could be done for Fiona if she were deaf, he had told Tara when she had arrived half an hour previously. He had a friend in Edinburgh that he wanted Fiona to see, and he was going to work on Morag and her family. Tara didn't doubt that he would get his own way eventually. She imagined that he usually did, and at that thought she felt her cheeks go warm. Why, she wondered, should she have a sudden memory of what had happened a few hours before? That thought was followed by the remembrance of when he had first woken and called her "darling" in his sleep. Who was the woman he thought she had been?

"No, Fiona," his voice disturbed her comfortable thoughts. "Not that one." He tilted Fiona's face up and held up a circle. "See, this one." And he nodded. Tara saw the girl's lips tighten rebelliously. That was a good sign. She had emotions; she could feel annoyed with him. He looked up quickly and winked at Tara as Fiona, after taking the circle from him, bent her head. She smiled back, suddenly happy. It left her with a comfortable glow that lasted several minutes.

"Tara, will you make some coffee, please?" He was looking at her again, and she stood up.

"Yes, of course." Suddenly she realized something. She was no longer conscious of her scar or of her limp. She had not once felt the need to turn her head a certain way or disguise her walk, which had always been agony to do. It didn't matter anymore, and she felt a heady sense, almost of freedom, as she went out to his kitchen.

It was a man's kitchen, she realized with a slight smile as she looked around her. No trimmings, no fancy mats or trays, just the essentials: coffee pot, cups, oil lamp on top of a cupboard. As curious as any woman in another's kitchen, she looked about with the valid excuse that she had to find coffee, sugar and milk.

He was well stocked with canned foods, which was sensible. She admired his use of space, everything was well planned and nothing was wasted. But then she opened the wrong drawer looking for spoons, and before she could close it she saw a photograph lying among odds and ends of broken gadgets, pens, and notebooks. *Men do keep things in odd places anyway*, she thought. She should have shut the drawer, but, instead she lifted out the photograph and looked at it. It was of a couple on a beach; the man was Jago, and the woman was a foot shorter, dark-haired and beautiful. They had both been swimming, and were laughing at something. Jago's arm was draped casually over her shoulders, and the woman was smiling straight at the camera as if to say, "Look what I've got!" Was this her? The woman he dreamed about? Tara swallowed and felt faintly sick. Now she had to make coffee and act normally, when she felt utterly wretched.

Jago looked at her when she carried the coffee in, and a frown creased his forehead. "Anything wrong, Tara?"

She managed a smile. "Nothing. Just a bit tired." The lie hurt, but the truth was even more painful. Nothing had changed, but she wanted to go back to her aunt's house. She didn't want to be here with him any more. She began to read the magazine, and had to concentrate hard in order to blot out the disturbing picture of what had almost happened at the Big House. The sickness was now shame, and, worse than that, humiliation.

When Morag came for her granddaughter, Jago went to the door with Fiona, and Tara heard their voices for several minutes. She looked around, wishing that she could just slip out of the back door. But he would probably come over to see why she'd left and she didn't want that to happen. The minute he walked in, she stood.

"Morag's an obstinate old devil," he began. "Won't hear anything about Edinburgh . . . ." he stopped, and walked across the room to Tara. "You look done in," he said. "Why don't you go home to bed?"

"Yes . . . yes, I will." She was edging away as she

spoke; if he touched her she would scream. But he didn't. He cocked his head in the way he had, and asked quietly, "What's wrong, Tara?"

"Nothing!" She gave him a tight, bright smile. "Nothing at all! Why should there be?"

"I don't know." He shrugged. "But there is. Is it something to do with Fiona?"

"Of course not!" That at least she could say with conviction. But if he asked any more questions. . . . He was far too clever. "I must go . . . really. J-just let me know when Fiona's coming again, and I'll be here. Goodbye, Jago."

He opened the door for her. "Thanks, Tara. Goodbye." And he gave her one of his searching looks.

She slipped around him and went out the door, clutching her purse like a weapon. She didn't see the expression on his face, because she didn't turn around, but she wouldn't have understood his look even if she had.

THE LESS SHE SAW of Jago in the future, the better. That was the decision Tara reached as she lay in bed that night. She knew now that it wouldn't take much for her to fall in love with him. Wouldn't he find it amusing if he knew that! Eventually she slept, and she wondered, just before sleep claimed her, how she would enjoy getting back to the typewriter and Damien Corbett. All that seemed tame compared with all that had happened since she last touched the keys.

She didn't see Jago for several days. The next time Morag was due, Tara wondered if he would call in first to make sure she was coming. Lalla was too engrossed with her new novel even to know what day it was, and she certainly hadn't noticed anything amiss. Tara was thankful for that. She had managed to immerse herself in her work and to push certain disquieting thoughts to the back of her mind. The morning Morag was due, all her worries came rushing back, and she found herself waiting with clammy hands for the knock on the door that would tell her Morag had arrived.

When it came she opened the porch door with a smile. "Hello, Morag," she greeted the small woman.

She couldn't help wondering what was in the other's mind as she returned the greeting with a knowing smile and the words, "Himself is waiting for you next door."

"Oh yes, I'll go now."

"Miss Baxter, she will be at her writing now, I don't doubt?"

"Why, yes, Morag. Did you want her? Is it urgent?"

Morag produced a crumpled envelope from the depths of her coat pocket. "It can wait," she admitted. "It is the invitation for you both," and she gave an important nod.

"Oh, how very nice. Er . . . to what?" Tara hoped she didn't sound too foolish.

"To the wedding party on Saturday. Did she not tell you? Tsk! I'll away in and put this on the mantel. Aye, well, off you go now."

Feeling dismissed, Tara went out along the path and knocked at Jago's front door.

"It's open. Come in," he called, and she pushed the door open, pausing to wipe her feet on the porch mat. There were fishing rods there, and she wondered when he fished. Then the inner door opened, and Jago stood framed in the doorway, dressed in his jeans and black sweater.

"Hello, Tara. Come in and sit down. How are you?"

"Fine, thanks." It was like talking to a stranger. She had managed to put him out of her mind; the nagging ache that she knew was jealousy hurt less that way. She had come up here to try to heal a broken heart, and it was no use going home with another one. She forced a smile for him and for the girl who sat patiently at the ta-

ble, waiting for Jago to bring her to life for a few short
hours.

"Good, I'm going to draw with Fiona today. She's got
some talent. I sent those sketches of hers off to a friend
in Edinburgh, and he's impressed. They're nearly normal for a girl her age . . . and considering all the terrific
drawbacks, *that* says a lot."

He went back to the girl, and Tara saw the papers
and crayons spread out as she went to her chair by the
fire. She had brought a manuscript to read, which would
be better than looking at him.

An hour passed before she looked up and said, "Shall
I get coffee?"

Intent on what the little girl was doing, he didn't look
up. "Please."

She didn't want to, but she had to open the drawer
again. The photograph had gone. Tara made coffee and
took it back along with orange juice for Fiona and
cookies on a plate.

When Morag came, Jago took Fiona to the door,
then came back into the room. Tara reached for her
purse but he said, "Wait a minute."

She stood still. "Yes?"

He ran his fingers through his hair. "I don't know
how to put this," and for a moment to Tara's surprise he
looked almost embarrassed. He walked over to stand in
front of her. "I heard you open the drawer again, so I
know. Did you . . . find a photograph last time you were
here?"

Tara stiffened and fought desperately to remain calm.
Was he going to humiliate her now? "Yes," she said. "I
wasn't trying to pry. I opened the wrong drawer when I
was looking for spoons. W-why?"

He smiled. "I thought . . . look, Tara, I don't know
whether you're interested, but that woman in the photograph is my sister. Her husband took the photograph."

The shock was so great that she felt the color drain from her face. He went on, "I just thought I'd tell you."

"Is that all?" She couldn't take it all in yet, couldn't take in his reasons for wanting her to know.

He nodded, and brought his hands forward to take hold of her arms. "Listen," he said, in a very strange voice. "Am I being conceited in thinking . . . it mattered to you, that snapshot?"

She couldn't answer, she just nodded her head wordlessly. Jago pulled her gently, very gently, toward him and kissed her. Then he looked down at her, and his smile was everything it should be.

"You were jealous . . . of a photograph?"

"Yes." She blinked several times quickly, for it would be ridiculous to cry.

"You little idiot," he said very softly, and hugged her. Tara put her arms around him because that was where they wanted to be, and the two of them stayed like that until he whispered, "Morag's eyes would fall out if she saw us now. We'd have to get married!"

That reminded Tara of the invitation. There was a crumpled-looking envelope on his mantelpiece as well. She looked at it, then at him. "Have you been invited to this wedding party on Saturday?"

"The *ceilidh* in the evening? Yes. And you? Good. I haven't even read it yet. Let's see . . . ." he reached over and opened the envelope to produce a postcard, which he handed to Tara. "Looks like another of her brood getting hitched. She's got eight or nine children scattered all over the Highlands and Hebrides. Should be a good do. The drink flows freely, from what I recall. They don't give you much time to buy presents, do they?" He flung the card and envelope on the table. "I'll get the ferry to the mainland tomorrow and have a look around. Want to come?"

"Yes, please," Tara answered promptly.

"All right. Ready at eight? We'll catch the nine a.m. ferry, and spend all day there . . . unless the weather's too bad, of course."

"Ready at eight," she agreed happily. The world was a brighter place—brighter and absolutely wonderful.

She left soon afterward, determined to do extra typing so that she wouldn't get behind with the manuscript. She knew Lalla not only wouldn't mind if she took a day off; she would also be glad to have the worry of buying a present taken off her hands.

Tara went to bed that night looking forward to the following day with a sense of joy. She had no premonition of what that day would bring, or of the discovery she would make that would change her life.

THE DAY WAS everything it should be. The sun shone, and the puddles in the road had dried up so that they were both able to wear shoes instead of Wellingtons for their walk down to the ferry. Jago put his arm around Tara as they walked along. Both wore macs, which were almost essential on the island, especially in early February. The sky was of palest washed blue, the tingling air as fresh as mint.

Jago jingled coins in his pocket. "Brought your money?" he asked.

"Mmm, yes. Why?"

"Wondered. Thought you might treat me to lunch."

She looked quickly at him, saw that he was joking and laughed.

"I don't believe in paying for men," she said, trying to sound prim.

He made a face. "Pity! And I thought you were an ardent women's-libber, the way you refused my offer of a drink that night in Kirkgarron."

"Oh! *That* night." She smiled at him. "I didn't know you then."

"Didn't like me either," he grinned. "And I didn't half fancy you."

She wondered if she was turning pink, and moved uneasily in his grasp. "Don't joke," she said faintly.

"I'm not," he sounded surprised, even faintly indignant. "Don't you know it's a challenge to a man if he thinks a woman doesn't like him? Especially if he doesn't know why, and can't see a reason."

"Is that why you kissed me on the ferry?" she demanded.

He began to laugh. "Partly! I wanted to see what you would do."

She was to remember those words later, and would know the truth.

"And you did," she answered. "You found out."

"Yes," he rubbed his cheek reflectively. "I miscalculated somewhat. You certainly pack a wallop for such a gentle-looking creature. You know something? You're only the second woman who's ever hit me!"

"Oh! And what was the other one for?" she turned wide eyes to him.

"Ah . . . better not. Not now. Maybe one day when I know you better." It was all lighthearted, and it set the mood for their journey across the water to Kirkgarron, where they took a bus to a larger fishing village. They looked around the shops and bought their presents before having a late lunch in a cosy pub. Afterward they left the parcels at the bus depot and walked along the beach throwing pebbles into the sea and feeding the gulls with cookies while the breeze tugged at their hair and stung their cheeks. Everything was so perfect and beautiful that Tara wondered if it could last.

Eventually they caught the bus back to Kirkgarron and the ferry home. In the tiny cabin, with just the two of them and their parcels, Tara fell asleep leaning on Jago's shoulder, while he sat with his arms steady and firm around her, breathing in the faint seawashed scent of her hair.

When they reached his house, he said, "Come on in and have a drink. Lalla won't have missed you yet, she'll still be writing."

It was seven o'clock and already dark. The faint stars kept vanishing in a cloudy sky. "All right," Tara agreed. "Just for a few minutes."

He lit the oil lamps, and Tara was surprised at how well two of them lighted the room.

He grinned as he carried in an oil stove and lit it. "I don't want electricity here," he said. "The place has got a life of its own with these lamps, and I can read by them as well as by anything else. Sit down, Tara. I'll make coffee, and we'll have something a bit stronger with it." He took her coat and hung it on a chair. "Have a look at a book or something while I'm in the kitchen."

She sat in the chair near one of the lamps and looked along the bookshelves beside her. As she lifted out a book, a brown folder fell out from where it had been wedged on the shelf, and as she bent to pick it up, several loose sheets fluttered to the floor. She could hear the distant clatter of cups from the kitchen and the sound of a drawer opening and she smiled to herself. The sheets were covered with bold handwriting, and she knew without being told that it was Jago's. It is impossible for anyone not to glance at a few words of a printed page, so it was unfortunate that the sheet she picked up should have written on it what it did. . . .*and the bitterness is mainly caused by the sense of rejection by fiancé— possibly much more than by facial scar—slight anyway (cosmetic surgery possible? Check). Not sure re leg. Could by psychosomatic. . . .* By then Tara couldn't have stopped reading if she had wanted to. She knew, with a sick, certain knowledge, that every word referred to her. She went on reading the terrible words, horrified at seeing everything set out in a clinical way even if she didn't understand what all the words meant. Then with shaking fingers she put the sheets in order and began to read everything from the beginning just as Jago came in. He was about to say something until he saw Tara's face. He put the cups down on the table and came over to her. When he saw the folder, the color left his face.

"Dear God," he said quietly. "I thought I'd burnt it."

Tara stood up slowly, every limb aching and trembling. "What are you?" she asked. "I know what *I* am now. I'm a specimen in a laboratory . . . b-but what are *you*? You're not a teacher or a doctor . . . not with those notes." The hurt was so deep that she could hardly speak. She had to force the words out, but she found the strength from somewhere, because she had to know.

"Tara, give them to me. I—"

She snatched them away. "No. I'm going to read them properly." She hugged the folder against her. "Answer me!"

"It was only at first . . . those first few days, I had to. . . ."

"What are you? A psychiatrist?"

"Yes."

She took a long deep shuddering breath. "I knew, I should have known. Shouldn't I?" The tears glistened and fell down her cheeks. "I should have guessed . . . that remote look you had sometimes . . . and I . . . I thought then there was something, but I didn't know you'd go so far . . . when . . . when you tried to make love to me at the Big House . . . ." She saw him close his eyes, saw the drawn harshness of his face, and something inside her cried out. "Was that an experiment, too? Was it?"

"No. You know . . . by then I knew you, knew what I felt about you—"

"You liar!" her voice was lower and more intense.

"How dare you lie now! That's why you kissed me on the boat too. Is it all here in the notes? All of it?" She had to press her hand to her mouth to hold back the sobs, and Jago took sudden hold of her.

"Tara, don't. Tara darling, listen to me now. I'll tell—"

"No! Don't touch me . . . ." His hands burned like fire through the sweater she wore, and she wished she were stronger, much stronger, because she wanted to hurt him as badly as he had hurt her. "Take your hands off me!" She wrenched herself free and the folder fell to the floor, the notes fluttering out like grotesque confetti.

"It's all here, isn't it?" she said. "Every detail about me, and how I look and act. You can keep them, and study them. I don't want to see them now . . . or ever!"

"Don't you think you should listen to me for a minute?" he asked her, and she saw him as she had never seen him before. She saw and hated every inch of him.

"While you tell me more lies?" she shot back. "No. First you're a teacher, then a doctor, then a relative of the laird, now this. . . ." She kicked the papers contemptuously. "I've had enough of them. Put them in a book. You should be good at that."

"I've never lied to you, ever," he said. "And I won't now. All I told you is true. It's up to you whether you believe me or not. Your aunt told me about you before Christmas. I knew at Kirkgarron who you were. That's not why I came back. But when I realized it was you, I wanted to help you. Isn't it instinctive to want to help others? And I did, didn't I? You no longer hide your face or feel self-conscious about your leg—"

"Shut up!" She caught him a stinging backhanded blow across the mouth with her right hand. "I won't listen. I *hate* you!"

"If it makes you feel any better, go ahead, hit me." The mark showed; she had caught him with the ring she wore, and blood glistened on his lip. But she didn't want to touch him again. She shuddered.

"And let you feel you've helped me?" she jeered. "Then you can put it in your notes. . . ." Suddenly she was too overwhelmed to say more. Huge waves of realization washed over her. She bent her head and covered her face with her hands. Stumbling blindly, she went to the door and ran outside.

BY THE TIME Saturday came, Tara was composed and back to normal, on the outside at any rate. She had had to tell Lalla a little of what had happened in order to explain her white face and shadowed eyes. Lalla had listened, as always, and had gone to see Jago afterward. But Tara refused to let her mention him, and Lalla wisely kept her own opinion of the matter to herself. She grieved for her niece and for the man next door, whom she knew well enough to realize that the last thing he ever wanted was to hurt Tara.

The wedding was Saturday afternoon on the mainland, and only the close family were going, for the ferry held a limited number. The whole island, however, was going to the *ceilidh* in the evening.

Tara knew Jago was going, and had told Lalla at first that she would stay at home, until Lalla had answered that in that case, so would she.

On Saturday, the two women were talking, and Lalla said, "Morag was telling me before about a man who's going to this party, by the fascinating name of Ruari Mhor. He's a red-haired giant of a man from what I can gather. In the Merchant Navy. He comes home about twice a year and creates havoc."

"In what way?" Despite herself, Tara was intrigued. After the sense of being betrayed by Jago, she had thought that nothing could matter any more. She had cried that night after the perfection of a wonderful day had been ruined by the discovery that she was not, and never had been, anything but a case history to him. She was like another Fiona to him, but the hurt was more bitter because with Fiona he didn't pretend anything; with her he was genuine. With Tara he had gone so much deeper, had feigned affection, and even more, had let her think . . . . Why, he led her to think that he was falling in love with her. How cruel, how unutterably cruel! She determined, there and then as she sat with Lalla in the warm sitting room, that she would let him see that it hadn't worked, that she didn't care. Only then would she ever be able to hold her head up in front of him.

Maybe in a way it would be a good thing for her to go to the party. Running away was no use. She had done enough of that, and now she would grow up and be a woman, with no regrets for what was irretrievably past.

"Well, dear," Lalla had that look on her face that Tara knew well, the expression she wore when another character was about to be found for a book, "he's quite one for the girls apparently, and they for him. And he's a fighter too. You know what Gaels are like when they've had a few drinks."

"Yes, I remember." Tara managed to laugh now, and with it came relief. "You've told me often enough. Oh, Lalla, of course I'll go this evening. And don't worry about Jago. I'll even speak to him, then he'll see I don't care." She took a deep breath.

Lalla looked faintly alarmed. "Are you sure?" she said. "You don't want to overdo it. I mean. . . ."

"I know," Tara nodded, calmer now with the resolution. "Don't worry. I've got to do it for my own peace of mind. You've helped me a lot. Perhaps in a way he . . . Jago . . . has, too. I'm not going to undo all that now. I've had a few days to think about it, and now I've decided." And she smiled at the older woman, who stood up and touched Tara's shoulder.

"I'll go make us coffee," she said. "I asked Morag to order me the taxi so we wouldn't have to walk to the village tonight. I took a chance, for I guessed somehow we'd be going. And I'm so glad, Tara, glad you're being sensible. You're doing the right thing, I know." She smiled and went out, and didn't see the fleeting look of pain that crossed Tara's face.

THEY WERE READY at seven, and Tara stood in front of the mirror in the living room putting the finishing touches to her lipstick. Lalla looked at her, affection creasing her face. "Er . . . Tara," she began. Tara looked around quickly.

"What is it, Lalla?"

"Well, as you're . . . er . . . going to speak to Jago, would it be all right if I told him he could share the taxi?"

Tara shrugged, "Of course." But when the older woman had gone out she bit her lip, faint butterflies of apprehension hovering about. Would she be able to bear it . . . bear him being close? She would have to, and maybe it would be a good test before the evening itself began.

She stood back from the mirror and surveyed herself critically. She wore a floor-length dress of deep red flowered courtelle, with a V-neck. It had been her favorite, months ago, and this was the first time she had worn it since the accident. Nervously she smoothed her skirt. It brought back memories, but the self-consciousness was momentary. She lifted her head high and smiled at her reflection. She had known she looked good in it before, and now she looked good in it again. Her soft blond hair curled gently forward, and her cheeks had filled out slightly, because here she was always hungry.

She looked beautiful and desirable and utterly feminine.

She stiffened slightly as she heard the porch door open. Then Lalla came in, and Jago was with her. Swallowing hard, Tara looked at him.

"Hello, Tara," he said.

For a moment she thought she wouldn't be able to answer, her throat had tightened so much. Then she managed to speak. "Hello," she answered. "Excuse me," and she swept out of the room and ran upstairs for her coat. Her heartbeat was rapid, but she had got the first awful moment over with, and she knew she could cope now.

She went to the bathroom window at the front of the house, and looked out to see if she could see a car's headlights. The sea glinted in the moonlight, and the distant mountains were harsh black outlines against a starry sky. It was all so beautiful, but she couldn't stay here looking at it. She must go down and let him know that he couldn't hurt her any more. She flicked her hair back and set off downstairs with her coat—the dark blue coat she had worn on the day she had first met Jago—over her arm.

He was standing by the fireplace with a glass in his hand and a cigarette in his mouth. He wore a tweed jacket and fine gray worsted trousers, and in a white turtleneck sweater he looked startlingly attractive. Lalla was nowhere to be seen and Tara swallowed a momentary panic. She dropped her coat over a chair and went to the window. She could see his reflection in the darkened glass and he hadn't moved, hadn't turned to watch her.

Then he spoke, "Fiona's coming on Monday with Morag. She won't let me teach her without a woman being there. Will you come or not?" She saw him turn slightly, but she didn't look around.

"I want to help Fiona," she answered. "Yes. As long

as I can read." And she didn't need to add, "Because I don't want to talk to you."

"Thank you." He swallowed the last of his drink and flung his cigarette into the fire. Tara turned around.

"Where's Lalla?" she asked.

"In the kitchen making coffee." She saw the healed scab on his lip, as well as the shadows under his eyes as though he slept badly. She hoped it was true.

"Oh," and she smiled very faintly to herself.

Lalla brought in coffee, which they drank, and just when they had finished, the taxi honked outside. Lalla switched off the lights and they went out into the crisp darkness, Jago carrying the two presents, which Hamish flung in the front seat. Tara got in first, because she wasn't going to sit next to Jago, and then they were on their way.

The party was being held at the island's only pub, which was the one place big enough to accommodate Gaela's seventy-odd inhabitants. It was noisy already when they arrived. The music had begun, and heads turned to watch them come in, followed by Hamish, who was also a guest. Tara knew without being told that she and Jago were a cause for speculation. It was something in the air, in the discreetly warm smiles they were given as Lalla greeted everyone. *If only they knew the truth*, thought Tara. *How ironic. No doubt the whole place assumes we're lovers.* She wondered if Jago was aware of it, but figured he wouldn't care anyway. As she smiled in answer to a greeting from an elderly lady who looked remarkably like Morag, she thought suddenly, *He doesn't really care about anything. Everything is logical and emotionless to him, able to be reduced to a formula on paper. Perhaps it's part of his job, being like that, and not getting involved.*

She watched him discreetly as Morag introduced him to the bride and groom. He stood there talking to them, perfectly at ease, a tall attractive man who was even now being eyed by several girls who stood in a giggling bunch in a corner of the large room. Tara's heart did a funny flip, although she didn't know why. Then she noticed the big man who stood by the bar, a pint glass in his hand, frankly appraising her. She felt herself go warm, as warm as the red hair he flaunted. It could only be Ruari Mhor and she knew what Lalla meant about him having an eye for women. He lifted his glass to his mouth, and his eyes narrowed before Tara turned away.

Morag came up, and the jukebox began blaring again, as Tara and Lalla went to meet the shy couple who looked as if they wanted nothing so much as to get away.

There was dancing and drinking. Jago bought them both whiskies before they trooped into a side room to see the presents. After that, in a Paul Jones, Tara found herself being partnered briefly by the red-haired man. It hadn't been her imagination before. The awareness was there all right, in the way he held her during that brief encounter. Tara didn't like him. She was instinctively frightened of him, but at the same time felt it was somehow nice to know that she wasn't completely devoid of attraction. The evening passed, and the room grew warmer and more smoky. Jago was enjoying himself, or at least appeared to be as much as he could, she thought. Wasn't everything, all human behaviour, just a lot of statistics to him?

Ruari Mhor got Tara into a corner during a particularly hectic dance, and held her prisoner with his arm.

"Let's away outside for a wee while," he said thickly. He had been drinking a lot and Tara hadn't missed the wary glances from other men, nor Morag's disapproving look when he had stumbled once and sent glasses flying. They knew him and were used to him, but all the same, Tara knew that Morag wished he'd come a week later.

Jago, busy dancing with a pretty girl who wore too much make-up, seemed completely unconcerned with anything Tara did. Some part of her wanted to cry out to him, "Look, someone thinks I'm attractive. A real man, not a head-shrinker." She smiled and laughed, and thought that maybe she was having a good time after all. Her first Highland wedding! It wasn't what she had expected, but it would be interesting all the same to tell her mother and father about when she wrote.

Lalla was busy talking to some of Morag's relatives in a corner. She had her "writer's" face on although she appeared to be listening intently and was nodding in all the right places. Tara knew that her mind was really miles away, shaping and forming a character for her book. And she sensed too that it was Ruari, who had clearly decided that Tara found him irresistible and who would not accept her refusals to take a walk outside.

Then at one point Tara knew she had to get away for a while alone. The smoky air pricked her eyes, and her head was reeling with the unaccustomed alcohol. Jago had vanished and her lips tightened. Was he with a girl? She didn't care, but she didn't want to see them either.

Tara slipped on her warm stole and walked quietly outside. The cold air hit her with icy needles and she shivered, pulling the stole more closely around her. It was a clear bright night, and she decided to walk across the paved yard as far as the wall, look over it, and return. Her head throbbed and she put a hand to her forehead. What was the use? It was an ordeal, this evening, but she was determined to stick it out. . . .

"So you came after all." Ruari's voice came from behind her, and she whirled around, startled, and found herself held by a pair of hard arms.

"Oh, Ruari! You frightened me!" It took her a few moments to catch her breath. She didn't want to be out here with him where there was no one else around, although the windows of the pub shook with the noise from within.

She tried to move away, but he held her, laughing. "Ah, come on, you're a fine bonny lass. Don't go all coy on me now." His whisky-laden breath was on her face as he lunged at her and kissed her hard. Her arms were held too tightly, so she kicked his shin.

"Let me go!"

"Ow! What you wanna do that for?" This, clearly, had never happened to him before. He bent to rub his leg and Tara twisted away, but not fast enough. One long sinewy arm came out and grabbed her. "Hold it, little spitfire. Nobody kicks *me* an' gets away wi' it." And then Tara saw the tall dark shape looming up from somewhere near the pub and heard—oh, blessed relief—Jago's voice.

"All right, you heard the lady."

Ruari released her to swing around, and saw Jago. He laughed, "Ach, you. What do you want, Sassenach? Do you not know where you're not wanted?"

"Do you want me to go, Tara?" Jago asked.

"No!" She hadn't intended it to come out so sharply. "No," she repeated. "I . . . I only came out for some fresh air. I want t-to go back now." She didn't care if it was Jago, she wasn't staying here with this drunken red-head, who was making her more nervous by the minute.

"Right. Come on, I'll take you in," said Jago, and held out his arm. Ruaru struck it away, and in a brief, unprintable two-word epithet, told Jago to leave. The lamp at the edge of the car park cast a dim light, but Tara saw Jago's face change and heard his indrawn breath. A strange excitement filled her.

"I don't like your language," he said in his calm voice. "Not in front of a woman. Tara, go on. I'll follow you later."

"Like hell you will. . . ." and Tara heard a stream of

Gaelic. She didn't know the language, but he wasn't commenting on the weather, that was certain. She began to move away, because instinct told her what was about to happen. This strange excitement pulsated inside her. She didn't want the men to fight . . . and yet. . . .

And then, astoundingly, she heard Jago reply in the same tongue. It shook Ruari, she could tell, for he peered more closely at Jago as he muttered, "Who the hell *are* you?"

Tara noticed two things at practically the same moment: both men were the same height, and the pub had gone deathly quiet. Faces were peering at the window now, and she could sense the excitement.

Ruari lashed out with his right arm in a blow that would have felled a tree, but Jago moved quicker than the red-haired man, and went in swiftly. He caught Ruari once, twice, under his chin, rocking him.

Groggily, and vile-tempered now, Ruari shouted "Right, boyo, that does it. You—" But that next word was lost as his head cracked back and he went sprawling to the ground. Tara was rooted to the spot in horror. This was awful, and yet there was something fascinating in the sight of Jago—calm, impersonal Jago, who never got annoyed or lost his temper—reaching down to yank a half-conscious red-haired giant to his feet. Ruari hadn't once hit him. It had been over in minutes.

Noise broke out, and then footsteps were coming nearer, and voices were raised in excitement as everyone began to discuss what had just happened. Tara suddenly felt sick, and turned away to lean on the low wall and stare blankly ahead at dark shadows on the hills. She was trembling with reaction, and put her hand to her mouth. If only she hadn't come out. . . .If only. . . . Too late for that. She started violently at the touch on her arm and turned to see Morag.

"Oh, Morag!" She wanted to burst into tears. "I'm ... I'm sorry ...." she began.

"Sorry! Ach, what is it? By God, he's a bonny wee fighter, yon man of yours. Best entertainment I ever ... ach, an' we never knew!"

"You're not mad?" gasped Tara. "It's ruined your party ...."

"No! Away wi' ye. Can't we always expect a wee brawl or two, especially at a wedding. An' no one's ever seen Ruari Mhor off his feet before." She patted Tara's arm briskly. "T'will give us something to talk about for awhile. Aye, and mebbe that red-haired braggart will not be so keen to boast in future. Come away in, girl, you're shivering. ..." And she led Tara back inside.

It was past eleven, and the party was beginning to break up. Perhaps that had been the climax, thought Tara, seeing the islanders donning coats, saying their goodnights, and going over to speak to Jago, who, she suddenly realized, seemed to be the hero of the hour.

There wasn't a mark on him. *There wouldn't be*, she thought wryly, and was suddenly sobered to think that the fight had been over her. The least she could do was to thank him, but she didn't want to. She would have to force it.

Half an hour later they were walking home. Lalla had been one of the audience at the window and was bursting to talk about the incident, but in view of the constrained atmosphere between Tara and Jago, had to content herself with comments about the reception and the buffet supper they had eaten earlier. Lalla asked Jago in for coffee when at last they reached the house. Tara knew he was about to refuse, and said quickly, "I'm going straight to bed, so feel free."

"All right, thanks." He looked at Lalla, and Tara caught the glance, but didn't understand it, for there was something there. ...

As soon as they were inside, Tara kissed Lalla. "Good night, love. You don't mind?"

Lalla winked at her. "Of course not. Shall I bring you up a drink?"

"No, thanks, I'm dead tired." She turned to go out, and Jago said, "Good night, Tara."

She faltered in her steps, but just for a second. "Good night." She couldn't say his name, not for anything. She had no intention of ever saying it again.

CHAPTER SIX

THE NEXT DAY they slept late, and when eventually she woke, Tara felt better than she had for days. She slipped on her dressing gown and went downstairs to make tea. She remembered, as the kettle boiled, that she had heard Lalla's and Jago's voices for what had seemed like ages before she eventually fell asleep, and she wondered what they had found to talk about for so long. Not that it mattered to her, for she really didn't care. But she found out, partly anyway, when she took a cup of tea to Lalla, who was still in bed.

Her aunt stretched and yawned. "Oh, my dear, how nice. Put it down there. That's it. Mmm, lovely," she struggled up and reached for her wrap. "Sit down on the bed. I've got something to tell you."

Tara obediently sat down. "What is it?" she asked, expecting something about the party.

"Morag's told Jago he can take Fiona to Edinburgh to see his specialist friend!"

"What? Oh, that's wonderful. How did it happen?"

"Because of the fight, apparently! Morag was very impressed by a man who could actually knock Ruari out. She had a quick rethink and a chat with her son, who was at the reception, though I don't remember which one he was. . . . "

"Yes? And when's he taking her?"

"Well," Lalla gave Tara a look that should have warned her. "Well, this is the awkward bit. Obviously she's got to have someone . . . a woman . . . with her . . . and . . . . " she stopped.

Tara stood up. "No," she said. "Oh, no!"

"And Morag says," Lalla ignored the outburst, "that it can only be you, for Fiona likes you, and—"

"No!" Tara went to the window in great agitation. She turned around. "Lalla, you know I can't, not after what's happened."

"I know, dear. So does Jago, believe me. We spent hours going over it last night, and it puts him in a very awkward position because she needs to see this specialist soon. Each week's delay could affect her eventual treatment—"

"Stop it!" said Tara weakly. "Please. Let me think." She put her hands to her face, but she knew that she really had no choice.

She turned to Lalla. "I want to speak to . . . to him," she said. "Will he be up?"

Lalla nodded. "Yes, I think so. Are you going now?"

Tara looked down at her dressing gown and smiled faintly. "Not like this. I'll get dressed." And with a last look at Lalla, she left the room.

SHE KNOCKED at his door. There was something else nagging at the back of her mind, and she had to have an answer to it; it couldn't wait.

He called out, "Come in," and she hesitated, then slowly opened the door and entered. The living room was empty, but sounds came from the kitchen. "Won't be a minute . . . . " Then she heard his footsteps and heard him begin, "Did you tell—" He came in and stopped. "Oh, it's you. Good morning."

"Yes, she told me about Edinburgh. Tell me, is it one of your plots?"

Jago looked at her. He wore a brown dressing gown over blue pyjamas, and was barefooted. His hair was untidy and he needed a shave. Perhaps he intended having one after he had drunk the tea he held. "I don't follow," he said. "Do you want some tea?"

"No, thanks. This trip to Edinburgh that I have to go on . . . is it so that you can have me discreetly examined as well by another of your friends?"

There was a slight tightening of that dark jaw. "What do you think I am?" he asked quietly.

"I know what you are, I just want an answer."

"Of course not. Morag told me last night that I can take Fiona. It's as simple as that. There's no one else I can ask to go. Besides, the girl likes you. You know that, so does Morag. I want to go soon, before they change their mind. This week. I'll phone my friend today from the village. I tried to phone him last night from the pub after she'd given me the go-ahead, but he was out. That's how keen I am. It has nothing to do with you except purely as a chaperone for her."

"I don't need to tell you why I don't want to. But for Fiona's sake, I'll do it." Tara turned away. "I'm going now. You'd better let me know what day we'll be going, and I'll get some things ready. How . . . how long will we be away?"

"Two nights."

"Right, I'll tell Lalla. Goodbye." She opened the door before he could move to do it, and went out. She was committed now, but she still didn't trust him, not at all.

IT ALL HAPPENED QUICKLY. That evening Jago came to the house while Tara was listening to a radio play. Lalla had gone upstairs to make a few notes about "Red Ruari" as she had christened him. The soft strains of the play's closing music filled the room as the rap came on the door, and she went to open it.

Jago stood on the porch, and it was so dark she could scarcely see him. She took a deep breath. "Do you want Lalla? She's writing—"

"No. I've just phoned. We can go tomorrow. Can you do it?"

"I . . . . " she hadn't intended to ask him in, but the surprise took her breath away. She backed away slightly. "You'd better come in . . . it's a bit sudden . . . . "

He pulled off the hood of his anorak as he came in,

but made no move to unzip the coat itself, as if he knew he wasn't going to stay. "I've just come from Morag's now. They're packing some clothes for Fiona, and they'll have her ready at nine."

"Then I'll be ready, too. When? Eight?"

"If you will." He had a very steady gaze, but it was quite different, like a stranger's, she thought. *Not like last night,* she thought. *He came to life then, just for those few minutes of the fight. He was a real man, tough and aggressive.* "Take some warm clothes. It's freezing in Edinburgh."

"All right. Where will we be staying?" She hadn't intended to ask, but his mentioning clothes made her wonder.

"That's all taken care of. Well, I'll go—"

"Just one more thing. How much money will I need?"

He had half turned, but he slowly came back. "What for?"

"Everything. Fares, accommodation, meals. Just to give me an idea."

He waited until she had finished speaking, and a flicker of something she couldn't understand touched his eyes. "I shouldn't worry about that."

"I'm not letting you pay for me," she said clearly and pleasantly, but with cold determination as well. "I'll pay my own way. Fiona . . . . " she shrugged, "she's different. That's your business. But not me."

He inclined his head slightly. "As you wish. But to save time, I suggest I let you know what you owe when we return."

Tara nodded. "All right. Is that all?"

"Yes. I'm going."

There was something else she had to say to him and it might as well be now. And if it came out reluctantly, she didn't care. "Thank you for g-getting rid of Ruari last night."

He paused with his hand on the door. "That's quite all right. I wasn't sure at first if I was interfering or not."

She swallowed. "No. No, you weren't. I would have managed to . . . to push him off eventually, but . . . well . . . ."

"Would you?" There was the slightest trace of a smile at his mouth, but it didn't reach his eyes. "You might have had a few shocks first. Some men don't like having to take no for an answer. Good night." And he was gone, shutting the door silently behind him. Tara stood there, seething. Just for a moment, there had been a thin thread of arrogance in his tone, and she hadn't liked it. She took a deep breath and went to pack some clothes.

THE TRAIN LULLED Fiona to sleep soon after they left Kirkgarron. There was no direct route to Edinburgh, and they had to change at Inverness, but not for two hours. The coach was an open one with tables, and Tara sat next to Fiona. Jago was opposite, his long legs stretched slantwise under the table. Rain pelted down outside, and Tara looked out the window, seeing the gray mountains pass them in a wet blur. They were the only ones in the carriage, and she carefully avoided meeting Jago's eye. Not, she had to admit, that he was making any great effort to look at her. He was at that moment busily engaged on the *Times* crossword, and Tara had an open magazine in front of her, which she kept trying to read. They would arrive in Edinburgh by late afternoon. She didn't know what would happen then, for she didn't like to ask, but she was sure that he would have everything planned to the last detail. She glanced at the sleeping girl beside her and her mouth softened. Poor little lamb! Did she guess what was being done for her? Did she wonder where she was being taken, by these two comparative strangers? If she did, she had showed no outward signs of apprehension when

Jago and Tara had arrived at the small whitewashed house where she lived. She had gone immediately and trustingly to Jago and put her hand in his, and Tara had seen Fiona's mother bite her lip and turn away, distress written on her pleasant features.

Within minutes they had been on the ferry, and within a half hour on the train. Now, with the miles speeding past, Fiona would soon be further away from her home than she had ever been before.

Suddenly Tara wanted to tell Jago that she knew how much he was doing for this child. But she couldn't. The barriers were too great now ever to be surmounted. They were invisible, yet as strong as any steel walls. Tara had made up her mind to that, and nothing would ever lessen the pain and shock she had had that night when she had discovered she was merely a human guinea pig to the man who now sat opposite her. He knew, that was certain, and his apparent indifference only seemed to confirm her conviction. It was odd, even so, that he remained so courteous. His manners were perfect, Tara had to admit. Opening doors, carrying her suitcase, and Fiona's pathetically small carrier bag, helping them on and off the ferry—none of it seemed forced. It came naturally to him, and that was a point, however slight, in his favor.

"Do you want a cigarette, Tara?"

"No, thank you."

"Do you mind if I smoke?"

"No, of course not." Maybe he had read her thoughts. She nearly smiled, and it seemed as if his glance rested briefly on her face. She composed her features and looked down at the magazine quickly. Eventually, she closed her eyes, wishing for strength to get through the ordeal of the next two days. If he stayed like this, it would be all right, but if he tried to talk to her . . . . She turned and looked out the window, seeing nothing but a gray drizzly blur. He wouldn't, would he? Would he?

Tara ran her tongue over suddenly dry lips, and heard him say, "Do you want a drink?"

"What? Oh, no, thanks. Not yet. W-when we arrive in Inverness. How long have we got to wait for the connection?"

"About twenty minutes. Plenty of time."

Then there was silence again, because there was nothing more to say. Tara dozed lightly after a while, and had strange dreams.

AFTER THE QUIET of Gaela, Edinburgh seemed enormously loud. The noise couldn't affect Fiona, but she stared around her wide-eyed and apprehensive as they went out into the bitter cold of a February day. She held tightly to both Tara and Jago. The coat she wore was not really thick enough, but Tara knew that she was wearing two pullovers underneath, a fact she had discovered when she had taken Fiona to the toilet.

Jago hailed a taxi, and they were off. Fiona sat with her eyes glued to the window, and Tara sat closely beside her to avoid contact with the man leaning forward to direct the driver.

The journey was long. Edinburgh was a gray, beautiful city, full of trees and small parks, and Tara began to relax. She wondered what the hotel would be like, and hoped that it would be one of the major ones.

When the taxi stopped, it was outside a terrace of imposing Victorian houses, all with several bells on the porches. Jago paid for the taxi and then he said, "This way," and ushered them up the steps. Inside was a deep, rich carpet, and a door on either side of the hall. He produced a key, opened the door on the left, and stood back. Tara knew then, but she went in anyway, because she had no choice, and held tight to Fiona's hand.

"This isn't a hotel," she said, looking around. The apartment was large, with its own hall.

"No," Jago agreed. "It's not. It's my apartment."

"I'm not staying here. . . . " she began.

He opened the door and added, as if she hadn't spoken, "Are you coming in? The child's tired."

The living room was spacious, elegant and thickly carpeted. The furniture was beautiful and well cared for, and the pictures on the walls were of good landscapes, the sort Tara enjoyed looking at. But she was too agitated to take it in. She faced him.

"You know what I mean," she said as she ushered Fiona into a chair.

"You usually manage to make yourself perfectly clear," he answered, and the irony was well concealed, but there. "But I see no point in paying expensive hotel bills for two nights when this place is as well equipped. There are two bedrooms . . . I'll show you. Twin beds in one, for you both. Bathroom, kitchen, this room. I've got books, color television, everything you need. Fiona's never seen TV in her life. She can see the children's programs here, but she couldn't in a hotel."

Tara felt as if the ground was slipping away from under her feet. She looked around, saw Fiona's eyes traveling over the room, and she knew that she had lost.

Jago looked at his watch. "I'm starving. Do you like Chinese, Indian, or plain old fish and chips?"

She bit her lip. "Anything, but Fiona's mother gave me a list of her likes and dislikes. Just a moment." She opened her bag and took out the folded sheet of paper, smoothing it open.

She read it quickly, then passed it to him. "It doesn't say anything about foreign foods, but then I don't suppose they've ever had any. I think she's better off eating something plain. It says she likes boiled eggs. Do you have any?"

"No, I'll go now and get some. Do you want to come, or will you wait here?"

"We'll wait." As if he expected her to choose otherwise!

"All right. I'll switch on the television and the fire. I'll bring back milk, too, for coffee. If you want any now, there's powdered in the cupboard."

"No, thanks." She would wait.

He went around the apartment, switching on soft gold-shaded wall lamps, the television and the huge log-effect electric fire. Then he looked around. "I won't be long."

She heard the outer door of the apartment close, and waited to see him go down the steps. Instead there was silence. Faintly, from the back, a door slammed, and Tara realized he had a car. That felt funny, because she had only seen him walking, and had never connected him with driving. It was logical, however. The apartment was in the suburbs. Wherever he worked—if he did work, and she was beginning to wonder about it, because what man can take holidays whenever he chose?—there would be a good distance to go. Tara went closer to the window, but not close enough to be seen.

There was a park at the end of the road, quite close to the house, but it was almost hidden from sight by the sleety rain.

Tara shivered and turned away. A cartoon film had come on the television, and Fiona, in the act of taking her coat off, stood transfixed, a look of complete wonder on her face. Tara laughed and eased the sleeves from the girl's thin arms. She opened the first door, and found it was a coat closet, so she put both hers and the little girl's inside, and went to sit beside Fiona on the couch. After a few minutes, she heard a car outside, and turned to look. It was a black Mercedes sports car, a luxurious vehicle that spoke of money. She saw Jago lean over to pick up a bag from the seat beside him.

She turned away. Well, now she knew. She heard the door slam, heard his footsteps, then he came in. Faint white specks were melting on his hair as he took off his anorak and put the bag of groceries down on a chair by the door.

"I've got eggs, milk, bread and butter . . . oh, yes, and cheese. I saw it on the list. And I've brought some food back for us. Would you like to come to the kitchen and sort out what you want?"

"Yes." She was hungry too, and knew Fiona must be, although the little girl never asked for food but just accepted what was put in front of her.

They ate in the kitchen, and Fiona bolted down her boiled egg and bread, clearly eager to get back to the magic box of color that so fascinated her. Jago nodded, and waved his hand toward the door of the living room. "Yes, Fiona, you may go."

Then there were just the two of them. He had brought back four cartons of Chinese food, and stuffed pancake rolls wrapped in aluminum foil. It was all piping hot and quite delicious. Tara helped herself from each carton and poured soy sauce over everything. It would all have been wonderful, except that she was with the wrong person. Just at that moment she was too hungry to care, and she noticed that Jago put his food back very efficiently, too. When at last they had finished eating, she had to say what was in her mind.

"You know I wouldn't have come, don't you, if you'd told me we were going to sleep in your apartment?"

"I know." He was standing by the stove, watching milk and water boil in a pan. He turned to Tara. "But in that event I would have booked us in at a hotel. I was determined to get Fiona here, one way or another, and I have."

"Do you always get your own way?"

"Not always." He turned away as he said it, so she couldn't see the expression on his face, but the dry ironic tone made her feel warm.

Quickly she said, "What's happening today?"

He turned then. "Nothing. I mean, not with Fiona. We're going in the morning to my friend's clinic. We'll be there all day, most likely, and then come back here. We'll set off Wednesday morning for Gaela."

"You have a strange job that lets you waltz back and forth across the country. Do you actually work?" She knew she was verging on the personal, even the rude, but a reckless impulse made her go on. It was as if she wanted to see how far she could go. He was busy pouring coffee into two mugs. Then he turned, set Tara's cup before her, put his own down, and drew up his chair.

"Right," he said. "You're obviously bursting to know, so I'll tell you. And when I've finished, if you have any questions to ask, ask then. In that way, you'll know, won't you?" He smiled, and she wanted to hit him. There was no humor in it, no warmth, just a movement of his facial muscles, and she was suddenly aware of his extraordinary power and strength, so she sat very still. In spite of everything, she really did want to know.

"I do work. Here in Edinburgh, at the University occasionally, where I lecture in psychology. But my main employment is with one of the biggest industrial firms in Europe. I work on a contractual basis, that's to say that I do a certain amount in a certain time. When, where, or how I do it is my own business. I compile questionnaires—the type used by many big firms to test that the people they want get the right jobs. To put it more simply, I help to fit square pegs into square holes." He pushed the sugar bowl across to Tara. "I work on Gaela sometimes during the day. I find the atmosphere there ideal. I don't practise in psychiatry, nor as a doctor, but

I assure you I am qualified in all three fields and can prove it.

"My grandfather was Angus Cameron, Laird of Gaela. He was an unhappy, bitter old man who turfed my mother out because she wanted to marry a penniless fisherman. After she died, leaving my sister and me living with our father in Cornwall, he must have had a change of heart, because he spent thousands tracing us. He left me a small fortune, as well as the Big House on Gaela."

"So you see, if I wanted to, I could move into it tomorrow and never work again. I might eventually do just that . . . move into the Big House, I mean. But not to laze around.

"I'm planning to have the house fixed up and converted into a convalescent home for sick children . . . those from broken homes, perhaps, or with mental disturbances. I've got a lot of things to think about before I do it, though."

He swallowed his coffee and stood up, and, for some reason, he was the nearest thing to angry that Tara had ever seen. It puzzled and disturbed her, as had his words. She now knew all about him, or as much as he wanted her to know, and the picture formed was disquieting. He was a single-minded man with a sense of purpose that was almost frightening in its intensity. How could she ever have thought she was anything to him other than a cold statistic? She turned away, unwilling for him to see her face. Carrying her empty cup to the sink, she said over her shoulder, "Thank you for telling me."

"No questions?" Mockery tinged the query.

"No." She looked at the table. "Shall I wash up?"

"No. You're my guest. Go and join Fiona. I'll show you to your room afterwards."

Without another word Tara went out of the kitchen.

FIONA WAS ALMOST asleep at half past seven, her head heavy as she tried to watch the television.

"Come on, love," said Tara, touching her on the shoulder. "Bedtime." She pulled the rolled-up pyjamas from the top of the bag and took the little girl into the bedroom. Minutes after that, she was tucked snugly in bed.

It was later that an odd, disturbing thing happened, jolting Tara once again.

The television was on, and she had been idly watching it because she didn't want to read or talk to Jago.

He went out at nine to put his car away. The sleet had stopped, and the ground outside appeared to be covered with a gray slush. She shivered at the sight of it as she stood by the window for a moment and she wondered what her parents were doing. How surprised they would be if they knew she was in Edinburgh, less than 250 miles from home. Jago had a phone, and she decided to ask him when he returned if she could call them. She looked around her and saw Fiona's luggage still on the chair, and went over to see what the child was to wear the following day.

Gently she lifted out the clothes and a lump came into her throat. There was a clean well-darned pair of gray socks, clean undershirt and pants and a warm dress. It was the dress that brought sudden tears to Tara's eyes. Clearly a hand-me-down, it was of brown wool, and very plain, even though it had an embroidered flower on a pocket. Something told Tara that this was Fiona's best one. She didn't hear the door open, or the footsteps. In her mind was a picture of Fiona as she would look tomorrow, and a rush of sadness overwhelmed her. Poor little scrap! What had she ever had out of life? Love and affection, yes, undoubtedly, but precious little else. Certainly she hadn't had the help she so badly needed, nor the understanding.

Tara laid the dress on the chair and covered her face with her hands.

"What is it? Tara?" Suddenly she was being turned around, and she started violently and tried to pull herself free.

"Oh!" She couldn't speak, and the tears came freely now as Jago lifted her hands from her face. She shook her head wordlessly.

"Are you ill?"

She managed to compose herself sufficiently to nod toward the dress on the chair.

"It's that . . . her clothes. I was just looking at them and thinking."

"I see." He spoke quite gently, and without more words she knew that he understood. "If I hadn't made them believe that Fiona's train fare would be paid by the National Health Service, they wouldn't have let her come. They're proud as well as poor, Tara."

She fumbled in the pocket of her gray pantsuit for a hanky, and found it. She turned away quickly then. The moment of intimacy must not last. "I think I'll go to bed. I'm tired," she said. "I may read for a while. Do you have any fiction?"

"Over there. Help yourself." For a moment she was reminded of that dreadful time at his house on Gaela. She went over to the bookcase and knelt down.

"Can I make a phone call to my parents?" she said, and half turned.

"Sure. You know where it is. If you're going to phone and then get ready for bed, you won't mind if I go across the hall to visit a friend, will you?"

Mind! "No, of course not."

"It's the door facing mine. If you need anything, anything at all, knock. I'll be there."

"I will. Thank you." But she didn't turn when she said it, and she waited for him to go.

SHE FELL ASLEEP before he came back from his neighbor's, and in the morning when she woke she wondered where she was. Then she sat up quickly. She was in Edinburgh, sleeping in Jago's apartment. He had shown a faint, disturbing trace of humanity again the previous night, which was disconcerting, to say the least. She didn't want him to be human. It was much easier if he just stayed the way she expected him to be.

She crept out of bed to see Fiona, and checked the time on her watch. It wasn't quite seven, and she wanted a cup of coffee more than anything. But she had no dressing gown, and her coat was in a cupboard in the living room. She could have kicked herself for not thinking of that!

She looked down at her nightie, which was two layers of filmy nylon. Although short, it was adequate. Quickly she crept out of the bedroom on bare feet that buried themselves in the lush carpet. When she reached the door of the cupboard, she looked up to see Jago watching her from the kitchen doorway. He was fully dressed in matching black sweater and pants.

She said quickly, "I came for my coat . . . . " When she had slid it on, she could look at him. "I wanted a cup of coffee," she said breathlessly.

"I've just made tea. Want some? Or must it be coffee?"

She buttoned the coat up. "Tea will do, thanks. Are you always up so early?" It was easier to talk than just stand there. His face had been devoid of expression when he had been watching her.

"No. But I have things to do before we go. There won't be time tomorrow. Did I wake you?"

"No, I don't think so. Fiona's fast asleep. Will . . . will these tests be at all . . . disturbing for her?"

"Nothing will hurt. She'll be X-rayed, given a comprehensive medical, tested to check her reflexes and so on—all the things to try and eliminate what's not causing her problem. She'll also have a very detailed hearing examination. There are parts of that I would prefer you to stay out of, but I'll be there all the time, don't worry. I'll be with her."

Tara took a deep breath. "I wanted to be sure," she said slowly. She closed her eyes for a moment. Jago poured out two cups of tea and handed her one.

"Toast? I'm making some."

"Please." She sat down at the red formica-topped table and spooned sugar in her cup. "What will happen if you're right, and there's nothing wrong with her except deafness?"

"She'll have to go to a special school for a few years. I think she's above average intelligence. I'm sure she'll be able to lead a normal life eventually."

"Could there be any hope in an operation?"

He shrugged. "Obviously that's something Kirk will want to discover."

"Kirk?"

"John Kirk. The specialist friend we're seeing today."

There was a faint but distinctive smell, and he turned to the grill with a muttered oath, pulling out two pieces of toast with blackened edges.

"I don't mind it well done," Tara said quickly. "Then I'll go and get washed."

"No hurry. We don't leave until nine. I'll be working in my bedroom after I've eaten, so you can get ready in your own time."

He put more bread under the grill, and Tara slowly began to butter that which was already done. She was beginning now, at last, to realize all the precise implications of what was going to happen today.

TARA SMILED at the pretty young nurse who brought her tea. "Sorry, no cookies," she said, as she passed the cup to Tara. "But there's a candy machine in the reception hall."

"No, thanks, this is fine," Tara smiled. She had stayed with Fiona for the preliminary medical, and now Fiona and Jago had gone off together, leaving Tara in a clean, warm, and completely impersonal waiting room of the clinic where Dr. Kirk was apparently well esteemed.

Magazines were piled on a table beside her, and she put the cup and saucer down on them, conscious of glances from several other people, who perhaps felt that what was good for one should be good for all. It didn't matter. Tara looked down at her feet, unable to read because her thoughts were with Fiona and what was happening to her. She must be frightened, because to her all this must be strange. And there was no way of explaining to her, as you could to a normal child, what was going to happen.

Tara bit her lip, seeing again Jago's face as he had told her it would be better for her to wait until she was wanted because they were going to do very delicate hearing tests and concentration was essential.

They had been in Dr. Kirk's office at the time. Fiona, swathed in a multicolored terry towelling robe, was sitting on Jago's knee, her arms around his neck and her eyes intent on his face. It was almost as if, Tara thought suddenly, she knew he was helping her without words being said.

He had said, "We'll be an hour or more. I'll be with her all the time, but I'd prefer you to step in the waiting room until we send for you."

"All right." She had watched his hands on Fiona's shoulders: strong hands that had knocked down a bully; gentle hands that could hold a child or a woman and not hurt them. The door had opened and the moment passed, as John Kirk, a thin, voluble Scot, came in and nodded. "We're right now, Jago." He grinned at Tara.

"And wipe that look off your face, lassie, we'll no' hurt her."

"I know," she had smiled faintly at him. "I'll go to the waiting room . . . . "

Now she straightened her legs. She realized, suddenly, almost with a sense of shock, that she had not once since leaving Gaela been conscious of her scar or her limp. And she knew suddenly why they didn't matter any more: she had someone else to think about. And if it didn't matter now, then it didn't have to matter ever again. Tara lifted her hand to her hair, to smooth it away from her face, and she knew she was free.

IT WAS BITTERLY COLD when they came out to the parking lot at the front of the clinic.

Jago looked at Fiona, who was shivering slightly. "Stay there, I'll go get the car." He ran down the steps and along the rows of parked vehicles until he reached his own.

A few minutes later, with Fiona snugly tucked into the back of the powerful car, they were driving along the road home. Then Tara looked around as Jago turned left instead of keeping straight on. Before she could speak, he said, "We're going shopping."

"Oh," she sat back again and turned to see Fiona sitting wrapped in a blanket in the narrow space at the back. She smiled at her.

"Was she good?" she asked.

"Very. No temper, no tears, nothing. It was as if she knew."

"Yes," Tara agreed, remembering the office. "I think you're right." He had said nothing about the tests, but she had to ask one question. "Can . . . can they do anything for her?"

"Yes. There's a lot of information to be fed into a computer, and those X-rays to be checked, but John says definitely. He agrees with me. She's very intelligent."

Tara let out her breath in a long sigh of relief. "Oh, I'm so glad!" Tears sprang to her eyes. Jago was too busy concentrating on the traffic to look at her, but he sensed her mood. He smiled slightly, but he said nothing.

It wasn't until they were in one of the larger and more exclusive Princes Street stores that Tara began to wonder why they had come. She had vaguely imagined he needed food, but they were in the children's wear department, and Jago looked at her.

"I'm going to buy this poor kid a coat," he said. "Will you help? I'm sure you have a better idea than me . . . . "

Then, seeing Tara's face, he added, "Don't say it. I'll cope with the parents when we get back . . . tell 'em I got it on the National Health or something," and he grinned down at Fiona, who smiled back.

"Yes. I'll help." She looked down at the shabby gray coat Fiona wore. "A tweed one would be best, I think."

"I'll leave it to you. Look, I'll sit here and have a cigarette while you wander around, okay?"

Tara took hold of the little girl's hand and they went off, leaving Jago to sit down gingerly on a giltbacked chair that looked as if it might collapse under his weight.

Strange emotions churned inside Tara. Her heart beat loudly, because he wasn't really so impersonal after all. She knew it now, and was disturbed.

Fiona didn't understand what was happening at first, but soon began to enjoy herself trying on coats and parading in front of a mirror. When Tara held out the warm lovat tweed, she knew right away that it was perfect. It fitted splendidly, and had a good hem, and good pockets. Fiona herself looked up at Tara as if to say, "Please, this one?"

It cost almost fifteen pounds, however, and Tara swallowed. Taking a deep breath, she went over to Jago with Fiona proudly walking beside her and said "You didn't say how much we could . . . er . . . go up to."

"No, because it didn't matter. Is this the one?"

"Yes. We both like it. Do you?"

"Looks fine to me, but I'm no judge."

Tara held up the price tag on the sleeve, and he winced. "I'm in the wrong business I can see. Right, we'll have it. She can keep it on." He lifted a finger and a saleswoman glided over oozing smiles.

They were outside, walking along Princes Street with Fiona in the middle, when Jago stopped outside a restaurant. "Are you hungry?"

"Yes," Tara nodded. They had eaten in the staff canteen at the clinic, but that had been at noon. It was now almost five-thirty, and the streets were thronged not only with shoppers, but also with workers hurrying home. Jago's Mercedes was in a parking lot near the station, and Tara saw the evening stretching ahead blankly, for there was nothing to do now except wait for morning and the train back to Gaela.

"Then we'll eat here. They make good food."

They went in, Jago opening the door for Tara and Fiona and following them in. Tara walked proudly with her head held high, and she didn't mind if he noticed the difference. She would never be ashamed again, never brush her hair forward in case anyone saw her scar, nor make the effort to disguise the limp. It wasn't important.

She was herself again, a whole person. She would tell Lalla tomorrow, then she would finish typing the Damien Corbett book and go home. She knew now that Lalla hadn't needed her as much as she had needed Lalla. And she couldn't stay any longer on Gaela with Jago as a next-door neighbor.

IT WAS ALMOST ten, Fiona had been asleep for hours, and Tara was watching a play on television. Jago had gone to his neighbor's, because Tara had insisted. A phone call had come for him, and he had asked if she would mind if he went over with a message from a mutual friend. "Look," she had said, "if you want to visit your neighbor, please do. There's a play I particularly want to see . . . didn't think I'd get the chance when I read about it in the paper last week . . . . " and she had watched him go with a great sense of relief.

But now as the play neared its end she heard Fiona cry out, and went immediately in to her. The girl sat up in bed and started sobbing loudly.

"All right, love, I'm here," Tara soothed her, but looked worriedly at the door. If only he could hear, but the walls were too thick. She switched on the light, saying, "I'll go for Jago . . . . " knowing that Fiona couldn't understand anyway. She ran out quickly, leaving all the doors open and knocked loudly on the door opposite.

A tall blond girl opened the door a few inches. "Why . . . hello?" she began, puzzled, as Tara tried to collect her wits. She had expected a man. But there was no time to wonder now.

"It's Fiona . . . she's upset . . . can Jago come over?"

"Oh, it's you! Sorry, love . . . Jago!" then she turned back to Tara. "He won't be a moment. Will you come in?"

But Tara was already retreating. "No, I'll get back to her. Thank you . . . . " and she fled. It wasn't until later that she realized the girl had been wearing a dressing gown over a nightie.

Fiona soon settled down after an aspirin and some warm milk. Jago looked down at the sleeping girl, her face still slightly flushed.

"Over-excitement," he said succinctly. "She'd had a very busy day, don't forget. She'll be as right as rain in the morning." He looked at his watch again. There had been, thought Tara, something very professional about the way he had looked at it when he was taking Fiona's pulse.

"Mmm, I won't go back now. Too late. Want any supper?"

"No, thanks." Tara's mouth was dry, and her throat ached. She didn't want to look at him. What he did was his own business, of course, but the girl had looked like an old friend. And why not, if they were neighbours? But there was a numb coldness inside her that wouldn't go away, even after she had gone to bed. She lay awake for ages, listening to the distant sounds of traffic before falling asleep. She knew she had to get away from Gaela; away from Jago Black, as soon as possible.

CHAPTER SEVEN

THERE WAS SO much to tell Lalla, and so much more that couldn't be said. Tara knew what had happened to her now, and the knowledge was upsetting. She was almost at the end of the book, and it would be nice to have finished it. It wouldn't be running away, for she was now cured of what had been troubling her when she had arrived on that misty isle not so long ago. Perhaps thoughts of Jago would fade in time, like that mist.

Tara carefully avoided seeing him, and as he wasn't going to try and teach Fiona until the results of her many tests came through, Tara didn't have to make any excuses.

He had accidentally touched her hand when they had been getting off the ferry on their return to Gaela, and that slight contact had sent dizzy spirals of sweet pain shafting through her.

Tara had steeled herself to type quicker than before. She could not wait to get away, and yet she didn't want to go straight home. She felt the need to be alone, to have a kind of breathing space of a few days before she faced her parents and let them see that it was all right now.

Lalla was, as always, sensible and to the point. "Why," she said, as she watched Tara pack, "don't you stay somewhere in a hotel for a few days? I know a super one just a few miles outside Inverness. It's a country mansion, a mile from the road . . . quiet and comfortable. You'd get your mind adjusted to going home and finding a job again."

"You're an angel! A wonderful person, Lalla—and I'll come again as soon as I can, as long as h-he's not here." Tara bit her lip. "You understand, don't you, Lalla?"

"Yes, I understand." On the other woman's face came a softly reminiscent look. "And I promise, before you ask again, that I won't tell him where you've gone. That is, of course, in case he even asks."

Tara gave a slight smile. "I don't think he'll even know I've gone," she admitted. "He's got a plate full with Fiona and her parents now. Oh, but he was marvelous with her."

"That I can well believe. Well, I'll away to my writing. Shout if you want me, dear." She went out and left Tara alone to her thoughts.

THE HOTEL WAS nice, and everything that Lalla had promised. *It's the ideal place for a honeymoon,* thought Tara, suppressing a pang at the idea. She had had to take a bus from Inverness to the village and walk almost a mile up the drive, but it was worth it. Gradually she adjusted to her new state, and ate, not well, but enough. She went for tiring walks before tumbling into bed utterly exhausted.

She knew Jago hadn't seen her go and maybe didn't even yet know of her departure. On the morning when the taxi had come to take her to the ferry with Lalla, she had seen Jago striding up the hill just after breakfast, and she had touched her lips with her fingers and blown him a faint kiss of farewell. Unwitnessed, unseen, unheard, her brief words softly said, "Goodbye, my love." She had watched him go and had had to blink furiously at the agonizing pain. But it would go away. It would fade as surely as the pain of David had, only quicker, and she would start a new life soon enough.

The next morning Tara bathed, and went down to breakfast late. It was a fine cold day, and there was a good bookshop in the village that she wanted to browse around. She wondered if Lalla had given Jago the money yet. She had roughly estimated the cost of her journey and food, and had written out a cheque for him.

She had given it to Lalla with strict instructions not to give it to him until he called at her house. Otherwise he might think she wanted him to know she had gone, and of course, she didn't.

She set off walking, and was half way down the village's main street when she saw the church door open and stood still, remembering the last time she had been in church, on Gaela. It would be nice to reflect quietly for a few minutes on what had happened since then.

As she walked slowly up the path, the bus from Inverness came down the road; she heard it, but didn't look around. In a few days she would get on that bus herself, and go back to the city, to catch a train home. . . .

The inside was cool, quiet, and beautiful, a sharp contrast to that sad little shed on Gaela. Tara sat in a pew half way down the aisle and let the peace of the place wash over her. She wondered if the dry sharp pain of unrequited love would go away. Gradually her mind grew calmer, and the thought of Jago became clearer, yet strangely less painful.

And then she turned quite slowly, because something was making her, and she saw him standing just inside the doorway, watching her. She thought for a moment that she must be dreaming, and made a soft sound. Suddenly he was walking toward her smiling and then he was beside her in the pew.

His hands went out to touch her face as he said, "Hello, Tara." Still unbelieving, she lifted her hand to see if he was real, and he caught her hand and held it, then raised it to his mouth and gently kissed her palm. "I love you, Tara," he said, and somehow the words were no longer unbelievable, but *right*.

"And I love you. I always have," she answered softly. "But how did you know I was h-here?"

He looked around, softly taking it all in. "I've got a lot to tell you," he said. "And I want to kiss you, but I can't here. Come, let's go outside." He stood up and held out his hand for her. Together they walked out into the cold sunlight, and then, outside, he took her in his arms and kissed her. "Let's go back to your hotel," he said, "and talk."

"Anything you say." Tara was still too dazed to think.

There in the large empty lounge with its many couches and rugs, and a huge fire roaring up the chimney, he told her what Lalla had done.

"I asked her, but she wouldn't tell me where you'd gone until I told her what I've just told you," he said. "And she said she'd promised you she wouldn't tell, and then she dropped a card on the floor. I picked it up; it was the name and address of this hotel. So I assured her that I would respect her promise and pocketed the card. That was last night. I got the first train this morning."

"Oh, Jago," she leaned against him and he put his arm tightly around her. "I knew I loved you when we were in Edinburgh, but then . . . then . . . that g-girl opened the door opposite, and I knew she was . . . . " She stopped. He began to laugh.

"Sally? You didn't let me introduce you, did you? She lives with her husband. They're both at the university, so I know them well. I was talking to him while she had a bath or something."

"Oh, Jago!"

"Listen, Tara, before we go any further. Those notes . . . I want to tell—"

"No," she twisted slightly around. "I was a fool . . . it doesn't matter, truly."

"But it does . . . and I'm going to tell you now." He moved his arm so that it held her more securely. "Listen, the first time I saw you . . . the very first time, on the train . . . with those youths, I wanted to kill them, and all I could do was look, as if it were nothing. I wanted to help you then. Also, with my training, it's instinctive to take notes, to get things down on paper. You can see everything more clearly then . . . so I made notes. I knew even then that I was strongly attracted to you, and I knew that before I got too close to see things in perspective I had to get it all down in black and white . . . . " He stopped and rubbed his face. "Oh, what the hell! I'm putting it badly. But the point I want to make is this; those jottings were finished. I was going to burn them because I suspect Morag goes through my desk occasionally. She came in as I took them out of the drawer, so I pushed them between two books. She never touches my books—a bit frightened of them, I think— and Fiona was with her. That was why it went out of my head. But you know, don't you, that I wouldn't have hurt you for the world? I've never wanted to hurt you . . . ever . . . and never will. Do you believe me?"

"Jago, you make me ashamed. What can I say? Everything you've done has been . . . " she shrugged helplessly, "has been right. You're a wonderful person, and I don't . . . I don't . . . . " She stopped, too near to tears to go on.

"Oh, my darling, my precious little idiot. Don't you know? Don't you think I know how you feel? All I've ever wanted to hear from you was those words you said in church: that you love me, too. Besides that, nothing matters. Will you marry me and live in the Big House? Will you, Tara? If you want me to get down on my knees and do it properly, I will—"

"Oh, Jago. Yes! And no, don't kneel on that rug, you'll get covered in dog hairs—" Her next words were lost as Jago proceeded to silence her in a most effective and delicious way. They didn't even see the proprietress come in to tell them lunch was ready. She took one look, smiled, and went out again, closing the door very softly behind her.

Golden Harvest

Stella Frances Nel

"A friend in time of need," was how Uncle Bart described Grant Saxon. That hadn't been Jane's impression of him from their first confrontation, and she had treated him with disdain.

He was a forceful power in the South African community, obviously admired and respected. Yet Jane was puzzled and angered by her own response to him, especially believing that he was not free. When she discovered her misunderstanding, her attitude seemed laughable.

The knowledge, however, came too late and she had said too much—for Grant's interest was diverted now by the arrival of the beautiful Mara. And Mara stated her claim in no uncertain terms.

CHAPTER ONE

THE CHILD SAT perfectly still on the sun-warmed rock, quite unaware of the creepy thing that was slowly making its way to the exposed part of her thin little thigh. Tangled hair shone red in the bright sun and her sleeveless shirt hung over brief shorts. The girl's slight body tensed as the first tug vibrated her fishing rod and Jane realized, with her heart in her mouth, that the moment would come when the fish swallowed the bait and the child would strike, leaning back with the movement. Right within reach of that tiny, poisonous tail!

Jane Wheeler slid quickly and silently down the bank; a sweep of her arm pushed the child off the rock just as the line became taut in the water. She made a wild grab at the ratchet-whirring rod that had been flung aside with a yelp of fright at her sudden onslaught.

"Sorry, chicken, I had to do that. Don't be scared—take your rod, he's still on the hook. I'll explain in a minute why I tackled you!" Jane was out of breath with her double effort, but she managed a wide smile at the startled little redhead. With one hand she held the line taut, her other hand stretched out to grip and guide the child's confused fingers back onto the rod. A keen fisherman herself, Jane knew the thrill of landing a fish all on one's own, scorpion and fright not excepted!

She released her hold and stepped back to watch a remarkable recovery as the little mite switched her attention to the effort of bringing in her catch. The hooked victim was zig-zagging in a most alarming manner, being equally determined not to be landed. As the excitement mounted Jane forgot her own disheveled state and was ready with a willing hand as a good-sized Yellow flopped on the bank. The two girls knelt down, the young one holding the fish while the older girl extricated the hook from a gaping mouth.

"You sure had luck, chick. I've tried twice at this same spot and only netted a couple of gillie-winkies!" Jane's brown eyes met the large gray ones for the first time. "I'm Jane Wheeler, from across the river."

"I'm Sandy—Sandra Saxon." The little redhead was excited and stroked the quivering fish with a hesitant finger.

Curiosity overcame pride of achievement. "Why did you push me off that rock? I didn't even see you—"

"Come, I'll show you. First put your fish in that bag; he's quite likely to jump back into the water." Jane waited and then led Sandy to her former perch, found a stick and started to poke in the crevices. The tiny red devil came out fighting, tail curved in an arch across its back. "Scorpy was about three millimetres from your thigh, and believe me, that tail is loaded with venom. I was stung once and for more than a week my elbow and arm was horribly swollen and burned like fire. If you're allergic it can be quite dangerous. Look at him—if he gets any angrier he'll sting himself!" Unwilling to kill the creature, Jane hooked her stick in the circle of the arched tail and swung it across the water, releasing the stick as well.

"Why didn't you kill it?" Sandy asked in surprise.

Jane scuffed the grass with the toe of her moccasin. "Well, you know how it is. He's so tiny and rather valiant and . . . and—"

"I know egsackerly how you feel," Sandy confided. "Matter o' fact I feel like putting my poor fish back in the water, but," temptation fought with pride, "I'd like Grant to see it."

"That's different, fish are legit game," Jane compensated.

"Legit—?" Gray eyes circled the child's face and then

brightened knowingly. "Oh, like having married babies, its legitimate to keep him?"

"Wherever—!" Jane covered her astonishment with a grin. "Well, I guess it's the same . . . er . . . principle," she added under her breath, "if you have a licence."

"Mara explained the difference, so it's all right. Mara is my mother. Thank you for saving my life, Jane." The upturned face was piquantly grave.

"You're from the Estates, the Saxon family?" Aunt Janet had spoken of the vast orange orchards and cattle ranch across the river. On her two excursions to this part of the river Jane had marvelled at the march of orderly trees and the insidiously sweet scent of orange blossoms that invaded the air and nostrils.

"Yes, Mara is mod'lling pretty clothes in Johannesburg, so I'm having my holiday with Grant—it's super!" Sandy smiled happily. "Are you on holiday too?".

"No, not quite a holiday. My mother has been very ill and we came here because the climate will make her better quickly. We come from Port Elizabeth. Is Grant Saxon . . . " Jane whirled as a flurry behind them drew her attention.

"Miss Sandy, the Boss said for me to go with you and you didn't wait for me!" A reproachful black face peered at them through the parted clump of pampas grass.

"Oh, Lemmy, you took ages and—come and see what I catched," Sandy answered inelegantly, clutching the dark hand to drag the young African to her net bag.

"Wow, that's too good!" He smiled in amusement. "Let's go now. Lena cooks, you eat, hey?"

"Yes, Lemmy." Sandy turned to Jane. "Will you come again tomorrow if Grant lets me come? He's going to smack my launching pad, if he knows I slipped 'way from Lemmy. Will you come, Jane?"

Jane pursed her mouth sternly and a small hand was

lifted appealingly. "I know what you're going to say. If you weren't here that scorpy would've bited me, and I'm naughty 'cos I slipped away from Lemmy. I promise I won't do it again . . . please, Jane?"

Jane bit back a smile. "Okay, mate, but let's make it the morning after tomorrow. I've some work to catch up with tomorrow."

"That's fab. If Grant 'llows me to come I'll be here at seven o'clock. 'Bye, Jane." At the top of the bank Sandy turned to wave at her new friend.

Jane walked back along the river to the stepping stones where she had crossed over and recalled, with a smile, the worldly way Sandra Saxon, aged approximately nine years, had repeated her mother's lesson on the law of legitimation. Mara Saxon, modelling pretty clothes in the golden city. Uncle Bart had remarked that Saxon Estates was one of the largest and wealthiest in that area, so it could not be financial embarrassment that took Sandy's mother away from her home. The child's affection for Grant Saxon was very evident, even though she had grimaced at the thought of a heavy parental hand on her "launching pad." Jane did not approve of parents who allowed their children to call them by name instead of the loving and cosy "Mum" and "Daddy." She herself had a loving mum, but was denied the presence of a comforting daddy.

The girl's thoughts turned inwardly to memories of her own misery and shock when her mother had nearly died of pneumonia. Elizabeth Wheeler had lost her husband five years previously. It was a bitter blow for her and Jane, losing a loving husband and wonderful father respectively. Elizabeth went to work for a thriving departmental store and, within a year, had become their top buyer in the rag trade. They maintained their standard of living and she was able to see her daughter through a typing and bookkeeping course.

The terrible rain and flooding of Port Elizabeth, the destitution and ravage that followed, would long remain in the memories of its inhabitants. The savage swirl of waters had trapped Elizabeth's car as she was returning home and her consequent battle against the elements had resulted in the inflammation of lungs that had never been very healthy.

Her brother-in-law and his wife had sympathized and urged Elizabeth to make her home with them. The climate was ideal and there were towns within easy reach if Jane wanted to continue working. They personally would be only too thankful if Jane would consider helping on the farm, for Aunt Janet had hurt her back and needed young hands to do the chores she could no longer handle. Also a companion to their two sons when they were home from boarding school was welcome.

Bart Wheeler had met them at Nelspruit and they had called at the hostel for his two sons, Anthony and Michael, whose holidays coincided. The remainder of the trip was done in his roomy car. That had been two weeks ago and already Elizabeth looked better, with color in her thin cheeks and brightness in her eyes as she became interested in her new surroundings. Jane had not quibbled about giving up an interesting job for the sake of her mother's health; they had made a tidy sum from the sale of their house and furniture and Mum was not ever going to work so hard again. Not while she, Jane Wheeler, was capable of caring for her.

She approached the farmhouse from the backlands, through lush green lucerne and past the henhouses and runs—that was her chore tomorrow, to clean out that mess! In the kitchen doorway she stopped short as two startled miscreants dropped the lid of the biscuit barrel with a loud clang.

"Tony—Mick! It took me all day to bake that lot. It's supposed to last for weeks, and look at your bulging pockets! Give—you're not that hungry." Jane made a sudden dive at them.

Tony, with the superior skills of a fifteen-year-old, sidestepped neatly behind her and clamped long arms around her slender body, pinning her flailing arms. Twelve-year-old Mick dropped and curled around her ankles, taking great care not to crush his bulging pockets.

Tony hissed in her ear, "Good strategy, what? You were saying, sweet coz?"

"Let me go, you hooligans! Put back those tarts and biscuits . . . ." Jane panted in her effort to free herself.

"Darling Jane, we haven't had it so good for years. Mum hasn't baked for simply ages—well, since she hurt her back. Are you going to deprive us of delectation while the going's good?" Tony nuzzled her ears and nipped delicately on a rosy lobe.

As Jane jerked her head away, long chestnut hair fell forward to obstruct her vision and her shirt worked its way up under the pinioning arms to bare a tanned midriff. Mick was trying his best to plait her legs. A large shadow blocked the outer door just as Jane gave a peculiar judo grunt and subsided limply, catching her tormentors off guard. She whipped Tony's leg up, he lost balance to fall on top of his brother and the girl rolled out of reach.

The shadow surveyed the jumbled mass. "Boys, you're slipping—a mere schoolgirl can do that?" it inquired sarcastically.

Jane peeped through a curtain of tumbled hair and hurriedly pulled her shirt down. The shadow resolved into a tall, massive-shouldered stranger.

"Is there a sober warder in this asylum with whom I can consult?" he asked, and stepped over the tangled heap to help himself to a fistful of biscuits.

Jane hopped lightly to her feet and swept back a cascade of nut-brown hair. Tony extricated himself shamefacedly while Mick explored the damage in biscuit-filled pockets.

"Hi, Grant. That was a sneak defence we weren't prepared for from this female . . . er . . . schoolgirl." Tony hastened to justify their downfall, a sly grin sliding over Jane.

Wood-smoke eyes surveyed her critically. "Do they teach judo tricks at the schools now?"

"Yes—I mean no." Couldn't this dark stranger with the startling contrast of gray eyes see that she was no schoolgirl?

Tony remembered his manners. "Meet cousin Jane Wheeler, the mighty atom from Port Elizabeth—she baked those cookies. Mr. Grant Saxon of Saxon Estates."

"Oh? I was given to understand that your cousin was a working girl. Is there another sister? Your baking's not bad, Jane, but your method of discipline is somewhat drastic." He sounded so tauntingly arrogant that Jane felt immediate hackles rising and stiffened her back haughtily.

"Reprehensible behavior requires drastic methods, Mr. Saxon. Thanks for the wild compliment on my baking. How do you do." Her rumpled appearance belied her manner, but she managed a natty sangfroid as she leaned over the table and selected a cigarette from the box that rested there.

A dark eyebrow shot up as Grant Saxon watched her action. He hesitated for a measurable, mocking moment, then leaned forward with his lighter.

"Advanced methods at the schools, surely, or are the superintendents ignorant of the fact that their scholars smoke?"

Her schooldays being well in the past, Jane could answer in all honesty. She took time for a slightly defiant puff on the offending weed. "No, the teacher lacks knowledge of my ignominious habits. I've also noticed that parents are more advanced, teaching the very young the laws of legitimacy and . . . otherwise. Tony, you may keep what you have taken, but remember in future, be moderate with your colossal appetite or no more bakings from me!"

Grant leaned against the dresser. "That center crack sounds suspiciously like Sandra's gossip. Her mother certainly has some odd notions that could fall under the category of modern teachings. Sandy told me about the lady," he stressed the last word, "who saved her from an awful fate. Where was Lemmy—he's supposed to watch her every move?"

Sandy had evidently not disclosed the full story. "He was around someplace. I happened to be above her on the bank—and got there first." Jane didn't care for his sarcastic stress on the "lady" part. Her cheeks felt hot as she visualized Saxon's first glimpse of her on the floor with the boys, hair wildly disarrayed and her shirt practically around her neck! Anyway, he had no right to come barging in at the back door, like a tramp. He was the great Saxon of Saxon Estates and should behave accordingly. Furthermore, if he thought Sandy's mother's notions were odd, why didn't he nip them in the bud?

Mick moved to the door. "If you're looking for Dad he's down at the pig runs. I'll go call him." Tony followed hastily.

Grant Saxon and Jane Wheeler took stock of each other. Her hazel-brown eyes lowered before the compelling, levelling gray stare. First she had noticed the dark frame of thick eyelashes and an almost black ring around the outer rim of blue-gray iris. Irish eyes, smudged in with a sooty finger. Sandy's hair was red, so she obviously had her mother's coloring. He had a strong, square jaw, well-defined mouth and black hair that looked alive and springy. He was indolently at ease in his contemplation and Jane felt prickles up her spine, as if this tableau would stretch through eternity if she did not make the first move to break it up.

"Would you care to step through to the living room, Mr. Saxon? Uncle Bart should be here any moment. Mum and Aunt Janet have gone to Kiepersol, I think, on some mysterious jaunt. I'll make coffee."

Grant turned in the passage doorway, filling its frame with lengthy leanness. "There's evidently been a great deception. You're not so schoolgirlish after all, not with all those ins and . . . outs. A bit on the skinny side . . . how is your mother?"

Jane straigtened indignantly and tried to flatten her "ins and outs." She answered coldly, "My mother is much better, thank you. The change of air is most beneficial."

"Good." Grant frowned darkly. "I had intended to speak to Bart concerning a responsible post for Elizabeth Wheeler's daughter; he had assured me she was a reserved and competent young woman. But now," he looked disparagingly at her scuffed moccasins, rumpled shirt and long, untidy hair, "I'm having second thoughts." He disappeared down the passage, leaving an infuriated young woman absolutely speechless!

She rattled the cups with a quivering hand as she heard her uncle greeting the insufferable man with easy familiarity. Post for a responsible person indeed! Grant Saxon had caught her at a disadvantage. He was absolutely beastly, and she would take great pleasure in telling him exactly what to do with his job at the first opportunity. Just let him dare approach her . . . !

Jane firmly intended to help her aunt straighten out the sadly neglected homestead; since her fall poor Aunt Janet hadn't been so active and her normal duties had fallen into a state of disrepair. After all that was back to normal then Jane felt she could consider an outside post. With the money she and her mother had saved and collected she could afford to invest in a small car, for future transport to wherever employment took her.

For some obscure reason Jane slipped into her room, intending to change into a cool frock. The reason was clarified when she held up a daffodil cotton with tan saddle-stiching; she wanted to show Grant Saxon that she could look all of her twenty-one years! With an abrupt movement she thrust the dress back on its hanger. He would guess her intention and jump to the conclusion that she was angling after his job—to the devil with appearances! Jane tucked her plaid shirt firmly into the old jeans, retied her hair and walked back to the kitchen. For good measure, she ran a finger across the blackened kettle and thoughtfully stroked her forehead. (She simply must tackle that kettle and stove, they were in a shocking state.)

She stomped down the passage with the tray and managed clumsily to spill a satisfactory amount from the brimming cups as she set it down on the low table between the two men. She smiled sweetly in their general direction and turned to leave, but her uncle stopped her at the doorway.

"Oh, Jane, just a minute, dear. I believe you've met Mr. Saxon, in the kitchen?"

"Yes," Jane acknowledged stonily. Teller of tales, her eyes shot silent accusation at the lanky, khaki-clad visitor. He returned her gaze blandly and the deliberate smudges suddenly felt like hot brand marks as gray eyes circled her face and a smile glimmered on well-cut lips.

"Grant came to find out if you were interested in office and general work, on the Estates. It would be conveniently near—"

"Me?" Jane opened wide eyes in astonishment. "Why, Uncle dear, a girl of my tender years couldn't possibly cope with such a responsible position. Thanks all the same, Mr. Saxon." She smiled vaguely, turned on her heel to leave and caught the loop of her jeans on the jutting lock of the door. She jerked savagely and proceeded down the passage to the tune of a deep male chuckle . . . !

Later, as Jane rinsed the cups and helped Alphina, the buxom maid, prepare the vegetables for supper, she looked through the window and caught a glimpse of the two men beyond the lucerne lands, at the edge of Bart's orange grove. Grant Saxon was gesticulating with his arms and her uncle showed evident agreement with whatever was being expressed. Alphina followed her gaze.

"The big boss is very particular about that fruit. The field hands have to be careful with it."

Jane took a second look. at the figures. "Mr. Saxon seems to be giving the orders, not the Boss?"

"He's *mongaka*, the big boss, miss Jane," came the astonishing reply.

"You mean Mr. Saxon is . . . those trees belong to him? But this land belongs to my uncle!" Jane was utterly bewildered.

"Yes'm, I dunno for sure. . . ." Alphina shrugged plump shoulders and turned to the stove. Jane gazed at her back in perplexity. This was something that had to be explained more clearly, as soon as possible.

She had no opportunity that afternoon, for Bart Wheeler went off in the car and only came back in time for supper. Elizabeth and Janet also came late and, at the table, excitedly revealed the secret of their jaunt to Sabie—a knitting machine, to be paid for and used jointly. A visit to various shops and friends had resulted in a batch of satisfactory orders for knitted garments. They intended to widen the list of customers, from Nelspruit and Barberton to a wide circling of Lydenburg,

Graskop and Pilgrims Rest. Elizabeth's eyes shone as she and Janet outlined their big plans and Bart remarked wryly that one little machine was not going to be sufficient if all their ideas bore fruit. He was pleased to see his wife bright and lively again; she had been rather depressed since her fall down the steps and the coming of Elizabeth and Jane had cheered her considerably.

Elizabeth felt that the profits she and Janet hoped to make on this knitting venture would help toward her and Jane's keep; her independent spirit demanded a return for her brother-in-law's and his wife's goodness in providing a home for them. Janet would also benefit; she knew spans of busy wives who would be only too pleased to pay for what they considered a tiresome chore, and her back could stand this particular labor.

"Grant can give his measurements, and Sandy's. I'll insist he be one of our first customers," Janet declared, with a determined glint in her eyes.

"What about his—Mara—isn't it? Why can't she knit for them and stay at home where she's needed, instead of modelling—"

"Oh, that one, you wouldn't find her burying all that glamor in the wilds. The world's axis would slip the day Mara Saxon takes a knitting needle in her hand!"

Jane was genuinely puzzled. "It can't be much of a life for Sandy and Grant, with her away most of the time?"

Bart looked thoughtful. "Well, Jane, it's always been her job, since before her marriage, and she loves it. Sandy is much better off at boarding school than being towed along where her mother's work takes her. Grant doesn't mind, he's very fond of Sandy and she loves spending her holidays on the Estate. So everyone's happy. Grant had word from Mara, she's coming for a long rest when her present assignment is completed. She's very beautiful—red hair and the most remarkable green eyes."

"And Grant Saxon is satisfied with the arrangment? If she's so beautiful he surely would want her with them?" Jane felt she was harping on that theme, but she felt an irresistible urge to find the reason for a man like Saxon allowing his wife to flit around at will. He looked strong-minded, virile and sure of himself, not the sort of man to let any female boss him around. . . .

Janet gave a small, mirthless laugh. "Quite frankly, she has an unsettling effect on Sandy and, I'm almost certain, on Grant as well—although he clams up mighty quick when it comes to a discussion on Mara's not-so-fine points. Mick, stop stuffing your mouth like that, a body would swear you're starving!"

Tony started to laugh, caught Jane's stern eye that warned against revealing their morning tussle and subsided meekly.

Lying in her bed that night, Jane's thoughts nagged again on the Saxon setup. The man was definitely good-looking, and in the brief time she had been in his presence, Jane had instantly become aware of a vibrant aliveness about him; such a man would surely want his beautiful wife at their home constantly, not only at spaced intervals? Especially with a young child to care for and love?

Uncle Bart and Aunt Jane seemed to have accepted the state of affairs with an indolent contempt that Jane found hard to understand. They were usually very proper about the sanctity of a home and all it entailed. Jane snuggled deeper. What concerned her most was the set-up right here at Mimosa. Alphina must be wrong in her facts . . . she would speak to her uncle in the morning.

CHAPTER TWO

JANE REELED IN and came to sit beside Sandy, taking care to sit outside striking distance: Fishermen were known for frustrated anger when their bait was taken only to have some chump get in the way of the strike! She cast a glance at the large hamper that Lemmy had so carefully deposited in the shade of a willow. Judging by its size, enough tucker to feed an army . . . she had only brought a flask of tea and homemade biscuits. Tony and Mick had begged to join them, after they had wheedled her destination out of her, and Jane warned them to bring their own vittles. They had the "disgustingly menial" job of cleaning out the pig runs, so would be down much later. Jane had cleaned the hen-houses the day before and felt she had earned the right to enjoy her early start with Sandy.

Yesterday Bart had left early and had come back fairly late, tired and grumpy, so she could not speak on the subject that was causing her worry. Jane could not bring herself to approach her aunt on the matter and decided to speak to Uncle Bart after supper tonight, when he was relaxed and enjoying a quiet smoke on the veranda.

Sandy intercepted Jane's glance at the hamper. "Lena packed lots 'cause Grant's got a big appetite—so've I, but I don't get fat. Do you like chicken sammidges too, Jane?" The little redhead had taken an immediate fancy to her new friend. She was different from her mother, who wouldn't be seen dead in the worn shirt and blue shorts that Jane was wearing.

"Grant—what has his appetite got to do with the size of your hamper?" Jane asked sharply, her suspicions aroused before Sandy confirmed them.

"He's coming to have tea with us. I did tell him about my fish after all. Last night I told him 'cause my conscious was guilty." Sandy looked piously for approbation.

"So why is he coming to tea?" Jane smiled her approval of Sandy's confession while she thought wryly, he's coming to check the child's safety with that scatterbrained, juvenile Wheeler girl. . . .

"Because I'm as keen on fishing as the next, and a break is indicated, in the presence of two charming ladies." Grant's deep voice floated down the bank and Jane turned a startled face to the lithe figure towering above her.

Color flooded, then receded most annoyingly in her cheeks; the mere presence of this man reduced her reactions to teenage ditherings. Something about him, a magnetism she could not define, rang bells of warning; look out, Jane, watch out, there's danger in the air. She recoiled inwardly from this ominous feeling. What danger could he have for her? She didn't even like him; he was . . . exasperating!

Grant dropped negligently on to a rock a yard away from her and flicked his hat back rakishly, amusement lurking in discerning gray eyes as he waited for her tongue to unknot.

"Good morning, Mr. Saxon," Jane murmured stiffly, and was relieved when Sandy placed her rod in the cleft stick and launched herself like a saucy rocket at him, diverting his attention momentarily. The youngster plopped on to his lap and twined thin arms around a tanned neck. "Can we eat now, I'm starving to death! Did you bring your rod? We haven't been lucky yet—Jane says Tony and Mick are coming too—mm, you smell delicious!" She sniffed ecstatically and burrowed deeper into the open neck of his shirt.

Jane felt sudden laughter bubbling as she noticed a

deepening color rise up the exposed neck to suffuse and brighten well-shaped ears. Her own poise was regained at the thought that even a wealthy, temporal Saxon could not always control nature's embarrasing blushes! He did smell rather strange—a mixture of green orange leaves, hay, shaving soap and tobacco—an intriguing combination. "Cut it out, you little squib, that's my Chanel Number Five you're busy licking off. I didn't shower in it for your benefit!" Grant tickled the child into a state of delighted hysterics.

Jane swallowed the bubbling laughter and asked demurely, "A new sort of bait for the fish, Mr. Saxon?"

"A new sort of bait, Miss Wheeler, period." Over the tousled head wood-smoke eyes dwelt on her with deepening speculation.

Jane made a deliberate show of tilting her head to study the trees, scrub and river as if in search of something or someone and then turned back with an expressive shrug of her shoulders. A feathery prickle started up her spine at the amused stare that had replaced the speculative shine in his eyes. She was annoyed at the queer breathlessness that tightened her chest and the words that were meant to be uttered nonchalantly came out rather stiltedly. "What a waste of good bait, and so expensive. Sandy may as well enjoy it."

"Unappreciative girl! Doesn't it send your senses reeling just the tiniest bit?" Grant dared mockingly.

Jane stood upright and dusted the seat of her shorts. The man was out to bait her; time must hang heavy on his hands with the absence of his wife. But she, Jane Wheeler, was not going to be a temporary target, not by a long shot, for the amusement of any flirtatious-minded man!

"It certainly does not, Mr. Saxon," she retorted, and walked away from his unsettling presence to open the flask of tea. Arranging the cups in a precise row, she shot off a quick backward glance. Grant was tying Sandy's ribbon with great concentration and calling to Lemmy to fetch his rod and tackle.

Sandy came to help Jane open the hamper and they set out plates of chicken and cucumber sandwiches, hard-boiled eggs and ripe tomatoes. By the time this was done, Grant had his line in the water and was settled very comfortably against the jutting root of a willow tree.

He looked so relaxed with his rather scruffy hat edged over his eyes that Jane forbore to call him. Instead, she walked over with the plate and steaming cup. Grant tipped his hat and watched lazily as she set it down within his reach. "Thanks, Jane. Have you attempted a catch yet?"

"I gave up just before you arrived, Mr. Saxon."

He squinted up at her, "You may call me Grant," sounding so condescending that betraying color whipped her cheeks.

"Big deal!" Her retort was only an indignant whisper as she turned away, followed by an involuntary squeal as a lithe body turned like a steel spring and her ankle was caught in a vice, making her come down inelegantly on her seat.

"Girls always fall at my feet even without bait lure, didn't you know?" Grant jeered, and brought a tanned, disturbing face closer. "Sit still now, there's a good girl, and tell me why you're so very prickly. Are you like that with every stranger you meet, Jane Wheeler?"

Her heart began an absurd beat; his dark nearness was causing a strange effect . . . . Jane sat perfectly still while she tried to analyze her emotions. She did not like him very much; he was too arrogant and sure of himself; his derogatory manner infuriated her—and he was a married man with a small daughter.

"Well, Jane, is this hate at first sight?"

"I don't hate every stranger on sight, Mr. Saxon."

"Grant."

"—but then strangers don't usually treat me in an offensive manner." To her own ears Jane sounded absurdly prim, but that was exactly how she felt. A primness that covered quite unexplainable wavering emotions.

"My dear girl, have I offended you? I thought you liked horseplay, having seen you with the boys. . . ." Grant tried a penitent look. "Did I hurt your delectable little ankle or is it your neat posterior that pains—or just your vanity? Actually I had to make a grab, you're like a will-o'-the-wisp, in order to have a serious little chat."

"If that's your idea of an apology then I fear you haven't had much experience in that fine art, Mr.—"

"Grant." The interpolation came firmly.

"—however, I will accept it as such." Jane extricated her ankle from his grasp, brought her knees up and encircled them with her arms. "What do you want to talk about, what serious discussion could you possibly have with me?"

A banshee yell rent the air. "Your line, Grant, your line—just look at it!" Sandy screamed. Grant shot toward the singing ratchet and rod while Jane flattened herself in a good imitation of a starfish.

"Well, what do you know!" Grant exclaimed as they viewed the shining, wriggling fish with dark markings across its back. "A Black bass, no less!"

Tony and Mick appeared on cue, to admire enviously. They were all for settling their bait then and there, but Grant allowed for tea and vittles before the ants invaded everything. The children were obviously fond and at ease with him and his comradely way with them was uncommonly surprising and pleasant to watch. He did not mention the supposedly serious discussion again until just before they packed up. Lemmy went off loaded with gear and the empty hamper. Grant took Sandy's hand and repeated his invitation to run Jane and the boys home in the Rover that he had parked under the trees.

"No, thanks . . . Grant," she still stumbled slightly on his name, "I . . . we enjoy the walk and Mick promised to show me clumps of montbretias and agapanthus growing wild further downstream." Within the past two hours Jane had overcome her strange antagonism, which had melted somewhat under his rather devastating personality. Grant Saxon could be quite charming when it suited him.

"Yes, I know the place. I'll be around later. I must see your uncle about certain things and I'd like you to be present. It concerns you as well." It was politely worded but sounded like a definite demand, and Jane watched him and Sandy disappear over the bank with mixed feelings. She simply could not account for the butterfly condition under her ribs.

One thing for sure, she was determined to have a talk with her uncle before that broad-shouldered, rangy man arrived. Jane felt there might just be a connection between that subject of discussion and her state of mind.

The car was parked at the side of the house, so her uncle must be home. Elizabeth and Janet were setting up the knitting machine in the study, which had been drastically converted to suit their needs. Bart's books and disorder were stacked neatly in a corner cupboard, his writing desk stood outside the door on the enclosed portion of the verandah. Janet assured him he would do far better there, it was so much cooler, and the poor man perforce agreed to this invasion of his territory, in the interests of Business!

Jane took her uncle's arm and persuaded him to walk with her to the bench under the trees in the back yard. Bart sat down and watched her quizzically, aware that his niece had something on her mind. "Spit it out, Jane. If I can help—here I am."

"Uncle Bart," Jane studied her interclasped fingers, suddenly hesitant for fear he might think her presumptuous for sticking her nose into what did not concern her. Anxiety and a sincere wish for clarification made her lift her head and continue, "Uncle, please don't think it's cheek or mere nosiness and interference on my part—would you care to tell me if Mr. Saxon has some hold on you? Is he perhaps a part-owner of your orchards and lands?"

Bart Wheeler studied the intense young face and gold-flecked brown eyes that withstood his scrutiny with a levelling sincerity. He withdrew his pipe from a jacket pocket and started to tamp down the tobacco with a stained thumb. "What did you hear, and how, Jane?" he asked quietly.

"Alphina was rather confused on the set-up here. She happened to mention something about—Grant—being the big boss when we were watching you and him through the kitchen window, two days ago. I didn't want to question her or Aunt Janet, but I'm rather puzzled. She seemed to insinuate that he owned all the land."

"Oh." The pipe drew to his satisfaction and Bart spoke through a cloud of fragrant smoke. "Grant Saxon is the big boss, Jane. He owns the land, house, in fact the entire property."

Although her suspicions were finally confirmed a ripple of astonishment contracted her throat and she stared at him wordlessly. Bartholomew Wheeler had lived here for more years than she could remember and there had never been a hint of evidence that he was in need, financially, or planning to sell his beloved farm.

"Why, Uncle?" she managed at last.

"Well, dear, it's rather a long story, but I'll put it as

briefly as possible. I wanted to spread out, tried my hand at tobacco and chose one of the worst, driest years. A complete flop it was, and I, who should have known better, also committed the unpardonable sin of neglecting my orchards. The results were black rot in the orange crop and a tobacco disaster. The expense of the tobacco sheds and new equipment put me badly in the red. Grant came to my aid and, being a decent chap, gave me a share in the business and took over in his own capable way. He's convinced that those sheds will still be of use and will pay their way when the young tobacco crop he planted matures. I'm also on his wage sheet, all his chaps are provided with good living quarters and he insisted that I remain here, in my own home. Don't look so tragic, Jane. It's a satisfactory partnership and arrangement. The lands adjoin, to Grant's benefit, and Janet's and my roots have not been disturbed by having to consider the possibility of moving. It could have been bad, if someone else had taken over."

Jane watched him attend his pipe in the silence that followed.

"Meaning," she stammered slightly, "that you live here, only while you're willing—and able—to work for Grant? What happens if you become ill and unable? Do you lose all this, your heritage—"

Bart put a rough brown hand on her knee. "Don't be so upset and concerned, Jane dear. I have no intentions of giving up or losing my health. Grant and I get on very well and I'm not badly off financially now. He's a good, generous man, although a hard driver, and quite rightly so. I was very fortunate to have him as my neighbour and I feel deeply in his debt—not financially, but for helping me keep my head above water at a critical time. A friend in time of need. I didn't mind selling out my heritage—as you call it—to such a man and still have a share in it all. Actually I'm better off now, the load of responsibility has shifted; not that I want to shirk the work, but I'm getting older and he's a young man with more advanced ideas . . . a man with a great store of vital enthusiasm. Tony and Mick will learn more from him, and I have Grant Saxon's word that this will remain our home for life—with a pension clause in our contract." He smiled confidently into the eyes that had mirrored mixed emotions at his explanations, with an intensity that varied their color from gold to almost black.

"Yes, I understand, Uncle. Thank you for your confidence." Jane's lashes dropped to her hands again. "Mother and I coming here, are really interlopers on Saxon property—"

"Just a minute, girl, let's get this straight: Grant knew that Janet and I wanted you to make your home with us; we're allowed to invite our families into our private homes. He practically demanded that we send for you and Elizabeth, not only to visit but to make a permanent home with us. Which we were very happy to do, so don't let me hear any more of that sort of talk or I'll be very angry!" Back in his mouth, the old pipe belched smoke like an upgrading little engine.

Jane smiled a beguiling apology but persisted on the tangent of her mind. "Do all the people on these estates work exclusively for the owners?"

"Of course, that's understood. He can't provide for outsiders and his men are happier when they have comfortable homes right on the job."

A startling thought struck her. "Was that why he—Grant— mentioned something about a job for me? Is it a real job, Uncle, or simply a made one to put me in a working category, not to be listed as an outsider?"

Smoke belched again, but her discerning relative understood and considered.

"I don't think it's a put-up job because, to my knowledge, the offices are short-staffed. Two girls are down with 'flu and one is leaving for Nelspruit to get hitched. If Grant mentions it again you can take it from there, if you feel so inclined. But remember, it's not necessary for you to seek outside work. There's plenty for you to do right here, and you've already shown your worth with the chores you've undertaken. On the other hand, you have high qualifications in your own line of work and due respect should be given in the right direction. So, if such an opportunity is offered," twinkling eyes creased at the corners, "Grant pays damned well for services rendered!"

Jane smoothed an affectionate hand down his sleeve. "Thanks, Uncle Bart, for being so patient with me. I do understand, and I think you're very brave to be so philosophical about your losses. Your loyalty to Grant Saxon is commendable—but anyone with half a brain can see the advantages of being in a position to snap up fertile adjoining lands!"

For the second time that day a certain adjective was used when her relative said rather reproachfully, "Jane, don't be so prickly about our neighbour. Get to know him before you judge too hastily. You didn't mention anything, but Tony told me that Grant spent the morning with you at the river; that's most unusual and surprising—he's forever too busy to relax for a moment, never mind a full morning! A hard business man, difficult to assess at first or second meeting. His prestige is high; he's regarded with respect throughout the eastern Province. Really a good chap. Come on, Janey, why the prickles—did you have a tiff with Grant?"

Jane jumped up suddenly and showed pearly teeth in a wide smile. "Listen to that list of virtues! And you're so right about me being hedgehoggy; firstly, he found me on the floor in a dishevelled state with the boys at our first meeting, brought me most unbecomingly down on to my seat this morning, treats me with amused contempt and makes me feel ludicrous most of the time. Who wouldn't prickle? But for your sweet sake I'll endeavour to remain upright on my two feet as from now on and show due respect for such a paragon—"

"Starting right now. The paragon approaches," Bart advised as a low-slung, high-powered car purred up the driveway.

The door opened and long legs unfurled, followed by the rest of a lithe body. Grant Saxon clicked the door shut, saw them and started to walk toward uncle and niece.

"Wow!" said Jane, her eyes glued to the sleek lines of the car. She ignored the driver.

"Car or driver?" Bart teased.

Brown eyes swivelled to the driver and Jane very nearly repeated her exclamation. He did look rather dashing. Brown tight-hipped trousers accentuated the slim hips and length of strong rangy legs. A tan polo-necked pullover, a mixed texture of wool and some silky stuff, contrasted sharply with the blue-gray smokiness of dark-lashed eyes. Grant moved with indolent grace. And Jane Wheeler felt a silly flutter in her breast as she watched him approach . . . .

Well, any female, unless she were made of solid granite, would admire and feel a certain flutter at the sight of such broad shoulders, supple free-muscled stride and male vitality! Jane sternly put an end to the lyrical waxing of thought and forbore to answer her uncle's teasing remark.

Instead, she concentrated on composure and the quelling of rioting butterflies under her ribs, stuck a determined smile on her lips, and let her eyes wander back to the car.

Grant lifted a saluting hand, then turned slightly to follow the direction of the girl's eyes.

"Like it?"

She lifted her chin to meet his questioning glance. "If 'tis permitted to use expressive slang when referring to that well-bred, sleek, autocratic, fabulous automobile? Definitely a snazzy job!"

His laughter, deep and vibrating, immediately disturbed and caused new havoc amongst the winged insects that Jane had managed to quell only moments ago.

"Bart, the lady approves!" Sunshine lent red glints to dark hair as Grant inclined his head. "In appreciation of her outright and sincere flattery may I suggest Jane be given fifteen minutes to change into attire suitable to the occasion and I'll proceed to prove that performance equals beauty?"

Jane turned wide, bedazzled eyes to Bart. "The inland dialect is so charming, but so hard to follow. Do I understand rightly—we are referring and acclaiming the beauty and merits of the car and that I've been invited to share those delights . . . ." She stopped abruptly. Now she had left herself wide open for whatever was coming. Her admiration for the car had been open, but she had not voiced her thoughts on the man . . . that tongue of hers would always try to outsmart the rest of her!

Yes, "whatever" was coming. Jane was treated to a cool, amused, analytical stare, a diabolical eyebrow lifted knowledgeably.

"I realize my inimitable charm is quite as devastating; my performance can equal same, but," Grant sighed regretfully, "we were discussing the car. Maybe at some future date. . . . Yes, Jane, you're coming with me to the Mission Hospital. I suggest you slip into a dress, if you own one, my dear. You look very . . . cute in shorts or jeans, but it would be more circumspect to confront the medical staff and patients properly attired, don't you think so?"

Jane's soft mouth opened and shut rather like that of the poor fish that had lain panting on the bank.

"Well! Of all the . . . ." even white teeth clamped hard on a runaway tongue.

Bart touched her arm hastily. "Janey, don't argue, run along and change before you're hijacked bodily, just as you are. It can happen, take it from one who knows."

"On your way, a small request, for Janet and your mother to join us with coffee, while we wait for you? Fifteen minutes?" Grant bowed politely.

Jane's slim hands came defiantly to her hips, and Grant Saxon took a reflective step forward. She backed hastily, turned to look at the car and decided to capitulate. "One's prepared to put up with anything for a ride in that beauty"—amending quickly as a dark eyebrow shot up again—"sorry, by anything I mean being ordered around. It's rather late, can we make it to the Mission and back in time for supper?"

"Dr. David expects us to stay for dinner, so there's no need to hurry back," Grant stated calmly.

"But he doesn't know me or expect—"

"He's expecting both of us. I phoned him."

Jane was transfixed and silent with the audacity of the man!

Grant Saxon lifted a negligent arm and studied his watch. "Twelve minutes to go."

She walked indoors breathing exasperation and gave her aunt his message through clenched teeth. Under a quick shower and while she dressed, Jane took stock of her jumbled emotions. She could quite easily have stood her ground and refused to go; this was a civilized world—and Grant wouldn't have really forced the issue, to lift her bodily as her uncle had warned? A niggling thorn in her mind pricked her into admission that she did want to go with—she compromised—in that sleek car, just to experience its performance and to meet the interesting people at the Mission.

Two doctors, according to her aunt, and an attractive Sister-in-Charge, nurses and clerical staff. Dr. David Muller, the elderly popular head, dedicated to his work, and his young assistant Dr. Peter Davis. The Sister, Pat Somebody—Jane could not recall her surname—was young, blonde and attractive.

Yes, she would go with Grant this time only, but she wouldn't let it become a habit. Uncle Bart didn't seem to think it strange for his niece to ride around with an attractive family man; he evidently trusted the estate owner considerably. However, she would refrain from accepting any further invitations, if they were forthcoming; she might become the target for unsavoury scandal if she were seen gadding about with Saxon too much, especially if his glamorous Mara heard of it! On second thoughts, maybe Grant was making this trip, taking this opportunity to have that talk that was mentioned earlier on?

Jane took a last quick survey of the reflection in the mirror. Shoulder-length hair brushed to a silky sheen, a glimmer of eye-shadow and pearly lipstick. The short-sleeved cinnamon sheath showed the youthful contours of her slim figure and boosted her morale considerably after the derisive way her scruffiness and questioned lack of dress had been commented upon.

Slim feet went into her newest buckled shoes, and with the comfort of feeling clean and well-groomed, Jane lifted her head proudly and descended the steps to where her family were in a worshipping huddle around Grant's car.

He was smiling at Elizabeth and turned to glance at the girl, taking in the slim brevity of her mini-dress, the wet shine of buckled shoes, and the shining fall of hair and delicacy of features. His expression altered infini-

tesimally, something Jane saw but could not define but
that sent a feathery play along her spine.

With great ceremony Tony opened the car door for
Jane and Mick dashed to do the same for Grant. Elizabeth smiled at her daughter and dropped a wicked wink
of approval in the direction of the owner of the super-
car. Only Jane saw it, but it was so blatant, so unlike her
conventional mother that the girl wondered for a
shocked moment if Elizabeth knew that her daughter's
escort was married. Of course she knew; they had discussed Mara and there was young Sandra to prove it!

The family waved cheerfully as the powerful car
glided swiftly and silently down the avenue of pines.

The man behind the wheel did not offer small talk
and Jane pushed back the puzzlement of her mother's
strange behavior to relax and enjoy the feel of comfort
and power the "snazzy job" instilled. She was entranced
by the lovely scent and orderliness of orange trees
stretching into the distance. The variable greens of pines
and gums sloped lushly up the hills and closer, on the
sides of the road, wild flowers peeped out in many brilliant colors amongst tree ferns and wild creepers.

Inevitably, her eyes were drawn back to the long
brown hands manipulating the wheel with sure, firm
ease. She lifted her head slightly and studied his neck
and profile, relaxed yet revealing strength and certain
arrogance that commanded one's attention.

Grant turned his head suddenly, met her intent gaze
and his teeth gleamed whitely. "Up to expectations?"
The smile deepened into an unexpected dimple. "And
I'm referring to the car."

Jane straightened from her relaxed position. He really
was a tease, but he had caught her studying him and
teasing seemed to be part of his nature.

She answered naturally and enthusiastically.

"Absolutely super, marvellous suspension—it's like floating inches off the ground, and the engine's so silent. Synchromeshed?"

Grant's eyes crinkled at her enthusiasm. "Automatic transmisssion, air-conditioned, button-control radio. You name it, this baby's got it!"

"You will show me the engine some time?" Jane closed her eyes dreamily. "If I possessed a baby like this, I would travel all the time and see Africa. I bet these seats are convertible, the backs lower to form beds—you did say name it?"

His chuckle came deep and infectious. "Caught me out first shot! No convertible seats, I'm afraid. I wasn't thinking of sleeping when I bought this car. Do you like travelling, Jane?"

"No more or less than most ordinary folks. This car is highly conducive to such thoughts—one wouldn't tire easily on long journeys. I have visited the Cape and Natal, but inland, further north and east is still just an enchanting dream to me."

"You should travel the Summit Route some day. It begins right here on your doorstep."

"I've heard about Mount Anderson and the Pinnacle at Graskop. The Bridal Veil falls and Devil's Knuckles—Jock of the Bushveld route—"

"Blyde River Canyon and its Nature Reserve, and God's Window . . . ." Grant continued as Jane paused for breath, "the Devil's Pulpit. Near Bourke's Luck are the Potholes, a series of rockpools at the confluence of the Blyde and Treur rivers.

"They've built suspension bridges, and if you're prepared or brave enough to venture on them you have a clear view. A visit to Mount Sheba is a must—I believe two brothers from Kenya have built a fabulous hotel and the view is breathtaking. Then there's Kowyn's

Pass, which drops roughly one thousand five hundred feet down the escarpment within a matter of two miles and was named after a Bakwena Chief.

"I've now made up my mind," Grant went on, "to take you on that trip. It's been quite some time since I last travelled that way, and with this car and your enthusiasm I'll see and appreciate with new eyes. However, our humble Mission lies ahead and it's time to come down to earth and meet a dedicated mortal—David Muller."

Jane had been so mesmerized by his deep voice and travelogue that she only realized now that they were beginning to wind through a number of white-washed buildings. Spaced at intervals, the long buildings were evidently wards for the sick and ailing. A number of Africans were either sitting or walking about in a type of long white shirt with blue, knitted skull-caps on their thick black hair. Grant followed a sign and pointer indicating the doctor's quarters and offices.

Her eyes saw groups of tiny children, but her thoughts ran on Grant's sudden decision to take her on that Summit trip. It would be wonderful, but definitely not just the two of them? He could only mean when Mara came home. Jane Wheeler found her thoughts dribbling to a stop with unaccountable heaviness. . . .

CHAPTER THREE

GRANT USHERED JANE through the reception office where orderlies were busily engaged. The Staff Sister greeted them with a pearly smile of recognition for the Estate owner. She was clad in a crisp blue and white uniform with ranking blue belt and her white cap sat jauntily atop curly black hair.

"Sister Marion," Grant put a hand on Jane's shoulder, "this is Miss Wheeler who, with her mother, is now living with her relatives, Mr. and Mrs. Bart Wheeler."

Sister Marion hesitated for only a second, then clasped Jane's outstretched hand. "I'm honored, Miss Wheeler. You wish to see Doctor Muller, please come this way?" She spoke to a passing nurse in dialect and then politely motioned the two visitors to precede her down the cool stone-floored passage.

A door at the far end erupted violently and a blonde, uniformed girl turned sharply in the opening and straightened her cap while she spoke indignantly to an unseen occupant.

"I promise you, Peter Davis, if you lay a finger on me again I'll report you, so help me!"

"Well, what have we here, young Pat? Someone molesting you?"

The girl whirled with a startled squeak, a hand to her mouth as Grant spoke directly behind her.

"Grant Saxon, you devil!" She lifted a shaking hand to tuck another wisp of gold under her cap. "Sorry, you startled me—"

"You seem to be between two devils, then, my beauty," Grant drawled, and towered over her slight figure to peer into the room she had vacated so abruptly. "Can only be one other and sure 'tis he, Pete the Knife! Do I smell nasty competition, sweet one?"

"That man couldn't compete with a—a zongololo!"

"That man" came into view. "Certainly not! That creepy has a thousand arms and I only have two." Peter Davis surveyed his hands disgustedly, looked up and caught sight of Jane in the background. A delighted eyebrow shot skywards.

"Move over, please, can't have my patients waiting. Grant, old boy, do you mind, your manly bulk is impeding progress—take Sister Pat away and smooth her feathers. I accidentally tipped her cap—no offence, y'know."

Grant moved negligently, but his voice came with a sharp bite.

"Superintendent Wheeler has come to look into reported negligence and misbehavior on the part of the staff. She has now registered first-hand knowledge. . . ." Amused interest lurked in gray eyes as he watched the abrupt reaction of Doctor Davis and Sister Marais.

The Mission staff stiffened to attention. Peter ran a finger along his collar, buttoned the top button on his white coat and the blonde, petite Sister flushed to the tips of her ears and twined her hands nervously behind her back.

Peter's former rapt but now startled gaze shifted for a moment from the lady "superintendent" to Grant Saxon. He caught the mocking light in wood-smoke eyes and relaxed indignantly.

"I thought she was too young and unspoilt-looking to be a dreary inspector. You're an unmitigated goof, Grant, frightening the curl out of Pat's hair and right into my toenails! Wheeler? Elizabeth? No, this must be Jane, old Bart's niece. How do you do, Jane Wheeler. I can see by the innocent surprise on your face that you weren't on to this dirty trick Grant tried on us. Peter Davis, at your service." Her hand was clasped tenderly.

"Not so much of your kind of service either. She's under my care. Jane, this is Pat Marais, Sister-in-Charge between times of warding off unwanted approaches of various males in the neighborhood."

Pat Marais acknowledged the introduction and immediately slanted blue eyes back to Grant. "Excluding yours, Grant? Your approaches are the most difficult because," her dancing gaze swept back to Jane, "his are never there to ward off!" Slender shoulders sloped regretfully.

"Why didn't you tell me about this torch you're carrying, honey?" Grant teased, and Jane was more than ever convinced that, for a family man, he behaved most outrageously. And his bland statement that she, Jane, was under his care, designating himself calmly as her keeper—well!

"You've felt the scorching heat of my torch, but you remain hard, uncaring and unbeguiled, damn you, Saxon! How did you get into his clutches, Jane?" Pat wanted to know.

With all the flirtatious banter and the openly admiring eyes of Peter Davis fixed on her, Jane felt that things were getting slightly beyond her. She answered Pat airily enough in a conspiratorial whisper. "His car, Sister, lured me as inexorably as a bird is hypnotized by a snake. Absolutely magnetic, you know?"

Sister Marion had vanished from the flippant company and now an adjacent door opened and an elderly man in a white safari suit appeared, his hand outstretched to meet the firm clasp of Grant Saxon.

"Sorry to keep you waiting, Grant. I could distinctly hear my staff putting up an inferior show of entertaining, but couldn't free myself sooner to rescue you and . . . ." He turned to Jane and a quick, piercing eye circled her face and rested for a long moment on her honey-flecked brown eyes.

"How do you do, Dr. Muller." She found herself

stammering under the close scrutiny of those piercing blue eyes.

Grant's deep voice interposed, "Enough of this mutual admiration stuff. My feet wants up and my hand craves to clutch a glass of something wet and cool."

Jane's hands were dropped. "Jealousy gets you nowhere, old chap. Come, I've finished for the day, I hope, so let's move to my quarters." He turned to his silent staff. "You two may join us at dinner if . . . I repeat, if you manage to complete your duties and stop wasting hospital time on horseplay!" Jane's hand was tucked firmly in the crook of a wiry arm and they proceeded down the passage. Grant lowered a wickedly superior look on the two open-mouthed victims before falling into step beside Jane.

David Muller's quarters led off the main building under a connecting, open-sided canopied walk. The lounge contained scattered armchairs covered with faded but clean floral cretonnes, a few small tables and a long bookshelf that stretched across one entire wall. A battery-operated radio occupied one corner, next to it a low table stacked neatly with a small selection of records.

The doctor led Jane to his best armchair and Grant sank his length into the depths of another, across from her. A sharp clap brought a white-clad house-boy and David communicated his guests' choice of drinks. The two men chose whisky with ice and Jane settled for an iced passion-fruit. A silence that held a companionable quality enveloped the three occupants while they waited for the return of the house-boy with the tray. He set the tray on a table and withdrew.

"How is young Sandra?" David inquired of Grant.

The sun-browned Estate owner leaned his dark head back comfortably and grinned lopsidedly, "Just fine. She has a new friend who's also keen on fishing, and that's tops with her. Her friend is the sole subject of discussion at all times . . . how she saved Sandra Saxon from an agonizing death, how this understanding friend allowed her to land her first catch, which incidentally grows with each telling. How she, Sandy, pleads with her Maker every night to change her own 'orrible red hair to a nice, polished berry color. This amazing friend truly doesn't mind getting dirty all over, and wonders never cease, she doesn't squirm or shudder away from threading nice juicy earthworms on to the hook. Quite unlike her mother, who's stuffy about a bit of dirt and squeals at the sight of a dear little worm. Sandra has a great pash for her new friend!"

Two pairs of eyes were on Jane. Her face had turned a bright pink, but she lifted her chin and outstared them defiantly.

"I like her too, very much. We would like to explore, your permission permitting, the gully and stream below the pines. We want to start a nature book, with pressed specimens and notes on what we see and find."

David spoke before Grant could pass comment. "That will be fine, I'm sure Grant won't mind. It's a good thing for the young to learn about nature at first hand. I'm very glad Sandy has found such a friend. Not many older girls would bother with the things that children find exciting and wonderful. Tell me about the rescue from agonizing death?"

Jane's heart warmed toward the discerning doctor and while she explained she also silently wondered what Grant's thoughts would be on the comparison between mother and friend. Sandy would think it disparaging, but he would pass it off as a comparison seen through a child's adventurous eyes; he would rather have Mara just as she was, glamorous and fastidious, of that Jane was quite sure.

"That must have made our Sandra's day! And the

glamorous Mara, have you heard from her, and how is the modelling profession progressing?" David voiced the direction of her thoughts.

Grant became intent on the golden liquid in his glass. His reply was laconic, but Jane noticed a pressure of hand that whitened the knuckles of the one holding the glass.

"She's doing well. Her tour ends this weekend. We can expect her soon; she's finally bought another car and insists on driving herself, instead of my usual motoring down to fetch her. Wants to show off her driving prowess, I guess."

David's eyes narrowed slightly as he watched the tip of Grant's glass.

"That means she's finally overcome her aversion to driving, since the accident?"

"It means just that. Positive proof of a fault in the steering column, not her, caused the tragedy." Grant's lips were compressed.

"Yes, well." David smiled again. "Coming back to Sandy and her friend. Mara's going to be slightly ruffled at the competition. Sandy's worship has never wavered before. Come to think of it," his blue eyes rested on the uncomprehending girl opposite him, "those pretty feathers could be ruffled quite considerably!"

Grant Saxon lifted his head and stared at his friend for palpitating seconds before he stated with a cold finality, "If you're harping back to a certain personal subject, I assure you the question doesn't arise, nor ever will."

"Okay, Grant Saxon, don't knock your block. Just a reminder that no man can say with complete confidence that he's impervious to the insidious guile of the fair sex."

Jane looked from the cold, closed face of Grant Saxon to the crinkled eyebrows of the older man in complete bewilderment. She had absolutely no idea why the teasing tones had suddenly become something that left a gleam of icy steel in wood-smoke eyes. She knew nothing of what they were alluding to when they spoke of Mara and accidents and ruffled feathers. Surely the doctor couldn't mean that she could cause a rift somehow? That was unthinkable and in bad taste, not the sort of thing she would expect of David Muller. No wonder the cold look had come into those eyes! It had also spoilt the air of ease that had pervaded the room . . . until Mara Saxon was mentioned.

She turned with a sense of relief as voices heralded the appearance of Pat Marais and Peter Davis. David expelled a gusty breath and smiled at the pair while he called for more drinks.

Grant subsided deeper into his chair, lit a cigarette and allowed the smoke to drift across his face while he contemplated Jane in a disinterested way, almost as if he did not see, as if his eyes were turned inward to match a secret brooding thought.

Jane turned a bright face to the newcomers, angry and bewildered at the stony, lifeless feeling under her heart. When they finally sat down to dinner Peter Davis made a point of engaging her attention, and it was not hard to return his friendly banter.

Pat Marais revealed gay social abilities as well, although she seemed somewhat obsessed with Grant and flirted outrageously whenever opportunity offered. His riposte had a derisive, mocking quality that only incited, instead of curbing her enthusiasm. Jane knew her own insides would curl up if a man returned her teasing with that certain inflection of voice that Saxon knew how to use to a fine art. He, a family man, evidently enjoyed a bit of offside bird-baiting in the absence of wifely restrictions!

The thought made her sniff contemptuously, harder

than she intended. In the sudden silence that befalls most conversations, that sniff came loud and clear!

All heads swivelled in that direction. Grant, directly opposite her, leaned over and studied Jane with concern, the dark ring rimming the outer iris of his eyes blending into blue-gray pools.

"This is no time to start a cold, Jane."

Jane squirmed at the sudden all-round scrutiny and answered with some asperity. "Of course not. Can't one sniff in medical company without the worst being immediately diagnosed?"

Grant said coolly, "I'm not included in the medical category, but Dr. Muller will bear me out, there's been a wide outbreak of Hong Kong 'flu in this vicinity. Did you have the precautionary injection last year? That was a mighty unusual sniff, young woman!"

"Well," she retorted, guilty color making her feel hot, "that was simply an unexpected, ordinary snort—sniff—not a cold or impending 'flu—take my word."

"I could take a test—prompt attention and all that?" Peter's eyes twinkled in anticipation.

His superior slanted an ominous eyebrow at his assistant. "Very commendable, but quite unnecessary, Dr. Davis. I know every nuance of various sniffs, and that one sounded suspiciously like a . . . disdainful snort. Now, I wonder," a piercing eye circled the table and came back to his slim, delightfully blushing guest, "what caused it?"

Jane's lashes fanned her cheeks in confusion and she started to pleat her napkin with unsteady fingers. Pat laughed suddenly and waved her hand across the table to break the spell of staring eyes.

"You see how it is in a small community, Jane. Everything you do is analyzed, even a sniff isn't allowed to pass unnoticed. Join me on my afternoon off, we'll creep into a bush hideout and sniff and snort disdainfully, disgustedly, vulgarly and to our hearts' content at everything and everyone we yearn to sniff at!"

Everybody had to laugh at her comical, commiserating expression, and Jane was very conscious of the moment when the direct gray gaze of Grant lowered as he leaned back in his chair. Only when he offered cigarettes did she lift her eyes to refuse mutely. David put a hand on her shoulder.

"Joking aside, Jane, we've really had a run of the illness and three of my office staff are flat on their backs. Have you any experience of clerical, elementary office work, and are you, by some miracle, free and willing to help out?"

Her beech-nut hair swung into a pleased affirmative, but Grant Saxon cut across her reply with astounding, maddening coolness.

"Sorry, old boy, we're also drastically short-staffed. Jane may, if she's willing and not too tired, give you a hand one or two afternoons a week if you're truly stuck. Otherwise, she'll be kept horribly busy in my own office!"

Under the mesmeric smile directed at her, Jane slowly expelled the smoldering breath that threatened her bosom to bursting point. Doctor Muller shrugged rueful shoulders.

"Trust big Saxon to be first on the field! Talent of any description simply gravitates to the Estates, or should I say, is sucked in before any other poor devil gets the chance. Well, I'm grateful for any crumbs of help, every bit helps, I'll accept your offer, Grant, if Jane agrees."

Smoke drifted up steadily from a brown hand and a dimple line deepened as Grant continued to look at the stunned girl.

"My new assistant will be up to her ears, but I'm sure she'll take pity on your suffering. I'll give you a ring on her free time and bring her over myself."

Peter said, "That's how the cards fall, Janey. Your life gets mapped out regardless; don't look so stunned. Has Mr. Dynamite forestalled me, or have I still the chance to invite you to the Club dance two weeks from now?"

The trend of talk and impudence of Grant's cool declaration had indeed stunned Jane and her eyes were still mutinous when she switched from the hypnotic gaze to look at Peter. Sanity returned as she mastered her thought and tongue.

"Thanks, I'd like that, Peter." She managed to repress the sarcasm to a minimum, to turn her lips upward. "Mr. Saxon hasn't forestalled you at all. He's rather overpowering at times, but surely not omnipotent?" Turning to Pat, whose bright inquisitive eyes had jumped from one speaker to the next, "Are you going to this dance, Pat? What are they like? Is the attendance good? I haven't even seen the Club."

Grant interposed, "Quite respectable, my dear. Pete may be quite a lad with the girls, but he'll look after you—no need for girlish qualms."

Jane raised furious eyes and thought wildly: You, Grant Saxon, should be the last man to jeer at Peter's way with girls, you're way ahead of him! And not even free to be that way; you're the one I would have girlish qualms about. Stating in that lordly manner that I'll be working for you, without even asking me first—we'll see about that, Saxon! Not everybody is a softie!

Through a mist of boiling thoughts she became conscious of Pat speaking.

"The only man I'd bow down to doesn't ask me, so I'll take up the first offer that comes my way, being an eager beaver when it comes to dancing. My boss will probably put me on night duty to save my innocent soul and prevent me from making an ass of myself!"

"I'm quite sure you'll not lack escort, Pat. If this one man in your life is such a stodge, my advice is forget him, he's not worth further thought," Grant comforted.

Pat looked at him through slitted eyes. "Yeah!" she gritted, "how closed and dense can a man get? I suppose Mara will be here by then, so you're accounted for?"

An imperceptible pause followed before Grant said with careless equanamity, "Don't try to be too perceptive, Pat dear, it's unbecoming in the young. I may show up. Depends . . . ." he turned to David and inquired after the health of the Estate hands who were in the Mission for treatment.

Jane again felt a sense of puzzlement at some mystery in the atmosphere. The Mara situation definitely intrigued. All was not as it should be in the Saxon household, of that she was becoming very aware.

Later, Pat curled up on the couch in her bedroom while Jane visited the bathroom. She washed her hands and joined the blonde Sister, looking around curiously at the cosy room. "Nice pad you've got here, Pat. Do you live in permanently, and have you a family in this vicinity?"

Pat uncurled and stood up, stretching her body languidly. "Mum and Dad live in White River, I visit as often as permits and I've two younger brothers. Real stinkers, those two, but I love 'em all! I like it here, plenty of work but interesting. What do you think of Pete Davis?" she asked in a sudden tangent.

"Peter? I haven't had much time to delve deeply, but he strikes me as a good sort," Jane answered cautiously.

"He's okay, a good doctor but an awful flirt." Pat spoke offhandedly and shot another question, "What do you make of Grant Saxon?"

Jane became more cautious; that question came with deeper intensity. "There also I plead short aquaintance. He's slightly masterful—very sure of himself."

"And yet you're already on his wage sheet . . . and visiting list? Do you like him?"

Jane grinned suddenly. "Come now, Pat, one visit to

the Mission, that's all! As for the wage sheet, I . . . ." she almost blurted out the truth, that she herself had heard of that for the first time tonight. Something held her back. "I do need the work and it's close at hand, practically on my doorstep, so to speak, very convenient all around. As for liking the man—well, it's hard to say."

"I couldn't agree more! Grant Saxon is a strange man, you either fall madly or hate him like hell! He's a real paradox, one can hate and love him at the same time, and as elusive as the proverbial will-o'-the-wisp. I'm beginning to believe that Mara is the only one . . . ." Pat stopped and dived to a lower drawer to extract a few tissues.

Jane waited and found her body tensed for the conclusion of Pat's beliefs. Her companion straightened up, tucked the tissues into her pocket and said casually, "Shall we go?"

Feeling highly frustrated, Jane came to a decision. "Pat, what happened in that accident, with Mara?"

Pat paused in the doorway. "Oh, didn't you know? Mara was driving—rumor has it that she was slightly intoxicated, but I hear now that some driving gear was faulty. It's being investigated . . . poor John was killed instantly."

"John?" Jane felt shock streak through her system.

"Of course, you never knew him. One of the best, an awful tragedy, and Grant was absolutely and still is inconsolable. He loved his brother very dearly. John Saxon was two years younger than Grant, but they were like twin souls . . . except where Mara was concerned. I hear she's coming back, and if I know her, she'll have her way, fair means or foul. Grant would be most annoyed if he heard my gossiping, but, just for the record, I can't stand that female. Let's go!"

Peter had been called away to attend a slight emergency and Pat hurried in his wake with a wave of her hand. David Muller walked to the car with Jane and Grant.

"Remember that offer of help, Grant," was his parting reminder as they pulled away.

Jane waited until they were on the open road, steeling herself to question Grant's statement and foregone conclusion that she would accept his plan of employment. Somehow the heat had gone out of her resolution to confront him with angry reproaches. Since Pat's rather muddled explanation her heart had softened towards this tall, sun-browned man. Sorrow did not sit on his shoulder, but he must be grieving inwardly at the loss of a beloved brother. She still had no idea of where and when the tragedy had occurred nor how Mara became involved. Nevertheless she felt a strong wave of sympathy for Grant Saxon and decided not to probe further into his affairs or try to solve the puzzling Saxon set-up.

He disarmed her completely in the next few seconds.

"Jane, I'd like to thank you and say I admire your self-control for not letting me down in company. I saw the surprised anger on your face and, quite frankly, I surprised myself. I had no intention of startling you with that bald statement, fully intending to discuss it with you first. Remember the confidential talk I mentioned this morning? When David pleaded lack of staff and I could see your coming acceptance—well, it simply had to be said."

Her reply was not immediate and Grant lifted his foot off the accelerator, slowing down to glance at his silent passenger. "Don't be angry, Jane. I'm asking you now for your help at the office. Bart told me you would be seeking your type of employment, you live conveniently near and further transport will be provided. I really need your services desperately. Jane?"

The assured, self-contained Grant Saxon actually apologizing and pleading! Her silly heart, already softened by sympathy and now made more malleable by his disarming explanation, capitulated completely even while her mind urged caution. If Pat had not told of his bereavement. . . .

"I'm not angry any more, but I certainly was astonishingly so, at your apparent high-handedness. However, I accept your explanation, and when would you like me to start?"

"Thanks, Jane Wheeler, I like the way you cut corners. As soon as possible?"

"Can you send for me tomorrow, and do I wear an overall?"

"Atta-girl! Transport will be waiting at seven-thirty and you're not going into the packing sheds . . . my office is reasonably clean, so no overalls!" The car shot forward under pressure from a well-shod foot.

He left her at the front door with a smile and a word of thanks for her company. Jane leaned against the closed door until the diminishing sound of the car had died away, then walked slowly to her room with very mixed and undefinable emotions clouding her mind.

CHAPTER FOUR

THE BIRDS WERE CHIRPING boisterously when she returned to her room from an early morning shower. Jane opened the windows to their full extent and leaned out precariously, filling her lungs with pure, dewy air.

She twisted back for her brush and lifted her hair, allowing the fresh breeze to tingle her scalp while she brushed the long, nut-brown strands. The new, sparkling morning gave her a feeling of buoyancy, a sense of fitness; she felt capable and ready for her new job and whatever else this day may hand out. She completed her toilet, then walked quietly down the passage and tapped softly on her mother's door before entering.

Elizabeth opened sleepy eyes, then came fully awake as she realized it was not her morning tea as expected but daughter Jane, trim and businesslike in a neat dress instead of the jeans and shirt that were usually standard morning gear. "Wh-what's happened, darling? You're dressed."

Jane smiled reassuringly. "Not to worry, Mother. You are surveying a girl with a JOB! The Saxon Estates have acquired a brilliant new hand." Her smile turned mischievously gamin, "I hope! I'm going to have a cup of that aromatic coffee I can smell brewing and then someone'll probably be here to pick me up. I've just nipped in to let you know and I'll give you more details this evening."

She leaned over her astonished mother, gave her a kiss and a pat on the cheek and disappeared before one of many questions could formulate on the opened lips of her nearest and dearest!

Her uncle was seated at the kitchen table, a large cup of steaming black coffee under his appreciative nose.

Bart raised shaggy eyebrows at his niece's neat appearance. She was usually up with the lark, but this was not her morning rig. Like a dewy bud, for sure, in her yellow linen dress with collar and cuffs that matched the highlights in her hair.

"Morning, Jane, going somewhere special?"

"Good morning, Uncle Bart." Jane poured a cup of coffee and settled on the chair opposite him. "I'm a working gal, no less."

"Well, well, the boss sure doesn't waste time, I'll say!"

His tone unaccountably flustered her, taking it so for granted that it could only be Grant Saxon that had hired her. A resentful wish fluttered for a moment, that she could inform him that she was being employed by the Mission or somewhere else. Oh well, Grant had been her escort the previous evening, so it figured. . . .

"Yes, he certainly doesn't. I think I was hijacked into this, last night. He declared, in front of witnesses, that I was a new addition to the Estate. If he hadn't been so fast and given me the idea that I would be letting the side down by denying his statement, I'd most probably be doing a spot of duty for Doctor Muller instead." A sliver of indignation was evident in her explanation.

Bart assimilated her news, drawing deeply on his pipe. A strong chuckle mingled with pipesmoke. "I see . . . Grant and his devious ways. He strikes fast and you find yourself loyal, willy-nilly, even while wondering what hit you!"

Jane sighed. "How right you are, Barty dear. Now, about my chores here—can I change them from the morning to the evening?"

"Oh, don't worry about all that. I forgot to mention that I've hired a local handyman, Flip Olivier—bit of a rover, can't stay in one place for long but good at whatever job's going. You should see him on a tractor, slices the ground like butter. He'll be available twice a week for the heavy work, cleaning the hen and pig runs and the garden. Not the sort of work for a girl anyway."

"Oh, Uncle, I didn't find it such hard work," Jane smiled, "just very smelly."

"I don't care greatly for the man," said Bart, "but he prefers to earn his keep that way, does the rounds of all the farmers, and we take turns to feed and pay him."

A vehicle stopped at the side of the house and Jane rose hurriedly and grabbed her bag. Bart walked with her to the Land-Rover from which a driver descended. He greeted them politely and swung round to hold the door for Jane. She settled herself and waved to Bart as they proceeded down the drive.

Tom, the driver, handled the Rover competently and Jane still felt that curious exhilaration as they sped through the sparkling countryside. All too soon they drew up beside an imposing and dazzlingly white colonial-styled house. Jane felt quite awed, thanked Tom as he held the door open for her, then stepped back a few paces to view the graceful gabled frontage.

"Tom, do we have to stop here? This is Mr. Saxon's home and I'm supposed to go to the offices."

"Yes, ma'am, this is Mr. Saxon's home. My instructions were to bring you here." He pointed to a row of neat, white-painted, red-roofed buildings some distance away. "Those are the general offices, but the master's private office is here, if you will please come this way?"

He accompanied her and stepped back slightly at the wide, shallow steps flanked by tall pillars that led on to a cool, spacious verandah. They faced the heavy, superb oak door that fronted the house. It opened as if a signal had passed and Jane faced a lean pale woman of indeterminate age. Tom touched his cap and retreated the way they had come.

"Miss Wheeler? Please come in. I'm Minna Du Toit,

Mr. Grant's housekeeper. He asked me to show you to the study and serve tea, he'll be right with you."

"Jane, Jane!" A small body hurtled through an open doorway and Jane gasped as the missile contacted her solar plexus with breathtaking force. "Gee, I'm glad to see you what are you doing here are we going fishing and why aren't you wearing your jeans?"

"Sandra!" Minna Du Toit grabbed the hurricane with steely fingers while Jane bumped against the wall, searching for lost breath.

"Toicky, let me go, that's my friend Jane. You know I told you about her. Jane's come to visit me 'n she's awful pretty in that yellow dress, isn't she just, Toicky?" Fierce hands tried to free Sandy's captivity.

"Hullo, Sandy. I'm glad you like my dress and I'm very pleased to see you, but this isn't a visit. I've come to do some work." Jane smiled at the excited child and lifted her eyes to catch a peculiar expression on the older woman's face; very fleeting, but the pale eyes had definitely darkened and warmed to some inner emotion.

"It's a very nice dress, Sandy, but that's no way to treat it or your friend. Good morning, Jane, I'm positive you'll need a cup of tea after that attack." Grant spoke from the doorway that Sandy had hurtled through. He had evidently witnessed the whole scene, including Jane's breathless stumble against the wall—clumsy as usual!

"Good morning, Mr. Saxon," she answered primly, while those wretched butterflies started winging crazily at the sight of broad shoulders and freshly shaved, sun-browned features. His dark hair was damp but sleekly combed and a slight aura of shaving lotion gave impact to the lean, male look of him. Jane pulled herself up tartly; this was no way to begin the day! He was her boss and her emotions must be controlled if she intended showing her excellent business acumen.

"Minna, we'll have tea in the study. Sandy, scamper off and finish your breakfast. You may share Jane's break for tea at ten o'clock if she desires your dubious company."

Sandy meekly allowed "Toicky" to lead her away. Jane could not resist a wink of assurance at her little friend before turning to follow Grant. His lips quirked slightly, but he made no remark at her gesture. They walked through an L-shaped lounge on deep, autumn-shaded carpeting. The furniture was old-fashioned, its coverings green and the wood shining tamboti. Sun-filter curtains of orangey yellow filtered the harsh sun-light to a muted glow. Jane sensed atmosphere in this house; it was elegant yet homely and comfortable. Slid-ing glass doors opened on to the verandah and Grant paused to wait for her, noticed her interest, and a small smile deepened on well-cut lips.

"Sandy can show you the rest of the house later, if you're interested. It's a very old house and has its inter-esting points. This way, Jane." Grant led her out on to the verandah to the door of his study. Part of the veran-dah had been bricked across to accommodate the study. Inside, he showed her to her desk facing a long window. Through this she could see a vista of trees, shrubs and well-kept lawns. Filing cabinets and a larger desk occu-pied more space and a grand new typewriter rested in splendor on a corner table.

"This will be your desk. I've been here since dawn, clearing the mess left by Miss Ames, an excellent secre-tary but muddled in her ways. Comes of having mar-riage on the brain, addles it somewhat. You haven't any such thoughts, Miss Jane?" The question bounced abruptly across the cleared desk.

"Good heavens, no!" she retorted, raising startled eyes to meet the hard, penetrating gray stare.

"Good." Grant turned and slid open a drawer of the

cabinet. A batch of files were dumped on to her desk. "When you've had your tea, look through this lot and compare the opposite figures to see if they correspond. I've found a few discrepancies in them, due no doubt to Miss Ames's state of mind. We can't allow any margin of error in this business, the whole lot will have to be scrutinized again. Can do?"

Jane had started to page the top of the pile. "Of course I can do," she remarked, faintly nettled. This was small stuff she could almost do with her eyes closed . . . so he needn't be so condescendingly anxious, as if she were a rabbit at the game. Jane sat down without further ado, ignoring the large figure across her desk. Grant stood for a minute longer, studying the shining bent head of his new assistant, then moved to his desk, scraped back his chair and became immersed in the work before him.

Two hours later the scrape of a chair disrupted her concentration. Grant stretched his arms and made a gesture of distaste at the work on his desk. "I sincerely hope Ames bungles her honeymoon as much as she muddled this lot—it'll serve her right! Teatime, Jane, half an hour to get into the sunshine. Minna will serve it on the lawn. I'll join you presently." He leafed through her file. "Good going, girl," and he walked out across the verandah into the lounge.

Jane stretched likewise and went out and down the side steps that led directly on to the lawn where she had seen Sandy. The housekeeper came across the grass and indicated where she had placed the tea. Jane poured her tea and relaxed on the cushioned, wrought-iron chair. Her gaze wondered back to the house; it had been the family home for a long time. Where did Mara fit in . . .

"Toicky said I could have tea with you if I brushed my hair and washed my hands." Sandy held out two small hands for inspection and swung a neat ponytail.

"That's great, Sandy," Jane approved and poured for her little companion. The child was in a talkative mood, prattling happily of all the happenings since their last meeting. She took a wisp of tissue paper out of her pocket and opened it carefully, revealing a rainbow butterfly wing found on one of the shrubs. They studied it, two heads close together.

A shadow fell across their heads as Grant leaned over to scrutinize Sandy's find. "A gossamer-winged spring-azure, at a guess," he remarked, while his eyes lifted to a more interesting study of the older girl's quite delightful curve of soft but firm cheek. "We could check, though, I might be wrong. Tea, please, Jane."

Sandy wrapped her treasure, palmed two sandwiches and munched contentedly, her bright eyes roving from one grownup to the other. "Ooh, this is nice, my two best friends and Toicky's sandwiches." She wriggled comfortably.

Jane smiled at the odd coupling and surprised a similar quirk on the man's lips.

"Not long now, Sandy, then your mother will be here as well. That will be grander still, hmm?" she asked, and stared in amazement as the child opened her eyes wide and choked on a mouthful of bread. Small hands trembled as she put down the cup, spilling half its contents.

"Yes—yes, I 'spect so," she stammered, and Jane glimpsed a wet gleam of tears as the child turned suddenly and streaked across the grass to disappear into the shrubbery.

Amazement struggled with anxiety as Jane turned to Grant. "Whatever came over her? Oh, gosh, Grant, did I say something to upset Sandy? I thought she knew and would be pleased to talk about her mother . . . coming soon . . . ." her voice tailed miserably.

Grant ran irritated fingers through his hair. "Sandy knows Mara is coming, but something upsets her every time we mention her mother. I can't understand what's come over her lately. She gets in this sort of tizzy, clams up and dashes away, just as she did now. Almost as if she's afraid of—something."

"I'm awfully sorry. Shall I go after her?" Jane rose uncertainly and took a few hesitant steps. Grant stopped her with an abrupt movement of his hand.

"No. Leave her. She gets over these spells quickly. Perhaps you could sound her out, after lunch. As her special friend you may be in a position to extract her confidence and find out what's bothering the child." He straightened out of his chair. "Time's up, back to the study—the sooner that muddle's cleared up the happier I'll be."

Jane forced the problem of Sandy's behavior aside and concentrated on her work.

An hour passed and then Grant stretched out of his chair.

"I've finished my bit here. Take an hour off at midday, Minna will provide lunch for you and Sandy. I'll be back some time this afternoon," he paused at the door. "If you could go with the child to her room, after lunch, presumably to rest, she might just disclose her problems. Try anyway, you'll be doing me a favor as well."

Jane nodded willing assent and Grant disappeared down the steps.

After lunch, at which Sandy appeared again, Jane asked her to show her the rest of the house. The child eagerly complied and they made a tour of the rooms. The bedrooms, numbering six, were airy and furnished mostly with beautifully grained local wood. The kitchen was a housewife's dream and two bathrooms sparkled with white tiles and fittings.

Grant's room was austere, neat, with a three-quarter bed covered by a tweedy, striped bedspread. A room for one person only . . .

Sandy hung back when they reached the third bedroom and remarked tersely, "Mara's room."

Jane peeped in at the blue and white confection. It was superb; blue wall-to-wall carpeting, paler blue curtains and a white suite. The large bed covered with a blue valanced spread. A very feminine room indeed.

"And now for your room, pal." Jane turned away from the splendor that dazzled her eyes and clasped Sandy's hand. The child opened her door with a flourish. "I like my room best and Grant said he'd keep this room for me for ever 'n ever, even when I'm old 'n can't walk any more!"

"Why shouldn't he?" Jane wondered aloud, and duly admired the bright covers on twin beds, the dazzling array of animals that marched across the walls and the pretty pink curtains. "Can I rest on one of your beds? It looks so comfy, and I do like your room best of all," she added quite truthfully.

"Even better'n Ma—the blue room?"

"Indeed I do. Here I feel I can toss off my shoes and relax, cosy and comfy." Jane suited her words to action and stretched out to wiggle her bare toes.

Sandy watched her warily for moments and then a relieved sigh blew through her lips. She moved to a dolls' cot and lifted her baby doll carefully and settled on the other bed, the doll nestling in the crook of her arm. She said, "I wish you were my mom."

"Why, love?" Jane asked, keeping her voice carefully casual. "Your mom is beautiful and loves you dearly."

Sandy eased her "baby" tenderly. "She's very pretty and I 'spect she loves me and I did long for her, but," the small voice tightened curiously, "but now I don't want to see her, ever again!"

Jane sat up slowly and came to kneel beside the bed where Sandy lay with her face pressed into the pillow.

"Sandy dear, I'm your friend and it hurts me to see you're troubled about something," she stroked the bright hair soothingly, "and if you don't want to tell me I don't mind. Sometimes it helps if one can confide in a friend, and I do so want to see you happy all the time."

A muffled sob broke the silence. "You are my best friend, but I can't tell anybody that my mother did something to my daddy 'n I'll never forgive her."

Jane felt her insides twist and tighten at the despair in the small voice. What had happened, what had this child seen or overheard to make her so miserable? She remained outwardly calm and spoke soothingly.

"Never mind, sweetie, you needn't tell me any more if you don't want to, but I am sure you have something all higgeldy-piggeldy on your mind. Tell you what, you tidy your hair and then you can sit with me in the study while I finish my work. Have you any nice books to read?"

Sandy sat up and brushed the tears away with the back of her hand. "Can I really sit in the study with you? Grant never allows me into the study."

Jane wished silently that Sandy would say "Daddy" instead of "Grant." There had been a deep feeling in the child's voice when she so unconsciously gave her secret away, partly, and mentioned "my daddy." She said brightly, "I'm sure he won't mind just this once, if you sit quietly and read. I'll go now—find your books and join me, hmm?" She was probably breaking a strict rule, but didn't care. Grant could blow his top if he wished, but he had asked her to speak to Sandy and even though she had not progressed very far. . . .

Jane approached her desk with this thought in mind and came to an abrupt halt. Sandy's trouble was connected with her parents; how could she, a stranger, delve deeper to find the basic cause and then have to confront Grant with her findings? It was evidently a personal thing; she would tell him quite casually about Sandy's animosity toward her mother and suggest he settle his own problems. It would be most embarrassing for herself and Grant would certainly not thank her for baring a possible skeleton in the marital cupboard!

Sandy tiptoed into the study and Jane smiled as she indicated the small table and chair she had carried in from the veranda. The child settled down, her troubles forgotten in her sense of importance at having been admitted into forbidden territory.

At four o'clock Jane corrected the last page. She and Sandy again enjoyed the tea spell under the trees. The child was content to play with Lemmy when Jane walked back to the study. What could she occupy herself with now? Scratch around to find something to do or would that annoy her boss? Her problem was solved by the appearance of Minna.

"Mr. Grant phoned. If you've finished the work he gave you, you may spend your time as you wish. He'll be back to run you home." The housekeeper turned to depart, but Jane called her back.

"Just a moment, please. Thanks for the message. May I ask in which way I must address you—Miss or Mrs. Du Toit?"

The slight, neat woman took a few steps back into the room and her gaze hovered over Jane's head. "I'm Mrs. Du Toit. My husband passed away many years ago and I took the post of nanny to Miss Mara in her father's home. When she married she didn't want—Mr. Grant offered to take me as housekeeper and I've been here ever since." A smile pierced the sternness of her mouth, making her look years younger. "You may call me Minna if you like. Sandy started the 'Toicky,' her version of Du Toit, and most everyone has adopted that name now."

Of course Jane did not belong to this household so she would not be invited to be so familiar. She decided to stick to formality until she and Minna knew each other better. Under the prim manner lurked a friendly though somewhat suspicious soul. She was fiercely loyal to Grant and Jane wondered what her attitude to Mara would be; her cut-off sentence about Mara not wanting her after her marriage sounded hurt and strange, yet she was still under the same roof as her former charge.

Jane tidied her desk, did a quick spot of dusting across the filing cabinets, wondowsill and other surfaces, closed the study door and then wandered into the garden. Her heart started an erratic beat as the Land-Rover came to a halt and her tall, gray-eyed boss unfolded lithely. She simply must stop that magnetic charm of his from interfering with her senses; it was dangerous—and useless. No future in it whatsoever.

A few lengthy strides brought him to her side and the dilapidated hat pushed to the back of his dark hair gave him a rakish appearance. His hands lifted slightly and Jane had the curious illusion that he was about to say something quite shattering and that her own hands were lifting without volition to meet his! They weren't doing anything of the sort, they were merely clenched in her pockets, and he did not utter any heart-stopping words. But that illusionary moment was to remain indelibly fixed in her memory.

Grant's hand continued its upward movement to remove his hat and run fingers through heat-dampened hair. "Hi, Jane, finished that lot? I hope we'll now be able to make sense out of them." Did she sense skeptic sarcasm, or was she being just too sensitive lately?

"Amuse yourself while I have a quick shower. The eastern water tank gave trouble." Grant turned away and vaulted three steps with a long-legged stride.

Commonplace greeting and words. Jane lifted rueful shoulders; the man would find everything in order; he evidently didn't regard office girls with high esteem. He was disgruntled with water tank trouble and the fleeting moment was a figment of her imagination. Nothing of world-shattering importance could possibly be said or exchanged between her and this . . . family man.

A soft toot of a car horn brought them back from their stroll. Sandy dashed across the driveway to where Grant was standing beside the car. "Please, please, Grant, may I come too?" she pleaded sweetly.

"Sure thing, poppet. Run and tell Toicky first." The tall man smiled at the flurry of heels and turned to Jane. "The kid imagines she's Miss World when she rides in the back seat. Never in front with me, her chauffeur. Children have wonderful imaginations."

So have some silly grown-ups, thought Jane as she took her seat. *My imagination almost jumped the gong not twenty minutes ago!*

A breathless Sandy deposited her small self in the center of the back seat. "Thank you," she said grandly as Grant opened the door for her, and the man bowed politely.

"A pleasure, ma'am."

Back at the Wheeler home he joined Bart in the pumphouse. Jane and Sandy walked into the house to see how "Operation Knit" was faring. Elizabeth looked up from an intricate pattern and her soft eyes smiled a greeting, and rested on Jane with a querying tilt. Her daughter circled her thumb and forefinger in the traditional manner and edged Sandy closer.

"So far so good, Mom. Meet my friend, Sandra Saxon. My mother, Sandy."

Sandy pressed closer to Jane's body, but managed a shy, "How do you do, Mrs. Wheeler."

"Hello, Sandra." Elizabeth beckoned the child closer. "Just look at this lovely design. Of course I'm only practising, getting the hang of it, but it's proving quite fascinating to watch it grow."

Jane laid an affectionate hand on her mother's shoulder. "How many millions have you and Janet turned out today?"

Elizabeth laughed and put a casual arm around Sandy's waist. Her natural gesture allayed the child's shyness and she too bent forward to study the growing pattern. "My dear Janey, production nil today. Give us time to conquer this monster and then talk about output!"

Janet called from the veranda, "Coffee for the working gals!" and greeted Sandy with a comradely hug. "How's my girl enjoying her holiday?"

"Fine, thanks, Auntie Janet," Sandy answered, completely at home now with her three companions. Elizabeth noticed that the youngster stayed as close as possible to Jane, intent eyes fixed on her vivid face as she gave a quick résumé of her first day of work at the Saxon Estates.

Tony and Mick, expert artists of foodsmelling, arrived on cue, dusty and dishevelled from some mysterious excursion. They greeted Sandy in the casual, lordly manner that boys have toward mere tender females; but soon bore her off with them. The three females relaxed in their chairs to discuss the day's duties and gossip.

Bart and Grant eventually joined them and Janet invited the big man to stay for supper. He declined, "Thanks, Janet, not tonight. I have to investigate some trouble at Block Six and that gypsy, Olivier, seems to be the cause of it." His glance travelled from his hostess to Jane, then to Bart. "Watch that chap when he comes here and send him off, pronto, when his job's done. Idling is his downfall—see that he parks his ramshackle caravan a good distance from the house." Again his smoky glance flicked over to Jane.

Bart caught the glance and nodded. "I know Flip . . . I've hired him before, as you know, and my eyes are wide open."

Grant stood up, prepared to take leave. "I'm not too happy about it. He's a slippery eel and it's time we all gave him a walking ticket. Jane, walk with me to the car, I've a few instructions to lay out for tomorrow." Bart was about to accompany him but withdrew, and Jane, obeying her boss's command, walked beside him down the steps.

He briefed her as they walked. "I won't be with you tomorrow, but will set out the most urgent work for you to tackle. Sorry about that, but I'm sure you'll manage. I have to do a round of the packing sheds and blocks. By the way, how did you fare with Sandy, get any sense out of her?"

The sudden flush on her cheeks irritated Jane and she looked past broad shoulders that were too close for comfort. Grant walked, his eyes curious and then alert as he watched the confusion on her face. "Come, Jane, out with it," he requested quietly and lifted his hands to her shoulder. The grip tightened as she struggled to formulate her reply. "It can't be as difficult as all that—I can see you've succeeded in getting somewhere with her. Let's have it, and don't try to spare me!"

The flush receded and her cheeks paled miserably as she fixed her eyes on the lower button of his safari jacket. "Well, I didn't persevere very far, Grant. She did confess that—her mother—did something, and she'll never forgive her," Jane stopped and bit on her lower lip.

"Sandy said that she wouldn't forgive Mara for something she—Mara—did? What?" The hard hand gave her shoulder a slight shake.

Jane lifted her head at last. Her own hand came up and she tugged the restraining grip from her shoulder. "Grant, you're hurting me!" Her lashes lifted and she faced him squarely. "It's a family matter and I'll not say more or probe any further. Sandy has a great affection for you. If you treat her gently, she'll be willing to discuss and reveal her problems to you."

He said softly, "You know more than you've told me, sweetheart. And you're not going to tell—is that so? Well, I admire your reticence if it's an embarrassing subject. My apologies if I've involved you in a delicate family matter. Say and do no more. I'll attend to Sandy's problems and promise to treat her with the utmost gentleness. Don't look so woebegone and appealing; it does things to my morale." Grant raised his hands to circle her throat, moved them slowly to tilt her mouth, and the next moment Jane felt his lips on hers.

Transfixed and silent, she suffered the coolness of his mouth on hers. A shock of awareness replaced the unease that had rippled down her spine only moments before as she felt unaccustomed response on her own warming lips. A current of power, vibrant and devastating, came from the hands that circled her throat and exploded against her mouth . . .

Grant Saxon withdrew his lips and his hands slid down to her shoulders. Wicked steel gleamed in his eyes as he said whisperingly, "You pack a hidden punch, honey—built-in atomic power, perhaps?"

The flame in her cheeks deepened; the tumult in her pulses receded at the derision in his voice. Jane mastered her senses, thoughts and tongue and stepped back with supreme indolence, ignoring the flags of color on her cheeks. She smiled sweetly above the angry frustration—or something she could not define—that raged within.

"You don't do too badly yourself . . . darling. Do you always allow things to have their way with your morale so easily?" she asked mildly, feeling anything but mild, and brought her hands up expressively. "Nice tips a girl gets for imparting family secrets!"

Grant's expression changed with thunderous intensity. He put a hand on the car door and said bitingly, "Nice, did you say? Such a milksop word, my dear. We'll have to grade the family secrets—the bigger the secrets the better the tips. I reckon we've made a damn good start, the future's fast becoming bright and exciting. Do a bit more delving, love, for our mutual pleasure?" He slid behind the wheel, started the motor and leaned across to open the passenger door for Sandy. "Hop in, poppet. Enjoyed your outing?"

"Yes, Grant. 'Bye, Jane, shall I see you tomorrow?"

Her mind a whirlpool of emotions, Jane had stiffened to rigid control at the audacity of Grant Saxon's treacherous suggestions. Suggestions that belied the thunder on his face. His expression was now blandly taunting as he and Sandy waited for her reply. A longing to strike the taunting look from the dark face and shriek like a banshee almost overcame her. Instead, she said stiffly, woodenly, "I'll be there, Sandy. I don't chicken out easily. Transport being available." Her challenging look rested on the man at the wheel.

Grant's face softened into a slow smile. "Yes, my atom, transport will be available. I reckon you've got what it takes, in more ways than one. Pity you'll be deprived of my company so soon, but," the sun wrinkles deepened at the corners of his eyes, "work before pleasure, y'know. 'Bye now."

Jane watched the dust of the departing car and vowed furiously to bring the driver down from his pinnacle of insufferable ego and audacious self-assurance.

CHAPTER FIVE

JANE STOPPED TO TWIST a ripe tomato off its stem; they were quite delicious when eaten straight off the bush. She watched the water coming down between the furrows and looked up to see who was directing its course. The man was leaning on his spade and the early morning sun gleamed in blue eyes that were studying her with insolent admiration. An inexplicable shiver recoiled down the girl's back, but her feet did not falter as she approached. She had to pass him in order to reach the side driveway where her transport would arrive at any moment. Jane loved this early morning walk through the fruit trees and vegetable garden. She bit into the fruit and strolled casually, keeping her eyes on the rows of greenery. Flip Olivier raised a hand to his hat.

"Good morning, miss."

Jane raised her eyes briefly. "Good morning, Mr. Olivier." He could only be the subject of Bart and Grant's discussion two days ago.

"Tomatoes are good this year, hey? Oom Bart told you who I am then . . . . Pleased to meet you, Miss Jane. You are liking our part of the country?"

"Very much, thank you." Jane indicated her desire to walk on. The man hesitated for an insolent moment before stepping aside to allow her passage on the dry strip between the furrows. She turned around out of common courtesy when he spoke again.

"The land is good if a man has water to cultivate, but the seasons have been very dry these past few years."

She nodded and looked towards the horizon. "They have been, the need for rain is great. My uncle says when that haze starts on the mountains there should be a change in the weather."

The pale eyes lifted from her face to study the direction of her eyes. "It looks promising, we must hope for it to come soon."

A hum of a motor heralded the approach of a vehicle and Jane smiled at Flip, feeling a small sense of relief at the interruption. He seemed of a mind to hold her in small talk and that nibble of recoil still played on her spine when the hypnotic gaze circled her face and figure. She turned her back and walked quickly around the corner of the veranda, took her bag from the canvas chair where she had deposited it earlier on and waited for the Land-Rover. Tom greeted her with a smile and they proceeded to the Saxon Estates.

Grant was not in the office when she walked in from the veranda entrance, which she now used instead of coming through the house. This would be his third day of absence. She had not seen him since the day he had brought her home and taunted her on kissing tips. Her work was laid out every morning, so he obviously hadn't disappeared into the blue. Jane was strangely relieved when he failed to appear; how to treat a boss who kissed, then taunted his new employee? The anger inside her might have exploded with dire results—for him!

Yet, as she prepared for her day's work, Jane felt the loss of his magnetic presence; some strange exhilaration inside her seemed to feel the need to cross swords with this audacious autocrat who played on others feelings while he waited for an absent wife. She was still determined to topple him from his high and mighty perch, and a slight sense of frustration probably had a hand in her feeling of loss!

The obvious thing to do would be to ignore his manner as she normally would with any other self-assured egotist. She had made short work of them in the past. Except . . . that kissing episode, which really meant nothing to her or Grant, had not been exactly repulsive. Be honest now, Jane Wheeler, it was only his mocking and flirtatious ways that riled her considerably. Was she a square to object to married men dickying other girls? Grant had teased that pretty blond Sister at the mission—had he kissed her as well, and did she raise an objection?

Jane swore softly but decisively under her breath as she looked for the elusive square of Tippex to correct a typing error, determinedly wiping all thoughts of an irritating boss from her mind to concentrate on the letter forming under her usually nimble fingers. At this rate she'd be fired before any perch tilting could be accomplished!

Her mind nagged again when she sat down to lunch with Sandy. Had Grant discovered the skeleton in her little cupboard, or had he disregarded their talk on Sandy's troubles? The child was listless lately, off her appetite and hung around Jane when permitted; had he been too harsh or was she merely missing him—where did he go during the course of the day, and what did he do in the evenings—spend his time in the study or take time off to give her the enjoyment she obviously found in his company? Sandy caught Jane's speculative gaze, answered her thoughts with uncanny timing.

"Grant is so tired when he comes home every night, do you know he's got millions of—what do you call that kind of sheep when they stand against the mountain 'n in the valley they look like lots of grey stones? He's got to ride an awful long way to see them 'n then come back every night to stay with me."

"Merinos. Millions, Sandy? Where?" Jane asked.

"Well, not 'xactly millions, but 'n awful lot. They're near where the forest begins, the gove'ment Forestry, and it's cool 'n the hills look like bread dough. My next holidays I'm going with him, he promised, for a whole week. There's nice bungalows 'n a swell stream where we can fish 'n swim. Will you come for a ride this afternoon, Jane? You can ride on Dicky, he won't throw you 'cause he's old. Can you ride, Jane?" Sandy pepped up at her own proposition and waited anxiously for her friend's verdict.

"Golly, Sandy, I haven't mounted for years and will most likely fall flat on my face regardless of Dicky's age! What's your pony's name?" Jane side-stepped delicately.

"Sugarbush, 'n he's getting fat because I've been too busy fishing to exercise him. You can come and look at him 'n Dicky and I'm sure you won't fall off. Tony 'n Mick says he's too 'crepit for them."

Jane laughed. "Probably for those two hell's angels, but he sounds just right for me!"

She channelled their chat away from horses and riding, a sport that had never appealed greatly because she had a slight fear of the large animals and suspected her seat was at fault. "I've got a pile of work and simply must finish it today, so I'll get cracking and maybe I'll find time to look at your horses before Tom takes me home."

"I'm cross with Grant," Sandy stated flatly.

Jane felt her heart constrict at the sudden bald statement and looked silently at the pout of the young mouth.

"I'm really cross because he makes you work all day 'n we can't go fishing."

"Oh, Sandy dear, I'm sorry about that, but even if I wasn't working here I'd have to work somewhere, so please don't be cross with him. Anyway, I don't work on Saturdays and Sundays, so let's make a plan." The constriction lifted and Jane leaned her elbows on the table. "I suggest you ask Toicky if you may come with me this afternoon. Uncle Bart or I will bring you back in the car. We'll go down and do a spot of fishing or swimming and I'm sure Grant won't mind."

The pout was gone in a flash, an eager face was lifted. "Oh yes, Toicky'll let me go!"

"Well then, eat all your salad in case she objects on that score." The housekeeper entered right on cue and Jane decided to do the asking.

"On one condition, miss, Sandy must finish all her food." One look at the young one emptying her plate fast told of the conspiracy and Minna turned an approving look on Jane. "You have a way with this one—pity the bribe can't be used thrice daily! Take a rest after lunch, Sandy, if Mr. Grant isn't back by the time Miss Jane leaves I'll tell him where you are."

"Thank you, Mrs. Du Toit. I'll take good care of her and bring her back. No need for Mr. Saxon to fetch or send for her."

"Right, miss. It gets a bit lonesome for the wee one."

"And I'd like to take her out for the day on Saturday if I may—"

"Oh dear, begging your pardon, there's a message for you from Doctor Davies, not to forget he's calling for you on Saturday for the dance. And I don't think it will be suitable to take Sandy on Saturday," Minna hesitated, suddenly agitated, and Sandy interposed anxiously, her fork halfway to her mouth, "Why not, Toicky, why not on Saturday?"

"You know perfectly well your mother will arrive either Friday or Saturday, that's why."

"Oh, hell!" Sandy dropped her fork with a clatter.

"Sandra! That's very impolite and rude!" a shocked Toicky scolded her.

"Well, I mean it. She won't take me fishing 'cause the sun burns her 'n the ants bite her 'n—"

"That's quite enough, young lady. Your mother hasn't seen you for a long time and will want you to stay with her while she's here."

Sandy remained stubborn. "She sees me 'n slobbers—

I mean kisses me all over and then follows Grant all over the place."

"Sandy, I'm sure you're wrong about her attentions towards you—and as for following Grant all over the place, that's understandable—isn't it? I mean, she sees so little of him as well," Jane said, and found a small "oh, hell!" in her own heart at the thought of Mara's imminent arrival.

A shadow crossed the young face as Sandy said in a subdued way:

"Lemmy says a woman's child is 'of her own flesh 'n blood' and Grant isn't, so why does she close the study door 'n won't let me in 'n send me to my room when they sit on the veranda at night, 'n put on her prettiest things—and even so, what she did . . . ." a small trembling hand clamped her mouth shut. Jane was at her side in an instant.

"All right, love. Your mother will probably be tired from her long trip, so I'll personally ask Grant if you may spend Saturday with me. I'm going to the club with Peter Davies in the evening, but my whole day will be free to spend with you." Jane's eyes dared Minna to contradict her.

Minna looked from the challenging brown eyes to the down-bent head and brought her hands upwards in a hopeless gesture. "Be it your responsibility then, miss," and turned away muttering a low, "You don't know nothing yet."

Jane turned back to speak firmly, hiding her puzzlement at the child's flare-up about Grant (jealousy after all, in a lonely heart?) and the strange way Minna had looked at her. "Come, Sandy, no more of this. You'll only make yourself ill and then you can't come with me this afternoon. Have your rest now and I'll see you at teatime and we can plan what to do, fishing or swimming, mm?"

"Yes, Jane." A watery smile played on Sandy's face as she obeyed meekly.

Now she'd embroiled herself, but good! The type-writer rattled to keep with Jane's thoughts; her mind urged caution in dealing with this household while her heart wept for the young one. She was already biased against Mara Saxon, and that wasn't fair; Sandy's mother might be quite a charming person and the very person to still her daughter's strange grudge with a per-fectly simple and reasonable explanation (what had she done to "poor Daddy?") Children did sometimes be-have in an incomprehensible manner, especially an only child. It could be pure and simple jealousy of Mara's way with Grant or vice versa. Or an overheard disagree-ment between her parents could be built up in her mind to abnormal dimensions and the blame placed on the mother's side alone.

Grant Saxon, for all his clam-like reserve on "Mara-talk," for all his dickying technique with other females, must be experiencing an inner delight at the return of a wife and wouldn't take kindly to a disgruntled daughter disrupting the happy homecoming!

A painful sensation threaded through Jane's breast as her mind pictured that homecoming. It had absolutely nothing to do with her, this reunion. She was an out-sider looking in, purely and simply that. So why did a mental vow to keep on her guard against something—or someone—persistingly hammer in her mind as she gazed absently out of the window, waiting for the inex-plicable pain in her breast to pass?

"COME ON, SANDY, last one in is chicken!" Jane poised, lifted her arms and cleaved the waters to their clear depths. Moments later a small body came hurtling down and they surfaced together, gasping at the contact of cold water against warm bodies. Their hair, unrestricted red and brown seaweed, floated and framed their faces as they turned on their backs in pure bliss.

A bliss that was rudely shattered by two brown rockets that landed over and under, jetting sprays of stinging water on to upturned serene faces and causing havoc amongst the mermaids! Tony and Mick laughed with glee as Jane retaliated instantly and the ensuing water battle became hilarious and breathless. The boys were wary of Jane's former judo tactics and also gave thought to Sandy's smallness, so the girls promptly took advantage and had their enemy in full retreat to surrender ignominiously on the grassy bank.

Grant Saxon's eyes darkened as he watched the girl in the pool. They flickered from her hair to bare shoulders and back to long slim legs moving languorously in the clear emerald water. Jane saw the towering figure on the rock ledge and brought her feet down to caress the pebbly bed of the pool. Wet mermaid hair dripped gleaming jewels on to her golden shoulders. She brushed wet tendrils from her eyes and more rare jewels sparkled on her lashes, turning nut-brown eyes to amber, to glow like a panther's eyes.

Her every nerve tautened as they faced each other in silence, his smoky gaze holding her mesmerized. She shook off the fairy net and started to walk out of the water, and the silver jewels sparkled down her back and breast to disappear forever at her feet. Grant stood a moment longer, as if he too were held in a steel web, before he stepped down and reached for her towel robe.

Wordlessly he held it in readiness and Jane turned gleaming shoulders to be enveloped in its warm softness. "Water sprite, golden nymph, lead I to thy jewelled palace, for I wouldst fain come willingly, holding thy tender hand, even unto my last breath," Grant chanted gruffly and stepped back to grin at the astonished expression in her luminous eyes.

"Quite the romantic, Mr. Saxon? Strange how outer appearances can belie the inner, sensitive being." Jane put her arms into the robe sleeves and stooped for her cigarette case.

"Absolutely fantastic, Miss Wheeler. You should know. One moment ago a panther looked out of your eyes and now—now there's nothing. Pity, he looked engaging." He lit her cigarette and the smoke wreathed between them.

"And who could believe in a poetic soul by studying the exterior?" she quipped coolly.

"Study must dig deep to extract the full value—does my rough exterior bother you at all? Take no notice, be the ernest archaeologist, the soul-seeker, and I'll be—"

Jane interrupted hastily, "Not at all. I was only generalizing. We had a whale of a time in the water and Sandy's an absolute eel. Who taught her to swim so well? Didn't Minna tell you that I would see her home? I managed to finish that pile of work you left. You're back early today." Her tongue wilfully hastened in all directions without coalition on her part and Jane allowed it to take a further plunge. "Can Sandy spend the day with me on Saturday?"

Grant made the familiar gesture of hooking his thumbs into the pockets of his trousers while his brows lowered quizzically. "Shall we take it in sequence? I agree the water's terrific. I did. Yes, Minna told me, and also very perceptive of you to notice my early return." Dark brows drew closer together and Jane waited for the curt reminder that precious Mara would be home. "Saturday . . . yes, I guess she can. But aren't you going to do any shopping, hairdressers and all that jazz, dicky up for the dance?"

"I do my own hair, and have no shopping to do." Jane hesitated and drew on the cigarette between her fingers. "I thought her mother might object to her absence so soon after her arrival—I mean—"

"I gather your meaning, but doubt if Mara would mind particularly. She'll be here on Friday and will probably go to town for her beauty treatment, not being so versatile as you in that way. No home touch for a model, only the best professional care." He watched the swing of damp hair as temper started and held up a belaying hand. "Now don't go off your rocker, I'm not critizing your abilities, merely stating a fact. Now where was I? Your action's so provoking . . . Sandy has my full consent to visit with you on Saturday."

"Thank you, Grant." He would be delighted to have his wife's attention focused on himself without distraction. Jane immediately reproached herself for the mean thought, for she sensed instinctively that Grant was anything but mean or mulish toward Sandy.

"Your aunt invited me to supper, I accepted, so that answers for Sandy's transport home tonight."

"Oh." She would have to suffer his aggravating presence all evening. Could she do a bit of quick perch tilting . . . or did she really want to do so? His wife would be back soon and all his charm would be channelled in the right direction, leaving no opportunity for side-stepping.

"What a dramatic reaction!" The taunt was back, but he turned away at once.

At the table that evening Grant's paricular charm had a personal touch for everyone but her, or so Jane imagined. Elizabeth was obviously taken in by his attentiveness and the rest were already besotted, so Jane did not attempt a battle that was sure to be a dead loss without support.

She surprised herself by enjoying the evening. Sandy started a hilarious game of telling a tale, exciting or memorable, in each one's life. Sandy had fallen out of a fairly high tree and a passing turkey had broken a dangerous fall by strutting conveniently and innocently under the path of her descent. Imagination ran riot when she described the bird's fright, screams and loss of feathers! Tony and Mick relived the time they had bunked hostel after lights out for a midnight picnic at Tadpole Dam. Unfortunately the party became too boisterous, they were covered with mud, sneaked through an open window and nearly caused a snooping matron a heart attack when she confronted the weird creatures in the bathroom.

Elizabeth recounted her battle against the elements during the floods of Port Elizabeth and Janet created gales of laughter on the agitation of a favourite hen who brought out a clutch of ducklings and watched, with angry, ruffled feathers, her brood sail gaily on the dangerous waters of the pond!

Grant demanded a romantic episode from Jane, but she ignored the remark and said, "Don't try to skip your turn. Surely you, too, have a past episode, dangerous or romantic, to relate?"

An uncanny silence suddenly reigned. Laughter crinkles disappeared as Grant's face sobered abruptly. He offered his case to Bart and lit both cigarettes before answering.

"My affairs of the heart are not for tender ears, my big moments lie in the future." He looked at his watch. "And it's long past poppet's bedtime. I called in at the Mission, by the way, David Muller sends regards and hopes to see you at the club on Saturday. Are you all coming?"

Bart said, "Surely. It's the highlight of the community, ladies dressing up and the men's chance to watch the girls go by!"

Janet turned to Grant. "You'll be there?"

He pushed back his chair and held out a hand for the sleepy child. "If Mara has her way it's a certainty. How is Olivier doing?"

"All right so far and somewhat subdued . . . that other matter settled?" Bart asked in return, and Grant nodded.

Jane forbore to mention her encounter with the man in question; it was of no concern to Grant Saxon, and Olivier had been polite to her, though even now the thought of his pale eyes sent another uncomfortable shiver down her spine.

Man and child gave thanks for the dinner and pinpoints of red rear lights finally vanished in a cloak of darkness.

FRIDAY PASSED UNEVENTFULLY except for Jane's uncontained curiosity every time a vehicle was heard in the driveway. And yet, in spite of her curiosity, she hoped fervently to be on her way home before the arrival of Mara Saxon. Grant was not to be seen in the morning, arriving in time for lunch, and later he positively prowled, fiddled absently amongst his papers and then disappeared for long intervals.

Minna thoughtfully kept Sandy in the kitchen, occupationally intent on a baking venture. At afternoon tea the young miss proudly presented a plate of lopsided scones which Jane duly praised. They were really good, though queer-shaped. Grant was not present.

Tom was with him when the Rover pulled up in the late afternoon. Jane settled the cover on her typewriter, scooped up her purse and walked down the steps. Tom moved behind the wheel and Grant stepped aside to lift a casual hand as the vehicle drew away. Jane, assured his mind was full with the imminent return of a beloved one; obviously no time wasted on attentions to a mere female employee today! She tried hard to divert her thoughts as they drove through entrancing greens, beside sparkling streams . . . somehow their appeal did not register and she felt a flattened sense of depression.

The telephone was shrilling the Wheeler code when she entered the house and Peter Davies' voice greeted her as she lifted the receiver.

"Hi, Jane, how's our working gal?"

"Just fine, thanks. How is the great healer of bodies?"

"Cussing and stitching madly. The entire African nation are going through an era of falls, fisticuffs and what-have-you, resulting in broken bones and dislocated anatomies. I swear they do it just to keep this medico exercised and his thoughts away from a certain charming lass. Still on the subject of this lass, how is she passing her time, and is Saxon slaving you to death—and did you get my message from Toicky?"

"Yes, I got your message, though I doubt if you will make it with all those bones to grind."

"Phelange, femurs, pelvis and skulls can do their own knitting tomorrow night—I'll be on your doorstep at the stroke of seven, come floods, 'flu or famine!"

Jane laughed lightheartedly. "Right, doctor, you'll find me on the second step to the right, arrayed in my best and nestled in the wistaria. Will you recognize me, or should I clamp a red rose between my pearly teeth for identification?"

"I'd recognize you draped in poison ivy, sweet one!" Peter declared with confidence, and Jane laughed again as the receiver positively vibrated in her hand.

"A stinging prospect, not to be considered for one instant. Listen, Peter, my folks are all going as well—wouldn't you rather I meet you at the club, more convenient and time-saving for you?"

"Positively not, my pet. Deprive me of that extra pleasure? Oh dash, I'm being stabbed by steely glares from the boss—'bye now, see you tomorrow." The line clicked in hasty termination.

SANDRA ARRIVED AT AN early hour the following morning, complete with collapsible fishing rod and a case containing her bathing kit.

Jane thanked Tom and invited Sandy to join her in the kitchen and help with the sandwiches for their outing. The aroma of new bread, sizzling bacon and tomatoes made her small nose twitch hungrily, so Jane promptly set another place at the table.

Sandy declared that she had been to excited too eat her porridge at home.

Bart had breakfasted and departed; Janet, Elizabeth and the boys were still in the throes of waking up and dressing so the two girls had the kitchen to themselves. Jane buttered hot toast as she ventured the question that had hovered on her lips since the child's arrival.

"It was good of Tom to bring you; now we can get away sooner. Did—did your mother come, yesterday?"

Sandy bit into the luscious buttery toast, savoring it slowly before she answered. "Mara—Mom came in time for dinner last night 'n she was pleased to see me. She says I look better 'n not so scraggy any more." She chewed reflectively. "I'll never be as pretty as her, though, I don't think . . . I was very polite 'cause Grant said I should be. He talked to me last night 'n asked if I was troubled about her."

In the silence that followed Jane asked casually, "And you told him what was troubling you?"

"No, I didn't, but he was awfully nice and said to trust and tell him when I was good 'n ready, and anyway he 'spected my feet were in the wrong boots 'n I must be sure of my . . . my . . . ."

She hesitated, and Jane supplied, "Facts?"

"That's right. I must be sure before thinking wrong things about anybody. B-but, Jane, I can't tell anybody what I heard 'cause it's awful and—" the young face looked downcast, "I was sneak-listening. "

"Eavesdropping, Sandy?"

"Yes, and I'm 'shamed, but I did hear that—what I heard." Sandy's lips closed tightly.

"Okay, Sandy, you were nice and polite, and that's good. I'm proud of you. We'd better move. The day doesn't wait and it's glorious in the sun and I want to catch a terrific tan today."

They took the short cut through the vegetable garden and lucerne lands. Jane felt a familiar crinkle in her spine as Flip Olivier straightened up to watch their progress. He made her so nervous.

The girls had a blissful, uninterrupted day. They swam to their hearts' content and basked on the sun-warmed rocks. Sandy's joy was complete when she landed four small fish and Jane showed grateful appreciation of the large one that obligingly hooked itself on her line when she was inattentive and sleepy with the sun's soporific effect.

The sun was a giant orange ball on the fir-clad hills when they reached home again. Tom timed his return trip neatly and Jane waved cheerfully to her little friend, then dashed into the house to wash her hair and prepare for the night's entertainment.

When she finally walked into the lounge the entire Wheeler clan voiced their approval. The African sun had given her skin a golden glow and the simple yet daring apricot midi shimmered in swirls from her slim waist, showing bare shoulders to perfection. Shining nut-brown hair was drawn up and away from high cheekbones to fall from the top of her head in swirly coils. A single smoky topaz on a fine chain nestled in the visible cleft of softly firm breasts. Matching earrings captured the light and reflected in her tawny-brown eyes. Wispy gold sandals completed the enchanting effect.

Peter arrived in his own sleek sports car and Jane's eyes approved the well-groomed look of her escort, while Bart proposed a drink before departure. The doctor, in turn, was mesmerized by the delightful vision that would be his companion for the evening and his normal, easy chatter became slightly erratic. . . .

The trees encircling the club grounds were festooned with colored lights and the beautifully kept lawns were edged with masses of geraniums that lent color to a very scenic setting. A white-clad waiter drew chairs together for the new arrivals and Jane looked inquiringly at Peter; did he want to join the family or had he expected a table for two?

Peter was quite happy to join the family circle.

The band swung into sound in the spacious hall and couples lost no time in enjoying the inviting beat of the drums. Peter danced well, held her lightly, and Jane knew she was going to enjoy his company. They returned to the veranda to find Pat Marais and escort had joined the party. Her partner stood, tall and gangly, obviously a farmer, or so Jane deduced when she felt the hardness of a calloused hand as Pat introduced Julius Davenport. Jane's eyes wandered farther afield, but she saw no sign of another tall, lithe figure . . . a figure she had been unconsciously seeking since her arrival at this gathering.

Janet and Bart decided to try out their "atrophied" legs while the others rested. Long drinks sparkling with ice were deftly served by the same waiter who had delegated himself to the special care of their tables.

A movement along the entrance of the veranda distracted her attention. Grant Saxon was walking toward them and he looked wonderfully handsome in his dark suit and immaculately white shirt. Her eyes moved to focus on the woman at his side.

Beautiful became an understated word in describing the titian-haired woman who walked with the haughty grace of a queen . . . ravishingly lovely, green eyes emphasized with subtle makeup, Mara Saxon's green wet-look dress showed every sinuous provocative movement of her perfect body. She was openly, coolly aware of her attraction and a long slim hand rested with possessive assurance on the dark-clad arm of her escort.

"Well, shake me down, the goddess appears once more on the scene. Wonder what havoc is brewing this time," Peter said in Jane's ear.

"Are you immune to havoc, dear doctor?" Jane turned to him in her effort not to stare so blatantly. Her heart mocked, *You've seen enough, Janey. . . .*

"There are havocs and havocs, sweetie, you being one of the pleasanter ones—but that one is a dangerous, snaky, bedevilled witch and, if I guess rightly, will concentrate her charm on the rocky one at her side!"

"So what, Peter Davies? Is it so unusual? Or are you of the school that believes in marriage swaps?" Jane asked sharply, with more heat than she realized, and Peter raised astonished eyebrows.

"Jane! Whatever are you saying, or insinuating?"

"Hello, Jane," a deep, familiar voice said at her back, and she turned to look up at Grant Saxon.

Peter and Julius stood up politely as Grant drew Mara forward. "Meet Elizabeth and Jane Wheeler, Mara. Elizabeth is Janet's and Bart's sister-in-law and Jane is her daughter. Two charming ladies, very welcome and an asset to our community."

Mara Saxon inclined her head in gracious acknowledgement (only an experienced, trained model or a lady of inborn grace could make this gesture without embarrassment.) Jane wouldn't dream of emulating, so she merely smiled at Grant's flattery and then at the beauty at his side. Elizabeth did likewise, although her curiosity was more apparent than her daughter's.

Mara said, "How nice to have more feminine company in this rough, hard-bitten slice of country.

Sandra's quite taken with you, Miss Wheeler, and used pretty persuasive powers on Grant and me to allow her to spend the day with you." She sighed provokingly. "I guess it's to be expected, when one is away so much, for a small child to transfer her affections to someone closer and willing to do the childish things that children adore."

Indignation flooded through Jane. "We must all be very childish, then," she riposted, and laughed gaily. "All my family love fishing, swimming and exploring. Even Grant has joined us and he doesn't strike me as being exactly childish!" *Put that in your pipe and smoke it,* thought Jane inelegantly.

The green eyes transferred from the smoky topaz on Jane's breast to the man at her side.

"Sweet of you to allow the girls to charm you away from your precious work, dear Grant. I'll have to learn from them, their ways and wiles, to lure you into doing the things I love to do." Mara's incredible lashes fanned her cheeks. "Though they're anything but childish." Her smile remained gracious, but Jane definitely detected a thread of venom interlaced with the sweetness.

Grant's eyes narrowed slightly at the interchange, but he answered laconically, "When will you realize that I'm quite impervious to guile from the fair sex?"

Says who? Jane's mind questioned impudently. *You, Grant Saxon, can dish out guile by the bucket, so what makes you so impervious on the receiving line?* Luckily Peter interposed before her indignation found tongue.

"Ha, and another ha! Not even you are infallible or immune, Grant. Not one of us—I've found my weak spot, and revel in my weakness." His eyes rested on Jane.

Pat suddenly looked nettled and her retort came unexpectedly. "Your trouble, Pete, is that you're riddled with weak spots, like . . . like a tea-strainer!"

It was Peter's turn to look exasperated and Jane felt the air vibrate with tension and a forthcoming battle of wits and sarcasm. She stood up and smoothed her apricot skirt. "Come on, Julius, let's not waste the effort on the part of the band while these two run through the holes of said strainer!"

Grant had to step aside for her to pass and his glance seemed to rest for the first time on her appearance. Gray eyes circled her hair, to bare shoulders to her bosom. A subconscious stream of awareness, or memory, surfaced impetuously as she compared the look in his eyes with that of Olivier and was further shocked to find that it did not repulse her as those pale eyes had done. The feeling down her back was there, but not of repulsion . . . it contained a strange, unholy excitement that made her very aware of her own body and his closeness.

Jane stepped past Grant and took the hand of Julius Davenport.

Other perceptive female eyes watched Grant's scrutiny and the girl's reaction. Mara kept a smooth smile on her lovely lips and a caressing hand on his arm. "We're keeping our friends from their enjoyment, darling. Shall we find our table?"

Julius grinned down companionably at Jane as they circled the floor. "Quite a dish, I'll say! Like a slinky green mamba—dear Mara didn't like your crack about childish things. I watched her eyes turn several shades of green. You know, Jane, I suddenly yearn to invite her out to my place and put her through the ropes—fishing, swimming, riding, climbing, and watch how she comes out at the other end. I also have an uncontrollable urge to find out what childish things she loves to do!" Julius closed his eyes in mock ecstasy and Jane's humor was restored by his comical expression.

How dared her own body betray her like that? Grant

had a magnetism that attracted greatly, but she was not merely another magnetized steel pin, to be drawn so easily . . . Mara would be, was the recipient, the one who surrendered to the magic of belonging. Jane brought her mind back abruptly from the devastating, treacherous trend it was taking. She turned and found that she would be seated with her back to that other table where Grant and Mara were sitting.

Pat and Peter were back on amiable terms; Bart and Janet were talking at another table; the boys were out on the lawn and there was no sign of Elizabeth. Pat started the laughter and hilarity between the four of them when she discoursed on her and Peter's escapades in and out of the Mission. Peter was not slow to follow her lead, and their wily ways with Dr. Muller, more often unsuccessful than otherwise, caused shocked merriment between the two listeners. Peter and Pat looked often at each other for collaboration and Jane thought with certain affection, they were right and good for each other. Under all this wit and sarcastic comebacks something else was blossoming, slowly but surely. Peter's sweet way with her, Jane, was only the attraction to a new face. She came out of her matchmaking reverie as Grant politely requested the next dance with her.

CHAPTER SIX

"YOU'RE A GOLDEN GIRL tonight, Janey."

Over the arm that held her she saw Mara dancing with another man. So now that "glamor girl" was dancing with someone else he dutifully took the opportunity to dance with his employee? Well, his employee had a great urge to dance with her boss, to find out if her spinal trouble was indeed a symptom of his nearness or merely some dreaded disease. She absorbed the feel of his arm, the steel strength of the hand that held hers, the latent vitality of the man's body and decided she hadn't the qualifications to judge or diagnose the rubber in her bones.

She lifted her eyes from an earnest study of immaculate shirt. "Apricot, not golden. You color-blind, boss?"

He gave her a little shake and his voice roughened. "I am not your boss tonight, and don't think this is a duty dance . . . oh yes, your mind is an open book. Apricot or golden, what's the difference, you still look good enough to eat. As luscious as the golden harvest on my trees."

Open book! Invisible covers were shut in mental haste and Jane queried gravely, "Round and juicy?"

"Yum." He matched her gravity.

"Your—girl—is quite beautiful, Grant."

"My girl?" His eyes flicked her face. "Meaning Mara?"

"Who else?" Jane countered.

"As you say, who else? Mara always looks chic and beautiful."

"And I don't." It was not a question but a flat statement.

Grant brought the hand that was holding hers down under her chin and she was forced to meet his direct gaze.

"No, you don't. That's why it's a pleasure to see you looking so enchanting. A man can't and doesn't want to eat cake every day."

A mounting flush spread from her neck to ears. Mara had only arrived the day before and already he was passing outrageous remarks to her, Jane! Had she given him cause to believe she was easy prey to loose flattery? Or did he belong to the brigade of compulsive male flirts? Not something special as her betraying heart would believe? Her eyes glowed with amber fire as she said in a small, cold voice, "Grant Saxon, after this dance is over I'll thank you not to approach me again."

Grant remained silent and only a slight tightening of his hand over hers gave clue that he had heard. The music stopped and the arm around her waist forced her to walk with him to a side door and out under the stars.

Grant dropped his arm. "Enlighten my darkness," he said simply.

Jane knew a moment of puzzlement as she looked at his tall, straight body and direct gray eyes. "You're being obtuse," she whispered huskily, "because you want to stay that way. You're perfectly aware of the reason behind my request."

"Jane," Grant put his hands on her shoulders. "Jane, are you hurt because I said you weren't chic and enchanting every day?"

"No, Mr. Saxon, don't deliberately misunderstand. Enjoy your cake while you have the opportunity, it's not always available."

Jane felt a sliver of fear as the hands on her shoulders tightened with painful force. His breath was warm on her face as he jeered softly.

"A most profound observation, golden one." He drew her closer. "Maybe we can soothe that ruffled, jealous heart with a certain anodyne?" She was drawn inexorably closer and then his mouth got in the way of her furious denial.

The starry heavens became a crazy kaleidoscope and the girl shut her eyes and forced her traitorous body into rigid stiffening control.

Grant Saxon lifted his mouth from her bruised lips. His eyes were black in the starlight and his hands suddenly, caressingly gentle on her back and shoulders.

"Janey, why are you fighting so stubbornly? I know you're attracted as much as I am and I've no intentions of trying to seduce you, sweet and alluring as you are. Why the angry barrier and oblique words? Why, Jane?"

Tears of angry misery made her eyes luminous. Jane knew without doubt that she loved this indiscriminate man. Knew, too, that if she lost control, every nerve in her body and mind would respond joyously and she would forget that he belonged to another!

Her approach choked on heartbreak. "If you can still ask that then I can't answer. Does conscience or loyalty mean nothing to you? If not, please don't choose me as recipient of your—favors!"

Grant stepped back and with deliberate, ominous restraint lifted his cigarette case from his jacket pocket. He allowed the smoke to wreath past his eyes before he spoke again.

"I can't begin to understand what you're implying, but it sounds highly insulting. My patience is wearing thin, and if you've turned out to be neurotic about romance and such things, my apologies. Though, being obtuse, I failed to sense it. It's not a habit of mine to get so close to a girl and my sense of perception seems to have deserted me." He looked across her shoulder and his face closed and hardened like a granite image.

Jane whirled to follow his glance and Mara and Julius were within two yards of them. Her heart began a dull beat as she saw the green glitter of the redhead's eyes . . . she was still suffering from the shock of Grant's grim onslaught and would now have to bear the brunt of Mara's anger. Had she misconstrued the whole setup by blaming the wrong party? Was this the reason for Mara's long absences from her home—her husband's dalliance with other girls, despite contradiction that it was not a habit of his?

Mara's mouth wore a thin smile. "So cool under the stars. Julius and I decided to explore the possibilities, and we find—others are doing likewise." Julius's eyes widened at the falsity of her words; she had demanded that he accompany her. Mara continued sweetly, "You don't look as if you've found it very romantic, Jane. Grant told me about his obliging little secretary. Has he been lecturing you? He's so obsessed with the affairs of the estate. You look quite sweet when your feathers are ruffled, dear."

"How right you are, Mrs. Saxon. We were in the midst of solving an enormous, universal problem. But it usually dwindles to petty proportions when faced squarely, have you noticed? Grant will grasp my point when he stops being—obtuse." The lowered dark brow touched Jane with strange fear. She walked to Julius's side, masking her apprehension under an appealing smile.

Julius drew her hand through his arm. "Nothing romantic about our little walk either. Mara's found what she was looking for." He disregarded the icy look from greeneyes at his failure to back her reason for coming out and smiled at Jane. "Enough fresh air? Come and dance with me."

"A pleasure, Julius." Jane held her head high as they walked, arm in arm, across the velvety lawn.

Her apricot skirt whirled gracefully as he executed complicated, expert turns, and she lifted her eyes once, to meet Grant's mocking smile across her partner's shoulder. Mara's gleaming head nestled against his cheek. She was taller than Jane (her head only reached his heart). After that, someone suggested champagne and Jane imbibed with uninhibited gaiety. She was frothy and gay, laughed a lot and her dazzling wit became as sparkling as the "bubbly," and if it was slightly forced only Elizabeth sensed this and wondered briefly what was boiling in that young breast.

Grant leaned nonchalantly against a veranda post, Mara at his side, Julius in earnest conversation with them. Jane was too far away to hear what was being discussed, but a sidelong glance showed Grant's gesture of consent and Mara's dazzling smile bestowed evenly between the two men. The cacophonous music and chatter blasted her ears, her nerves jumped in the pit of her stomach and she felt weary and deflated with her attempts to mask her emotions. The champagne brought a throb to her head and she wished desperately to be alone, anywhere in the soft cloak of darkness, in absolute solitude. To examine the burst of knowledge that had come to her when Grant had held her under the stars; torture herself with this new, blinding torment. This she wanted to do with almost sadistic urgency, having the curious illusion that in doing so she could exorcise the love that rioted in her heart, kill it stone dead before it became overwhelming, completely and slavishly insuperable.

JULIUS DAVENPORT REJOINED them with a satisfied glint in his eyes and Jane studied him with some trepidation when he threw her a conspiratorial wink before disclosing his plans; they were all invited to spend the Sunday at his home. His grandmother would welcome the company; she was in her seventies, hale and hearty except for troublesome arthritis in her hip that kept her from visiting too often. She dearly loved company, so would they all come, gladden her heart and enjoy themselves?

The Wheeler family accepted the invitation. David

said he would take over morning duties and allow his two assistants the day off.

Julius whispered in Jane's ear, "I'm starting my campaign on the queenly Mara."

She felt exasperation rise and whispered back furiously, "Leave her alone, Julius. You'll only cause trouble and I think there's enough of that in the Saxons's life. Anyway, I don't want to come. I've had my day in the sun and all this . . . I'm tired and completely—"

He interjected rudely but with a humorous twist to his mouth, "Shush, sweet one. I'm merely going to crack that case of superiority complex ever so slightly; under that glamor and scheming red head must be something worthwhile. And you simply must come and visit my grandmother. She and I would appreciate it greatly."

"Why don't you leave Grant to crack his own way to her worth?"

"My good deed," Julius grinned, "help him and enjoy myself into the bargain! Will you come, Jane?"

She felt dispirited and wanted to go home, away from the intrigue that seemed to be affecting everyone. "Yes, I'll come, Julius."

Peter said, "What are you two conspiring? Jane, you're looking pale. Say the word and I'll take you home."

"Thanks, Peter. That overdose of bubbly's finally catching up with my liver and I'm suffering in consequence. Do you mind?"

"Not at all. I've had enough as well." He collected her beaded purse and wrap and Jane waved a casual hand at her circle and walked away quickly, before any objections could be voiced.

AN INSISTENT TAPPING on her bedroom door brought Jane out of a heavy sleep and her traveling clock showed just after six o'clock. Oh, bother! It was Sunday.

Why couldn't she be left just for one morning to sleep
on and on? Her heavy spirit lifted a dark head to remind her of the promised jaunt to Julius Davenport's
homestead. She had taken one of her mother's sleeping
pills the night before, or rather, in the early hours.
Taken because Jane suddenly feared the outcome of
that inner insistence to torment her heart in solitude.
She knew with painful conviction that nothing in the
world could exorcise the unwelcome love that had entered her unwary heart. A number of times she had believed herself to be in love, but when it hit her like this
then she instantly recognized the gold from the dross.

And of what earthly, or heavenly, use would this remarkable knowledge be to her? Absolutely, hurtingly
and hopelessly none whatsoever.

Her decision to stay at home (primarily because
Grant Saxon would be there) was overruled by an un-
sympathetic family and she eventually subsided list-
lessly on to the back seat of the car next to two horribly
boisterous boys. The magnificent scenery on the Sabie
road failed to arouse her normal enthusiasm; this was
part of the Summit Route that he had mentioned and
she would never travel it with him, as promised.

The Davenport home was built in the old tradition,
with modern additions and appliances discreetly blending. The wide veranda overlooked a sloping lawn and
the pool nestled in a hollow surrounded by indigenous
shrubs and trees. Jane aroused herself to take note only
when Elizabeth drew her attention to the intensity of
varied greens and wild natural beauty of a carefully
planned landscape.

Mrs. Davenport sat in an old, comfortable chair on
the veranda. Julius, incongruously clad in wildly colored Bermuda shorts and blue T-shirt, looked fit and
brown as he ambled down the steps to greet his guests.
Pat and Peter were already there and voiced their long-

ing for the tea that was being held back to await the lazy laggards, so Julius decided not to prolong the torture. Fresh tea could be made for the Saxons if and when they arrived. Tony and Mick hastily greeted the old lady and their host, then made a beeline for the pool. Thirst being quenched satisfactorily, the adults followed suit with the exception of Jane, who chose to laze in a deckchair and visit Mrs. Davenport. Pat declared she was being chicken after her night out and Jane lazily agreed, closing her eyelids serenely against their jeers.

The two of them chatted companionably, and then Julius's grandmother took Jane into her bedroom and opened a heavy stinkwood chest. With reverent hands she lifted a beautiful crocheted bedspread that was nestled in tissue and sprinkled with aromatic camphor. The wondrous work of love and art had been handed down to each succeeding generation and now awaited the future wife of Julius.

"And my wicked grandson will soon reach his forties and still hasn't found a girl to suit him. He'd better make haste, for I'm determined to hold a grandchild—I mean a great-grandchild in my old arms," she smiled mischievously, "and I'm getting mighty weary of waiting, being selfishly eager to meet up again with my dear departed in the delightful hereafter! Come, help me fold this again. My old ears are still good and I can hear a car. Must be Grant. I haven't seen young Sandy for over a year now—"

Jane followed slowly and stood beside her to watch Grant, Mara and Sandy walked down to the pool. Mara appeared self-possessed in a short towelling wrap and the man beside her, in light safari suit, strode with indolent, loose-limbed grace. Sandy flung her own small beach coat off her shoulders as she reached the edge of the pool, hesitated a moment while she obviously looked around for her friend; the watching girl saw

Elizabeth wave toward the house and all three new arrivals turned. Sandy waved madly and Grant started to walk back alone. He would naturally be coming to greet Mrs. Davenport. Jane thought desperately for a way of escape.

"Mrs. Davenport," she gripped the arm nearest her, "I don't want to speak to Grant Saxon, not just yet—don't waste time asking why, just give me an out, please, darling?"

Darling Mrs. D. took one quick look at the troubled brown eyes of her companion and said, "Go through the house and find the back door. To the left of the house is a row of fig trees, the pigsties are beyond them. See if Mama Pig's not squashing her young litter. There's also a new clutch of chicks just come out . . . that's all I can do, dear."

"Mrs. D., you're an absolute doll—thanks!" Without a backward glance Jane disappeared into the cool haven of the house.

She found the downy yellow chicks and fondled them one by one while their ruffled mother scolded loudly. Jane left them and walked on. Mama Pig lay contentedly on her side while the little ones, twelve of them, fought hungrily at the exposed milk bar. Finally they all found a place and Jane leaned on the low stone wall, listening to little grunts of satisfaction and watching the tiny forepaws kneading swollen udders to excite the flow of milk. She leaned over perilously to see where the out-of-tune squealing came from. The sow moved her hindquarters, and Jane saw the thirteenth piglet, squashed under a heavy haunch!

Without further thought she jumped over the wall and approached the family, talking soothingly to the sow. A quick heave and the squashed, angry one was clear, unhurt except for his hungry feelings. But now things began to happen . . . Mama thought this red-shirted human was doing the hurting and came clumsily to her feet, scattering babies right and left, and they in turn voiced their disapproval in no uncertain terms! Jane stepped back from the advancing menace, her foot skidded in a puddle and she found herself sitting neatly wedged in a trough of swill.

A tall shadow moved on the wall. Sandy and Grant Saxon were studying her in equal astonishment.

The child's control was not so great as the man's and a high giggle escaped. "We heard the row and came to see—oh, Jane, what are you doing in there?" Her giggle exploded in convulsed laughter.

Through clenched teeth Jane said, "I'm watching the pigs," and eyed them haughtily. She was firmly jammed and was not going to let anyone be entertained by her struggle to extricate herself. Damn him, oh, damn him to hell—and Sandra could join him there for being so inquisitive!

Grant bent down and leaned laconic elbows on the wall. "I grant you the other pool is a bit crowded and sympathize with your wish to be alone, dear Janey, but not with your alternative choice," he said.

"Go to hell, Grant Saxon!" Jane hissed between pearly teeth.

"Language, dear, in front of the child too!" he reproached, softly taunting.

"And take her with you!" she riposted in cold fury.

"Oh, Jane, don't be cross, but you do look funny. Are you hurted?" Sandy's laughter subsided at the look on her friend's face.

Jane forbore to answer and turned her head to watch the wretched sow, cursing inwardly at the cause of her embarrassment; she would have let the piglet suffocate gladly if she had but known the outcome of her kindly rescue.

"Need any help, Miss Wheeler? You look slightly

stuck . . . ." Grant began conversationally, but stopped as furious nut-brown eyes stabbed him.

"I'll thank you to leave. Go away!" Wilfully her voice betrayed her too, coming in a husky croak. Grant moved behind her back, leaned his long length down and slid two hands between her upper arms and body; a quick heave and she was out and up. He steadied her while she found her footing. The swill runnelled down her jeans and squelched into her shoes. Jane kept her back to him when he released her, fully aware of the odorous picture her posterior presented.

"Thanks," she said bitterly.

"Sandy, show Jane to the outside shower and bring her bathing suit and wrap . . . and some nice scented soap," Grant added thoughtfully.

Jane turned her head to watch his receding back; there was a definite quiver to the broad shoulders! She stamped her foot in sheer frustration and her shoe squelched back happily.

Sandy complied promptly and sympathetically, then waited outside the roughly built workers' shower while Jane soaped herself thoroughly with the "scented" soap. Feeling sorry for her outburst toward the child, Jane made amends by recounting her rescue of one piglet that resulted in her predicament. Sandy passed in her towel and bathing suit and when Jane emerged she saw a maid soaking her clothes in a laundry tub. The maid smiled shyly when Jane thanked her and promised to have them dry and ironed right away.

Sandy skipped back to the pool and Jane walked over to Mrs. Davenport and told her about the smelly climax of her attempt to keep out of Grant's way. The old lady tried to keep a sober face, but the twinkle in her eye could not be denied.

"Grant didn't tell me. He ambled past with the assurance that the pigs were fine, that you and they were on very cozy terms! I'm sorry I couldn't keep him here with me, but Sandy demanded to find out what the fuss was about and he decided to accompany her. I'll have to give you that particular piglet as a memento of the furor he caused!"

"Thanks for the kind thought, but I never want to see him again, and if you leave him on my doorstep I'll promptly strangle him," Jane threatened.

There was much cavorting in the water when Jane's reluctant feet finally brought her to the pool's edge. With the exception of two: Mara lay on her back, dark glasses protecting her eyes and the brief white bikini accentuating the lines of her slim loveliness. Grant, darkly tanned in blue trunks and smoking on the far side, had evidently just emerged, for his hair and skin glistened wetly.

Jane greeted Mara briefly and a slender hand lifted in acknowledgement. She scanned the upturned face with a quick sweep of lowered lashes and found no signs of derision or mocking smile and concluded that Grant had not tattled, as yet, about her adventure. He was biding his time, waiting for a suitable moment, no doubt. She didn't dare to glance at him but shed her wrap to stand poised, young and clean-limbed, before executing a smooth cleavage into the water.

Everyone had tired of water battles, for which Jane was thankful, being in no mood for that sort of thing, and soon they climbed out one by one, leaving her to wallow in the silken, cool water on her own.

She was very aware of the tall figure standing at the far end and stayed at her end, floating with her eyes closed.

It came as a shock when she felt a rippling movement at her side and opened her eyes to find him floating alongside. Jane immediately made for the edge and rested her arms on the warm slate, allowing her feet to sink down. Grant followed promptly, did likewise with his arm close to hers.

"You're hair floats and resembles seaweed, and you're a slick chick in the water. Feeling more aromatic now?"

A searing look was her answer, but it seemed to have no burning effect on the man's tough hide or stony feelings. An imperceptible pause followed before Grant continued coversationally, "That unfinished business last night—I'm still trying to figure out what you were doing your nut about and why it took such an insulting trend."

Jane interlocked her fingers tightly. "Leave it be, Grant. Call it a silly episode, anything you want to, but forget it. I apologize for any insult, apologize for whatever you think needs an apology."

His direct glance held genuine curiosity. "Haven't you been kissed before and enjoyed it without behaving like an outraged innocent?"

"I have, I'm no innocent, and it's still no concern of yours. If you can't or won't figure it out—my attitude—on your own, then I can't help any by going into details." His nearness brought a breathlessness to her words.

"For heaven's sake, child, what details? I can only conclude that you've formed some nasty hallucinations about me or, another alternative, I revolt you in some way."

"Oh, heavens!" Jane wondered if he had a blindspot in his makeup; there was genuine puzzlement apparent. If he only knew how opposite to revulsion were her feelings toward him, how eagerly she would have cooperated if he were of single status! She turned her head away, silently mute.

Grant studied her closed face for a moment longer, then impatiently ran his fingers through his wet hair, expelled deeply and said, "Very well, Jane, I'll not trouble you further. If you persist in being obstinate about this, there's no point in persuasion and it becomes rather boring." He slipped under water and a slight rippling on the surface showed his progress to the other end. There was a tightening of muscles in brown arms as he lifted himself out of the pool and then walked to where Mara watched and smiled invitingly.

Jane couldn't isolate herself any longer from the party on the lawn and forced her body to obey good manners by walking around on the warm slates to join them. Bart, Janet and Elizabeth had left, to dress and sit with Mrs. Davenport. Mara now prepared to follow suit.

She stood up and smoothed her hands sensually over the satin skin of her arms. "I've had enough of the sun, my skin blisters easily."

Julius barred her way. "But you haven't even been in the water, darling."

"That's for the birds, and I do feel rather worn out from my late night." Her glance played lightly on Grant's upturned face.

"We all had a good late night . . . getting too old to play?" Julius taunted.

"Oh, let up, Julius. Julius, put me down." He had suddenly lifted her in strong arms and was striding toward the pool.

"Put me down, Julius, don't be so juvenile!" Her voice seemed to dwindle on the last word and only her tormentor saw the sudden terror in her eyes. Mara Saxon was afraid of water!

Grant said, "She can't swim, Julius."

"Well, I'll be damned! What price all those lovely bathing suit ads? The sooner she starts learning the better and it'll be my pleasure to teach you, young woman!" Julius lowered her to her feet and tugged playfully at the coil of hair on her neck.

Mara moved away irritably and her mask of sophistication dropped for an instant as she glared at him, knowing that his action had exposed her one weak spot. All John's and Grant's attempts to teach her had failed miserably; she was absolutely terrified to enter water over four feet in depth. So now this swim-mad party knew she couldn't swim and, to lose face in front of others, even though it was only that dippy Peter and Pat and Grant's sulky secretary (what was she doing out under the stars with Grant, last night?) But the tiny look of contempt that had come into Julius's eyes when he put her down . . . she was used to admiration in all men's eyes . . . to lose face was one of the major crimes in her book and jet-set circle!

As if he knew what was going on in her mind, Grant said casually, "It's no crime not to be able to swim, Mara."

"Thanks, Grant." Mara fluttered her eyes gratefully. Julius bent down to pick up his shirt and said sharply, "Not a crime but a necessity, don't you think? Fortunately Sandy can swim like a fish, so probably won't need your help some day, but you might just topple from one of your poses and land in deep waters!" He glanced at his watch. "I reckon we should have a light lunch and start on our walk, as planned."

Pat explained to Jane about the proposed walk. The younger people were going up the mountain and Bart, Janet, Elizabeth and Mrs. D. would take the car later and meet them at a designated spot for a picnic tea.

Jane's clothes were clean and ironed and quite "aromatic." Sandy was the soul of discretion, merely winking gravely when Jane appeared in her jeans and shirt. Had Grant warned the child or was it her own finer feelings for her friend's pride? Thoughtful, if it was he, but she would reserve judgement in case Grant was waiting to burst the bubble himself!

Mara's wish to come later with the car was downed in

chorus, and her face was quite sulky when they finally set off. She kept shaking her wispy sandals and made good use of Grant's willing arm. It became obvious that she was holding them all back and soon the boys, Sandy and Jane lost patience and forged ahead. Pat, Julius and Peter caught up with them and Jane looked back to see Mara sitting on a rock while Grant knelt at her feet, shaking the offending grit out of a sandal.

They walked and climbed for about half a mile when Julius stopped with a shrug of irritation. "I'm going back to relieve Grant, his patience must be wearing thin. I'll carry the flipping girl, if necessary!" He turned on his heel and disappeared down the incline of trees and jutting rocks.

After negotiating a stiff, rocky climb that shortened even the breath of the very young, a sharp drop stopped them on the brink of a clear stream cascading down to misty, green depths.

Jane stood on the lip of the gorge. She stood alone, a remote figurehead carved by the wind that whipped her hair into a silken pennant and molded her shirt to slender firmness.

Her nerves signalled his approach before her ears registered the firm stride and crackling of leaves. She knew instinctively it was Grant, even before she heard him warn Sandy to be careful. Jane turned her head and saw fires of anger in wood-smoke eyes.

His voice was steel as he gripped her arm and pulled her back roughly. "Get back at once and stay with the party. Don't you recognize danger? A slight lift of the wind could put you off balance; then dizziness could plunge you to the bottom of this gorge . . . if you haven't any sense, at least Peter or the boys should know better!" His face was granite-hard and pale.

Jane stepped farther back and the iron hold on her arm slackened. Her heart started knocking unevenly as his words brought home the danger and her unthinking foolishness. She drew a jagged breath and whispered contritely, "I'm sorry, Grant, I really had no fear . . . d-didn't realize—"

"At least you could think of others, their feelings if something should happen to one of the party."

Jane went a trifle pale at the cynical contempt in the rough voice. He might as well say outright that only she could cause catastrophe, for it was there in his tone. She suddenly resented his attitude and the color crept back into her cheeks; after all, she had apologized most contritely.

"Did your—Mara give you a bad time? If so, don't work your spleen off on me. I'm sure I was quite safe until you frightened the living daylights out of me." Dark brows drew together and she added hastily but offhandedly, "I'll be most careful as from now, no need to go jump down the boys' throats."

Grant Saxon's eyes narrowed. "You're the sort that positively invites a man to shake you till every bone in your body rattles, Jane Wheeler!" he gritted, and turned sharply.

Jane took the child's hand and followed slowly. Sandy said thoughtfully, "I wonder why ever'body's so cross today. Mara is cross 'cause her feet hurt, you're cross with Grant all the time and h-he's not nice today."

Jane stopped impulsively and put her arm around the small shoulders.

"Sandy dear, I'm a real misery today and I know it. Thank you for not telling anyone about my mishap this morning. I guess that's why I'm out of sorts. It's very humiliating to be found in a pig's trough, particularly by Grant. I wouldn't have minded if it was only you—it must have been very funny—my sense of humor seems to have deserted me."

Sandy returned her smile. "You're not a misery, Jane,

but . . . since Mara came . . . ." the young voice hesitated and Jane interposed quietly, "Why don't you call them Mummy and Daddy? I'm sure they would love—"

"But my daddy is dead, Jane."

CHAPTER SEVEN

QUIETLY SPOKEN WORDS, which took a full moment to register, then coursed through her body with shocking rigidity. Jane fought the threatening lockjaw and paralysis of nerve centers.

"Sandy," she whispered at last, "whom . . . what are you . . . what did you s-say?"

The child's eyes were lowered and missed her companion's distress. "Ever'body knows my daddy's gone to h-heaven. When my . . . Mara was driving his car, there was 'n accident 'n my daddy got killed and Toicky 'n Grant said he's gone to heaven." The slight shoulders trembled in Jane's arms. "I think it's her fault 'cause she fought with Daddy a lot, so God took him away from us. I was good 'n loved him awfully, so why did God punish me too, Jane?"

Troubled eyes looked up trustingly and Jane sought desperately to collect shocked wits, to find the right answer.

"God is good, Sandy, never forget that. Th-there must be a reason for taking your daddy. He wasn't punishing her. He needed your daddy too. . . ." She stopped, at loss for words or comfort. The tumultuous shock she had just experienced left her bereft of sane thought.

"I never called my daddy John, but my mother likes me to call her Mara." A small chin lifted bravely. "I'm going to ask her 'bout the accident 'n if she was under the influence and fighting with my daddy."

"Who told you that?" Jane asked urgently, through a second upsurge of emotion.

"Nobody. I heard Flip say to this other man, down by the hedge, that 'madam was under the influence 'n they had this accident' and the other man said 'boozed up again 'n fighting,' 'n I knowed they were talking about Mara. I think I'd rather ask Grant 'cause I'm frightened to ask her, 'n I think maybe Flip is 'n awful liar. Jane, will you come with me when I ask him? I feel all wobbly inside, but I'd like to know 'cause he said people must always be fair to ever'one."

"He's quite right, and I'll come with you," Jane suddenly remembered the night at the Mission when Grant had discussed a fault in the steering with David and felt justified in continuing, "You'll find that things are not at all as you were led to imagine. Not today though, darling, because we're visiting the Davenports—after work, tomorrow," a swift thought crowded out shock; maybe, after today's contretemps, she wouldn't have a job! "Come now, the others must be waiting. We still have to walk to the road to meet the car for our tea."

Well, she had committed herself and would have to keep her promise to be with her young friend, when she confronted Grant or Mara with her important question. She hoped fervently that they were in a position to settle Sandy's troubled doubts. Grant had told David that the fault had been in the car, not the other. The "other" being Mara, a woman incapable of driving safely?

They teamed up with the rest of the party before she could assimilate her own shock at hearing that Grant was not Sandy's father after all. Julius and Mara had caught up as well and the lady was evidently in a furious temper, not quite so immaculate now, her hair tied back with a piece of string, extracted handily from Julius's pocket, her fair skin deeply flushed from sun and exertion. Julius was carrying out his plan with vengeance. Jane felt a quiver of sympathy for Mara run through her.

Her mind and thoughts were a tangled mess; however hard she struggled to find the pattern, the worse became the skeins. Jane walked mechanically, only answering when addressed directly, her feet finding their way blindly.

Not one of her family had contradicted her when she had coupled Grant and Mara as Sandy's parents; Pat had mentioned John's accident and said that when Mara came back, she would have her way; Bart had described Mara; Sandy always mentioned Grant by name; everybody took for granted that Mara would accompany Grant to the club dance and not once had he disputed their right to take it for granted; Mara had her own room in the Saxon household. In fact, she was mistress of the house but not married to the master of the Estate.

What an almightly misconception she, Jane, had been laboring under—and suffering!

And, her heart shrivelled, insulting a perfectly innocent man. Dear God, no wonder Grant Saxon, after asking her to clarify her insulting remarks, had become angry, contemptuous and bored. She, who loved so desperately, had killed all chances of reciprocation by repulsing his advances with highly insulting advice. She had even told him to go to hell! Oh, why, through all that had been said and transpired, hadn't anyone been more explicit on the relationship of the two Saxons?

Simply because they were not to guess that she didn't know—oh, damnation!

Jane must have cried out aloud because Peter asked solicitously, "What now, Jane?"

"I banged my knee, Peter," she lied brazenly.

"There's a doctor in the trek, love," he enlightened softly. She grimaced at him and continued on her way. "Never known such a grumpy, silent party—can only be last night's leftovers,'" he muttered.

She stopped at the road edge and looked back. Grant was still at Mara's side. Something was irregular about the situation—Mara had a perfect right to live in her late husband's home (with her brother-in-law). Now that Jane had their relationship in perspective, she recalled snips of gossip and hints: that Mara had her claws bared for Grant, that he had loved someone who had let him down . . . It could only be Mara, and he still loved her. If her conjectures were facts, why hadn't he married? A suitable time had passed since the death of his brother: was there a governing law against a man marrying his brother's wife?

And why did he bother to flatter her, Jane, and kiss the way he kissed her last night? She had watched him tease Pat. Did he kiss her as well, because he couldn't have the one he really wanted?

Her intent gaze had settled on the man uppermost in her thoughts. A dark eyebrow raised as he intercepted her inward preoccupation.

"Seeing ghosts, Miss Wheeler?"

"No, Mr. Saxon. Lost visions, that's all." Julius called and Jane turned away before Grant could delve deeper.

The car was parked in a shadowy bay scooped out of the side of the towering mountain. A driver had driven the roomy station-wagon. Janet and Elizabeth were setting out tea and scones on a folding table.

Mara drew attention as she started to count the newcomers aloud.

"Janet, Elizabeth, Mrs. Davenport and Bart, plus driver. That makes five. There's room for me, for the return trip. I flatly refuse to walk back, and don't ever invite me on a big walk again. It's for the birds and—"

"Childish and juvenile?" asked Julius sweetly.

"As for you, Julius Davenport," a graceful body whirled to face the old lady, "your grandson, Mrs. D., is quite uncivilized, he handled me like a—a sack of maize, an absolute boor and . . . and—"

"Patient, long-suffering and perfectly charming!" concluded Mrs. D.'s grandson, his smile dazzling.

"Shut up!" Fury made her fiery. "May I accompany you back, Mrs. Davenport?"

"Surely, my dear," said that lady equably.

"Chicken!" sneered Julius, but did not pursue his taunt.

"You see, Jane, everybody's mad today," Sandy whispered.

Jane nodded complete agreement. She was the maddest, most miserably mad of the lot.

Peace reigned while tea and scones disappeared down thirsty throats. Jane desired a lift back as well, but in the face of the jeers that had met Mara's demand, she stifled her own request. There wouldn't be room anyway.

Her step was not so buoyant as they set off on the return trip. Peter and the boys seemed to be the only fit ones left. She, Pat and Sandy stayed together, followed by Julius and Grant. The trail back, on a different route, was steeper and required concentration, for which mercy Jane was thankful. It kept her mind away from the startling disclosures that Sandy's amazing words had revealed.

Mara had freshened up considerably by the time a tired group reached the homestead. She walked down the steps to Grant, who held Sandy's hand in his, and bent down solicitously.

"My poor little girl, is she worn out? I'm an unthinking beast, I should have let you come in the car as well. I think we should leave soon, Grant."

A bit late, thought Jane cattily, to act the anxious mother now, Mrs. *John* Saxon. And felt a ripple of pure jealousy at the cosy trio they made.

The trees were throwing tall shadows, and they were a long way from their respective homes, so all decided to take their leave. They thanked host and hostess, with the exception of Mara, who pointedly thanked Mrs. D. very sweetly and ignored Julius. He smiled nonchalantly at a backview of an exaggerated mannequin glide to Grant's car.

Grant spoke to Jane briefly. "Tom will call at the usual time."

She nodded her head and followed the boys into the back seat of the car.

JANE LAY BACK and folded both arms under her head to gaze unseeingly at the stars that winked impishly through her open bedroom window. Her recent findings were still too new and raw to share; she herself didn't quite know what it was all about and inner turmoil was an absolute kaleidoscopic mess. She sighed deeply, moved one hand to switch off the bedside lamp, cuddled both hands under her cheek like a tired child and closed her eyes. A pathetic plea flew from her heart to brain, to dispel that persistent image of wood-smoke eyes smudged into a strong, dark face. *Let me rest peacefully through the long night.* Tomorrow would come and Jane Wheeler must face the gigantic task of sorting out the upheaval, unwanted and sudden, that threatened her placid existence.

Sleep hovered over the troubled young face, took pity and lowered its gentle cloak. . . .

THE HASTILY FASHIONED Psyche-knot of nut-brown hair wobbled slightly as Jane lifted a proud chin when she entered Grant Saxon's study on Monday morning. He glanced up with an absent smile of greeting.

"The returns for that last shipment came in on Saturday—check and file them, Jane. I must take you down to the packing sheds soon so that you can have or form a clearer notion of what's going on—easier for you." His eyes focused absently on her tilted chin.

Which instantly made her feel absurd and quivery. "Good morning, yes, Mr. Saxon—Grant."

The smile became slightly pronounced, more sardonic at her obvious hesitation. "The weekend. . . interlude, with all mishaps have passed safely, I assume. No broken bones, regrets or vengeful aftermath?" Grant's fist thumped the papers before him, giving her not a chance to reply, even if she could (which was most unlikely). "Good, and so to work, my young rebel, to the slave-wheel once more!"

"Yes, boss," said Jane, grateful for his light manner yet bristling instantly at the knowing, sardonic smile on his lips. The bristling helped to settle emotions that had stirred at the sight of him sitting there, dark, rugged and heartbreakingly distant. And quite openly referring to her mishap at the Davenports', no regrets for the attempted flirtation. An interlude to slide over amusedly. He would never know how much more it meant; to discover he was not a married man after she had shown her contempt even while feeling his potent attraction. Her seemingly neurotic manner had surely dispelled any loving thoughts, if there ever had been any such toward her. And above all, not forgetting—Mara.

Jane lowered wistful eyes from the down-bent head of her boss and shuffled the papers on her desk.

An hour passed in comparative silence with an occasional crackling of paper. Jane's interest in the work at hand quickened and she gave an involuntary sound of disagreement when she came across an error of calculation in a final total. Grant looked up immediately, a deep frown of concentration furrowing his brow. "Let's see, Jane."

She picked up the offending paper and walked over to his desk to stand beside him, putting the missive down for his inspection.

"Show me what and where."

Jane leaned over, unthinkingly placed her one hand on his shoulder while she guided his quick eye with a finger of her free hand. Her hand blanked part of the figures and Grant moved it aside to look for himself. He retained her hand in his while they both mentally toted again. A tingle feathering up her arm diverted Jane's eyes and her glance shifted to the tip of his ear.

Mara chose that moment to drift in unannounced.

"Moral support because of a great deficit or merely—moral deficit?" Her dulcet tones floated across the study to startle Jane and Grant equally. Her wintry smile rested on the other girl's hands, one on the man's shoulder, the other nestling in his clasp.

Grant dropped the hand in his, to reach for a pen. Jane straightened abruptly from what could easily be misrepresented as a cozy pose.

"Morning, Jane dear. Please don't let me interrupt your . . . session with your boss. Grant, Sandy's being tiresome, insists on riding her precious Sugarbush this morning. Is it safe? I'm simply not up to haring around with her." Mara was superbly cool and chic in a willow-green catsuit. A green band circled her hair and the shoulder-length fall was flicked up to perfection, magnolia skin showing no bad effects of the previous day.

The girl at Grant's side felt that she, in comparison, suggested everything her name implied. Plain Jane. Here before her was someone who could exploit her finest points and beauty to the utmost. Experience had taught her to tone down or highlight with subtle finesse. Jane's skin glowed with natural, healthy sheen, her only makeup a pearly lipstick, but she felt like a naïve amateur compared to the artistry of this one.

Grant ignored or was unaware of Mara's sarcastic comment on Jane's proximity. His eyes approved the picture of languid grace she presented but were blind to the sparkle of venom that flashed for an instant in green depths before the woman shifted her eyes from the girl to the man.

"Sandy's perfectly safe with Sugarbush. Lemmy always rides with her and she won't wilfully do anything foolish," he smiled at his sister-in-law, "and I can't see you being much help if any rescuing's to be done."

Mara smiled back, her movements deliberately evocative. "You do know me so well, darling. I'm no dashing lifesaver. We'll leave Sandy to her own devices. Can I help here, or is your little secretary quite efficient in every way?" She laid stress sweetly but surely on "every."

Jane had moved back to her own desk, eyes lowered studiously on the papers before her. Under that bland mask she was fighting an incredibly brutal, pagan urge to clutch the heavy paperweight and hurl it straight between those insufferable green eyes, to shatter that mask of beauty and superiority!

"I've no complaints. Jane is every man's dream of the perfect . . . secretary." Grant's smile showed sudden wicked awareness of Mara's allusion to the cozy scene she had witnessed. "Thanks for the offer, but we're coping very well. Entertain yourself elsewhere and we'll join you for tea later."

Her dismissal was evident in the way he bent over the figures that Jane had brought to him. Mara's eyes swept critically over the other girl before she made an indolent exit.

"Bully for you, boss!" Jane commended silently while a little warmth circled her cold heart. She insisted on having her tea in the study because she became genuinely immersed in her work and had no inclination to watch the sorceress manipulate her willing victim. Grant did not insist, as he usually did, that she have a fresh air break. Jane felt that this was sure indication that he had changed—since Mara's arrival. The pattern was changing, for even Sandy failed to appear for the tea break that she adored sharing with her new friend.

Lunch was as usual, except that Mara and Grant did

most of the conversing, Sandy and Jane the quiet listeners, where before they had been spontaneous and cheerful in exchange of confidences.

And so the pattern of days proceeded. Jane became withdrawn and recoiled inwardly at any attempt on Grant's part to put their association back on its former natural, friendly basis. He sensed her withdrawal and gradually ceased trying, to become just her terse, businesslike, matter-of-fact boss. Just that and no more. Mara found many pretexts for drifting in and out of the study or merely sat out under the trees, reading, varnishing her nails or languidly watching Sandy at play. She livened considerably when Grant appeared and ignored Jane with the indifference of mistress towards menial. Jane seethed, but managed to subdue her feelings, quietly pursued her duties with serene composure. Grant Saxon was her boss, not Mara, and he paid well. She also tried hard to squash an inner conviction that she stayed on because it kept her close to him and her sadistic heart delighted in self-torture; there would be no difficulty in finding employment elsewhere, just as lucrative. Her mind considered seriously, but the rest of her rejected immediate action.

One afternoon Tom requested her to wait while he replaced a defective fanbelt. Jane assured him that there was no special cause for her to hurry home and started to walk down a shrub-lined path toward a grove of aromatic gum trees. The air hummed with bees in the treetops; gum-tree honey surpassed in flavor any other she had tasted. A taste of honey . . . on her lips, unforgettable, one night not so long ago, never to taste again . . . that was sweeter. Now unobtainable through her own stupidity.

Sandy ran down and joined her and they walked in companionable silence.

"Jane," Sandy's hand in hers tugged an invitation to

sit beside her on a gnarled stump, "Jane, you know, we've got no farther with my nature book 'n Christmas is nearly here 'n I've collected lots of wings and ferns 'n wild flowers. I do so want to complete a book to give to Grant for a present. You're always so busy," large eyes pleaded. "Will you help me? You promised. I've got it all set out in my room, but I don't know how to place 'n name them by myself."

Jane remembered her promise to the child and wanted to help, but the very thought of an evening in the house of Grant Saxon sent her nerves into quivering crescendo. For the sake of her pleading friend she would have to steel herself to remain one evening with Sandy in her room, while the child's mother disported her charm on a certain person under the same roof perhaps on that cosy swinging couch, a mere thickness of wall away. Why couldn't *she* help her daughter? She did absolutely nothing constructive around the house, unless being attratively at hand to delight the master could be construed as constructive . . . Jane shivered at the ugly change in herself; her thoughts and mind had developed a wicked will of their own, ruled by a rearing green head!

"Let's find out how long Tom will be, maybe we can make a start now and finish off another evening." Jane took Sandy's hand and they started back at a fast clip. Grant appeared around the corner of the house. Sandy saw him and suddenly stood stock-still, her hand jerking Jane to a stop as well.

"Jane," the name came on a slight gasp, "you're with me now. I'm feeling brave, so let's ask him—about Daddy!"

The hand holding hers tightened painfully. "No! Not now, Sandy, please."

Sandy's voice drifted loudly in sudden appeal. "Please, you promised!"

Grant's head turned, he stopped for a moment and then diverted his course toward them.

Sandy's hand tightened nervously and Jane felt her own back go rigid while every nerve protested at the child's nervous determination. The man came to a stop, two yards away, surveyed the unsure stance of both girls and his thumbs automatically hitched into his trouser pockets.

"What's happened now?"

Jane unlocked stiff lips. "I . . . nothing's wrong, nothing has h-happened. Sandy wants—"

She was unable to proceed and Sandy interposed stutteringly, "It's something I want to ask you. Have you got time to listen and . . . and can we sit down, please . . . my legs feel funny." She plonked down on the grass as if her legs had indeed become fluid. "It's about my . . . daddy."

Gray, probing eyes lifted from the small figure to Jane's stiff stance, circled swiftly to the house. A calculating dark-browed estimation of distance, possibly to see if Mara was visible or within earshot. Long legs folded as he haunched down on his heels.

"Okay, poppet, but before you ask, may I let you in on a secret? It's this; I've wanted very much to talk to someone, most of all to you, about John, your dad, and I'm so glad that you've decided to do so of your own free will. Sit down, Jane, you're in on this and, I suspect, the open sesame."

Jane refrained from a cold reminder that it was he who had asked her to delve into the cause of Sandy's misery. Instead she too sank silently on to the soft grass. Sandy sensed her perturbation and instinctive defense came in her words. "Grant, please don't mind if Jane stays with me. She's made me brave 'nuff to ask you about . . . things."

His eyes crinkled slightly at the corners as he noted

the swift fall of Jane's lashes, veiling her eyes. "Okay, kid, I accept your bodyguard. Shoot."

Sandra cast a nervous glance toward the house, looked back at Grant and gained confidence from his level, steady gaze. She said, with sweet determination, "I know Daddy died in a car accident when Mara— Mommy was driving. Was she—was it really all her fault, Grant?"

If Grant received a severe jolt at her unexpected question the only indication was a sudden deep pucker of dark brows. Jane gave him full marks for control, for there was no doubt in her mind that he had not expected this to be the cause of Sandy's display of misery and strange outbursts. She saw enlightenment dawn and compassion darken the wood-smoke eyes as he realized what agony of mind this small soul had endured. A brown hand came up in a slow, familiar gesture to brush back an unruly lock of hair. Jane had learned to recognize that simple action as a sign of deep thought, an aid to solving certain problems. Was every familiar gesture always going to affect her heart this way?

Grant answered with loving firmness. "Sandy, I'm terribly sorry that I didn't realize long ago, before you had to draw courage to ask this, that you may have overheard that particular version of the accident. It's quite evident now that you heard certain gossip that spread, untruthfully, before anyone was aware of the true facts." He paused long enough to lift a small hand that trembled amongst the grass blades into the firm clasp of his warm hands, and continued with slow deliberation. "Your father's death was caused by some fault—something wrong in the steering system of the car. Your mother happened to be driving at the time and was in no way responsible for the accident whatever you may have heard to the contrary. The car went through a bridge railing. Mara was . . . lucky—but your daddy didn't suffer, darling. God took him straight away. Do you understand, poppet?"

Sandy's eyes showed a glimmer of tears, but they held her uncle's gaze with steadfast faith. "Yes. I knowed you wouldn't ever lie to me, and I'm glad my daddy didn't suffer." She swallowed bravely. "I'm also glad m-my mother wasn't hurted."

The quiet silence enveloped three people and their thoughts. The man watched the small bent-down head while he stroked the fingers in his hand, one by one. Their silent listener felt her heart turn with sympathy and burned to have the right to lay her hands on each beloved head in wordless consolation. . . .

A sigh escaped the big man. "If only my poppet had asked me, or your mom, right away, all this heartbreak would have been spared, darling. Tell me, anything else worrying you?"

Jane's breast swelled at the pure, grave concern for his brother's child. Sandy lifted her head and said, equally gravely, "Yes, Grant. Now I'm worried 'n 'shamed of all the bad things that was in my head about . . . Mara."

Grant put a comforting hand on her shoulder. "Well now, it's all over, and you can make amends by showing your mother in all sorts of ways that you love her. How about starting right away by calling her Mummy, instead of Mara?"

Sandy nestled into the pressure of his palm, but uncertainty showed in her eyes. "Jane said the same at the picnic, but she likes me to say Mara 'n I don't think it'd please her awfully for me to call her Mom. Should I 'fess to her about my bad thoughts and ask for . . . forgiveness?" The very thought of this darkened her eyes with apprehension and Grant's discerning comfort came quickly.

"No, Sandy. It wasn't your fault, so you can't be

blamed for any bad thoughts. They were put there by silly gossip and it'll only upset her again, after all this time. Call her as you've done in the past if she wishes it and just be your natural sweet self, and everything'll work normally. I'm sure your friend will agree." His deep gaze lifted to the quiet girl at Sandy's side. "Not so, Jane?"

Jane had been silently applauding his handling of the situation, his forbearance in not questioning the source of twisted information, also regretting that he should have to be the recipient and consoler while the mother got off scot-free. A little girl who was afraid to turn to her own mother. . . . His question caught her completely off guard, she was tongue-tied as the blue gray eyes suddenly speared her.

Her eyes fled from his and she looked toward the house. Mara was walking down the steps with studied, indolent grace. She had most certainly noticed their huddle on the grass but was not aware of its grave cause and decisions. Jane stood up and brushed wisps of grass off her skirt. Her tongue unknotted at last.

"I certainly agree, nothing more should be said to anyone. I'm only sorry that Sandy didn't speak sooner. To labor under such misapprehension must have been simply awful—and lonely."

Grant straightened up as well and held a helping hand to Sandy. "We all do, at some time or other—and find our particular island of loneliness. Sandy braved the storm before it became too late. So few have that courage." He spoke almost indifferently, his gaze held by the woman walking toward them.

Jane also watched Mara while her heart echoed agreement. Her boat was surely wrecked on her particular island. And she dared not brave the storm; she would never receive compassionate treatment. Scorn would be her reward, derisive contempt at her temerity in hoping that she could get to first base ever—while there was Mara—his first love. And last?

Grant stood beside her, but they were miles apart, because of her ignorance. Perhaps, in spite of Mara, something sweet might have budded if she had known the true setup; she had felt that he was attracted. Her insults had withered the bud and drawn taunts instead of tenderness. Past events had baffled her completely and now she felt sick. An incredulous lump in the pit of her stomach as she saw appreciation lighten gray eyes as he watched Sandy's mother.

Stop! Stop deluding yourself, Jane Wheeler. You were a pleasing interlude in the interval of waiting. That star-studded night that blasted the truth to you meant very little to Grant Saxon!

CHAPTER EIGHT

"It's a promise, Sandy, I'll finish the pressing and complete your nature book." Jane squeezed the small hand in hers.

"'n you promise to write?" Sandy gave a small excited skip beside the car and turned to watch Mara and Grant descend the terrace steps. "I'm going to be extra good at school 'n then she'll be proud of me. That'll make up for my wickedness, won't it, Jane?" She voiced her plea and resolution in a small hurried whisper. Jane leaned down with a secret affirmative to both questions, then withdrew her hand and stepped back to allow Mara's farewell to her daughter.

"Sorry I'm not well enough to accompany you and Grant, sweetie, but truly my head feels like a carpenter's shop with every hammer banging." Mara stooped and kissed Sandy's cheek. "Be a good girl and I may come and see you the weekend after next." She stood back while the child settled into the front seat of the car. "Really, Grant, Tom or one of your other drivers could have taken her."

Jane cast a swift glance at Grant before she turned and made her way back to the house. His face had a grim set this morning; something had upset the master of the house. She had received terse instructions for the day and now she heard him reply to Mara abruptly.

"I have every intention of conveying Sandy personally. I hope your hammer shop will close shortly. Goodbye now." His tone was threaded sarcasm. The car swooped away in a scatter of gravel.

Jane worked solidly all morning. The silence was only broken by Minna with her tea and a remark that Mara was confined to her room, having taken pills for her headache. Lunch was quiet and solitary. Jane missed Sandy and kept glancing at Grant's empty chair. She tried hard to dispel the quivers of loneliness and despair that persisted and did not linger at the table, but walked briskly twice around the shrubbery before returning to her desk. Later in the afternoon she saw Mara strolling to the garage, dressed in casual slacks and sweater with a gay bandanna holding back her luxuriant hair. Five minutes later her sports car swept out of the drive and disappeared from view. Jane concluded that her headache was gone and she fancied a run to pass the time until Grant returned.

Tom was waiting for her; she had worked later than usual and the shadows had lengthened considerably—flamingo pink flared across the western sky as they wended home.

"There's Mrs. Saxon's car!" Tom exclaimed as they negotiated a wooded curve.

"Slow down, Tom, she may be having trouble with her car," Jane advised, and in the same instant recognized the man leaning negligently against the side of the car. Flip Olivier! Why in heaven's name had Mara stopped on this deserted section of road, and why was that man adopting such a familiar pose? Mara made a sudden movement, sliding her arms off the steering wheel as she watched the Land-Rover slowing to a stop beside her car. Olivier straightened up with a defiant deliberateness. Tom slipped from his seat and asked, "Anything wrong with your car, ma'am?"

Mara's eyes glittered greenly and a queer lilt made her voice strange. "Not now. This . . . gentlemen . . . fixed things. I'm on my way—not to panic." She engaged gears and shot away so fast that Olivier had to leap back to avoid flying particles of sand.

He recovered and watched the departing car for malevolent moments before switching his gaze to the occu-

pants of the stationary vehicle. Tom reseated himself
and Olivier sauntered around to where Jane was sitting
in complete surprise at Mara's abrupt departure.

"Some woman, that," he indicated and smiled at
Jane. "You're running late today, miss?" One foot
raised laconically to rest on the footboard.

"What happened to Mrs. Saxon's car?" Jane lifted
her chin and stiffened inwardly at the look in those pale
eyes.

"Just a slight . . . adjustment. I'm good at that sort of
thing." His eyes were openly gloating at some inward
thought. Jane passed a signal, and Tom nodded and
pressed the starter. "Much obliged, Mr. Olivier," she
said distantly, and for the second time that gentleman
had to step back fast!

"He's not a good man," Tom ventured after they had
traveled some distance. "Mrs. Saxon should be careful
and not stop for such a man."

"You're right, Tom, I'll tell her. Maybe he happened
to be on the spot to help her when she was stuck. Luckily it was just some small adjustment." Jane hid her own
disquiet at the encounter. She could still envisage the
glitter of green eyes and wondered what had passed to
bring that strange breathlessness to Mara's brief exchange. She felt relief at Tom's timely arrival to put a
stop to any mischief or intention of mischief. His polite
warning made it quite clear that Tom was fully cogni-
zant of the man's reputation. She would say no more
now but would drop a word in Mara's ear at the first opportunity; she might well be ignorant of Olivier's disreputable ways. That gloating look in his eyes meant
trouble for somebody! Her thoughts turned to Grant;
he had chastized Olivier only recently; it was quite possible that he harbored revenge, and what better way
than through Grant's household . . . Jane shivered suddenly, inexplicably.

The homestead was unusually quiet. Bart, Janet and Elizabeth had taken the boys back to school. Jane felt thankful for the quiet peace of an empty house; her mind was so muddled lately that she couldn't concentrate wholeheartedly on family fun or discussions—a quiet evening would prove blissful. Jane leaned back in the swing seat on the veranda and relaxed to the healing touch of nature, allowing her mind to blank out troubling thoughts. It was the only tonic; all the man-made medicine in the world couldn't cure the invasion of peace of mind and body . . . let what come later, she would find strength to cope. If leaving this heavenly portion of Africa was her only choice she would do so, even if her heart stayed forever, and wander far to other countries . . . the panacea lay in work, wearying mind and body to numbness.

A restful night coupled with an upward surge of spirits made her jump out of bed with the old alacrity. The morning was bright with promise and Jane felt lighthearted as though infused with new young life and the joy of being alive to greet a new day, whatever it might hold.

She was seated at her desk when Grant entered the study and her smile of greeting was filled with such warmth that the big man's sure step faltered momentarily. He returned her greeting with a look of wonder in smoky gray eyes, and the questioning focus remained on her bent head and fanned eyelashes as she studied the paper in front of her.

Jane felt his glance and traitorous color crept upwards. She was thankful that she had left her hair hanging loose and shining because the tips of her ears were burning to a crisp. She surreptitiously fumbled at her skirt, closing the gap that lay open over her legs, expecting sarcasm to erupt any moment.

Nothing happened and she dared a quick look. Grant

was frowning over a letter on top of the pile of mail. She relaxed, drew the typewriter into position and waited for instructions. Without volition her fingers played lightly on the keys "I love you—love you, darling—

"Stop that, for crying out loud, Jane! It's maddening on the nerves."

"Sorry." Jane stopped immediately and wondered what would happen to his nerves if he could hear the words of the classic her fingers were following. Minna came in with the tea tray.

"Mister Grant, Mara asks that you see her after tea. Her head's not so good."

"Very well, Minna. She's supposed to accompany me to Sabie today— tell her I'll be along." Minna nodded and left the study.

Jane stood up to pour the tea, her spirits unaccountably drooping. She carried his toward the desk and was stopped in her tracks.

"Stand quite still, Jane Wheeler!" Grant's command immobilized her into petrified marble. A dancing tempest smoldered in gray eyes as he surveyed her, from swinging nut-brown hair to slim stockinged legs and neat shoes. She stood there with posed cup, one dainty ankle and foot forward, eyes large and luminous. His eyes lifted back to her face and wonder flickered in smoky eyes.

"Nifty get-up," he mused thoughtfully. "But I think I should warn you —your skirt's come undone. I'll turn discreetly while you make the necessary adjustment."

Jane was released from her trance. She stepped forward, cautiously placing the cup on his desk. A moment longer and it would have landed on the carpet. She emphasized deliberately, "I'm so glad you approve. It's the in thing for office girls nowadays. Don't let the skirt worry you, boss." Said skirt swung away to reveal neat pants and shapely legs as she whirled back to her desk.

Those same legs felt mighty shaky as Jane sat down. And then she felt uncontrollable laughter well in her throat . . . his look was that of a fascinated rabbit confronted by a sinuous snake.

"Well!" A deep breath was expelled from well-cut lips. Grant reached forward to take his cup and the view from under her desk made his hand waver uncertainly. His eyes were raised piously. "How can any boss be expected to work under duress?" he asked the ceiling.

"Nothing to it, Mr. Saxon," his secretary intoned with maddening composure.

Grant put down the empty cup and strode to the door. "Now I must confront another vision, most certainly clad in the latest slumberwear. It's too much to bear. What's going to happen to my morale?"

Jane reached for a cigarette and smoked thoughtfully; she had to wait for further instructions. Ten minutes passed and he was back again.

"Did you find out, and how's your morale?" she asked curiously.

"Ravishing, m'dear, absolutely stunning." Grant kissed his fingertips delicately and irrepressible laughter shook the girl at the sight of a manly figure making like a couturier. Grant joined her merriment with a deep chuckle.

A breathless joy impeded her heartbeats. She wanted to whisper urgently; dearest one, I love your carefree chuckle, please laugh forever with me, I do love you so very much. But it would most certainly wipe that smile away forever if voiced aloud. . . .

Grant's amusement settled into a smile. "You should laugh more often, Janey, it's attractive and becomes you."

Almost an echo of the whisper in her heart . . . except for the loving part. She composed her features, clamped a lid on the protesting whisper and said, "Well, you're still in one piece, so let's get cracking so's I can earn my keep."

"Who's the boss here?" Grant grunted and walked to the window. "You, Miss Wheeler, will come with me to-day on a business trip. We leave within half an hour. Mara is unable to accompany me, I need feminine support, so that'll be your chore for today, I'll list your duties on the way. And," he turned suddenly to catch her look of utter surprise, "you're dressed for the part, fortunately!"

Jane controlled her surprise and began to feel distinctly nettled. Dear smart Mara was unable to oblige, so Jane Wheeler was a passable second best? She opened rosy lips. . . .

"Second choice very often turns out the better. I should have asked you to accompany me in the first place as you have a better grasp of what will be required as my accomplice. Mara offered, and you've been rather sullen lately, so it never occurred to me to invite you along with us."

Jane closed her mouth tightly; the man was psychic in his choice of words; second best, sullen, was she? Her mouth opened again. Grant leaned over her desk. "Darling, don't look like a fish. That was a compliment, however obscure it may seem to you. I'll put a call through to your mum, advising her you'll be late home tonight."

Jane watched his receding back. Mara must really have a bad headache if she was willing to forgo this trip with him, or did the thought of some hard work at the other end deter her? That was a cattish conclusion, Jane scolded herself, and spared a moment of sympathy for the ailing Mara, forgotten almost instantly as she considered that, although she was second best, this was going to be her day with him. Possibly not alone all day; the drive there and back; that alone she would savor and absorb into pages of memory; she would savor it for the time when she was no longer near, no longer able to see or hear, respectively, his smoky-gray eyes, tanned, strong features and deep voice. Jane reminded herself that, on awakening, she had felt this day would be special; take it as it comes and blast the consequences, the aftermath—the gods may never smile again!

Only then did she begin to think of the duties entailed and how her substituting would affect Mara if Grant had told her that he would take Jane instead. Oh, please, don't let her headache disappear within the next few minutes, Jane pleaded, crossing her fingers at the wickedness of thought.

"Ready, Jane?" Grant's figure filled the doorway.

"Yes, Grant." She controlled an urge to snatch her purse lest he detect the haste to be away before her wicked thought came home to roost. Grant opened the car door for her, then walked leisurely to the other side and climbed behind the wheel. He took a notebook out of his pocket, studied a listed column of figures while the girl at his side interlocked her fingers and watched the front door of the house, expecting it to open any moment to reveal the figure of Mara, dressed for travel.

At last he deigned to press the starter and they were away!

Grant's hands were firm on the wheel, the car purred powerfully as he negotiated the curves, sharp declines and hills. Jane found the lush scenery wonderful, but her eyes turned again and again to the strong brown hands that manipulated so skilfully. The urge to touch them, to feel the vibrant power course through her own fingers predominated, became almost an obsession. She forced her eyes back to the passing countryside. It was vaguely familiar; she recognized certain landmarks and realized they were nearing the Davenport farm. Jane re-

membered that day, her lack of interest in the route—
color rose in her cheeks at remembered happenings.

Grant's amused gaze flicked over her warm cheeks.
"Care to stop for tea? The old lady will be pleased to see
you again, if only to satisfy your anxiety about the progress of a certain little animal rescued under dashing
circumstances," he jibed softly.

Indignation deepened the tawny brown eyes that
lifted to meet his cool, innocent gaze. "Grant Saxon, I
don't want to know—I never want to see. . . ." The retort died on her lips as Jane recalled that neither he or
Sandy had taunted her or disclosed their hilarious
knowledge of her smelly predicament. A projected vision of the incident floated across her inner eye and the
humorous, the comical view as seen by an outsider
effectively stilled further retort and tilted her lips delightfully. Surprise lifted Grant's eyebrows as she continued, "I guess it was screamingly funny, I haven't
thanked you and Sandy for not broadcasting—for not
making fun of me. It was most humiliating at the time,
but I can see the comical side now."

"Comical, I agree, but," Grant added musingly, "you
looked quite adorable apart from the absolute hate
sparking your eyes to yellow fire. Disintegrating, what!
Hotter than the place to which you wished us—"

"Any girl would feel that way," Jane interposed spiritedly. "Especially if her predicament's discovered by
the very one who—" She bit her tongue sharply.

"The very one who . . . what, Jane?" The insidious
query was repeated when she did not answer and drummed against her ears hypnotically.

Her treacherous tongue vindicated itself ambiguous-
ly, "The one who's my boss, of course!" Her breath
expelled in little bubbles as a gimlet eye returned to the
road.

"Oh." Grant turned the car through white gates. "I

never thought you set such store in your boss's regard. Here we are, and there's Julius and horse . . . he's a great guy, don't you think?"

Jane's "Wonderful!" came with such relieved gusto that a surprised eyebrow was raised again. Grant made no further comment, for Julius was striding toward them. The car came to a stop and he stood ready to open the door for Jane.

Tea was a very pleasant interlude and Jane felt immensely cheered by the warmth of Mrs. Davenport's welcome.

Back in the car they said their goodbyes to Julius. He leaned down to speak to Grant through Jane's side window. "I'll be down your way in a day or two—got a spare bed?"

"Surely," Grant smiled.

He pointed out places of interest as the powerful car ate the miles and explained the reason for wanting a female companion. Mr. Dixon had come up from Johannesburg for the interview, and his wife and daughter would be with him. "I expect this interview to be of some length, so would appreciate it if you'll entertain the ladies. Dixon mentioned his wife particularly wished to visit a well-known citrus estate in that locality. Your knowledge, gleaned from working with me, should make it interesting for the two women and for you, gaining insight, so to speak, from a personal tour." Grant smiled at some hidden thought. "I would never have suggested that Mara take them, she hates walking . . . just as well you're with me. The car is at your disposal, to drive there and back. Inside the gates is where the walking starts."

"I don't know anything about citrus except book work, and that's no help! And you're askimg me to drive this car—she's far too powerful. My driving abilities are of the Mini standard, and that's gone rusty with disuse—I mean my ability to drive, not the Mini." Jane was hardly coherent with nervous anticipation of having to entertain two slick women from the golden city *plus* driving this monster, with two pairs of sophisticated eyes watching her every move—*and* what she knew about oranges, apart from drinking the juice, was anybody's guess!

Grant pulled her up abruptly.

"Nothing to it, once a driver always, etc., so stop dithering. A personnel officer will accompany your party through the estate, all you have to do is to look knowledgeable and charming. Not very much to that?"

"Oh no, Mr. Saxon!" Jane disclaimed sarcastically. Her trepidation returned as they drew up in front of the hotel.

Her anxiety was misplaced. The Dixons were unassuming and friendly. Grant knew the family from previous meetings and all three showed their approval of his feminine companion by drawing Jane instantly into their warm circle. Secretly amused and relieved, she realized it was she who was being entertained, not the reverse. A meaningful look passed between the older couple when Grant asked Jane solicitously if she would like to freshen up after the long hot drive. *Heavens,* she thought, *they've convinced themselves that I'm promised to Grant Saxon!*

To confirm her suspicions, just for fun, Jane smiled so sweetly and lovingly at Grant that he stopped in the middle of some ordinary remark and, poor unsuspecting man, couldn't remember where he had left off and had to start all over again.

After a leisurely lunch, Grant walked the three ladies to his car, winked intimately at Jane's nervous concentration as he indicated points to remember about this monster she'd be tackling single-handed. Her sullen glare at him was misconstrued as sultry by two occupants and he played right into their dreams by patting his "promised" tenderly on her cheek—also proof that he was aware of their turn of thought and deliberately playing up. Jane's glance would have withered a lesser man for she felt like biting the hand that patted!

"She's a wonderful girl—I mean driver. I have every confidence in my Jane. So competent," he remarked fondly—to step back hurriedly as the monster lurched forward in slender "competent" hands.

"Oh, my, this does take me back to my young days!" Mrs. Dixon settled back complacently from the sudden departure.

They arrived at the offices of the citrus estate in one piece with Jane's discovery that this was no monster after all, just a purring tiger, easily controlled. She patted the trunk gratefully, in passing, to join the party. The tour proved of considerable interest and the official allotted them most charming.

When they got back a smiling waiter passed on his message, "Mr. Saxon would take pleasure if the ladies would join them in the cocktail lounge." Jane thanked him with a return message; they would do so within ten minutes. Over cocktails, Grant regretted they could not accept the Dixons" invitation to dinner; they had a long run home, and he wanted to detour slightly to show Jane some fantastic scenery. The waiter had already been instructed to pack a hamper. Both men seemed highly satisfied with the outcome of their conference. The family would return to Johannesburg on the morrow.

Their farewells were cordial, with a pressing invitation to Grant and Jane to call on at their home when visiting Johannesburg.

Although the sun was casting long shadows, it was still hot and Jane opened her window fully to catch some cooler air. Grant guided the car with one hand while fumbling to loosen his tie with the other. His companion watched his efforts for a moment, then leaned over, removed the tie and undid the top two buttons of a still immaculate shirt. Grant smiled his thanks and ran a quick, clinical eye over her flushed face. Flushed from heat, unusual imbibing of drinks at that hour, and mostly from the little service she had just rendered; it had brought her very close for a few moments and his masculine magnetism did things to her!

They passed a sign indicating a garage one kilometer ahead, and without a word, Grant turned into the driveway and stopped the car.

"There's a ladies" room. Pop in and take off your skirt—I've noticed it's detachable—and your stockings and shoes. You'll feel mighty cooler then."

Jane sat looking at him and a brown hand nudged her not ungently.

"Come on, girl, don't gawk. The road's long and I want to show you something of interest," Grant urged.

It took her exactly seven minutes to follow instructions plus tying up her hair into a ponytail with the lace extracted from her shoe. Back in the car her modest feeling soon disappeared as Grant gave but a cursory glance of approval before turning his attention excluslvely on driving. She actually blessed him silently for his thoughtful suggestion. An hour passed, with Grant's deep voice coming at intervals, telling her about the deal with Papa Dixon and the outcome, a very satisfactory market for forest pines. Finally, a grunt of confirmation and he turned the car on to a subsidiary road, pointed at a sign on the grass verge.

God's Window.

Jane straightened in her seat with sudden excitement, eyes wide in wonder as they ascended under a canopy of breeze-stirred sentinels. A dappled hush of green, sprinkled with rosy overtones of a setting sun. Up and up they rose, by twists and turns between verdant greenery, with glimpses of blue sky resembling magical, faerie lakes. Grant brought the car to a smooth stop on a tiny open plateau. He led Jane by her hand up the last ascent and her breath caught at the sheer wonder of the scene that met her eyes.

They were surely gazing from a heavenly window, down, down at a world spread before enraptured eyes; to the right a red fragment of sun cast the most wondrous magic over misty blue valleys and gorges, to pagan artistry on pinnacles and escarpment. To the left, mile upon mile of untamed, wooded land stretched to the far reaches of hazy lowveld. The sheer magnetism of far, unexplored depths at her very feet, a world cloaked with beauty and mystery and an eternal peace, tugged at the girl's heart and made her step forward involuntarily.

A firm hand gripped hers, safely and surely. "Careful, child, one more step and the valley will claim you forever. Over there, in the distance and beyond, farther than the eyes can see, is the vast lowveld. The road that way leads past Bourke's Luck and the Potholes , Blyde River Canyon and nature reserve, through the Strydom Tunnel and on to Tzaneen and points further north. Beit Bridge and Rhodesia . . . ." Grant stopped. The hand in his was trembling and large brown eyes were caught in a mist of doelike agony.

Only it wasn't agony. The overwhelming scene, the solitariness of just the two of them, his hand holding hers with gentle strength and his voice speaking huskily as if, he too, sensed an All-powerful Closeness. It was a hypnotized ecstasy and just too much for Jane. The next moment she pressed her face against an immaculate shirt and wept with deep, sobbing gulps.

Grant's free arm lifted to encircle her slim waist. The warmth of his arm, right where she longed to have it, stopped her sobbing for a rending moment, and then the very nearness of his warm body reduced her to further misery.

Grant stood perfectly still and silent, a rock of timeless patience. Gradually the slim shoulders stopped shaking and Jane started to feel quite appalled at what she was doing. With perfect timing a large white hanky was thrust into her questing hand and a voice in her ear jibed softly:

"Janey, Janey, who would ever dream a tomboy with long nut-brown hair could turn out to be such a softie?" His lips touched the top of the head resting against his chest and nearly precipitated another display of tears. Jane turned in his arms and scrubbed her eyes and nose with a crumpled handkerchief. Her being cried out silently, willing him to say, "I love you, Janey with the long brown hair and soft heart."

Then he would find out how swiftly a long-haired tomboy could become soft, urgent and very feminine!

Grant said, "My navel's playing tunes on my backbone. Let's open our Pandora box and discover what Kasbeen packed for our delectation. I'm starving—come on, softie." He removed his arm from her waist and gripped the nape of her neck to propel her gently back to the car.

Jane stood like a bare-footed, chastised little girl, her back to him while he extracted basket and blanket from the depths of the car. Grant spread the blanket on tufted, springy grass, straightened up and stood with feet slightly apart, his hands on lithe hips, and regarded the drooped head, stiff back and long bare legs tapering from rounded hips to bare feet. A smile hovered for a fleeting moment as he watched one slim foot come to rest across the top of the other, as a small shy child would do. Some vagrant thought wiped away the smile and the man made a hopeless, negative motion toward the stiff back.

"Come now, Jane, not to worry if the makeup's slightly rainwashed. I can bear it, being more concerned with my stomach. Here's the flask and cups, do your thing." He dropped to the blanket. "I'm beginning to feel sorry I brought you here, had no idea it would affect you so wetly—"

Her body turned with a rush and Jane sank to her knees before him, grasping the handle of the basket until her knuckles shone white. Dew-wet eyes glowed with amber fire and parted lips showed pearly teeth in a smile although a usually firm chin wobbled only a little bit.

"Don't ever say that again, Grant. Or ever regret bringing me here; it was only with you that I could ever have had this glimpse of heaven, and I shall never forget it, to my last dying breath!" Jane spoke huskily, fervently, drew a deep breath and said softly, "Thank you, Grant Saxon." She sat down then, crossed her legs and drew the basket closer. The cups were set down with care and over the pouring of tea she added, as an afterthought, "I'm not a bit sorry about that disgusting flow of tears either."

Grant watched every movement and a full minute passed by before he lifted his hand to delve into the basket. They ate and drank in silence. Jane's eyes darted in exploration; of trees, foliage, bird twittering, rosy clouds, everywhere, with one exception; the man sitting opposite her.

Grant offered her a cigarette, leaned forward to light it. Her eyes rested on the steady hand and a sharp movement made her ponytail swing. She smiled brightly, "Thanks."

He lay flat on his back and closed his eyes, only lifting an arm to draw deeply on the cigarette between his fingers. Jane dared to look at him then. His lithe length, strong tanned arms in sharp contrast to white, rolled-up sleeves. High cheekbones, with fabulous Irish lashes fanning them darkly, mouth in repose still firm yet faintly vulnerable. His whisper startled her considerably.

"Why 'only with me,' Jane? Anyone could have shown you this place. It's here forever, you know."

"Well," she hadn't meant to reveal that little bit, so her cover-up had better be good, "I meant that coming here . . . with you . . . and my crying fit—well, I couldn't do that with just anybody."

"I get your meaning loud and clear. You feel safe with me, whereas another chap would take advantage of a perfect setting. You're quite delectable in shorts; why safe with me? Have you forgotten another time and place, when you were kissed very thoroughly by this safe person? We're very much alone, and your . . . wild . . . ways are most intriguing." Grant lifted his eyelids to squint through his lashes.

Jane shivered as though a bite of cold air had touched her spine.

"You're my boss—and who would do or even think anything wrong in this beautiful spot?"

His sudden laugh blasted the silence. "What wild reasoning! Bosses are human, exceptionally human, from the jokes I've heard, and this place is ideally romantic. And the way you turned to me, love, you can count yourself lucky I didn't lift you then and there, to carry you to some leafy bower and . . . ." he lifted his head to observe her hands clamped to her ears. "Very well, we'll leave the rest to your colorful imagination!"

Jane was on her feet. "Please don't trample with careless feet. May I pack now, it's getting late."

Grant stepped over the basket and gripped her shoulders. "Forgive me, I can't help imagining what some bounder could do to a trusting little atom such as you. Be more careful, will you?"

"Yes, Grant," Jane said, then continued with irrepressible spirit, "Not forgetting my judo . . . I could throw even you now, with the greatest of ease."

Her eyes held such unconscious appeal, with that bit of daredevilry lurking behind the innocence, that the grip on her shoulders tightened roughly and Grant spoke quietly, distinctly. "You may well have to use it within the next few seconds, I'm going to kiss you and if you're a sensible girl you'll cooperate, because I've been so good and deserve it, not so?"

The air became suddenly charged as a dark head bent lower and Jane felt cool, seeking lips on hers. Famous judo tactics were forgotten as her face lifted, of its own accord, her lips responded with heart-leaping urgency to the sweetest kiss ever given, and taken, in that Window of the Universe.

Grant lifted his mouth and looked for a long moment at the mouth he had kissed.

"I'll never forget this time and place either, Janey. Come on, let's go."

Jane lifted her bag and disappeared into the undergrowth, to walk back minutes later with skirt, shoes and stockings suitably adjusted. A quizzical eyebrow was answered with a smile, "The air is much cooler now."

CHAPTER NINE

Mara dislodged herself from the edge of Grant's desk and sauntered over to stand behind Jane. She watched nimble fingers on the typewriter, stifled a yawn and walked around to the front of the desk. Well, here it comes, thought Jane, and she was so right. . . .

Grant had not appeared this morning and Mara had prowled the study for the last ten minutes. Jane's "good morning" raised a curt query on his absence. Jane didn't know his whereabouts and said so. She worked composedly under the other woman's lengthy scrutiny, but could feel tension building.

"Got back pretty late last night." It came as a statement.

Jane said, "Mmm" and looked over her typewriter at the fingers drumming on her desk.

"I phoned last night and Dixon obligingly informed me that Mr. Saxon and his *girlfriend* had left before sunset. Have trouble?"

Jane's fingers paused on the keys. "No. We stopped for a hamper supper."

"How nice for you . . . quite a lengthy supper. Grant's an exciting man to share supper with on a moonlight night." The slight laugh that followed had suggestive venom.

Too true! Jane said aloud, "I agree. My boss is interesting and charming," she met the green eyes with a clear, direct gaze, "No matter whether morning, noon or night. What we working girls dub a real nice gentleman to work for," and continued her typing.

Mara's fist drummed on the desk. "Stop acting holier-than-thou, and stop that hammering!" Jane finished the paragraph and dropped her hands.

"Mrs. Saxon, my boss left me a pile of work, so I'll have to 'hammer' even if it disturbs you. I suggest you speak to Mr. Saxon if you're interested in his business trip."

"Why, you. . . ." Mara's beauty was marred by a sneer. "Mr. Saxon, is it? How businesslike—was it like that yesterday? Minna tells me you were wearing a snazzy hotpants job, and wasn't it just too, too handy that I had a headache and you all dressed for the occasion? Shouldn't you stay smart and stylish every day, just in case another occasion arises?" Her disparaging glance raked over Jane's simple cotton attire.

Complete amazement was tinged with a slight feeling of guilt as Jane dwelt on her emotional episode at that lovely place. Not planned, just a happening, but the fact remained and her cheeks colored at Mara's onslaught. To Jane it would remain an everlasting memory, but to others it would be regarded in a different light, according to their level.

Her silence seemed to infuriate the woman across her desk. "I've noticed your cow-like looks at Grant and attempts to draw his notice. He kissed you that night at the club, I know very well what a girl looks like when she's been kissed . . . Grant told me." Jane's indrawn breath told Mara what she hadn't known, only guessed. "Now get this straight," she leaned forward so that every nuance of her message would register. "Grant was mine long before John tempted me away. Only after our marriage I discovered that Grant was the one who held the purse strings and have regretted it ever since. Grant still loves me. His silly sense of decency is all that's holding him back. It will pass, I'm working on it. You'll never make first base—he likes kissing girls, but make no mistake, I'm the one Grant Saxon will marry!"

"Are you quite, quite sure of that, witch?"

Mara turned very pale and wheeled around with a

gasp. Julius Davenport walked into the room, to stand beside her, his eyes on Jane. She sat, quite stunned by Mara's cold-blooded message.

Julius leaned forward, both hands on the desk. "Don't upset yourself, Jane, this woman's brain is addled. I heard that bit about John and it makes me sick to my stomach; what will it do to Grant, if he finds out how mercenary she was and still is?" He turned and gripped Mara's arm, hard. "He believes you loved John and God help you if he ever hears otherwise. And stop pestering Jane, or I'll personally put a large spoke in your wheel."

"You wouldn't dare . . . Grant loves me and wouldn't believe you!" Mara wrenched her arm from his hard grasp. Unperturbed, Julius lowered it to encircle her waist.

"Don't ever dare me, lass. My great weakness is the inability to refuse a dare. Now, offer tea to your guest, like a nice girl—"

"Make that all round, Mara. Tell Minna I'm back, and we have a guest who'll spend the night." Cold gray eyes surveyed the scene. "I don't mind a little amour myself, but why choose my study? Julius, I presume you will be spending the night?"

Julius dropped his arm laconically. "Surely. I'm not one to let grass grow under my feet—and that, old man, answers both your questions." His smile was bland and friendly.

Jane could hardly believe it was the same grim Julius of a moment ago. Nor could she believe her eyes as a transformed redhead walked to Grant's side and smiled back at Julius.

"You know darling, I really don't think we should encourage this naughty man to visit. He's so—impetuous—as you noticed."

Grant moved to his desk and sat down. Gray, enigmatic eyes glimmered through the rising smoke of his cigarette. "You're welcome any time, Julius, and you, Mara, should know by now, how to handle impetuous cobbers."

"Of course, dear," said Mara in an astonishingly mild tone. "I'll see about the tea."

"I've actually brought those papers for you to scrutinize, Grant. You promised to look them over before I did anything rash, and time is of the essence," Julius explained his presence.

"I'll be here for about an hour, sorting this lot out and helping Jane with the day's logging," a clefted dimple showed unexpectedly. "Entertain Mara and . . . have your tea. I'll be with you shortly."

"Right!" Julius beamed, unabashed, and walked out of the study.

"Morning, Jane."

"Good morning, Grant." Jane slipped a clean sheet in the typewriter and closed her mind to the ordeal and scene she had just endured. But two sentences persisted insidiously, like a black fog, in the cracks of her mind; he kissed you at the club . . . and Grant told me . . . he likes kissing girls, but I'm the one he will marry.

Men who kiss and tell. He'll laugh with Mara—"You see, love, it was ridiculously funny, she simply fell weeping into my arms, so what could I do, etc . . . " If he did tell about the night at the club, who shouldn't he repeat this far more amusing episode? Oh no, she could not believe Grant was like that. Mara had made it up or seen them when she and Julius had appeared so suddenly. Jane had come to work this morning, reconciled to hug the memory of "her day" close to her heart. Determined, too, to establish a firm, friendly basis with her boss. The sweet taste of yesterday, his thoughtfulness, cynical humor, teasing—and then one kiss taken and given without thought to further liberties; these were hers to savor whenever she was alone or lonely. He'll forget, or vaguely remember a girl and a promise, "I'll never forget this time and place either, Janey."

Mara had spoilt the sweet taste by her degrading insinuations.

Jane squared her shoulders resolutely; there was nothing to be ashamed of, and no treacherous female was going to trample or bully her! She swung the carriage fiercely.

"Anything wrong, Miss Wheeler?"

"No. This darn thing is too slow."

"Stone the lizards, we are in a blasphemous mood this morning! Please, miss, I'll order another one right away, thank you ma'am. Was Mara the cause of this morning storm? How come she's scouting so early—not industriously minded that's for sure."

How right you are . . . *mischief* minded aptly described Mara's early scout!

That hidden thought made Jane say with some asperity, "You needn't be so facetious. I'll manage with this derelict, *and* I referred Mrs. Saxon to you. She's very interested in how you spent the day, and especially half the night!"

"Shall I confess all, do you think?" Grant asked softly.

"Don't you usually do that?" Her eyes met his squarely across the room.

"Do you always believe everything you're told?" he countered with uncanny sixth sense.

"I'm not concerned, either way."

"Very cheeky, this morning. I like my gals cheeky. Now, to tell or not to tell? I'll not tell," Grant decided.

"Bully for you!" Jane muttered nastily.

He studied her with critical concern. "When a girl backchats her boss in this manner it's a sure indication that she needs a change." Jane felt a cold chill down her spine. "You may have this afternoon and tomorrow off. Yesterday seems to have affected you badly."

"Understatement of the decade!" came out sotto voce.

"I beg your pardon?"

"Oh, nothing, Mr. Saxon!" This time her voice cracked on a high note.

"You are in a vile mood, sweetheart," Grant decided belatedly.

Jane kept her lips tightly shut while her mind screamed, "I'm not your sweetheart nor ever will be—how vile would you feel if someone attacked you the way your beloved did me—and oh, my darling, I do love you so desperately, and do you really kiss all the girls, and may you never find out that she married your brother for the money he didn't have. Perhaps it would be better, because then you would discover her true worth and turn to Miss Second Best on the rebound—and shut up, Jane Wheeler, you maniac!"

Minna brought the tea. Jane did the necessary in stiff silence, which nearly disintegrated when she put Grant's cup on his desk. He looked up and gave her a wink.

She set to work as if her life depended on it and looked up in surprise when Minna put her head in the doorway to announce that lunch was waiting. Grant had long since left the office. She had a good mind to skip lunch, since she was officially off for the rest of the day. Tom would be having his break now; Jane wondered if Grant had given instructions to take her home. Well, she wouldn't appear cowardly; she'd face them for lunch with her chin in the air. Thank goodness for Julius's presence; he was a dear, and Jane had a notion that, for all her scorn and for some reason, Mara was just a little afraid of him.

She was briefly amused at Mara's pretty chaffing of Grant about his late homecoming the previous night.

She ignored Jane and spoke to Julius only when absolutely necessary. He was completely unconcerned, directing his full attention on Jane. This, after a time, seemed to pique Mara; her dislike of him was evident, but, dog-in-the-manger, she wanted all the male attention.

Grant said, "Tom is at your disposal when you're ready to leave, Jane. Have a good rest this afternoon and tomorrow."

"How thoughtful you are, Grant! You do spoil your staff. I wouldn't have been so clapped after one little day's journey. Pity I had such a bad head and let you down so badly—I hope it didn't affect your business adversely." Mara accepted his offer of a cigarette.

"On the contrary, all went exceptionally well. Jane was the right sort for the Dixon family and she did some legwork on the citrus estate which I doubt you could have accomplished, my dear Mara." Grant leaned back and blew smoke rings.

"Legwork?" Mara laughed. "I do believe Jane revealed quite some limb in the delectable outfit Minna tells me she was wearing."

"Quite a bit and, as you say, delectable," Grant returned blandly.

"Most distracting for the poor little guide. Did he fall hard, or don't they provide guides any more?" Spots of color high on her cheeks showed that Grant's needling was prickling. Mara looked directly at Jane.

Jane said clearly, "As a matter of fact he did. A most charming man, tall and handsome. So persistent, but understandably regretful when I had to whisper that I was already spoken for."

"Oh, is that why Mrs. Dixon referred to the 'girlfriend' so romantically?"

"When did you speak to Mrs. Dixon?" Grant asked abruptly.

Mara lost her poise for a moment. "I . . . I phoned, darling. Worried, you know. It was late, and one does begin to worry."

"You need never worry your beautiful head about me. I'm grown up now and perfectly able to help myself."

"One-track mind the dear, sweet, nice-minded girlie," Julius observed and stood to hold Jane's chair.

"I would like to take you home, Jane, if you don't mind. It's a short run and a visit with Bart and Janet would be pleasurable. May I?"

"Thank you, I'd like that," Jane smiled and turned to Grant. "Thank you too, boss, for the time off."

"What are you doing this afternoon, Grant?" Mara asked.

"Completion of labor sheets. I suggest you go with Julius. It's boring for you here alone."

"No, thanks, I can entertain myself. We could take a run to the club this evening, hmm?"

"Can do." Grant was noncommittal.

"That will be great," Julius counted in with superb disregard of Mara's green glare. "How about it? Want to make a foursome, Jane?"

"No, thanks, I'll catch up on neglected chores and stay with the family. My mother and I are almost strangers lately!"

"Sorry about that, but suit yourself, lass." Grant and Mara made no comment, so Julius took Jane's arm and led her to the door.

"Stop me if I'm interfering, love, what was Mara so fussed about when I walked in this morning?" Julius asked as they walked along.

Jane hooked thumbs into the pockets of her jeans, in unconscious imitation of Grant when thinking. "She was ferreting the reason for our late return last night."

"Did you enlighten her?"

"I referred her to Grant. For your information, we made a detour to God's Window and . . . stayed longer than planned."

"Hmm," Julius accepted this in a small silence, then said, "That wasn't all she wanted. How did John's name crop up?"

Jane lip twisted mirthlessly. "You heard her. I was informed in no uncertain terms that Grant Saxon was her property, before she—married his brother—and I must refrain from making cow's eyes and . . . angling for him."

A hand on her arm halted her rapid stride. "Jane, stop me if this is an imposition, but, seeing you've confided so far—are you in love with Grant?"

Jane stood quite still under his disconcerting scrutiny. At last she raised her lowered lashes and Julius read the answer in amber brown eyes.

"Grant belongs to Mara." Her lips trembled and pearly teeth clamped hard on her lower lip.

Julius said sharply, "He does not! Not yet. I'll exchange a secret with you. Grant is not going to belong to her any more, because I'm going to make her my woman. I know all her faults and she's not everybody's idea of the ideal woman, but I happen to fancy that redhead for a wife!"

Jane gasped, became dumbfounded as she stared at her companion. The set of his jaw finally convinced her that Julius was in earnest.

"But, Julius," she exclaimed at last, "what about Grant? You can't do that to him! Anyway, they're in love with each other—and I'm not belittling you, Julius, but nobody will succeed in taking what belongs to Grant Saxon. Mara said he was only waiting for a decent period to elapse before . . . proposing."

"Who says!" Julius interrupted rudely. "My grasping, greedy redhead doesn't know the meaning of love. I've known her for a long time, but I was too poor to be noticed while the Saxon wealth was floating before her beautiful eyes. Yes, she and Grant were close before she suddenly upped and married John. If he's a man, as you so fervently declare, in complete command of any situation, why did Grant allow her to slip through his fingers? Because he loved his brother more and believed Mara reciprocated John's love for her? Which you and I know now to be a mercenary love, on her side. John worshipped her. He was an idealist; Grant was the realist and the one to build the estate to what it is today. Quite a shock for our heroine, to discover that the *younger* brother held the purse strings! John was not financially embarrassed, and Grant was overly generous, but . . . well, that was the setup. The present position is this: if Grant wants Mara he'd better get cracking, because I'm going to do my damnedest to take her for myself; dangle my own acquired wealth most illuminatingly and show her what a dazzling, charming catch I am. In fact, by hook or crook. And believe me, from the day she becomes my wife I'll shape and pound her into the finest wife any man could wish for. I like my women pretty, but I prefer them, at least a wife, to be a housewifely, loving and obedient female!" His eyes sparkled as Julius paused for breath. "All's fair in love and war!"

Amazement struggled with a certain amusement and affection for his determined air and became mixed with angry sympathy for Grant's relinquishment of sweetheart to loved brother. But he was free now to claim, if he still desired Mara. She was waiting to fall into Grant's arms!

"Are you going to warn Grant of your intentions? He is a friend of yours, I gather?"

Julius grinned. "Not I! Surprise is the element of success in my venture."

"How low can one get? I'll make it my business to warn him!"

"Equally, how high-minded can one get? Grant will draw the ace if it's so ordained. In the meantime this bod can try a bit of cardsharping. Anyway, why spoil your own pitch? Don't be a doormat, get in some fast bowling for your own side, sweetie. You'll be helping poor Julius at the same time. Grant isn't the kissing kind, but by jove, Mara and I saw you in a fine clinch under the stars, at the club, and if you didn't take advantage of a little frolic at Providence's window then you're soft in the head!"

Mingling through her mixed emotions and his mad suggestions in mixed metaphors, one warm fact emerged clearly: Mara had lied about Grant telling her of the episode at the club and Julius had stated positively that Grant was not the kissing kind. Where one lie started others could follow. . . .

Jane stared absently into Julius's eyes as she considered this aspect.

"Aha, I see the wicked struggling with the righteous." Julius came close and hugged Jane hard. "I could almost go for you myself when you look like that . . . if I wasn't spoken for, so to say. Something did happen yesterday." He felt her stiffen in his arms. "I'll respect your silence, but I'm going to use you and it'll cut both ways. We'll make those two so jealous, and wanta bet we both land with aces?"

Jane struggled free. "You're mad, Julius Davenport!"

"Yes, Jane Wheeler. Crazy enough to try any low-down trick. Come on, it's time to depart and plan my mode of attack." Julius grabbed a slender hand, started off with long, quick strides which forced his victim to abstain from angry protestations.

His verve for the impending attack bubbled over into practising on Janet and Liza. Julius lifted them in turn with a smacking kiss of farewell and chased Jane twice round his car before blocking her nimble feet with a long-legged leap in the opposite direction of her flight.

"See you tomorrow, my beauteous collaborator!"

Jane washed her hair and joined her mother and aunt.

"You'll have all the girls in the neighborhood gunning for you," teased Elizabeth. "A day and almost half the night out with your boss, Julius hugging you in the lucerne *and* Peter coming to take you out tonight. Pat's coming to keep an eye on things . . . all eligible bachelors, and you must hog the lot!"

"Well, a girl can't work all the time." Jane drooped wearily, then demanded sharply, "What about Peter taking me out?"

Elizabeth looked contrite. "Sorry, Jane, you were late last night. I didn't see you this morning and Julius's visit made me forget. Peter is coming to take you out. I think he mentioned the club; and Pat promptly invited herself. I accepted on your behalf."

"To the club?" Mara's suggestion to Grant flashed through her mind. "No, I'm not going."

"Why, Jane, have you made other plans?"

"I just don't feel like it, that's why!" Temper made her blood rise, she whirled in the door. "I'll phone Peter, right now—"

"The telephone is out of order," Janet said mildly.

"Oh, damnation!" wailed Jane.

"Oh, dear, I am sorry." Elizabeth clasped her hands together and looked so distressed at her daughter's reaction that Jane curbed her blood pressure and managed a weak smile.

"I did so look forward to an early night. Perhaps they'll be content to spend the evening here. I'd like that."

"Peter said something about visiting a patient in that

vicinity, love, making it a round trip, so to speak. Combining duty with pleasure were his exact words, I recall now."

"Oh, Mother, since when have you become so—so vague? If they're coming all this way to pick me up, I'll just have to go," Jane said helplessly.

Janet intervened briskly, "It won't do you any harm and you needn't make a late night of it. You're not working tomorrow so you can sleep late for a change. Get dressed, my girl; you can't go in jeans. Supper will be ready soon."

Jane was waiting on the veranda when Peter swooped up the drive. He looked freshly vigorous in tan slacks, open-necked shirt and sporty cravat. Pat was neatly cute in cotton sun dress, Jane in a patterned dress in autumn shades.

"Thanks for accepting my second-hand invitation, beautiful. I knew if I got Liza to accept on your behalf you wouldn't be able to wiggle out. Excuse the drag— she insisted on coming, and when Pat looks so beseeching a leech has nothing on her!"

"I'm glad you hung on, Pat. It's more fun this way." Jane cheered away the desolate droop of pretty lips, and Peter threw her a "spoil-sport" look.

"Is that what you think of me? Haven't you heard of two's company, three's a crowd?" he demanded morosely.

"Peter dear, how was I to know you yearned for a twosome?" Pat showed wide-eyed innocence. She turned to Jane and whispered, "I had to come, to protect you from a wolf. Don't be deceived by appearance, take it from one who knows."

"Yes, nurse." Jane smiled across at Peter's cocked ear. "She's only saying she's so wild about you, she can't bear to let you out of her sight."

"You traitor!" Pat hissed. "Don't expect a helping

hand when you land in deep waters. I'll revel in delicious revenge at your struggles."

Peter passed cigarettes and they smoked and chatted on the trip to the club. He stopped at the side of the building. "I'll see you lassies settled, then pop in to my patient. He's the caretaker and lives in that cottage peeping through the trees."

"Can't we wait in the car?" Jane hesitated beside the car.

Pat nudged her back. "And waste drinking time? C'mon, it's quite in order for girls to enter without escort. We can pass the time ogling other women's chaps and causing feminine havoc."

"Watch it, you alcoholic siren!" Peter armed them up the steps and seated the two girls on the deserted veranda. The waiter appeared; Peter ordered their respective drinks, a Cinzano on the rocks for Jane and vodka for Pat. Piped music and chatter came from the interior bar. "Stay put, don't move, I'll be back in two shakes."

"Don't kill him off in your haste, dear doctor," Pat offered Peter's departing back.

The Mission nurse leaned back and studied her companion with open frankness. "How is the job going, and how's Grant and Mara?"

"The job's fine, thanks. I've got the day off, tomorrow. Grant and. . . ." Jane stopped as a familiar feminine laugh reached her sensitive ears. "Grant and Mara are well, and Sandy is back at school. I think they're here with Julius, who's visiting for day or two. He seems rather keen on Mara."

"Is that so?" Pat rested her elbows on the table. "How blind can a man get . . . what's the matter, Jane, you're looking pale around the gills?"

"Don't be silly—this drink—I gulped too fast, hit my inside like a charge of dynamite!" Jane prevaricated, and breathed deeply to control a thudding race in her chest. She wished desperately for Peter to return before someone appeared and found them sitting alone. Pat was eyeing her strangely so she spoke with forced calm. "Just fancy, Pat, until last Sunday I was under the impression that Grant was Sandy's father."

"What!" Pat looked her amazement. "You thought she wasn't John's child?"

"No, no, I was—I thought that Mara and Grant were married, to each other."

"Goodness, it must have been a shock!" Amazement turned to curiosity. "You're in their house daily, Jane, couldn't you see if they were on—intimate terms—like husband and wife?"

Jane flushed and twisted the glass in her hands. "Mara has her own bedroom, and I stop work at five— I'm not there at night. Grant is very busy during the day and Mara wanders around, and calls him 'darling.' I'm merely telling you this to prove how easily a person can be mistaken."

"Your mistaken impression may well be rectified if Mara has her way and persuades Grant to take the plunge. They were close before she suddenly showed preference for John; he was a fine man, make no mistake, but I have my own personal suspicions of why Mara acted on that preference. Later, she couldn't show open regret because Grant was very fond of his brother and has high ideals concerning wifely behavior; Mara had to toe the line because she daren't lose face, to disillusion the one she really favored."

Silence ensued. Jane put the glass down, rubbed the tips of her fingers along the edge of the table. "I know that now. I told Julius not to interfere, not to . . . hurt Grant . . . all over again. He's determined to woo Mara."

"He doesn't stand a chance if Grant truly wants her for his wife." Pat confirmed Julius's own words.

"Julius is fully aware of that but prepared to try his damnedest and has declared intentions of using me to further his interests."

"How?"

"By trying to make her jealous—he says it might help us both to achieve our hearts' . . . Jane stopped abruptly.

"Well, well . . . that's how the land lies?" Pat's quick mind read the conclusion. "Are you going to connive?"

"I am not!" A slim hand closed convulsively as Julius spoke to Mara in the doorway leading to the veranda.

"Much cooler here and not a soul to contaminate the fresh air."

"I'm not a fresh air fiend and—oh, not quite deserted, take note." Mara inclined her head and Julius turned, dropped his hand from her arm and sauntered to the occupied table.

"Two angels disguised as mortals; luck is smiling at me tonight." He grasped the empty chair in front of him, pulled it back and turned to meet Mara's haughty green stare. "Come, sweet one, join the heavenly harem and proceed to entertain my lonely heart suitably."

"I'm sure the *angels* have their reasons for coming here unaccompanied. Stop spoiling their pitch, Julius." The innuendo was unmistakably insulting.

A smile remained on the man's lips, but his eyes were very cold as he replaced the chair.

"My apologies for the distress that remark may cause, angels."

"Hello, Mara, Julius." Peter bounded up the steps, stopped to study the redhead clinically. "State of rigor mortis? Join us in a spot of medicinal."

Julius said, "Thanks, Peter—later, if the angels permit. Right now Mara needs fresh air. Her head feels very . . . stuffy."

Peter watched the stiff figure being led firmly down

the steps, into the gloom of shrubbery. He sat down slowly. "What gives?"

Pat opened her mouth . . . Jane forestalled her. "Nothing, Peter. As Julius said, Mara isn't feeling too good. The—smoke in there affected her. She'll be all right and won't need your medical attention. We need you—look, our glasses are empty."

Peter nailed them in turn with alert appraisal. "Okay, I get the message. Waiter!"

"How is your patient?" Jane asked.

"He'll live. Speak to me, Pat. Silence doesn't become you . . . a slight case of lockjaw?"

"Lockjaw be damned!" Pat exclaimed. "Can you believe it, that—"

"That drink you had, Pat. You gulped it too fast, remember?" Jane interposed swiftly.

"Yeah? Oh, sure, it took my breath away; I remember. Now lockjaw, or tetanus, is caused by invasion of bacillus entering through wounds multiplying to secrete poison which travels along lymphatic vessels — something about nerves—to the spinal cord. Symptoms, some days after injury, spasms and stiffness of jaws . . . if untreated is fatal. Prophylactic dose of anti-tetanus serum should be injected, deep wounds thoroughly cleansed; skilled nursing required to feed patient without precipitating attacks." A deep breath, and Pat continued hypnotically, "Bacilli normally present in intestines of horses and other animals. Wounds or injury on heads should be treated by doctor—"

"I prefer a silent·Pat," Jane reckoned, while Peter gasped in awed wonder.

"The treatment is to prevent bacilli gaining foothold in wounds . . . dead, damaged tissue must be cut away and antiseptic applied." The little nurse waited modestly for acclaim.

Wonder turned to beaming satisfaction on the

doctor's face. "And I often despaired, wondered if my teachings ever penetrated! Jane, I feel the most extraordinary symptoms attacking me for this wonder protegée. Do you think marriage is the prescribed prophylactic dose?"

"I do," Jane advised

"No other cure?" he pleaded.

"No other known cure," Jane contradicted gravely.

"Will you marry me, protegée?"

"I will," said Patricia Marais promptly.

Doctor Davies coughed as if he had an obstruction in his esophagus.

"Yippee!" he croaked on an expiring note.

Complete silence reigned. The waiter placed the order and backed away with puzzlement on his face.

Jane raised her glass slowly.

"Congratulations," she whispered.

Grant Saxon cleared the doorway in time to behold an exalted nurse drain her glass, throw it over her shoulder on to the grass verge beyond the veranda wall and emit an excited "Yoicks!"

He came to a standstill within a yard of their table, to study the scene at closer range: Jane and Peter regarding each other blankly, Pat leaning back with eyes closed in rapture. She opened one eye slightly, saw him and murmured, "He's proposed."

"Accepted?" Gray eyes were fixed on Jane.

"Most promptly."" Jane raised her head to meet the smoky, intent stare. "Congratulations are acceptable."

"Congratulations," Grant gritted huskily.

Pat opened her eyes fully at his tone and saw him hypnotizing Jane. "You don't have to sound so grim, and you should be looking at *me*. After all, I'm the one that was proposed to!" she stated ungrammatically.

Peter found tongue. "Oh, God, what have I done . . . clobber me, pal, clobber me hard!"

Grant drew a chair and sat down with unusual care. "Accept the inevitable, Doctor. It happens, sooner or later."

Jane found herself unable to resist saying, "What will it be with you, sooner or later?"

"My dear Jane, fate has not revealed her plans, which is most probably fortunate for my peace of mind. But I am considering," his narrowed gaze held hers levelly, "some problems, peculiar problems to solve, which will make it later, no doubt." He beckoned to the waiter and ordered iced champagne.

Jane tore her eyes away and looked towards the shrubbery. His problems could only be certain formalities to observe, before marrying his brother's widow. She unclenched her fists, forcing her hands to relax on her lap.

Pat took Peter's hand in hers and stroked the top of sensitive fingers cajoling a weak smile to his lips. "You have five minutes to retract, before the champagne arrives, darling." She was in perfect earnest.

Doctor Davies looked long and hard into the eyes of his medical assistant.

"Do you know," he said thoughtfully, "I don't think I want to retract anything . . . Have you seen the pool by moonlight lately, Patricia? Come, let me show you, it's a beautiful sight."

"Yes, dear, but not via the shrubbery, it's occupied." They left Jane and Grant without apology.

"Someone else romantically minded in the shrubbery?" Grant asked, without interest, and continued without waiting for a reply, much to her relief. "For a moment there, I thought it was to you the good man had proposed marriage. I'm relieved it's not so."

"Why are you relieved?" Jane asked quietly.

"He's not the man for you. Secondly, I wouldn't want to train another secretary."

"Indeed? Can your superior knowledge describe the man for me?" Jane felt nettles rising at his bland superciliousness.

"Give me your hand, *chérie*," Grant leaned over to take her hand in his, palm upwards. "A very pretty hand, I declare," a questing forefinger traced the lines and Jane felt a shock of awareness tingle up her arm and jerked her hand. "Steady now, I can't read your future if you wriggle so much. Yes, there he is, tall, dark and handsome . . . very elegant, with flashing eyes. The very man to suit your personality. Davies would have been too—juvenile—for you. This one I see in your hand will be demanding, brave, fierce and will cherish unto eternity. Not a bad guy at all," he mused, "the sort I would approve of, if I were your mother. I advise you to start a trousseau immediately—he's already hanging on your lifeline."

"Oh, Mr. Seer, how clever! Can you foresee the extent of my family as well?" Jane was deliberately scornful, to cover a feeling that his mocking description described himself . . . excepting the cherishing bit.

"Family? Now, let me see—here's one, a girl with nut-brown hair like her mother, and a boy with flashing eyes . . . can't see the color. My stars! there's little feet pattering all over your fingers, I can't keep track of 'em all. Poor Jane, you'll become so weary of love and its consequences that, at the early age of seventy, I see a mug of poisoned ale being rammed down the old man's gullet. He expires dutifully, at last you're free to throw that maternity over the wall—but what is this? A stranger picks it up and returns it, bows over and kisses your pretty wrinkled hand, a greater love is born—and you start all over again!"

"At seventy?" Jane's laughter bubbled irresistibly.

"A very young seventy," Grant consoled, his lips curved disarmingly.

A movement across her shoulder caught his eyes. Jane followed his gaze and her laughter subsided as they both watched Julius and Mara walking slowly, deep in conversation. Jane turned back to find Grant still watching with narrowed, enigmatic eyes, absolutely unreadable.

Pat and Peter met up with the couple and ascended the steps together. Julius hesitated a moment when he saw Grant sitting with Jane, held Mara back to say something in undertones, then walked to the table still holding her arm. Peter seated Pat and drew two more chairs. The waiter appeared with a bottle of champagne nestling in a bucket of ice and glasses.

"Somebody celebrating something?" Julius inquired, quick eyes darting speculatively to Jane. Did he think, or hope, she was "conniving" faster than sound? Her brown eyes scorned negatively.

"Spot on, Julius, however did you guess? Pat and I have decided to take the plunge." Peter waited for the pop of the cork.

Grant unwound with ease, stood while the others settled in chairs and the glasses were filled. He lifted his own glass. "To Peter and Patricia, may their engagement be happy and their marriage everlasting."

Mara voiced a forced "Congratulations" and studied the amber liquid in her glass. Her green gaze rested on Grant at intervals and Jane guessed she was trying to read his reaction to her disappearance with Julius. He gave no indication of any feeling in the matter and Jane marvelled at his superb control. Nothing disturbed his equilibrium; any other man would surely show signs of anger, or contempt, toward one of them. Grant must be very sure of himself, or sure of Mara's loyalty.

Well, Jane sighed, that's how love should be, but she wished it hadn't been Julius, knowing he was going to do his utmost to woo Mara away from Grant. That would prove trying for Mara and Grant would be very angry, when he found out, angry enough to sever a good friendship. Somebody was going to be hurt in the process and looking at Grant's disturbing nonchalance, she suspected it would be Julius.

Grant requested a dance with Pat and Julius beckoned Jane. Peter took his cue and they drifted on to the small dance floor in the cocktail lounge. The piped music was soothing and a few couples swayed languidly.

Jane whispered, "Julius, you looked very cross when you dragged Mara into the shrubbery . . . how come she came back so subdued? What did you do to her, beat her?"

"I have a way with me, poppet. Women cringe when I lay down the law. I won't bore you with details except that I had a little hellion on my hands when I remarked, quite amiably, that girls who pass such remarks to others only cheapen themselves, the common trait reveals its true self. Oh boy," Julius's eyes sparkled reminiscently; "I almost had to hog-tie the filly, to prevent her from clawing out my eyes! After she quietened down I apologized for the rough handling and said there were other ways a girl of her spirit could vent surplus energy. A woman's inborn curiosity got the upper hand, so I propounded with great fervor on the most beautiful Arab stallion in Southern Africa. I owned that stallion; I glowed, I shivered ecstatically when dwelling on his finer points. Mara wanted to know what that had to do with her surplus energy. She used to be a fine rider. I don't know when last she mounted a steed, but her interest was aroused. I deplored the fact that Sheik, that's my stallion, wasn't getting the exercise he needed and her mettlesome spirit (no, darling, I didn't say meddlesome) would match his perfectly. She would look queenly superb mounted on such an animal. An open invitation was delivered with great courtesy, with an offhand, veiled hint that, being stinking rich, I wouldn't put it past myself to offer Sheik as a gift to one who could match his pride and beauty." Julius crossed two fingers against his partner's back.

"You beast, Julius Davenport!" Jane hissed, aghast at his temerity.

Grant lifted an eyebrow beside them. He had heard her exclamation quite clearly. Julius tightened his hold, kissed the top of Jane's head and said, "Quite beautiful, when she's angry," and whirled into an intricate step.

"If you insist on doublecrossing Grant with your beastly bribes I'm going to warn him!"

"My sweet girl, if Mara is open to bribery then she's not worthy of any man's love. Think of all the misery curtailed if he finds out now, and not too late. Warn him if you consider it necessary, but remember, you weren't present at the actual bribery; Grant heard your outburst, and you'll feel mighty foolish if he interprets your warning as jealousy of my little stroll with Mara in the dark."

"And I thought you were a nice simple farmer when I first met you!"

"Not so much of the simple, darling, but rather definitely nice," Julius summed up placidly.

Without leaving the floor they changed partners, Peter claiming his new fiancée and Julius bowing Jane over to Grant. They moved in silence to dreamy music and Jane savored the steel feel of his arms and male nearness.

"Julius is tall and, some would say, handsome," Grant said thoughtfully, above her ear.

"So are you," Jane quipped tartly.

"Thanks, Jane." He looked surprised. "How is your palm going to work that one out?"

"You're the teller of fortunes."

"Well, there seems to be an influx of handsome men

in your life. Don't fall for all of them and hope for the best, just because your palm says so."

"Oh dear, if this influx swarms around me, how will I know which is the brave, fierce one who will cherish unto being poisoned by my wrinkled hand?" Jane looked appealingly confused, even though her heart clamored that she was in the arms of the only one, right now.

"When *he* touches you, your palm will tingle warningly," Grant prophesied. And was stunningly ignorant of how very right he was!

CHAPTER TEN

A BENIGN SUN sent forth busy rays to sweep away morning mists from the eyes of another glorious day. Jane stood, barefooted, at her open window and watched silky, sulky puffs of candyfloss disperse reluctantly from the meadows to huddle defiantly in shadowed foothills, a last veiled resort against inexorable golden brooms. She felt a rise of youthful resilience warm her mind and body at nature's eternal promise.

An invigorating shower and hearty breakfast started a satisfactory morning, gossiping with Liza and Janet, catching up on her mending and just wandering around the house. She started a walk through the fruit and vegetable garden, but retreated when she saw Olivier busy in their midst; an encounter with him was not to her liking. Uncle Bart had mentioned that this would be his last day of work; then he would be moving on. Jane's thoughts dwelt on this man; Flip Olivier. His way of life, roving, working for others with no fixed abode or family to call his own; he was good with earth and growing things; did he ever yearn for a place of his own, a wife and children whom he could work for and find comfort in? A nomad existence sounded exciting, but it could be very lonely.

Two hours after lunch Jane announced her intention of walking to the river for a dip. Janet warned her not to wander too far and offered her company.

Jane promised and laughed at her offering. "My darling Aunt, I'm a natural in the bush, so don't panic. I've yet to get lost and snakes slide backwards at sight of me. One can't get lost here, with the hills, river and orchards as positive landmarks!"

She drifted in the cool, clear water for some time and

basked on a warm rock like a lazy rock rabbit. Back in shorts, shirt and sandals she decided a small exploration would be fun, keeping the river obediently in sight. A few specimens of interesting leaves and ferns were stowed in her haversack for future study with Sandy's nature book in mind. After supper she would embroider the linen cover she had cut that morning for the book. The ground alongside the river was damp with the close jostling of willow saplings, berry bushes, grass and stray gums and pines. Halfway down the bank she noticed a peculiar jutting root, most realistically resembling a cheeky elf with a fantastic red nose. Jane went down on her knees and her seeking fingers were intent on investigating a possible breaking point when a sudden loud nicker startled her. Unbalanced, she slid forward on her stomach and started her downward journey. A water-logged root obligingly met her wild grab and saved a mud-smeared victim from deep waters . . . by the time she topped the bank, back-sliding, crawling, clawing her way up, she was a sorry mess with a newly acquired bloody scratch from elbow to wrist!

A short distance away she spotted the cause of her downfall. The horse was tethered and nickered again, eyeing her with bright sympathy and apology. Jane walked slowly toward him, wondering to whom he belonged and what the unknown rider was about in this silent neck of the woods. The river bank was lower here, the water shallower. She spoke softly to the animal while bathing her arm in the cool stream. On the brink of stepping in to wash her legs she suddenly stood quite still . . . a distinct, feminine cry . . . not bird or beast? Again the sound reached her intent ears; not a cry but a female voice scolding—or frightened!

Jane moved softly and swiftly up a rise of pine trees, her feet cushioned on a blanket of fallen pine needles, to stop warily while her eyes travelled down the shallow clearing in front of her. A gypsy-like caravan nestled in the grassy hollow—a woman in riding clothes was leaning against the gaudy side, scolding the man facing her. Jane's breath escaped in amazed recognition.

Flip Olivier and Mara Saxon!

The man made a rough gesture, his voice carrying on the clear air.

"So why do you come here if not for a bit of jolly? You knew my pad was parked here. Chickening out—scared, Mrs. Saxon?" His laugh was ugly.

Jane started her silent approach while her mind could only register amazement at his attitude and Mara's presence. She watched him take a closer step as Mara raised the stock in her hand, to whip it brutally from her grip.

"Oh no, baby, you don't!" Mara pressed against the side of the caravan at the fury in his voice. "Your great brother-in-law has already insulted me enough. Do you think I'm going to let his woman beat me as well! You killed your husband because you're too fond of swigging—"

"That will be all today, Mr. Olivier!" Jane's command cut across his tirade.

Flip Olivier whirled to face the slight girl walking toward him, the stock upraised threateningly—to lower it as she passed him unafraid, to join Mara.

"Well," he sneered, "the birds're gathering like homing pigeons today!"

Jane ignored him. "All right, Mara?"

"Yes—I didn't expect—"

"Didn't expect, my foot! What you come here for, where nobody ever comes? You stopped your swanky car the other day to speak to me and I told you my pad was here—and lied to this bird about me fixing your car. And you, Miss High and Mighty, can't even pass the time of day with a lowdown gardener—" he pushed

Mara aside roughly to lay his hands against the boards on either side of Jane's shoulders, imprisoning her effectively. "You're free with your kisses, and that's no lie. I saw you at the club with Saxon and I saw Davenport hugging you in the lucerne. The way I figure, how's about my share, huh?"

The insinuation and venom enraged Jane to icy flashpoints of anger.

"I'll give you five seconds to remove your arms." Her acid contempt hazed the air between them. "I'm waiting."

"I'll do that for the price of one kiss—not being the greedy sort. One kiss and I figure you'll come back for more, baby."

Grant Saxon lengthened his silent stride down the opposite side of the glen. Mara took a step closer to Olivier. "Leave her, you—"

"Shut up. What about it, girl?"

Jane wasted no more time. With swift accuracy her knee lifted sharply and, while pain exploded from his lips, she turned to grip his arm with sure knowledge of her next move.

Grant lifted the man off the ground where his slim adversary had hurled him, head over heels! Jane felt a rigid shiver up her spine at Grant's savage, strangling grip and steely jaw.

She spoke with deceptive calm even though, flowing wildly through her breast, came a savagery to meet and meld with primeval delight at sweet conquest of evil. "Let him go, Grant, he's not worthy of anger, just a spineless rat."

His eyes cold dangerous ice, Grant shook Olivier in a steely grip.

"You two—has he touched—harmed either of you?"

"No. Didn't have time," Jane assured him laconically, stilling the erratic beating in her breast.

The man in his hard grasp was still grunting with pain. Grant flung him contemptuously against the wheel of the caravan. "Olivier, hear me. Report to Sergeant Mason within the next two hours. I'm allowing you that much time to report and leave this vicinity. If you haven't done so I'll sign a warrant for your arrest in connection with two counts of assault. Two hours. The Sergeant will be waiting because I'll advise him of your coming."

Jane beckoned Mara and started walking back the way she had come. "Just keep you mouth shut and let me do the talking," she advised softly.

"What . . . what are you going to tell Grant?" a pale-faced Mara hissed.

Jane stepped carefully on the carpet of pine needles. "I won't give you away," she answered shortly. They turned then to face the grim man, side by side.

Grant watched them in silence, hands on hips.

"I'm waiting."

Keeping her fingers crossed in apology to a listening, shocked Providence, Jane outshone the proverbial trooper. "We—Mara and I met at the swimming hole and decided to investigate up the river. We didn't know about the caravan until we walked slap bang into it."

"You can't see it from here, granted. Topping that rise it hits you in the eye immediately. Why didn't you turn back then?" Grant demanded sharply.

She turned to Mara questioningly. "Oh yes, we were talking and watching our feet. Snakes, you know."

Grant raised a sceptical eyebrow. "Only a woman could be so blind! Did you walk while Mara rode?"

Oh, heavens, the horse!

Grant continued, "Did you ride while Jane walked?" His eyes were on Mara and Jane held her breath. Did Mara know there wasn't room for a rider in that tangle of branches?

Mara brushed back a strand of hair. "I led him." And Jane coughed delicately to hide her expelled relief. Mara must have come off the road and led her horse right across the clearing, judging from his tethered position. Grant's horse or car must be on or near the road. Had Mara deliberately moved the horse to an unseen position?

"Why didn't you leave him at the pool?"

"Because there's a way out on to the road which is nearer home," Mara said unthinkingly, and Jane recoiled in horror at the gleam in smoky eyes.

She breached the chasm hastily. "Olivier told us before he started getting stroppy." His lips tightened grimly and Jane grabbed her throbbing arm. "Ouch, this scrape stings! That was a bad fall when I slipped down the river bank, wasn't it, Mara?"

"Real nasty. It should be taken care of." Mara managed her cue and Jane laughed out loud, in sheer relief.

"We weren't really two helpless women, Grant. Mara had her stock and I—other means, as you noticed!"

Grant stepped closer to scrutinize her arm. "This must be attended to at once. Mara, lead you horse the way you came . . . follow her, Jane, I'll be right back." He turned on his heel and walked in the direction of the glen.

"I'll lead the way." Jane showed Mara where she had slipped. "We're sunk if he questions Olivier. He's gone back for his horse, I suppose."

The redhead bit her lip and walked behind Jane, the horse following meekly. " What possessed me to be so damned inquisitive!" she exploded, as they followed the river.

Jane kept silent. Only Mara herself could find the answer to that and she, Jane, was mostly preoccupied with a bad vision of Grant questioning Olivier. The lies she had told! Her instinct, probably misguided, to protect

Mara had lead to deep deceit would sink farther into morass, Grant, being no one's fool, would ferret until one of them fell into the web of their own making. Now she was in the act of making a further fool of herself as she turned to Mara.

"Mara, if Grant does find out we weren't together, I'll say I was with Olivier and you came to my rescue. Understand? No matter what that man tells him, we stick to that. We'll reason further and say because he hates Grant he'll say that it was you."

Genuine wonder was in green eyes as Mara asked, "Why are you doing this for me?"

Even if Jane could have answered, which she doubted, there was not time, for over Mara's shoulder she saw Grant close behind them. They crossed below the pool and waited for him. He dropped the reins of his horse and studied the two girls.

"Found a more plausible tale to tell, perhaps nearer to the truth?" Two hearts dropped in unison, but his glance at Jane held only curious wonder. "You sure have a knack of muddling into the most awkward situations!"

Jane's face flamed at the reminder of her past encounters with him. "Don't I just!"

A smile tugged his lips. "That was an awesome judo trick you played on him . . . his painful silence when I passed by for my horse proved it! Why did he pick on you?"

Mara looked bravely pathetic as she stepped to Jane's side. "He . . . got fresh with me and grabbed my stock and turned on Jane when she wanted to help me."

Grant's level gaze shuttered from one face to another. "I have a queer notion that I'm being shacked. There's more to this . . . have either of you more to tell, not only for your own sakes but for the safety of other girls, helpless girls who can't defend themselves? Sergeant Mason can deal—"

"Nothing at all!" Jane's immense relief that he had not questioned Olivier and that they had no further reason for lies was only slightly tinged with guilty sympathy for other girls who could not handle Olivier the way she had done. Her gaze flicked to Mara; what might have happened to her if she, Jane, had not appeared on the scene? She had been frightened and that man had acted mighty nasty. . . . Grant interrupted her queasy thoughts.

"Very well, we'll ride back to Bart's house." He legged easily on to his horse and held out a hand to Jane. "Up you get, in front."

She allowed him to seat her, his one arm circling her waist. Every time she had been in an awkward situation this strong arm about her waist had been available. Here it was again, warm around her waist, awakening the fluttering wings in her insides, his chest hard against her back, his breath lifting tendrils of hair to tickle her left ear. Agony and bliss made a strange mixture— another golden opportunity not to waste. Jane closed her eyes and absorbed the comfort and male aura that enfolded her.

Jane turned her head sharply and watched Mara galloping ahead. Grant maintained the silence to the homestead.

Exclamations of concern came from Elizabeth when she saw the muddied state of her offspring and the girl had quite a time of it, trying to reassure her mother that all was well, under the raking eyes of Grant Saxon. Jane took thankful advantage when her aunt shooed her off to a hot, cleansing bath. Janet positively ordered Mara and Grant to stay for supper.

Mara was tidying herself in Jane's room when she returned from the bathroom. The redhead made as if to leave, but Jane invited her to stay. Mara sat down and silence ensued while Jane dressed, and moved aside for her to brush her hair and apply a pale lipstick.

"Please make use of these, and there's powder, if you wish." Jane smiled tentatively offering meager makeup. "It's not up to your standard, but any makeup makes a girl feel less defenseless."

"Thanks," Mara accepted stiffly. Jane waited in silence.

Mara turned at last. "Thanks," she repeated.

"Pleasure. You look better now, not so pale."

Lovely lips twisted in a ghost of a smile; Mara was finding it hard. "I mean, not only for the makeup but— thanks for what you did."

"You would have done likewise," Jane accepted casually.

"Do you really believe that . . . and would you ever find yourself in such a situation?" Mara asked obliquely.

"Never mind, it's safely past!" and Jane held up crossed fingers with a hopeful grin.

After supper they settled on the veranda in the cool half-light and conversation flitted desultorily. "Where's Julius?" Mara asked. Jane thought she looked more attractive without heavy eye makeup, more natural and rather pale, as if she still suffered from shock.

"He left after you suddenly decided to ride off on your own," Grant answered. "For some obscure reason, justified after the event, he seemed worried about you and would have followed. I stopped him. He left later than he intended, and his concern rubbing somewhat, I decided to ride out and meet you. Did you two have a tiff?"

"A slight altercation," Mara began loftily, then continued hotly, "I hate that man, stallion and all!"

"Stallion?" Grant showed surprise at her outburst.

"He suggests I ride Sheik in the contest, next month."

"He's a fine animal, Mara, and you would have to practise like fury to come up to scratch. Julius is very proud of Sheik, he must have confidence in your prowess—"

"Well, I'm not going to accept. It's too far to go backwards and forwards every day, I'm not staying here—and I'm going back to Johannesburg soon. A big fashion do between the houses—I've already accepted a contract."

The silence was electric.

Grant asked softly, heavily, "You're going back to your profession?"

"My usual procedure, isn't it?" Her eyes were intent on him, oblivious to company. "What would you have me do—any suggestions?"

"Plenty!" The violence of reply startled them all. "That place is not good for you. There's never been a dire need, financially, for my brother's wife to display herself to all and sundry. You'll not go back to pollution while there's a solid roof right here in clean, pure, country air!"

Mara smiled suddenly, fondly and wisely, as if some inner knowledge had proved satisfactory.

"Dear Grant, let's not embarrass everyone with our problems. We can discuss your proposition cozily at home, hmm?"

"Very well." His lithe body came upright and he held out a hand to aid her from the deep wicker chair. "Watch that arm, Jane, for infection. Bart, we can still use the horses—"

"No, I insist. Janet and I will run you home as arranged. The horses are taken care of and bedded for the night. Send those chaps with Tom tomorrow morning to ride them back."

"Right." Grant retained Mara's hand in his. "'Night, Elizabeth, Jane."

Mother and daughter stayed on the veranda. The sound of the motor died in the distance.

"Enjoy your outing last night?" Elizabeth asked.

Jane came out of her reverie with a hand to her mouth. "Oh, Mum, with all our gossiping this morning I forgot the latest news. Peter and Pat are going to be married. He proposed to her last night." She recounted the events that led to the proposal.

Elizabeth agreed that they were well suited. "I bet Pat was equally surprised when her medical malarkey achieved the desired effect! Seems to me there's more mischief in the air. Grant was very vehement about Mara not going back to Johannesburg. She's certainly angling for a proposal and the silly man may do just that, if only to keep her settled."

"Mum, one doesn't take such a big step just to keep the other settled! There surely must be love as well, on both sides!"

"Mara doesn't strike me as the sort to bother or give her all for love. No, she's too mercenary. Grant is a good catch any way you look at it, and Mara will get older, as is inevitable, and in her profession you're out once the first wrinkle shows, so she'll want a well feathered nest in advance."

"She's well provided for, Grant mentioned that. She doesn't have to marry for security," Jane protested.

"Some people are like that, the more they've got, the more they want."

For some obscure reason Jane wanted to defend the girl who had insulted her on two occasions within two days; in the study and again at the club. A girl, a woman who felt curiosity and excitement in a man like Flip Olivier; certain women were attracted to the animal aura of men like him. Surely not the well-bred widow of a gentle man, who had everything her heart desired, with one exception . . . and that, too, would shortly be hers, to possess and cherish. Cherish him, Mara Saxon, for I would that I could be in your shoes. . . .

"No, I don't think Mara is like that. Remember, they were sweethearts before she married John and . . . and Grant . . . oh, Mother, talk about something else."

The sudden appeal shook Elizabeth considerably. "My child, how I wish I could help. You do love him, and it hurts desperately, inside?"

Jane rubbed her upper arms, as if seeking comfort. "Silly of me, but beyond my control, and nothing can take it away. Even if I go to the other end of earth it will always be him. If, I mean when they marry I'll have to go—I couldn't bear—" She broke off painfully.

"We'll do that, darling." Elizabeth did not question or probe.

DOCTOR MULLER STUDIED the chart handed to him by his harried assistant. His eyes moved steadfastly down the formidable list.

"Hmm—quite redoubtable."

"Yes, sir, we're running short of antibiotics at this rate." Peter ran impatient fingers through his hair.

"I've put an urgent footnote to the supply order, Peter, and the call to Pretoria should be coming through any moment. Our biggest trouble is shortage of staff since those three nurses contracted the virus. I don't like the way it's spreading right under our noses."

"No, sir. But here we can take precautionary measures—it's the virulent spread in the district that's troubling me."

David agreed. "Davenports' housemaid was brought in yesterday and I've just had a call from Julius . . . his grandmother is poorly. She's not one to complain, but he's worried; characteristic pains, headache, aching limbs, sore throat. The tendency of pneumonia follow-up could be fatal to elderly patients. I'll take a run out there and check. She must have someone in constant attendance."

He rubbed his chin reflectively.

Peter said, "Most of the women in the district have their own household to attend but have offered to help whichever way they can. Pat is busy now, mapping out a plan for the free ones to tour around, spotting possible cases. Mara is on the loose—a bit of forceful persuasion from Grant may help."

"It might," David agreed sceptically and reached for the ringing telephone. "Dr. Muller here."

"David, Jessop has just called here, diagnosed 'flu as you suspected." Julius sounded very worried.

"How is she?"

"Not too good. Jessop gave an injection and left the necessary stuff. He can't supply a nurse for intensive care—this thing has become widespread—can you help?"

"I'm sorry, Julius, three of our nurses are down and Peter and I have been racking our brains. I suggest you contact Grant for two healthy young women, Jane and Mara, either of whom could help you. A sensible person is all you need, not necessarily trained, and you can stand over them, whip and all, to see that doctors' instructions are carried out implicitly. I'll be on call if Jessop is unavailable."

"Jane or Mara? Yes, well, if you're sure there's no one else. My neighbor's with Gran, but she has her duties at home and can't be here all the time."

"Try Grant," David urged the worried man.

"Thanks, I will." The telephone clicked.

TOM HANDED A NOTE to Jane on his arrival. She slit the envelope with mixed feelings; Mara and her complicity had been revealed and this was her walking ticket. No man would continue to employ a deceiving, lying girl as confidential secretary. The note was from Grant.

"Jane: Would you pack a case of clothes, preferably overalls, and be prepared to stay indefinitely? I'm up to my eyeballs with an invasion of influenza amongst the workers and Minna's down as well. Can do? Grant."

A relieved sigh escaped even as she pondered his predicament. It must be bad if Grant wanted her indefinitely. For a painful minute she wondered why things conspired to draw her closer than she wished and then asked herself if that was truth; what was her desire, which was the greater agony—to be closer or to avoid contact? She put the note into her pocket with a decisive movement. He needed her now and she was his to command. She instructed Tom to find himself a cup of coffee and whirled into the house to pack.

The study being deserted when she arrived, she instructed Tom to leave her case on the veranda and walked through the house to the kitchen. A slightly dishevelled Mara invited her to a cup of coffee and cigarette. Jane poured her coffee and sat down on the opposite side of the kitchen table, glancing around at the disorder of Minna's normally spotless domain. Mara inhaled sharp puffs of smoke.

"So what, I haven't a clue where to start, and Grant just disappeared."

"Have you and he had breakfast, and how is Minna?" asked Jane.

"Grant made toast and coffee and told me to help myself. He gave Minna some pills, she's sleeping, and that wretched maid, Polly, hasn't turned up yet. Now I'm supposed to make jelly and cook up barley water for Minna—he didn't even wait to tell me where the stuff is, never mind how to make it!" Mara's cigarette glowed fiercely.

Jane put the cup down and leaned her hands flat on

the table. "You can make a bed and dust? Well, do that and I'll pop in to Minna to see if all's well. Then I'll do the jelly, barley and clean up here. Polly will come in due course if she's not ill too, and so will Grant. By then we'll be ready for further instructions. Okay?"

When the big man walked through the open kitchen door later on he was met by the usual sparkle of shining cleanliness plus a delectable fragrance of peppercorn and bay leaves in the steak and kidney simmering on the stove. Cups were set in readiness for tea.

"Good work, Jane," he said gratefully.

"Good morning, Grant."

"Now, I'd appreciate for you two girls to be on call in case we can't manage. I'll try to find help with the household chores. We may need you in the sick bay. Seven employees are down with 'flu and more show symptoms. The mission is crowded—I'll phone David and find out what the chances are of moving them. We must put a stop to spreading infection. Both of you must take precautions when attending Minna—" the telephone stopped further instructions.

He came back with set lips. "Sandy is coming home; in fact she'll be here any moment; the schools have closed for the duration of what could well be an epidemic, and Angus McDonald called for his children at four this morning. He took upon himself to bring Sandy, being neighborly and a sensible man."

Almost on cue, a car stopped in the drive and Sandy jumped straight into Jane's arms. Angus, lean and freckled, was rueful when he heard he had brought the child from "the fat to the fire." Grant assured him he would have fetched her anyway, she was as safe here as conditions permitted. He thanked Angus for his forethought in saving himself a long trip. A quick cup of coffee and the McDonald clan were away home.

Sandy clung to Jane's hand after a quick, perfunctory

greeting to Mara and Grant, and was gravely concerned over her darling Toicky. Mara kept glancing at her small daughter, who seemed to prefer Jane to her relatives. Sudden perceptiveness made her aside to Grant anxious. "Isn't Sandy rather flushed, Grant?"

Jane's keen ears heard; she had noticed the flushed face but had passed it off as excitement at coming home so unexpectedly. Now she took a closer look and casually passed her hand across Sandy's forehead, brushing back the russet hair. Sandy sneezed explosively into her hand. "'Scuse me, Jane, the dust's made my throat sore 'n it was very hot. Can we go fishing tomorrow?"

Three adults exchanged glances over her excited head. Mara said, "Come along, Sandy, I've got a nice pink pill for that sneeze, you can take it and lie on your bed for today and then it will clear away."

"All day in bed by myself on such a—a grand day!" Sandy stamped a small foot, utterly unlike her normal, happy self.

Mara consoled, "I'll sit with you, dear," with a slight edge of irritation. The child sensed it immediately and her warm hand clutched Jane's hand spasmodically.

"Jane must—Jane can sit with me, then I'll be good— I promise. . . ."

Grant said firmly, "Very well, Jane can sit with you for just a little while. The office is closed today, but Jane has come to help the sick people. So be a good girl and help us by following instructions."

Jane walked with the youngster to her room and helped her undress. She became calmer in her bed and asked for her favorite books. While they chatted Jane's thoughts hovered back to the expression on Mara's face when Sandy insisted on Jane's company; a strange mixture of relief and injured ego . . . she hoped Sandy's preference would not further the enmity Mara had shown to her. So far there had been no insulting remarks this morning; there hadn't been time! Since the Olivier episode Mara was more subdued; maybe the shock of Grant appearing so suddenly on the scene had jerked her to a semblance of normality.

Jane heard the telephone in the lounge ring demandingly. It stopped and Grant's answering voice was muffled by distance. Shortly after the call, the raised tones of Mara's angry voice came clearly through the open door of Sandy's room.

"I absolutely refuse—I can't stand the man, he's a roughneck and I detest him!" Even her footsteps sounded angry as she walked toward her room.

"There's no one else. You will go and pull your weight in this crisis." Grant passed her door and entered Sandy's room. "Give poppet this capsule now, Jane, another in three hours' time." Mara's bedroom door slammed hard and his eyebrows drew grimly. "Julius has asked for help—his grandmother has caught this wretched thing."

Jane was concerned. "She's an absolute darling—oh, I do hope she has the stamina to fight the virus."

"Doctor Jessop called there, gave her an injection and capsules, but Julius needs a woman to tend her and the only available one seems to be Mara."

"You're sending Mara? Can she—I mean, I could go. I know—"

Mara stood at the door of Sandy's room, in a flaming temper that made her wild and beautiful and her teeth actually gritted as she cut across at Jane.

"You know what, Jane Wheeler?—do tell! That I'm incapable of caring for the sick and you're more capable and superior? I can look after Minna, Sandy or Mrs. D. just as well as any nit!" She turned to Grant. "She can go and I'll stay here."

Sandy's eyes grew large at the display of temper and

words. "No, Jane, please don't go away," she pleaded urgently.

"That's enough." The tall man stepped forward with a firm hand on Mara's arm to guide her back to her room. "Pack your things. Julius will be here at noon and you will accompany him, to care for Mrs. Davenport to the best of your ability. Upsetting the child is not going to do her good."

Mara's voice lowered to a wheedling tone, but Jane heard her say, quite clearly, "You may not know it, darling, but your *capable* Jane is quite gone on Julius. So why spoil her fun? You saw how eagerly she offered to go in my place, and Sandy will soon settle down with me when she's gone."

Jane gasped at the audacious lie and held her breath. A short space of silence followed, and then Grant said, evenly, "Sandy needs Jane at present. Julius needs a woman to help, not make love, so any selfish desires or grand passions can be suppressed for the duration of the illness. I'm needed at the sick bay, no more tantrums or arguments. Be ready for Julius!" His footsteps faded and stillness descended.

JANE WAS IN the dining room, deep in thought, wondering if a place should be set for Julius when Mara walked in.

She said, elaborately casual, "That remark about you and Julius—I thought it might persuade Grant to send you, instead of me. No go, nothing works when Saxon's mind is made up. I hate the thought of going." She evidently meant this explanation sufficient apology.

Jane bit back a hot retort and concentrated on placing the cutlery. There had been enough rumpus without prolonging this particular subject.

"I'm setting a place for Julius."

"I couldn't care less. You have my full collaboration to shove poison in his salad." Mara studied a fingernail. "You're probably dying for us to depart, so that you can have Grant to yourself."

"Don't be an idiot, Mara!" Jane retorted spiritedly. "There's work to be done, remember? The world doesn't start and end with larking around with some male."

"Keep it that way, with this particular male," Mara advised mildly and seated herself with a magazine.

The noon Highveld news was on the air. Four new cases of influenza were reported in Kiepersol, a batch of nurses were on their way from Pretoria to relieve the overworked Nelspruit staff.

The Davenport car rolled into the driveway. Grant unwound from the passenger seat, Julius from behind the wheel, and the two men vaulted the steps and entered the lounge.

They sat down to lunch and Grant and Julius discussed the whys and wherefores of measures taken to combat further outbreaks of influenza. Taken by itself, with all the antibiotics available, it was not the danger; that lay in carelessness of the victims contracting pneumonia. The consequent shortage of man-power put extra responsibilities on the shoulders of the healthy ones. Julius turned suddenly to Jane.

"Still love me, honey?" His eyes slid to Grant. "How about a swap, cobber?"

Wood-smoke eyes darkened as Grant studied the astonishing blush on Jane's cheeks. Mara's color rose as well, at Julius's obvious preference of company. A "dog-in-the-manger" assumption that, though she herself did not want to go, the idea that anyone should show preference to another was something that shook her ego badly.

"Grant would prefer that, but Sandy's taken such a shine to Jane that we felt it's best to humor her." Her green eyes dared Grant to deny it.

"I thought you wanted a nurse for Gran?" Grant's cynical look circled to Julius. He ignored Mara's remark.

"Indeed I do, but she does sleep, at times." Julius, unperturbed, gazed at Jane's flaming cheeks and her open, astonished lips.

"Well, Jane, if there was a choice, which would you prefer?" Grant's deep voice reached out with mocking, maddening coolness.

Jane tore her eyes from the cool steel of his gaze and flicked Julius a sweetly venomous smile. She said, "Someone—I can't think who, mentioned that passions and selfish desires should be suppressed for the duration."

"Is that so?" Julius looked surprised and perturbed. "That can only mean that when this emergency's overcome there'll be a lovely epidemic of suppressed desires catching fire all over the countryside!"

"Picture the holocaust," Grant said drily.

"Hot and beautiful! Oh well, dreams aside, I think we should be pushing off, Mara."

Jane pushed back her chair. "And I must take Minna and Sandy some baked custard—it's capsule time as well. Goodbye, Mara, Julius . . . give Mrs. D. my love and wishes for a speedy recovery."

"She'll recover with remarkable speed if I have any say in the matter!" Mara stalked to the bedroom for some last minute toiletry.

Grant came in late that evening, tired and grim-faced, and told Jane, at the supper table, that they were fortunate in having provided for just such an emergency, having a sick bay and well-stocked medical supplies.

After supper he disappeared in the direction of the office. Jane gave Polly a hand with the dishes, then settled Sandy and Minna for the night. Jane walked through the quiet house. On the veranda, she heard her typewriter clicking erratically in the study. She walked softly to the open door and watched Grant's clumsy efforts. Amusement touched her lips as he, aware of her presence, became more frustrated and banged the wrong keys. Finally he stopped completely to glare at her with dark-fringed Irish eyes. Jane moved to stand beside him, changing her amusement to a superior smile.

"Move over, boss, let someone who knows do the job." She nudged his shoulder none too gently and he moved with meek alacrity, to watch his efficient secretary in grateful awe as she inserted a clean sheet and ran her eyes over his notes . . . The last line typed, Jane looked up in time to see him stealthily slipping roughly scrawled paper on the opposite side to the one she had just completed.

"Oh—do you mind, Jane? Here's another one, it's got to be posted tomorrow—rather urgent, you know. You must be tired and it's an imposition, but—"

"Give, it won't take long when one can use all one's fingers. Go smoke your pipe, you're holding me up." Jane took the paper without looking up and so missed the strange expression that flitted across the man's face: Fortunately, for it might have demoralised her to the extent of complete inefficiency!

She addressed and stamped the envelopes, covered her machine and walked out, to sit on the low wall of the veranda with Grant, her head resting against a supporting pillar. The soft night breeze lifted her hair with caressing fingers while starshine gave her face the purity of marble and amber eyes a glistening, mysterious depth.

The minutes ticked by . . . (his arms were encircling her body, his warm breath was mingling with hers, he was speaking soft words of love, words that her heart longed to hear.)

"Jane, wake up, you'll fall off your perch. Jane!" She came out of her beautiful world as his hand touched her shoulder and his admonition reached her ears. Her legs lowered off the wall and her body came upright as she lifted eyes that were clouded with dreams. Grant put his hands on her arms.

"Jane, wake up. You look like a bewitched high priestess." He shook her gently. "Snap out of it, girl, you make me feel peculiar—are you all right?"

Her eyes focused as dreams departed, forcing back reality.

"Sorry, Grant—my mind seems to have left my body for a space of time. So peaceful and beautiful." Jane stepped back, out of the clasp of his hands. "Didn't you feel something, a space of time suspended in eternity?"

"I looked at you and you were cast in marble—as if indeed your soul had left your body, and I felt an urgent need to call you back." Grant shrugged broad shoulders as if he felt an entangling web. "Don't go all psychic on me, Jane. It gives me eerie shivers. I think we're both tired. But a cup of hot tea would go down well before staggering off to bed."

Jane said, through lips that had stiffened to meet reality, "That shivery feeling was in anticipation of again rescuing my clumsy self from another fall, this time from the wall."

Grant looked curiously at her. "You were dreaming. Did Julius match your ideals?"

"Julius?" Jane looked dazed.

"A girl usually dreams about the one nearest her heart."

"Now, how could you guess that, not being a girl?"

she hedged, unable to meet his statement with honesty. Let him believe anything about her and Julius, it mattered not a scrap to him of whom she dreamed. "You've been reading too many romantic novels, boss," she quipped flippantly.

"Did you dream about him, Jane?" Grant ignored her flippancy.

"No, I hadn't got that far—when you woke me." That wasn't a lie, she comforted herself; Julius might just possibly have come into her dream later, as best man! She turned away sharply. "I'll make the tea."

Grant shut the study door and followed her to the kitchen. He sat on the edge of the table and remained there when she finally handed him a cup of strong tea.

"I'll take mine to bed, Grant. I love sipping tea in bed, one of my many vices. Good night."

"Good night, Jane. Pleasant continuation of dreams," he called after her.

She steadied the cup in her hand while words tumbled inside; your humor would fade pretty quick, Grant Saxon, if you knew how close I came tonight, when I opened my eyes to see you so near, to throw myself in your arms and confess how deeply I love you.

Only you, dearest Grant . . . Jane drifted into tired sleep.

CHAPTER ELEVEN

"I'VE BROUGHT YOUR early morning vice, ma'am." Jane opened her eyes, saw him at the foot of her bed, tray in hand. Her hair tumbled back as she leapt out of bed, to jump back instantly as she awoke fully to embarrassed awareness of her flimsy shortie-pajamas.

He laughed and walked to the door. "I'll leave you to drink without offending modest instincts."

Jane waited for his footsteps to recede to a safe distance before jumping out of bed. The next half hour whirled by in a flurry as she showered, dressed in her neat mauve overall, brushed shining nut-brown hair into a severe bun on the nape of her neck, admonished Sandy to stay put while she flew to Minna's room, to apologize contritely for being so late.

Minna smiled weakly. "I really am sorry to cause all this extra work for you. I'm feeling much better today, only a bit shaky. Perhaps if I get up—"

"Nothing doing, my good woman!" Jane drew the curtains and turned to fluff the pillows. "We'll see what Grant says—he may allow you to sit in that cozy chair, later. You're not to worry about the work. We're coping and it's a break for me, really, from office work. You're certainly more efficient and I'll run fast enough for advice if snags crop up, Mrs. Du Toit."

"You may call me Minna—Jane—if I may call you by your first name. You're being very good to me."

Jane smiled at her and went off to see to her breakfast.

Breakfast over, she started on the bedrooms. In Grant's room she hesitated a full minute to allow her eyes to roam the room, taking in the neat austerity of bachelordom. Jane ran the duster over the wardrobe doors, dressing-table and stopped at the bedside table-cum-desk. Slowly she lifted the framed photograph.

So this was John Saxon. He looked down at the up-turned face of his wife with complete adoration. Slightly fairer that his brother, the lineament of his features showed distinct traces of an aesthetic dreamer. Mara gazed back at him with a small smile on her lips, glamorously photogenic.

Studying him closely, Jane's heart ached for the remaining brother, motherless and fatherless, and now the grief of losing a beloved brother. "Dear Grant, may you find the comfort that is God-given, and may she contribute her share of bringing and giving joy and happiness for both of you." She closed her eyes in an effort to visualize the man in the photograph. The face of Grant was imposed too strongly, so Jane wiped the frame and glass carefully, replaced it in position.

The telephone summoned and it was Julius. "Hi, Jane. Checking on the state of affairs—how's everybody?"

"Julius, I'm glad you phoned. We're all fine. Sandy hasn't caught it, thank goodness. Gran, how is she—and Mara?"

"Gran's tummy gave her hell yesterday and practically all night. She's as weak as a kitten today, But I think the worst is over, her temp is normal. Mara—well, I feel sorry for her. For the uninitiated it's not pleasant, especially nursing an old person, but she's been super and I'm fantastically surprised at the grit she's shown."

Jane sympathized. "I do hope it's over for the old dear now, Julius, and I fully agree that Mara deserves a medal." She sensed a presence and turned to see Grant leaning against the wall, his arms folded across his chest.

"Are you still with me, Jane?" Julius reminded in her ear.

"Yes, what was I saying? Oh yes—even trained nurses would find it distasteful, and her spirit is to be admired. I've got off lightly and Julius, Grant is here now if you want to speak to him."

"Actually Mara wants a word with him. She still hates my guts, although recent events almost made us sort of buddies, if you get my meaning! Right, Jane, put him on. Just a minute—any signs of the little green devil and—here comes Mara—tell me loud and clear how much you care for me, my little brown dove?"

Jane laughed and colored under the direct scrutiny of disturbing eyes. "Really, Julius! This is a party line! No signs of what you asked, and . . . well, I have a great regard for you—"

Grant levered himself from the wall and started to walk away.

"Grant!" Jane clutched the phone to her breast. He turned. "J-Julius wants to speak to you." She held the instrument the length of her arm. Grant walked back and took it from her, eyeing her flushed face with a gray, glacial stare.

"A great pity party lines aren't visual. Local biddies would derive ultimate pleasure—yes, Julius, you've put a becoming blush on tender cheeks and only I can see the delightful confusion—how regrettable. Now the maiden has stampeded in graceful retreat. What do you want with me?"

The deriding voice followed Jane and turned her ears a vivid puce. "I really do positively hate Grant Saxon at times," her lips moved angrily. "He's so sarcastic, horrid and—his bossiness is enough to shrivel any love a body might have—like a chameleon, nice one minute and then a Jekyll and Hyde—he makes me boil!" She tidied the magazines with precise angry hands—and realized she could hear every word that was being voiced.

"Hullo, sweetie. Why not—but you are, darling."

Saccharin and honey dripped from his tongue and the listener at the magazine rack muttered wordlessly, "Humbugging, Mara, watch it!"

"Everyone's doing fine—keeping an eye on Sandy, so far merely a sniffle. Hmm?—she's still here and kept busy—we'll see about that. She's just spoken to Julius— eavesdropping? That's nasty and I don't imagine she can hear what you're saying, so carry right on."

Jane made for the door leading to the veranda, her breast throbbing with a mixture of indignation and guilt. She was not interested in their honeyed talk and didn't care a fig what Mara was saying!

AFTER THE EVENING MEAL Grant once again made for the study. Jane cleared the table, helped Polly with the washing up and then walked out to study the closed door with curiosity. She longed to be with him, if only to help, but that door looked too forbidding, evidence that he wished to be undisturbed. She smoked one cigarette then went inside, bathed, brushed her hair and climbed into bed feeling weary, at odds with herself and the rest of the world. The sooner she decided on a definite course the better for her peace of mind; the bittersweet, close association in this house must end. Jane crossed her arms under her head and, under closed lids, a vision of a tanned, arrogant face and steel-gray eyes floated unchecked. Yes, far better to leave; distance would dim the picture, other work would numb, crush the yearning for. reciprocated tenderness. Before she made a complete fool of herself.

Tomorrow she would ask—no—she would tell him to replace her in the office. She would plan her future. A future in which Grant Saxon did not figure. . .

CHAPTER TWELVE

MINNA DUT TOIT was up and about. Sandy ran to meet Jane with her quota of healthy spirit and vigor and Polly's mother was back on duty, so Jane found herself back at the desk in the study. In Grant's absence—he was somewhere on the Estate—she tidied up the disorder of papers and found sufficient work to keep her busy till noon. He worked with her in the afternoon and just before closing time Jane set a firm chin and asked for five minutes of his time and attention.

Grant studied the set of her chin calculatingly. "Any chap with half a brain can reckon on a troublesome five minutes, if that chin's anything to go by," he sighed. "Fire away."

"I'd appreciate it very much if you would find a replacement for me as soon as possible, please."

"May I know the reason for this sudden wish to leave? Salary not good enough?"

"It's the best salary I've ever earned," Jane admitted.

"Well then, do I have to drag it out of you . . . what is or are your reasons?" Grant looked impatiently down at the paper on his desk.

"I have my reasons, private reasons." Jane felt stubborn and more foolish in the face of his impatience.

"Private? Hmm . . . like Julius, for instance?" Grant lifted wintry gray eyes briefly.

What could she say; that the sole reason was himself and her love for him? She should have planned her strategy beforehand. "He might just be one of the reasons!" came recklessly from her lips.

"I see. Respect and trust for an employer is not evidently to be considered." Grant held her defiant, mute stare for a coolly controlled space of time, and then shrugged a shoulder resignedly. "As you wish, Miss Wheeler. You'll kindly continue as usual until I advise you of the termination of your services."

"Grant!" Jane took a step toward him.

"Yes?" His eyes were blank, enigmatic.

"Please, I apologize if I've disappointed or angered you. I'm behaving very badly, but won't you just take my word that I would like to leave, without any special reason?" Her appeal came from the heart. He stared at her as if studying an alien specimen. "Please stay friends with me and understand."

Genuine puzzlement ousted the coldness from his eyes. "Other times I've known what to understand, but this . . . ! Friends are made for confidences."

Heartened by the warmer look Jane stumbled eagerly, "Grant, please accept that . . . it's something within me, something that must be withheld even from a close friend. . . ." she stammered to a tongue-tied stillness and watched him take a cigarette and light it smoothly and silently. Her voice calmed. "It has nothing to do with the Estate. I've been happy here and everybody's been very good to me, but I guess I'm what they call a career girl. There's no future here. I'd like to try my wings alone and farther afield. As for Julius—"

"He might clip them before you even find the chance to flutter them." A small smile played at the corners of his mouth. "I wouldn't have typed you exactly a career girl."

"How would you type me, then?"

"I haven't considered seriously, to be frank." As he was ordinarily a man of quick judgement, that bland statement hit Jane like a blow in her solar plexus; She was of such little account that he hadn't even bothered to "type" her! Grant continued almost absentmindedly, "But a random guess types you as a potential homebody, requiring a firm hand to guide and keep you out of mischief."

"Thank you very much! Your random guesses aren't always right on," Jane felt compelled to point out.

Grant's attractive smile framed very white, healthy teeth. "Time will tell. The agency at Nelspruit will give prompt and friendly service in the matter of supplying—replacement. Girls falling over each other for a job like this." He started to rustle the papers on his desk.

Jane walked back to her chair feeling inexplicably dampened by his noncommittal acceptance of her resignation. It mattered not greatly who did the office work as long as the female was fairly efficient. Oh well, she had asked for it and hadn't expected him to fall at her feet, begging her to stay because she was absolutely indispensable, highly valued or irreplaceable! A sad hollow made a lonely vacuum under her ribs and gave a disconsolate droop to her mouth when she forgot to guard her expression. She forgot quite frequently and, after a miserable time had passed, happened to raise her eyes to find Grant watching her quizzically.

"Do cheer up, lass. You look as if you have one big tummy ache," he said, densely unfeeling. "Mara's coming back tomorrow and Julius sent word that he'd be obliged if I slacken up on you. He desires some of your time and has much to tell you. That should cheer you up somewhat."

Which good cheer only made the hollow echo deeper against her backbone. "It sure does, he's a nice guy," Jane said sourly.

"Well, blow me down, the child sounds like doom. No joyous bells ringing, no butterflies fluttering?"

She managed a watery smile and Grant suddenly scraped back his chair, threw the heavy ledger on his desk and strode purposely toward her. Jane's eyes widened like a startled fawn when he gripped her arm and drew her to her feet. "Come on, Doc Saxon will supply the remedy. A dash of purifying air through hair and clouded brain." She was steered firmly through the door, down the steps and around to the back of the house. He bundled her into the car, and by the time Jane had recovered her breath they were out of the gates and away!

"My purse," she gasped weakly.

"To blazes with your purse. Unpin your hair and get set!" Grant pressed a button and the hood retreated smoothly to an invasion of late summer breezes which made of Jane's hair a flying silky pennant.

Up and up the winged monster flew, rounding hairpin turns and twisted pine-edged ribbons of road, down into breathtaking fairy valleys, verdant and lush with nature's bounty.

And then they were in a wide cleared space with a high steel structure towering above them. "Lookout tower." Grant switched off and looked at his windblown passenger. "Care for a bird's eye view, touslehead?"

The keen-eyed African keeper walked smartly to greet them. He had his own shack here and did constant patrol work. Jane felt quite breathless when she reached the top of the steep stairway and peeved at the ease and normal breathing of her companion as they stood on the high platform. The view was superb.

"Headache gone?" queried Grant.

Yes, her headache had gone. In the clear air, high above petty worries, who could not but feel exhilarated and cleansed. Of course, it could depend immensely on one's company; and whom would she wish for but the very one at her side?

Grant took the return journey at a leisurely pace and the evening star winked brightly at her paler satellites as they drew up behind a familiar stationary car in the driveway of Bart's home. "Julius, I do declare," Grant mused, with a sidelong glance at Jane. His hand fluttered an inch from the material covering her left breast. "Heart fluttering like a caged birdie?" He laughed at her indignant denial and mostly at her involuntary gesture of protecting her body from his hovering hand. "It's all right, honey, I only touch what's mine." He moved his arm across to open her door and Jane only just caught his murmured, "Very tempting, though . . . oh, strength, where is thy weakness!"

Mara waited languidly on the top step. Her green eyes were not so languid as they strayed from Jane's confusion to the tall figure of the man who walked toward her. "Hi, Grant," she said softly, reproachfully, and waited for him to reach the step below her. Two slim arms fondled across his shoulders and the man's hands lifted to encircle her waist.

Jane walked past them with a dazzling smile for Julius while her mind churned on six little words . . . "I only touch what is mine."

Julius had no such inhibitions. She was enveloped in a bear hug.

"Darling Jane! I was beginning to despair of ever seeing you again. We've been waiting ages. Minna told us Grant took you home and what do we find? No Jane, no boss. My thoughts were sadly following the elopement and dear Mara was just trying to console my great loss, by begging me to receive her affection to replace a lost love, when you materialized. Saved by the gong!"

Mara tore her green gaze from Grant's face long enough to glare at Julius. "If present company can believe that pretty speech then they don't know the shyster, or are themselves solid bone from the neck up!

"And where were you two this afternoon?" she demanded of Grant and Jane.

"Above the planets, touching the silver lining of a puffball," said Grant.

Mara's eyes flicked from his face to that of the quiet girl next to him. Her eyebrows arched with sarcasm. "Your poetic strategy may lure a little mackerel, darling," a sideways slant of her lashes at Jane. "I know them so well—was the puffball gratifying?"

"Absolutely, wholly satisfying." Grant lighted two cigarettes, passed one to Jane and drew deeply on the one between his brown fingers. "The silver came off on our fingers, never to be erased in our lifetime."

Bart came to join them. "Grant, I have some information from Sergeant Mason—could you spare a moment?"

"Surely." Grant excused himself and followed Bart inside.

"Flip Olivier is wanted for robbery, in Nelspruit. He managed to evade the police and all cars were stopped at a roadblock. A salesman admitted to giving a man of Olivier's description a lift. He got worried at the wild manner of the man and, on the spur of the moment, told him he, the salesman, would have to return to the hotel for an imaginary briefcase. The man muttered angrily and ordered him to let him off at that spot. The police believe he's headed this way. The sergeant is aware of his hatred for you and phoned your place. You weren't there, so he asked me to pass on the message, to be on your guard in case Olivier gets nasty. Derek Cross—you know him—his house was entered by an open bathroom window, quite a few valuables stolen."

Grant rubbed his chin. "Thanks, Bart. Wonder what made Olivier turn to robbery? A private house—hmm, I know the Cross family. Olivier is the type to seek vengeance when cornered, or when he imagines he's been ill-used. We'll have to do something about the womenfolk if the police haven't tracked him yet . . . I'll contact them at home. Keep a wary watch this end until you hear from me. Liza and Jane must stay at home tomorrow . . . I'll send Tom over tonight when I reach home, as an extra precaution. That day when I brought Mara and Jane home in such a dishevelled condition . . . they had a nasty encounter with Olivier . . . I'll find the whole truth from Mara if I have to torture her!" They walked back and Grant decided to leave immediately because Minna and Sandy were alone in his house. He cut short Julius's protest. "I'll take Mara home if you'd like to visit longer, Julius. A good idea because Bart can pass on the message from Sergeant Mason and you can contact your home as a precautionary measure. I must go now . . . thanks for the supper. Come on, Mara."

She was hustled into the car and swerved away in a flurry of gravel.

"What gives with the sudden haste?" Janet was intrigued.

"Nothing to worry about . . . I hope." Bart drew on his pipe, related the doings of Flip Olivier and Grant's instructions for safety measures. "The police may have tracked him by now, but if not, he has a grudge against Grant and therefore it may involve us. The mind of a man like Olivier works in devious ways, and that encounter Jane and Mara had with him will rankle in a wild mind." His eyes were on his niece. "The story is that he got fresh with you two and you used a bit of judo on him before Grant arrived on the scene?"

"Yes . . . Uncle," Jane answered. A shudder of apprehension went through as she recalled the man's nasty attitude and Grant's contemptuous order for him to leave the vicinity. A robbery put him outside the pale and his jealous, vicious mind would fasten on the estate owner as the cause of his downfall. Would Mara, in view of this latest development, confess the true details of that

ugly encounter in the woods to Grant? Jane had an urge
to tell her uncle all about it, but decided to await events.
The police might have caught him already, so there
would be no point in clarifying Mara's strange presence
with him. The truth was, Jane was still puzzled herself at
Mara's lack of propriety.

The burglar was forgotten as Jane lay in bed that
night. Her thoughts dwelt on Grant and Mara. When
would they announce their engagement . . . or
wedding . . . and why was he procrastinating . . . . Were
there still snags concerning a man marrying his
brother's widow? The way Mara had greeted Grant
showed clearly that she was determined on a showdown
and she had affected dislike for Julius in no mean terms.
Julius could forget about his vow to alienate her affections. If only the Saxons would declare their alliance it
would spur Jane on in her decision to leave . . . she was
only prolonging the agony of being near to him, allowing herself the exquisite torture of his sudden, lovable
traits of concern . . . like today when he hustled her out
for a breath of mountain air. Why didn't she stop being
a weakling for punishment, pack her bags and get out?
Why wait for the pain of their announcement? Jane sat
up and pounded her pillow to a softer bolster for an
aching head.

JANE WAS OUTSIDE, breathing fresh morning air, when
the Land Rover stopped in front of the house and
Grant's long stride covered the distance between them
with swift east. He saluted her with a hand on the brim
of his disreputable hat and Jane invited him in for a cup
of coffee. Janet and Elizabeth were at the kitchen table,
lingering over cups of aromatic coffee; the boys were
with their father in the backlands, taking care to keep
the house under careful surveillance.

The big man straddled a chair and Jane placed his coffee on the table.

"Thanks." A generous helping of sugar followed. "No sign of our vagabond. I doubt that he's in this vicinity. It's too hot for him. In his boots I'd streak clear across the country."

"Then I may as well get back to work . . . there's stacks waiting. Have you come to fetch me?" Jane looked down at her faded jeans and loosely hanging shirt.

"If you would, Jane. That's why I've come. Mara is edgy about the job she promised to do in Johannesburg. I can't take her all the way and won't allow her to drive alone, so the only thing to do is drive her as far as Nelspruit and put her on the train. A couple of hours and I'll be back. You needn't change, that rig's serviceable and you still have clothes at my place. I'm taking further advantage in asking you to stay on again until the scare is over or until Mara gets back, whichever's the shortest length of time."

"Sure, I'll do that," Jane said quietly.

Jane managed to wade through the stacks of work on her desk that had stealthily piled up in her short absence. She then took a breather by walking outside in the immediate surroundings of the house, keeping in mind Grant's explicit warning to all of them not to wander out of sight. She didn't feel like Mara or Sandy's company, or anyone's presence. She eventually walked into the house and met no one en route to the bathroom, showered and changed into fresh undies, green linen frock with saddle-stitching and thonged sandals. Her hair was brushed with uninterested ministration into a ponytail and she was not conscious that this severe style defined the pure lines of cheek and brow as no elaborate coiffure could.

Grant followed her into the dining-room where Mara and Sandy were waiting. He too looked freshly showered and virile in brown slacks, silk shirt and cravat. Minna, who was now fully recovered, put finishing touches to the serving dishes on the sideboard, from where the family usually helped themselves and did so now.

"Who were you speaking to on the phone, Grant?" Mara asked. "I was dressing so couldn't answer and then I heard you talking."

"Did you follow the gist of my conversation?"

"Of course not. One can't hear from behind a closed bedroom door."

"Well then, I'll tell you." Grant lowered his soup plate and sat down. "My talk was with someone who, most conveniently, will save you a trip by train."

"Someone going through by car? That will be fine. Who, Grant?

"None other than Julius Davenport. He's taking Granny for a check-up and we'll meet him at the crossroads and you'll be whisked off to your destination after he offloads the kids at their hostel . . . what's the matter, you look explosive?"

"I feel explosive. Why must it be that damned man, he's been in my hair far too much. I'd rather travel by train!" Mara exclaimed angrily.

Grant was amused. "Come now, girl, Julius is a fine chap and he sent a special promise to treat you gently and behave in a manner dear to the sensitive hearts of Victorian misses. After all, Granny will be with you."

"Oh, did he! I don't know which is the lesser of two evils . . . a trip by train or a few hours in obnoxious company." Mara drummed her fingers while Jane and Minna passed the roast and vegetables. "Excluding Granny, of course. I'll go with him only because she'll be with us and your mind will be easier. I know you always worry when I travel alone and he can save you considerable time and miles by taking the kids as well. And Jane need not stay here with Sandy and me away."

"Actually I'd prefer for her to stay, until Olivier is apprehended. Can't risk him accosting Tom on the road unless I personally take over the transportation."

"She can surely stay at home until the roads are safe?" Her bored question hid a slight crack of green anger.

"This is my busy time. I need Jane."

The following morning Grant passed on the news that the boys and Sandy would not be going back after all until a full complement of healthy children returned and no further outbreaks of 'flu were reported. He and Mara left soon after breakfast, with his promise to be back as quickly as time permitted. He had hesitated at the car door with his gray gaze on Sandy and Jane. "Would you two care to come along for the ride?"

"Yes, please!" Sandy dashed down the steps, but Jane stood her ground.

"Thanks, no, There's plenty of work for me, remember?" Jane waved to Sandy and walked purposefully to the office. Mara's affronted stare, at Grant's impulsive offer, floated between pages of calculations and notes. . . .

Such was her concentration that the piles of work lessened rapidly and shortly after lunch were satisfactorily completed. Jane walked to the kitchen in search of the housekeeper. Minna was setting out the tea cups.

They sat at the table and Minna enjoyed her occasional cigarette with Jane. "Minna," she said, wondering why she suddenly wanted to know, from this woman, something about the Saxon affairs, and if Minna Du Toit would deem it unseemly to discuss her employer. "Minna, was Mara really engaged to Grant—before she married John?"

Minna's questioning glance shifted from Jane's face to the tip of her cigarette, thoughtfully. She knew, instinctively, that this sudden probe would go further than one innocent question, she either had to answer that one and others or refuse to discuss the situation completely.

"Grant and Mara weren't exactly engaged, there was a sort of understanding. They've been friends from childhood and we—everyone took it for granted—you know how people are?"

"But weren't they in love with each other?" Jane wasn't sure now if she wanted to hear an affirmative answer or a denial and became confused and sorry that she had started the question. "Please don't answer if you think I'm prying into things that don't concern me. I won't mind at all."

Minna smiled at her companion's sudden shrinking. "It's all right, dear, the Saxon affairs are common knowledge and it all happened ages ago—I mean that part of it. What's to come no one but themselves know—at least, Grant believes he has a promise to fulfill." Minna's face became strangely sad, as if with some secret memory.

"Just talk about the family," said Jane. "What were his parents like? Did you know them well and were Grant and John nice little boys or utter devils?"

Minna sighed. "Mr. and Mrs. Saxon were a charming pair, and John was lively but sort of dreamy too. Grant was the little rapscallion—not what they call delinquent these days—full of lively curiosity about everything living and growing and happening. Their father passed away first and Mrs. Saxon did a mighty fine job of rearing her two boys to manhood. They loved her, especially Grant—I mean he showed his love more than John who was more reserved and sort of secretive. Mrs.

Saxon died after Grant came back from university, he passed degrees in agriculture and forestry or whatever it's called. He worked like a trojan on the Estate, it wasn't so big as now, and was with his mother when she had a heart attack and died in his arms. He went sort of grim after that and didn't laugh and enjoy life as he did before. I expect John felt as deeply, but he was away at college and we didn't see much of him until he came back and married Mara."

Jane sighed. A clear picture of the young Grant formed; unruly dark hair, gray questing eyes and a laughing mouth that became firm with grief and responsibilities. The image was stamped on her mind, never to be erased.

Minna said, "I was Nanny to Miss Mara. She and the household kept me busy, so I really can't tell you more about the Saxons. A real tomboy she was, and Grant and John were her constant playmates, Grant more so because John would come over, find a book and live a world of his own. Mara spent a lot of her time here too . . . what a time I had with that one!" She forebore to follow up that last statement and Jane did no more prompting.

"Grant escorted Mara to the odd entertainments, but she was often mad at him for not bending a knee at her every beck and call and for preferring to "slave," as she called it, on the Estate. She eventually left to take up a course in modelling, and did extremely well. As she was the only girl that Grant really noticed, we naturally presumed they would marry, and it surprised most of us when she suddenly showed preference for young John when he came home for three months." Minna looked through the window with a remembering, rather grim gaze. "Perhaps I did know . . . and didn't want to believe. We had a flaming row one day when I was presumptuous enough to accuse her of . . . certain things.

From then on she showed a sort of contemptuous indifference toward me. People don't like their secrets rammed down their throats, and I reared that child, so knew her very well." The housekeeper suddenly looked uncomfortable, as if she had revealed more than intended.

Jane was far too intrigued now and simply had to know more. "So Mara and John got married? Here?"

"No. John returned to Pretoria and Mara to Johannesburg. They motored back together and, some weeks later, the two households received telegrams announcing their marriage."

"How very deceitful!" Jane exclaimed scornfully.

"Well, I was surprised at John, I can tell you, but knowing madam's impulsive ways . . . anyway, John came home a short while later. What he said has never been revealed, but there was no change in the affection between the brothers. Grant actually acted as if . . . as if he were happy for John and unconcerned about Mara's preference. When Sandra was born Mara insisted that they make their home in Johannesburg and I suspect John was not pleased. Then came the accident . . . and Grant's promise to a dead brother." Extreme sadness clouded Minna's eyes.

"A promise to a dead brother . . . was Grant with John when he died?" Jane asked softly after elapsed moments.

"No, Jane. John was killed instantly. But I heard . . . I'm going to tell you this in complete confidence because I trust you and it's been a burden on my soul. I was the only one present when Grant uttered that promise." Minna pressed her hands together and leaned her forehead against them.

Jane sat quite still.

At last the gray head lifted. "I took him tea, one night, to his room shortly after the funeral, and he had John's photo in his hands—and oh, Janey, the grief was pitiable on his face. He said, taking my hand in his, 'Toicky, stay and bear witness to this pledge I make to a beloved brother. I will endeavor, to the utmost of my ability, to care for his family . . . his wife and child. I will comfort them in their grievous loss and may they never know want or lack of love as long as I live. Amen.' "

"Oh, Minna!" Jane laid her hands on wrinkled ones and the two women sat in deep silence.

Minna said, "John provided well for his wife and child, but my heart fears greatly that Grant will now marry Mara just to keep that pledge."

"But why does your heart fear, Minna? If they love each other surely that will be all right?"

"Do they?" Minna gathered the tea things. "Grant never once showed a grievance or jealousy . . . may he not be deluding himself that the old love is still there, merely because of that pledge and also for a secure future for Sandy, whom he adores? Miss Mara was dumbfounded when Grant inherited instead of John . . . she cares for Grant and has a thing about security." She lifted her eyes to Jane in a direct way. "Forgive me, Jane, but you, too, care a great deal for Grant?"

"I do, Minna," Jane admitted quietly.

"So you see, Jane, I don't know what will happen, I just don't know."

MARA TELEPHONED two evenings later and Grant joined Jane on the veranda after a lengthy conversation on the instrument. He gave a quiet chuckle as he took up a favorite seat on the wall. "Mara's having a spot of bother with Julius. He's evidently casing her place of work and making sure she's not being exploited by leering male buyers, and, she says, he even had the cheek to advise her not to model *revealing* garments."

"Julius, for all his advanced ideas, is plain old-fashioned and nuts!" Jane exclaimed. "Surely he knows that

Mara can look after herself. She's experienced in her job and has learned how to handle that sort."

"Well, according to her, he's making an old-fashioned nuisance of himself." Grant studied Jane for a long disturbing moment. "Does the thought of him being away and with Mara upset you?"

"Upset me?" She felt slightly bewildered by his abrupt question. Then remembrance came; Grant was still under the impression that Julius meant more to her than just a friend. "No," Jane met his eyes directly, "it doesn't upset me one iota. Mara's silly words that other day are quite unfounded. Julius is my very good friend and I love him as such."

His glance held hers and became almost like physical contact.

"*Love* him as such?" The emphasis on love was strangely questioning.

"Julius can be a staunch friend and there are different kinds of love. I love him in a what's commonly called platonic way—"

Grant cut across further explanation, "Do I rate a kind of love from you, Jane, and would it be platonic? Or haven't you made up your mind yet to which category I belong?"

"I—I don't put people into a categorical filing system," Jane declared, alarmed at the turn of questioning. His sudden probing might well unleash her wayward tongue into voicing irretractable avowals. She turned quickly back to the original conversation. "Julius is my friend, Grant, but I think you should watch him. I respect you, too, and I think you should know that he's trying to woo Mara away from you."

"Well, I'll be damned!" Grant came upright. "Thanks for the respect bit, but Julius wooing Mara? If that's what he thinks he's doing by dogging her footsteps—I'll be triple damned—wow! Jane, you're quite priceless, what a dear little old-fashioned word!"

"Call it what you like, but aren't you being just a little too sure of Mara? There's many a slip 'twixt cup and lip."

Sudden laughter came from Grant. He leaned down, took Jane's hands and pulled her to her feet. "I haven't heard that cliché for some time. Now who told you that I hold that particular cup?"

She felt again the electric tremor pass from his hand to hers and stammered confusedly;

"E-everybody knows that you and Mara—she told me—I mean she was your girl . . . ." and came to a tongue-tied stop.

"Do they now, did she tell you? And yes, she was my girl." Laughter was gone, replaced by searching stony eyes. "Quite a problem on my hands, wouldn't you say?"

"I don't see it as a problem, Grant. All you have to do is . . . ."

Grant interposed, "Honor a promise."

Jane dropped her eyes from the pain in his. She knew, from Minna, what he meant. But why should it be so difficult to honor that promise if he and Mara loved each other? "Are there legal difficulties?" she asked diffidently.

A short humorless laugh followed. "Doubtless there would be that . . . Mara spoke to you about her and myself? That seems to settle, rather definitely, one of my problems." Grant lit two cigarettes, passed one to Jane almost absentmindedly. "No wonder you were, some time ago, so indignant with Saxon, the sexy philanderer."

"At that time I thought you were married to Mara," Jane explained, and Grant listened in amazed silence.

"Again, I'll be damned! If you'd known then what you know now, would you have played along?"

"There's no point in pursuing the subject." Jane suddenly felt tired and weary of talk. "I'm going to bed."

His hand was on her shoulder. "Jane, if things were different, believe me, if they were—I'd stake my claim in no uncertain terms. Sleep well, child." Her shoulder felt the firm, gentle pressure of his hand and then he was walking down the steps and night swallowed the sound of fading footsteps.

So there were obstacles in his path to happiness. "If things were different . . . ." A dull ache followed Jane to bed.

CHAPTER THIRTEEN

DAYS FOLLOWED NIGHTS like gold and black beads in the hands of benevolent weather. Grant found work for himself, aside from the office, within the radius of the house. He did not believe that Flip Olivier, still at large, had left the vicinity of home ground. Jane asked tentative permission to return home nightly, but a curt negative came from her boss, which she obeyed with outward nonchalance. Inwardly, it was sweet torture to be with him constantly. Although there were no more intimate talks or quiet company in the evenings. Grant retired to his study or spent the hours after dinner perusing books and business circulars. Jane filled in the hours by chatting to Minna and helping Sandy prepare for school, retiring early.

Saturday dawned, clear and bright. At ten o'clock Sandra disappeared.

Jane looked up from the list of hostel clothes and toilet items she was checking when Minna walked into Sandy's room.

"Tea's ready, Jane, I thought Sandy was with you?"

"No." Jane fitted the list into the pocket inside the case lid and checked the metal fasteners. "Have you called outside? She was with Lemmy behind the garage about half an hour ago."

"I called and called but the little witch didn't answer. Up to mischief, I'll bet," Minna said distractedly. "I'm worried, Jane. Tom went to the compound on some errand and promised not to be away long. Do you think the children went with him?"

"Tom would have told us if he was taking them." Jane bit her lip vexedly. She straightened suddenly and made for the kitchen door. "I'm going to the storeroom." She ran across the yard, past the garage to the shed where, among other tools and equipment, the fishing gear was stored.

Two short rods and reels were missing!

"They've gone to the river against Grant's explicit orders! Oh, Jane," Minna wailed, "what shall we do?"

Jane's mind raced. "Not to worry . . . I'll take Mara's car. The child's wickedly talked Lemmy into a last fishing spree before going back to school. I'll tan her small hide with her own fishing rod when I find her!"

It took her a controlled five minutes to study the roadster gears, back out of the garage and swivel on to the road with a prayer in her heart that the youngsters would be where she hoped to find them. It was quite a walk and they must have left within the last hour. She'd have to leave the car on the roadside and cut through the grass and trees on foot.

The car flew under her trembling hands, and at a spot she reckoned would be nearest the river, Jane brought it to a stop on the grass verge.

The fishing rods were lying side by side in the favorite fishing place, somewhat haphazardly. Jane's heart gave a jump of relief but started palpitating unpleasantly with anger and then fear as she turned and searched and called without avail.

"Oh, God!" Sturdily shod feet faltered as a plume of smoke met her searching eyes. At right angles to her advance and the rising rock. "Not that, Sandy, not a fire, you stupid child!" Jane started running, her breath hammering more from fear than physical effort as she foresaw the destruction that silly action would start.

Then she was close enough to hear Sandy cry out . . . close enough to hear deep, uncontrolled laughter answer that piteous, frightened cry! Smoke veiled the figures and Jane tore past the outer rim of orange, leaping flames.

To come to an abrupt halt at the tableau that met her scorching eyes.

Flip Olivier towered over two very frightened children. Their hands were tied together with a grubby strip of stretched dry cowhide and he held the end of it in a tight grip. The man's pale blue eyes were alight with fascinated glee as he watched the crackling sparks fly.

Jane seemed to materialize like a genie out of the smoke and his glee was wiped out suddenly as he stepped back a startled pace before recognizing the furious demon that confronted him. Instinctively he dropped the lead from his hand.

Jane wasted no time. "Run for that big rock, kids! You, Olivier, take off your jacket and help beat down the flames. Move!" Her own jacket came down forcefully on the spreading rim of fire.

Flip Olivier's jacket came off in obedience to her peremptory order. He started to lift it and then dropped his hand and began to laugh again, a mad pitch of laughter that held a spice of insanity. "Gees!" he shouted, "I've scooped the kitty—Saxon's kid, his girl and a sweet fire to help him to hell!"

Jane ignored him and looked despairingly at the small headway her futile efforts had made and noticed that the fire was spreading in a circular run, with the rock slap in the centre. She turned back to glare at him in contemptuous anger. "Use your jacket, you fool!"

He suddenly lunged forward and whipped his jacket around her arms and body. "Nobody calls me names and gets away with it! Try your clever tricks now, Miss Mighty!"

Jane fought furiously, the hot breath of flames on their backs as they struggled on the uneven ground. Her efforts to loosen his hold only goaded him to further angry laughter. "I've waited just for this—Saxon has it coming—this will even up the score quite a bit. Better give up if you don't want to be burnt alive," he grunted as she kicked him hard on the shins. "Damn you! I'm joining the kids on the rock and you're coming with me if I have to drag you by the hair. Saxon's empire's going to burn like Rome did!"

Jane winced as his fingers viced cruelly into her upper arms. Quite suddenly she stopped fighting his straitjacket hold on her.

"You're right," she panted, "we may as well watch. The fire is right behind you—be careful."

Olivier slackened his hold suspiciously at her sudden capitulation and pushed her and himself away from the blasting heat of the approaching flames. The grass was higher and dryer on the rise to the edge of the rock. The children were huddled specks on its smooth grassless surface.

Jane stood docilely while Olivier still gripped the jacket, pinioning her arms. He turned his head to stare at the destruction he had started. Soon it would reach the trees and then the real fun would start. Dry wild brush crackled fiercely as hungry flames seized on them.

"Just dig that, sister," he said, mesmerized.

Jane acted. Her body and legs collapsed like to deflated rubber doll, completely and limply, bringing her tormentor down on top of her, completely off balance. Two feet hit his stomach, Jane's legs straightened and Flip Olivier flew through the air with a flail of legs and arms to land beyond her head. Then she was up and running for her life.

Olivier made no attempt to follow her.

Jane only realized this when she turned her head to see if he was gaining ground. He was still lying as she had thrown him and the fire was creeping very close to his head. She stopped for a stunned moment, and then began to run back. That trick couldn't —unless—his head lay at an unnatural angle.

"No . . . no!" She knelt beside him, the heat searing her skin. And then Jane saw the stone and the wound it had made when his head had contacted. No time for a closer look; he was either concussed or—her blood ran cold with terror—dead. She had to move him before the fire overwhelmed them both.

Slipping her arms under the limp shoulders, Jane began to drag him by straining and walking backward. He was a dead weight (her lips moved in silent prayer), but she managed to drag him a few yards before stopping to inhale fresh breath into her pumping lungs.

Two figures appeared beside her. "Please tell us what to do," Sandy sobbed. "We can help—Jane, you're both going to be burned!" Lemmy tugged at the man's legs.

"Wait, Lemmy." Jane looked back and glimpsed Flip's jacket, where he had dropped it. She ran back and snatched it from a lapping, fiery tongue, ran back and placed it on the ground above his head, then took up her former position, arms under the shoulders, and talked steadily to the children. "I'll lift him and drag him on to the jacket and then you two stand either side, grip the jacket tightly and drag with me. Now!" she managed with desperate strength to lift the inert body on to the jacket.

Heaving, dragging, straining, they started to make headway. At last they reached the rock, haven of safety, with hungry tongues of fire spitting dangerous sparks on clothing and hair in a last demon effort to capture its prey.

In various positions of utter exhaustion the three mortals gasped, choked in a pall of smoke and clapped feebly at clothing and hair. Flip Olivier lay as he had been dragged, inert and a bedraggled mess of torn, dirty clothing; his shoes had come off somewhere on the way and the backs of his heels were skinned and bloody. Jane became terrified of even looking at him . . . if he was unconscious at the start, not dead, then that struggle to rescue him had certainly worsened his condition. Her mind blanked at the thought and her body became too paralyzed to inch nearer to test his breathing.

"Thank you, kids, that was a stout effort . . . we're safe now." The dear smudged mites managed weak grins and then Sandy sat straighter and charged excitement took over.

"I can hear something, Jane, I can hear cars!"

The Land Rover, vengeance on wheels, braked to a halt on the ashes of a smoky but dead grassfire. Jane thought hazily, not a demon of vengeance but a mere haloed, heavenly astral vehicle, and the angel alighting could take over, body and soul and all.

Jane sighed softly, "They're getting mighty careless in heaven these days, darling, no wings . . . I killed him," and fainted in a very old-fashioned way.

She came to life with her head pillowed against a hard chest, exactly where that aching head yearned to be, vibrating against her ear with Grant speaking to someone. "Our firewatchers are on the ball, poppet. The alarm went forth at the first wisp of smoke. Now everything's under control."

"Is he dead?" Jane whispered to the chest against her cheek.

Grant tilted his dark head. "Feeling better? That was a silly thing to do, passing out at this stage—sort of anticlimax, don't you think? Lucky you postponed the first one until out of the burn, wise child."

Jane stammered, "When I saw you it—it just happened."

"That's because I'm more devastating than fire!" Grant quipped lightly, but the convulsive pressure of his arm belied the flippancy of words. "If you can sit up I'll help you to the Rover. The ambulance men are coming with stretchers."

Jane's eyes strayed to the quiet form and her stomach turned as she noted the jacket covering head and chest. Grant must have examined him while she was in her faint and the covering could only mean . . . Grant hadn't answered her question.

"How did they know to send an ambulance?" Sandy queried as she and Lemmy followed Grant and Jane to the vehicle.

"That's part of the fire-fighting unit, in case of casualties."

Grant settled them in the seats and prepared to walk away, obviously to meet the oncoming men.

Jane guessed his purpose; he wanted to speak with them and leave before they examined Flip Olivier. She simply had to know. Now.

"Grant, please wait for them. I want to know."

He turned away without further argument and joined the white-coated men. Vision was obscured by their broad backs and to Jane time became interminable, agonizingly endless before Grant lifted from his heels and walked back.

"He's alive, badly concussed."

Relief almost made Jane faint again. A small voice came from the back of her, "I think I'm going to be sick. . . ."

Grant lifted Sandy out. "Do so, poppet, you'll feel better." He held small shoulders while the child heaved; and Lemmy nonchalantly climbed out the other side and did likewise. Jane ached with tender pity for both of them.

At home at last, Minna and Polly were waiting, each taking a child in loving arms. Grant turned to Jane. His arms helped her from the Rover, wandered around her body and she was held close.

"Jane, Janey, how can I ever thank you for what you did for those children? What was in that madman's head?" The arms around her tightened as the big man seemed to lose control; as if his hold on her prevented, helped him from breaking apart and brought back sanity. His body shook as if in fever spasms.

"And you, Jane Wheeler, had to be mauled . . . thank God for your quick brain, clever tricks . . . and brave heart."

A measure of slackening came finally, one arm freed completely so that the attached hand could stroke back wildly disarrayed hair from off her face. Her nose unwound from his breastbone and air seeped back into her lungs. He tugged her hair gently back to tilt her face and look long and hard at her features, his gray eyes circling with a deep look of wonder in their depths. "Do you feel better now?"

"Except for a burst spleen, yes. Do *you* feel better too?" Jane countered.

"Burst spleen—" Grant saw the glint in brown eyes and his arm came away from her waist. "What do you mean, do I feel better?"

Jane felt like biting her tongue clean off for depriving herself of that exciting arm. Well, it was good while it lasted.

"An erupting volcano had nothing on you, Grant Saxon, a few seconds back! You've got it out of your system now; nobody was hurt except the villain and that was by accident. He hit his descending head on a rock and I'll pray for his recovery and repentance. Not too much damage was caused by his little arson game. Kids recover from shock rapidly, no lasting harm done and that's that!"

"That's all you know. Things are going to move my way at last." Grant took her shoulders, shook them slightly while some deep, secretive look made his eyes almost black. "I have a telegram in my pocket right now . . . ." he stopped and his eyes moved over her shoulder, "but that can wait for a more suitable moment. Take yourself to bath, girl, wash away your aches and dirt and I'll consider the bed-going bit." He winked deliberately and turned away.

AN HOUR LATER, bathed, changed, her hair swept into a neat chignon, Jane moved about the sitting room, Uncle Bart proudly at her side, and smiled composedly at the excited questions flung from all sides. Old friends greeted her with familiar pride and new friends were welcomed courteously. Through the open french doors a group of men clustered, Grant in their midst. His quizzical eyes strayed often, above their shoulders and heads to follow Jane's progress. Sandy and Lemmy, clean and exuberant, came in for their share of telling and praise.

Sergeant Mason cleared his throat selfconsciously. "I truly regret that I can't stay. This gathering that started off so fearfully is obviously going to turn into a jolly "do" and it's always my lot to have to push off when the going's good. However, duty calls." He bowed gravely toward Sandy and Lemmy. "The police personnel gratefully extend thanks to Miss Sandra and Master Lemmy for flushing out the enemy, which our entire squad couldn't accomplish!" He walked to Jane's side and put a large hand on her shoulder.

"Dear ma'am, on behalf of my colleagues, present company and myself, accept our deepest esteem for your brave act. I am personally sending a recommendation for citation to courage, quick acting in moments of danger and unbelievable compassion for a scoundrel who deliberately victimized two small children, committed arson and is a robber wanted by the police—and assaulted your person—"

"—vice versa," Grant cut in softly.

"Don't put an official off stride, it's illegal." Mason

waited for laughter to subside. "Again, thank you, Jane. I'm also deeply thankful that neither you or the children came to any harm. We'll call on you tomorrow, at your convenience for a little statement of events—will you be here or at Bart's home?"

Jane felt shaken to the point of tears at the sincerity of his intense and orderly speech and her own mind shook at the sergeant's unspoken conjecture of what might have happened to two innocent children. Grant answered for her.

"Miss Wheeler will be at her uncle's home tomorrow and you may call on her when she's rested suitably. Bart will contact you when she's ready."

"Thank you, Grant. That suit you, Jane?"

"Y-yes, Sergeant Mason. I'll be at your service any time in the morning." Jane stammered slightly. All of a sudden she was being sent home; of course there was no danger of being waylaid and something clicked in her memory . . . Grant had mentioned a telegram received this morning.

Her hand was shaken warmly and the sergeant took his leave. From then on she had little time for thoughts. She didn't realize that not only the stiff drink but shock was settling on her stiff shoulders. She stretched her eyes wide, closed them and repeated the exercise; opened them again to meet Grant's scrutiny across the length of the veranda. He put a hand, motioning for silence, and all eyes turned to him.

"This seems to be the time for more startling disclosures and, believe me, I have much to disclose. Firstly, Pat and Peter have finally settled their wedding date, three weeks from now."

Grant lit a cigarette, then slowly lifted a hand to slide an orange envelope out of his pocket. And Jane's insides curled witheringly as she remembered his remark about a telegram. It could only be from Mara; she was coming back. Grant wouldn't make a thing of it if it only meant her return; this was something of great importance and he could not wait for Mara's presence to announce the shattering news contained in that envelope.

Jane shuttered her mind while his maddening coolness iced through her veins. She had a fierce urge to scream at him, to get it over, let the hammer fall; let the knife cut sharp and viciously—damn you, get on with it so that I can go home and die alone!

After a million years Grant spoke and the words came strangely stilted: "Secondly, I have here a telegram," he looked up from the paper in his hands and, though his lips smiled, the challenging stare that pierced across space to transfix one girl held a grimness that belied his nonchalant appearance. "Another startling bit of news—Cupid seems to be working overtime."

He should have waited, Jane thought dumbly, for Mara to be at his side. She loved the limelight and would have been delighted in being the star of the day . . . .

"Julius Davenport and Mara Saxon were married in Johannesburg at ten-thirty, yesterday morning." Grant raised his voice above the sudden murmurings. "I'll read further, 'I married her to control mischievous intent. Stop. Love her madly and found surprising reciprocation. Stop. Don't be mad.'" Grant hesitated, his eyes strayed across the form in his hand, and then he folded the missive. "That's all."

Murmurs became prattle and Peter and Pat were warmly congratulated. Curious looks were cast at the Estate owner and conjecture written plainly on puzzled faces. Grant, quite composed and affable, began to walk toward Jane. Her eyes followed his progress hynotically. Three meters from her, heartbreak and shock collided.

Jane whispered sympathetically, "Oh, you poor dear man!" and Grant was there to catch her in his arms as she folded limply for the second time in one day.

Elizabeth walked with him to Jane's bedroom. At the side of her bed Grant turned, the girl still in his arms, and gave an anxious mother a beatific smile. "Tell the chaps to push off now, Elizabeth. I'll take good care of our Jane and bring her home in due course. You can all go home." His bright gray eyes took the sting out of the summary command.

Jane opened her eyes and hazily investigated the arm that circled her, the close warm body . . . and lifted her lashes fully; the bed was familiar, the setting sun comforting against drawn curtains and, most of all, the pure delight she experienced at the quiet voice in her ear.

"Sleep, child. Sleep, dearest one."

Jane blissfully obeyed and slept.

"IS SHE SICK—is Jane sick?" The frightened little voice penetrated. "Minna didn't want me to come, b-but I had to come. Is she very sick?"

Jane opened her eyes to a shaded lamp, felt the movement of Grant's head and closed them again quickly and just listened.

His free arm moved carefully to stroke Sandy's shining hair. "Jane is perfectly all right, poppet. Only very tired. Absolutely nothing to worry about."

Sandra breathed deeply. "Thank goodness—'cos it would be my fault if Jane is sick 'n then I'd die too. Do you want some tea?"

"No, sweetheart. You and Minna pop off to bed now and I'll stay with Jane and take good care of her till she wakes up."

"Okay, G'night, Grant." At the door, in a piercing whisper, "I'm glad Mommy married Uncle Julius 'n I'll teach him to be a fine new dad. And I think Jane belongs to you, 'cos you're sleeping with her!" The door closed.

"I'll say!" Grant shifted slightly to look at the face in the crook of his arm.

Wide open eyes stared back at him.

"Hello, darling," he said.

"Hello." Her voice held enchantment. "You're not to be mad at Julius and you don't have to console me. He didn't mean a thing to me—I just passed out because I feel so sorry for you."

"Yes, love, I know that. You have such a wonderfully compassionate heart."

Jane lifted her head from his arm and rested on her elbow to gaze at him earnestly. "You didn't finish that message from Julius today. Please don't let it hurt you too much, Grant."

"If I were hurt deeply, would you be willing to help me, Jane, to try and forget?"

Jane said miserably, "If that's what you would want."

"Would you give me anything I wanted?" His fingertips traced the contour of her face and lips.

"Yes, Grant."

"Unconditionally?"

Nut-brown eyes glistened mute confirmation.

"Say it! Say you love me unconditionally, heart and soul, with every breath in your beautiful body!"

Jane sat up straight, away from his thrilling touch. "I've loved you from the time I met you, so you might as well know. Even when I thought you were married. My mind was disgusted, but my heart was irrevocably yours."

"How lovely you are, my Janey. Julius did me one hell of a favor; I was beside myself with torment, because of a self-made promise—to John.

"Now I'm released. Julius, bless his scheming heart, released me from a course I almost took before you came, and when I saw you it became torture to contemplate sticking to that promise and I became a cowardly procrastinator. Thank God I waited! The telegram from Julius ended thus: 'I know where your heart belongs. Stop. Ask and ye shall receive. Stop.' "

Grant's eyes met hers levelly, a deep shimmering flame in gray depths.

"Dare I ask and will I receive, and do you know where my heart belongs, now and for ever, hazelnut?"

Jane's own breast became an erratic, joyous drumbeat.

"Do you know? Answer me, Janey. Well, come here and I'll show you!"

Grant pulled her down beside him and began to kiss her eyelids, worked his way to her smoothly fragrant neck, keeping her mouth for last, the sweetest of all.

Finally his lips lifted an infinite speaking space from hers.

"My darling dumb one, do you know that we belong?" he breathed, with rough passion, and Jane's answer was to seek his lips again with sweet ardor.

To whisper, "Yes, boss."

"This is why I must take you home . . . some time. And bring my wife back . . . soon."

Rocks Under
Shining Water
Jane Donnelly

Jenny had always been jealous of her sister. Caterine had everything—good looks, talent and a happy marriage to Paul Tremain.

Now there was no room for jealousy. For suddenly Caterine was dead and Jenny had gone to Paul's house in Cornwall to care for Timmy, his small son. Here, Jenny began to see the truth about her sister's marriage.

Had Caterine really loved this cruel man whose strong personality dominated those around him? When he taunted her with "you'll never escape now" Jenny realized that was the least of her problems. How had she dared to fall in love with him!

CHAPTER ONE

TIMOTHY WOULD AWAKE SOON. These days he always awoke early. Jenny Douglas lay still and silent on the settee that was serving as a bed in her living room. The clock said almost six; the door into the bedroom was slightly ajar; and soon the child sleeping in Jenny's bed would stir and whimper. Unless he heard her moving around he would quietly sob his heart out for his mother.

He was only seven, but he kept his tears for when he was alone—as Jenny did. If she had not had Timothy to consider the grief that welled in her now, choking in her throat and stinging behind closed eyelids, would have found relief in a storm of weeping.

Instead she held back the tears, as she did each morning when she woke and remembered. . . .

Two weeks ago the phone had rung downstairs and it had been Caterine. "Jenny? Can I come over for a few days?"

"When?" Jenny had been buoyant with delight.

"Now."

But it was midafternoon and the Cornish coast was a long way from this Midland town, so Caterine would be driving through the night.

Jenny had suggested, "It might be better to start first thing in the morning," but Caterine was positive that she needed a change of scenery right now.

"There's another storm blowing up and that'll be the umpteenth this month, and I need to get away before I go crazy from storms."

"The weather's foul here, too," Jenny sighed. "What a summer we've had!" It was a dreary day, rain was spattering on the colored glass panel of the front door, and her sister laughed derisively.

"You don't know what foul weather is."

Jenny laughed too, accepting there was no real comparison between inland storms when your home was protected by streets of buildings all acting as windbreaks, and the rage of elements around Caterine's house, high on the cliffs, overlooking the sea and the jagged rocks.

"So expect me with the dawn," Caterine had said, putting down the receiver, and Jenny had rushed out to buy a bottle of wine and food to stock the fridge with flair, because Caterine was not the girl to dine on fish fingers, the two lamb chops and half a pound of sausages that would have seen Jenny through the weekend.

"My sister's coming," she had told Louie Sumner, who lived in the ground floor flat with her husband.

Louie didn't know Caterine. The Sumners had only lived here four months. But she had seen the photographs and she'd said, "Nice! Will we get to meet her?"

"Of course."

And you'll both be bowled over, Jenny had thought as she staggered upstairs, arms around the huge carrier bag of foodstuffs. They wouldn't believe such a spellbinder could be her sister. Except for the nose—they did have the same nose.

She apologized in advance. "Heaven knows what time she'll get here, she's driving through the night. She is an idiot, but that's Caterine, everything's got to be now. I'll get down as fast as I can when she starts banging on the door. I hope she won't wake you."

"Not to bother," Louie said cheerfully.

When the phone rang again some hours later Louie had answered it and caroled up, "Jenny!"

Jenny didn't get many calls, although it was legally her telephone. She'd wondered, "Who is it?" as she'd hurried down, and Louie had shrugged and grinned.

"He wasn't saying."

It was Caterine's husband, Paul Tremain. He had a deep voice. He was a big man, with dark hair and solid build. Jenny never felt really relaxed on the rare occasions when she met him, but tonight the moment he said his name she was terrified. She knew he was going to tell her, "There's been an accident."

She said, "*No . . .* " shrilly as though denial could change it. "Oh God—no!" then, whispering, "How bad?"

Paul asked, "Is the girl who answered the phone still there?"

"Yes." If she had been alone would he have proceeded more gently, coming to it in circuitous fashion? Jenny's muted scream had halted Louie in her doorway. She stood now, pale, staring at Jenny.

Paul said huskily, "Caterine's dead."

Jenny crumpled. Her mind reacted so violently that it was like an explosion in her head. She dropped the receiver and it swung gently to and fro on its spiral wire. She covered her face with her hands, her short dark hair falling forward, then felt Louie's arms around her and heard Louie saying, "Come and sit down, Jen."

In their living room Bryan Sumner had the table covered with papers brought home from his work. He jumped up as Louie steered Jenny into the room and told him shakily, "Jenny's just had some bad news, Bry. There's someone still on the phone."

Bryan went out into the hall, closing the door after him. Louie was almost sure what the news was. Jenny had no one but her sister who was driving up here tonight, and she had the stricken look of a girl told the worst that could happen.

Jenny said, "Caterine's dead."

Louie had never met Caterine, but this was the house where Caterine had been born and there were the photographs of her and she had been on her way here to-night. It was nothing like the death of a stranger. Louie felt sick with shock and pity for Jenny. She said, "I'll get you a drink."

Jenny hardly heard, although she shook her head. She was numbed, frozen, unable to believe it. It was impossible to believe in a world without Caterine. Caterine was the shining one for whom the good things always happened. She had so much talent, all the gifts. Loveliness and love, a rich husband who adored her, Timothy . . . .

Timothy . . . . Jenny ran back into the hall, snatching the phone out of Bryan Sumner's hand. "Paul?"

"Yes, Jenny?" said Paul.

"Timothy wasn't with her?"

"No," he said quickly, and she handed the phone back to Bryan as though it had been his call she had interrupted. Caterine almost always brought Timothy. That was something to thank God for as soon as Jenny could feel anything again.

Louie made her drink hot sweet tea, and when Bryan came into the room he said, "God, what a terrible thing! Jenny, if there's anything we can do . . . ."

"Thank you," she said. "I'm glad you were here."

To have taken that news alone would have been unbearable, even worse if it had happened six months ago when their mother was alive. Mrs. Douglas had been an invalid for a long time, but if she had been strong and hale the news of Caterine's death would have felled her. Caterine was her joy, her favorite. Caterine was everyone's favorite, but Jenny hadn't resented it because she loved Caterine too.

She asked Bryan, "What did Paul tell you?"

He was wondering how much more she could take. She was a nice girl, quiet and pretty. She had always seemed sensible and calm, but he had never seen her in shock before. He didn't want to add to her distress by going into vivid detail until she was over the first blow. He said, "The car skidded."

"Where did it happen?"

"Not far from the house." All the roads were hazardous. Those leading down to the coves were no more than tracks. The only road into the little harbor of Tremain was steep and cobbled and ran like a mountain torrent when there were storms.

But Caterine would be taking the main road along the top of the cliffs. A storm was coming, she'd said when she spoke to Jenny. Another storm.

Jenny recalled the house as clearly as though she stood at an upper window: the main entrance faced the inland approach; there was a wide lawn edged with laurel and cedars and a thick yew hedge; and a drive opened onto the cliff road. Caterine would have turned right in her lime green sports car and skidded not far from the house.

Jenny asked dully, "What happened?" She could see the car, going over the cliff's edge, falling. When the sea was up the razor rocks below were hidden except for plumes of spray. In a storm the white-tipped waves reached like hands. It was a long way down.

Bryan gulped and Jenny's voice raised. "She went off the road? She went over the cliff?" He nodded, looking sick himself. Her brother-in-law had told him, "If you could tell Jenny how it happened before she reads it in the newspapers I'd appreciate that, and would you take care of her tonight?"

Jenny said stupidly, "She should have waited till tomorrow. Paul shouldn't have let her come if the storm had started and the roads weren't safe." Then she bit her lip. "I want to blame someone. Of course he thought it was safe. I just want to scream at someone."

But there was no relief and no redress. Everything

seemed so normal, as if nothing had happened. Upstairs her fridge was full of the food she had stacked away as she planned what they would do next week, she and Caterine and probably Timothy. Her family. Caterine, who looked like a young girl and would never grow old now and whom Jenny would never see again.

Jenny sat hunched, hugging herself in her own arms, asking herself, "What am I going to do?"

"You'll stay here with us tonight," said Louie gently.

Bryan agreed. He had assured the man on the phone that Jenny wouldn't be left alone, but he felt that for a while he should leave her to Louie. Louie half pointed at the papers on the table and Bryan gathered them together and took them into the bedroom, where he had a desk and sometimes worked.

He was supposed to have this lot in order by Monday morning, but he wouldn't. He kept thinking of Jenny and of the man who had just been explaining how his wife had died. Paul Tremain had sounded like an automaton, speaking with terse lucidity. Bryan couldn't have done that if anything had happened to Louie. He would have gone to pieces. But he had no doubt at all that Paul Tremain's self-control had covered a terrible grief.

Louie Sumner had grown fond of Jenny in the four months they had lived under Jenny's roof. After her mother had died Jenny had rented part of the house: the whole of the downstairs to Louie and Bryan, two rooms upstairs to a retired couple who were away this weekend.

It had been a godsend for Louie and Bryan, not long married and living on sufferance with his parents and two brothers, to find a furnished flat at a price that wouldn't grab the last penny. They were the first to apply and they took it on sight, waiting for the hidden snags to develop. When no snags did they blessed their stars and decided that the seemingly nice girl who owned the house really was a nice girl and honest in her dealings.

Jenny had been satisfied with her bargain. The old age pensioners upstairs were homely and kind, and Louie Sumner was bright and about Jenny's own age.

Jenny didn't have many friends of her own age. Her father had died the year of Caterine's marriage, and her mother had been an invalid almost that long. In the last three years Mrs. Douglas had rarely left her room, and Jenny had finally had to give up the secretarial work in a lawyer's office that had earned her an independent living. She had eked a pittance from home typing and there had been her mother's small pension, and Paul Tremain had made them an allowance.

Jenny had never enjoyed feeling like the poor relation, the hanger-on, but as Caterine said it was her money as much as Paul's. He had promised her all his worldly goods. Caterine had laughed and Mrs. Douglas had said it was sweet of Paul. It had kept Mrs. Douglas in comfort. There had been talk of getting a nurse in, but that would have cost more than Jenny doing the nursing, and her mother preferred having Jenny around.

Jenny couldn't regret that she had done all she could. She had loved her mother, although Mrs. Douglas had been a demanding and often querulous invalid, and at twenty-two Jenny was unlikely to step into the kind of job she might have had if she had stayed on as a working girl.

She stopped accepting the allowance right after her mother's death, although Caterine said that was stupid. Of course it wasn't charity and of course they could afford it. But under their father's will the small suburban house was now Jenny's—he had known Caterine would never need it, seeing the number of houses Paul Tremain owned—and Jenny planned to work.

She had gone to an agency, and during the last four months had done holiday relief for four different firms while she strove for confidence and competence. She was out of practice on both.

The phone rang again and Bryan went quickly through the living room. "I'll get it."

Jenny stopped breathing. Perhaps it was Paul again to say there had been a mistake, the car wasn't Caterine's. Or there had been a miracle and someone had noticed a flicker of heartbeat, and it was stronger now and Caterine had come to life again.

Bryan came back and said, "Jack Wilson," very quietly, apologizing that someone should be calling him on that phone at a time like this. Jenny thought, *I should have spoken to Paul.* If the car had gone into the sea how would they know for sure yet? She could have been thrown clear and lying above the water's reach. How could they know?

But she knew. She had a terrifying vision of Caterine, whole and happy one moment and the next plunged into a nightmare of whirling pain and choking darkness. Caterine, who had never been afraid or alone in her life.

The room began to disintegrate and she closed her eyes; Louie said softly, "Don't faint, Jen. Put your head down."

Jenny managed to open her eyes. "I'm all right."

Louie's own eyes were swimming with tears. Her voice was husky as she sat down on the small settee beside Jenny. "You were very close, weren't you?"

Jenny nodded.

"Do you want to talk?" Talking wouldn't bring Caterine back, but Louie was desperately trying to break through Jenny's frozen whiteness. Jenny shook her head, and Louie was the one who wept.

Jenny stayed with Louie that night. She took sleeping pills and slept little, and by the next day the neighbors had heard. Some of them remembered Caterine living here, although she had left home for drama school at eighteen and only came back for holidays. Then at twenty-one she had married Paul Tremain and joyously thrown up her promising career for love.

Jenny had been the only one with misgivings about that. She had been a schoolgirl and adored her talented sister, and when Caterine had told them before the wedding, "Paul doesn't want me to be an actress, he just wants me to be a wife," Jenny had thought he was asking a lot. He had been more than generous, and Caterine had always had everything she wanted, but Jenny retained a little resentment that he invariably made Caterine turn down the offers of small parts that still sometimes came her way.

Several people had thought Caterine Douglas had the makings of stardom. But Paul was obdurate, and Caterine didn't seem to mind. She had talked about it with Jenny the last time they were together, after Mrs. Douglas died. "It's flattering really, Paul's possessiveness. I wouldn't change him for any man I've ever met. He'd give me the moon if I asked for it. But," she had smiled as though she didn't really mind this either, "he's the master around Tremain, and he makes the rules."

The estate was his, but Jenny did not feel that should give him the ruling of flesh and blood too. She had never said so. It was Caterine's business and Caterine had always been happy. So had Timothy, their small son.

In the early years of the marriage Jenny and Mrs. Douglas had gone on holidays to the big house in Cornwall, but not after Mrs. Douglas became a confirmed invalid. After that Caterine would come here to see them, usually bringing Timothy with her.

Caterine's had been a wonderful life. Caterine had had everything to live for, and the neighbors kept saying so. It didn't make it easier for Jenny. All Sunday folk with nothing but pity in their hearts filled the small house. They wanted to sympathize, they wanted to help, and they sat with Jenny and talked about Caterine, and Sunday was a dreadful day.

The Monday newspapers ran the story. Paul Trémain was a rich man. Besides the house, Moidores, he owned farms, a flourishing tin mine and the village of Tremain. And Caterine was young and beautiful and had been an actress.

Any car skidding from a cliff top would have been reported, but pictures of the Tremains were easy to come by, and the big house made an impressive shot. And the cliffs with the rocks below.

It was because of the pictures of the cliffs that her friends tried to keep the newspapers from Jenny, although she had seen the rocks and remembered them and carried them in her mind's eye from morning till night.

The verdict was "Accidental death." The skid marks were plain. It was weather in which extreme caution should have been taken, and Mrs. Tremain, happily off on a visit to her sister, had possibly not given her entire attention to the road surface.

Jenny did not have to attend the inquest; it would have been a grim ordeal, and she was thankful to be spared it.

Neither did she attend the funeral, but that was because Paul phoned again and asked her if Timothy could come up to her for a few days.

By then the funeral would be over. The house and the village must be under a monstrous shadow now, and there would be heartbreak enough for Timothy when he returned to begin life without a mother.

Paul said, "He's asking for you."

He would know where Caterine was going. She would have told him, "I'm going to see Auntie Jen, only a little holiday. I'll bring you lovely presents back and you'll be good, won't you, and I'll phone you tomorrow."

Perhaps he had a wild childish hope that if he spoke to Jenny she would say, "Your mother's with me. Of course she's safe. They've all made a mistake." Everyone hoped that. Jenny had hoped, and she asked, "How will he come?"

"Rolf Perrie will bring him."

Rolf Perrie was manager of the tin mine. Jenny had met him years ago when she had gone on summer holidays. He had been a grave, rather gangling young engineering student, living with his parents on one of the smallholdings. She said, "Yes," and asked, "How are you, Paul?"

"I'm all right," said Paul Tremain. "You?"

"I will be. Why did it happen?"

He said, "I shouldn't have let her go. I should have stopped her."

"Don't torture yourself," she wanted to say, but even now she couldn't speak easily with him. He was too strong a man, too distant and powerful. She said, "No one could help it."

"No," he said. "Thank you for taking Timothy."

She said, "Thank you for sending him. He's all the family I have now." She put down the phone because she couldn't say any more: a tight band was around her throat.

Timothy arrived late at night. Jenny opened the door when she heard the car draw up and the man who stood there was Rolf Perrie. He had always been slow to smile, and now the long drive and the heartbreak of his mission made him look years older than his age, but she recognized him.

'Where's Timothy?"

"In the car. He's asleep."

The car was an estate model and she hurried out. Timothy lay curled in the back on a pile of cushions, covered by a red tartan rug. She knelt on the front seat and leaned over, feeling a rush of tenderness that made her want to reach for the child and hold him tight.

He was in deep slumber. By the light of the street lamp she saw his dark hair plastered to his damp forehead and his face shorn of all defense. He had always been a tough little boy, cheerfully belligerent, sparkling with mischief. But now he lay vulnerable and pitiful.

"I'll carry him in," said Rolf Perrie. "He's not been sleeping. You can understand that. As we came along he just went out like a light, and I tucked him up in the back."

He opened the doors of the back of the car, and Jenny leaned over to put her fingers around Timothy's. He opened his eyes sleepily, seeing her through a haze. Then he grinned a little. "Hello, mom," he said.

He thought she was Caterine. He wasn't awake yet; the light was dim, and there was that faint likeness between them. Then he blinked and saw her clearer and said, "Auntie Jen."

"Timmy." She mustn't cry. She tried to smile and her lips quivered, and he wriggled himself up and turned and scrambled out of the van, past Rolf Perrie. He was reeling with sleep, but he had remembered. He came around the van to Jenny, and she held out her arms and he stumbled into them.

They clung together. Her cheek was wet against the child's cheek, and he said suddenly, "Don't cry, Auntie Jen," although they were his tears.

"No," she promised. "No."

He took her hand and looked up at her. He had always looked like Caterine, with her gaiety and her bright charm, but now for the first time Jenny saw his father's face and thought—he will grow like Paul.

They went into the house and up to her room. She had a meal ready. She had arranged for Rolf Perrie to stay the night in a spare bed in the Sumners' flat before making the journey back to Tremain in the morning, but she had the meal here for the three of them.

She had hardly eaten for days, and Timothy simply pushed his food around. Rolf probably ate for courtesy's sake, for he seemed to have no appetite either.

She remembered his home was a long gray stone building. There were horses that Jenny and Lorraine Tremain, Paul's young sister, used to ride. Lorraine rode very well, Jenny had only been on horseback on those holidays and she was not a natural rider. Once she had slithered off when a horse moved suddenly and they had taken her into the farmhouse to have a glass of fresh warm milk and get her breath back.

She reminded Rolf, "Do you remember when I slid off a horse right into one of the pigsties?" This was really for Timothy, to coax a smile from him, and he grinned for her, but there wasn't much talking done.

Timothy looked tired, and it was plain that no one was eating any more. Jenny said, "It's very late, Tim. Bedtime now." He raised no objections.

He squirmed into bed yawning and she was almost sure he would fall asleep soon. He said, "Good night, Auntie Jen," and then, "You don't get real storms here, do you?"

That was almost the last thing Caterine had said to Jenny. Jenny said gently, "Not really. Good night, Timmy."

Rolf Perrie was still in the living room, sitting in the armchair, his head sunk low. When Jenny came out of the bedroom, closing the door, he said quietly, "Settled down, has he?"

"I think he'll sleep. He's worn out."

Rolf shook his head. "Dreadful business. Dreadful." He couldn't believe it either. He sounded bewildered,

"Mrs. Tremain, the last person you can think of as . . . ." He couldn't say "dead" to her sister. He said, "She was always so alive."

Caterine had enjoyed everything so much. It was a drab world for most, and tragic that someone who loved living should be extinguished.

There had been a photograph of Caterine on the sideboard; Jenny had moved it before Timothy came. She looked for it now without thinking and saw it in her mind, Caterine laughing.

"Best for the lad to be out of Moidores for a while," said Rolf. "It's a dark house these days." This house was dark too, thought Jenny, but at least there was human bustle and busyness outside, not the terrible loneliness of cliffs and seas and seagulls screaming.

Rolf Perrie cleared his throat and glanced at the closed bedroom door, then spoke in hardly more than a hoarse whisper. "Timmy, you see, he saw it."

"Saw *what*?"

"She said goodbye to them and went off in her car, and he ran upstairs to watch the car from one of the turret windows as far as he could." Jenny had only imagined the road and the rain, and the little car skidding wildly and falling, turning, but the child had seen it.

Rolf Perrie said raggedly, deeply moved, "He came screaming to the top of the stairs."

"Oh *no*!" Jenny's heart clenched. How could they ever hope to wipe out that memory from a child's mind?

"A storm broke just afterward," said Rolf, "and storms terrify him now. That's one of the reasons Paul wanted to get him out of Tremain for a few days."

"I'll take care of him," she promised and wished she could promise to keep the storms away.

She made up her bed that night on the settee and then in the darkness she opened the door into the bedroom and listened to Timmy's steady breathing. He was

peaceful yet, without dreams or nightmares. The nightmares would come with waking and she must be ready.
She left the door a little ajar and slept the listening sleep
of a mother with an ailing child.

She was awake first next morning, moving quietly
around getting the breakfast when he stirred. She heard
him stifling sobs and then he came out. He was not
weeping, although his face was smeared. He didn't look
as he had done while he slept, but as he had looked last
night telling her not to cry, holding his lips steady, not
with the wide gaze of a child but with the guarded eyes
of a man.

Timothy helped Jenny through the next week at least
as much as she helped him. There were no scenes and
no tears, but they both knew that the other suffered and
they both mourned.

Jenny filled the time. They shopped, cooked meals
and ate them. They took bus rides out of town, often to
places they had visited with Caterine. She couldn't always avoid that, and sometimes Timothy would say,
"Mom liked it here, didn't she?" as though they were
sharing with Caterine still.

On other holidays he had always been chattering,
running ahead, eager for any action going. But now he
was quieter and often now he reached for Jenny's hand.

She was going to miss him terribly when his father
fetched him home. Work and friends weren't going to
fill the void. Paul Tremain phoned each evening, always
at the same time, and Timothy would tell him what they
had been doing, but even Timothy was a little in awe of
his father.

When Paul handed the phone over to Lorraine or to
Ebby, the housekeeper, Timothy's tone of voice
changed. He loved them all, and they loved him, but he
was more at ease with the womenfolk.

Jenny understood that. She often spoke to Paul

briefly before Timothy took his call. He couldn't have been more courteous, but she always felt that Paul Tremain's usual reaction to any sort of obtuseness would be irascibility. She always half expected to make a fool of herself.

Tomorrow Timothy was leaving her, and when she woke this morning and remembered that Paul was coming today she couldn't hold back a sigh. She dreaded the moment of parting. It would be like losing her own child.

If Timothy made any sort of fuss at all—she hoped and prayed he wouldn't but after the phone call last night fixing the time of his father's arrival he had clung to Jenny like a limpet—if he did make a fuss Paul might be impatient with him and that would be heartrending for Jenny.

She put on her housecoat and went into her tiny kitchenette, and as she began to cook bacon she heard Timothy padding over the living room lino. "Hungry, Timmy?" she asked.

"No." He had eaten better these last three days. She had done a lot of planning to tempt him to eat without him realizing it was strategy.

She said, "I think I'm hungry."

He stood in the doorway, scowling, looking so troubled that she longed to comfort him.

"I don't want to go back," he gulped. "I want to stay with you."

She wanted that too. She had to keep the wistfulness out of her voice and speak lightly. "What about your father and Lorraine? Whatever would they do?"

He was torn between loyalties and Jenny said, "You must go home, Tim, they couldn't manage without you, but you can always come for holidays, and I'll come and see you."

He watched her warily. "You wouldn't be scared?"

"Scared?" she echoed.

"When the storms came." There was fear in his voice and in his small tense face. "Of the sea witch."

That old story. The legend Jenny had thought so romantic when she first heard it, at fifteen on her first holiday at Tremain, of an ancestor of the Tremains who fell in love with a sea witch and tried to keep her on land. But she escaped back to the sea and sometimes when the storms came sang her siren song that could lure anyone who heard it.

"Sea witch weather," they called the wildest storms along the coastline of Tremain, and the tiny island, inhabited by birds, that could be seen on the skyline from the harbor was the Witch's Rock. It was part of local folklore, like the wrecker tales. Timothy had never feared the sea witch before.

But that was before the sea took Caterine. In a child's mind something could have reached for that car.

Jenny decided that she must phone Lorraine and tell her. It was years since she had met Paul's sister, but Lorraine was only a few months older than Jenny and the two girls had been holiday companions years ago. Lorraine had been thrilled then with her dazzling new sister-in-law, adoring Caterine on sight, and she had stayed devoted to Caterine. Caterine's death must have been traumatic for her, and Lorraine was a delicate girl. In the long run Lorraine could be more affected than Jenny, who was physically stronger.

Lorraine would be mothering Timothy now. And Mrs. Ebsworth, or Ebby, the housekeeper. They would take good care of Timothy.

Jenny said gently, "The accident was because the car skidded. It could have happened anywhere; it was nothing to do with the sea. And the sea witch is only a fairy tale. You don't believe in fairy tales, do you?"

"No." He was emphatic on that. "Not in fairy tales," he added.

They went around the market that morning. The

stalls were varied and there was plenty to keep Timothy entertained. They had lunch at the Lotus Bough, because Chinese food was a change and going through the menu could be turned into a game.

Paul Tremain would be arriving in the evening, that was what he had said. He had declined the offer of a night's lodging and said he would book into a hotel, come around in the evening and collect Timothy next morning.

Jenny had said, "Just as you wish, of course," relieved that he was going to a hotel.

After lunch they went to a film matinée and then back home. It was hardly tea time, but outside the house there was a car that had to be Paul's. Jenny's heart sank as they turned the corner and she saw the car and Timothy said, "Father's here."

Louie came hurrying into the hall to tell them, "Mr. Tremain's come. He went up."

"Thank you," said Jenny.

Timothy walked on, not hesitating but not hurrying, taking the stairs with deliberation, and Louie said very softly, "I can see why the spare bed wouldn't have done for him."

The spare bed had done very well for Rolf Perrie, who had been most appreciative, but one look at Paul Tremain had been enough to tell Louie that this man booked into the best hotel in town as a way of life.

She was sorry for him, of course, as sorry as she was for Jenny and Timothy. But after she had directed him to the rooms Jenny had kept for her own she realized she had let him go without offering a word of sympathy. Intrusion on his personal tragedy was beyond her.

Paul must have heard their footsteps in the passage. Before they reached the door he opened it and Timothy went quicker. "Hello, Tim," said Paul.

"Hello father." Timothy looked very small hurrying toward the big man. Paul Tremain always had made things look small, Jenny remembered: rooms, people. He picked up Timothy and carried him into Jenny's living room, and Timothy grinned, arms around his father's neck.

When he set down the child, who went running into the bedroom to fetch something to show him, he looked across at Jenny, a quick and searching look, checking for what?

He asked, "How are you?" so it must have been concern, and she was touched by it.

"I'm well," she said. She had seen Paul last at her mother's funeral. Before that not for some years, and not since. He didn't change. The lines in the strong-featured face were deep now, but she wondered—*did you weep for Caterine?*

She couldn't imagine him weeping. She felt that he would have shut himself away and come back within a reasonable time, grief contained, to deal with the problems that had to be dealt with. Even the problem of death.

Timothy had pictures from the zoo—they had been to Whipsnade on Wednesday—and Paul listened as Timothy explained and went into long accounts of what they had been doing and what they had seen.

Jenny watched Timothy, loving him, realizing at last that she should be offering Paul some sort of hospitality and apologizing, "I'm sorry. Will you have some tea?"

"Not for me, thank you."

She said, "I'd better get ours."

"I do the cooking. I get the tea," said Timothy. "Sometimes."

They had cheese on toast today, which Timothy served and when it was eaten and cleared away Paul said, "We have to make an early start in the morning, Tim. You'd better have an early night."

Timothy pulled a face but went, dragging unwilling feet, to the bathroom, and when Jenny brought him back, pink and glowing, he kissed his father good night.

Jenny cuddled him and tucked him up as she did each night, and tonight he said, "You will come, won't you?"

"Of course," she promised.

"Soon?"

"As soon as I get a holiday."

That seemed to satisfy him. At least he snuggled down between the sheets and she went back into the living room. Paul signaled to her to close the door. As she did he said, "Thank you."

"For having Timmy? I don't know how I'd have made it through these days without him."

He was sitting in the big chair. She sat at the table and wondered what it would be like eating here alone again.

"They haven't been easy days, have they?" said Paul.

"I still don't believe it." There were still times when she didn't.

"I wish I could say I didn't." He would have seen Caterine, identified her.

Jenny asked quickly, "How is everyone? How's Lorraine?"

"Taking it badly," he said. "She's been very near to a breakdown." Lorraine had been shielded all her life; nothing like this could have happened to her before.

Paul said abruptly, "Jenny, have you any immediate plans?"

"Plans?"

He put it another way. "Is there any reason why you must stay here?"

"No."

"Good. Then will you come down to Tremain for a month or so?"

She hadn't expected him to suggest that, but she said "Yes" at once, without stopping for a moment to consider.

He looked relieved. She must be looking astonished because it was a complete surprise. He said, "Timothy is very fond of you, and I'm more than grateful for what you've done for him already."

Timothy had been bright and nearer his normal self just now, but Jenny tried to explain, "It wasn't all me. Most of it was getting away from Tremain. When he gets back he could be afraid."

"I know. But he has to come back and he has to feel secure again. If you could be around I think perhaps he might."

She said, "I'll try." She would do more than try. She loved her sister's child with fierce protectiveness and she was so glad of this chance to be with him, to help him, not to lose him. She had been so afraid she was going to lose him.

She got up, trying to put this into words, and Paul said, "Your time will be your own, of course, and I'll pay you what you'd be earning."

"You will not!" There was no reason for her intensity of resentment, except that she felt like the poor relation again. She snapped, "You're not employing me," and was horrified at herself because that was downright rude and, worse, could mean that he would say, "All right, forget it."

She said, "I'm sorry, but I don't want to be paid."

"Of course I'm not employing you, but I am taking you away from your employment, and why should you be the loser?"

Put like that it was more unreasonable than ever, but she couldn't pick up a salary for being with Timothy.

She said, "I'd rather not, if you don't mind. I do have some money coming in from the house." She ventured a weak smile. "And I presume I'd get room and board?"

"Then that's settled," he said.

Jenny left with them next morning. She had packed after Paul left last night and asked Louie to send on the mail, giving her the phone number of Moidores. It had been that simple. No one was going to say, "Don't go, Jenny," because she had no really close friends. Caring for her mother all those years had kept her from making friends. She was a free agent now, rootless although she had lived in this house all her life. It was not the kind of house that put down roots.

She went out of the front door with Timothy skipping by her side, and knew she wouldn't care if she never saw the place again. Although of course she would see it again. She was only going to Tremain for a little while. This was still her home.

Timothy was beaming. When she'd told him his delight had sent him leaping around like a crackerjack, and she had had a hard time calming him before his father arrived. Paul wanted her to help Timothy back to a calm and stable way of life, not get him so over-excited that he was as near to tears as laughter.

But he calmed down when he heard the car—his father was a restraining influence—and jogged out still talking about how smashing it was that Auntie Jen was coming.

It was a long drive, although the car went superbly. Paul didn't join in the conversation. In the back seat Jenny and Timothy chattered together and read a book, and Jenny spun stories and made up games. Paul could have been a chauffeur or a taxi driver. Unless Timothy spoke to him he didn't speak, and then he would answer, mostly with information. Most of Timothy's remarks were along the lines of "What's that? Where are we? Why is it?" But everything Paul said had an economy that dealt with the subject and closed it.

They stopped for a meal, eating at a good restaurant that seemed to be crowded but where a table was quickly found for them; and as Jenny helped Timothy with his selection she met the appraising glances of two well-dressed women at the next table.

Maybe they were thinking she looked too young to be Timothy's mother—although Caterine had looked no older, only lovelier. Maybe they would decide she was the au pair girl; her clothes didn't match Paul's, which spoilt it as a family group.

Making weak jokes to herself helped to keep her spirits up. She was glad to be here with Timothy, but she was only here because Caterine was dead, and that thought was never out of her mind.

Paul must be thinking that too. Physically he was with them, but his thoughts were not. Jenny made no attempt to draw him into conversation. She was here for Timothy and she confined herself to the child.

Timothy tired before the end of the journey and slept, huddled against Jenny, so that they drove for miles in silence, skirting the holiday resorts, coming on wilder lonelier country, where the roads were narrow and twisted, lined by high hedges through which every now and then they glimpsed the sea.

Jenny had not been to Tremain for years, but she remembered her first sight of it, and she looked for landmarks.

Tremain was a small natural harbor. For centuries fishing had been the livelihood of the men who lived in the little granite houses clustered around the quayside or clinging to the steep sides of the gorge. But now the tourist trade reached here in summer. There were shops, an artists' colony.

Rounding one spur of the coastline you could see the

lights of Tremain in the gathering dusk, and on the cliffs just beyond, above another cove, you could see the house.

Moidores dominated the skyline. It was rather narrow and high. Early Victorian Tremains had renovated the central part and raised it. The wider, lower parts had been left; some converted to outbuildings, other parts crumbling away, their Tudor beams exposed to the elements.

Facing the cliff edge a row of trees had once been planted as protection against the winds from the sea. There were gaps where some had gone with the crumbling cliff, others slanted with parts of their roots showing over the edge.

It had always seemed to Jenny that this was the true front of the house, facing the sea. Not the house that faced the road, with its curved drive, smooth lawns and well cut hedges.

In the driver's seat Paul Tremain stayed silent, and they passed the little signpost pointing down to Tremain with the notice beneath "No cars beyond this spot," and drove on along the cliff road.

There must be clues to pinpoint the accident: a hedge smashed, a fence repaired. Jenny couldn't look, but as they went through the gates and down the drive she glanced up at the turret window through which Timothy must have watched the road.

The lights were on in a number of rooms, and Jenny said softly, "Wake up, Timmy, we're home."

He woke easily. Once he had needed shaking awake, but not now. He opened his eyes and blinked the drowsiness out of them and sat up.

The front door opened as the car stopped and the housekeeper, Mrs. Ebsworth, came out. She was a tall woman, rawboned, with iron gray hair drawn severely back and a smile of surprising sweetness. Timothy went running to her and she bent to kiss him, then straightened to smile at Jenny. "My, it's a long time since we've seen you," she said.

"You haven't changed a bit," said Jenny. It wasn't that long, it was just something to say because Jenny was choked with emotion, and the grip of Ebby's hands told her the older woman was too.

They went into the hall, and a girl ran down the stairs—Lorraine. She was as fair as her brother was dark, as fragile as he was strong. She was a very attractive girl and she and Jenny had been good friends in the old days.

Paul said, "Jenny will be staying with us for a while."

"Isn't that smashing?" said Timothy. Ebby nodded and smiled, agreeing. Lorraine stood at the bottom of the stairs looking at Jenny with a startled widening of the eyes. Then she came forward and put her arms around her and kissed her and said, "Hello, Jenny, it's lovely to see you."

But Lorraine's first reaction had not been welcome. Jenny was not sure what it had been.

CHAPTER TWO

"YOU SHOULD HAVE TOLD ME," Mrs. Ebsworth said severely. "I'd have had a room ready."

She clicked her tongue at Paul and he said, "The room next to Timothy's."

So he hadn't left here intending to bring Jenny back with him. He must have made up his mind last night. She was a surprise to the women of the household, although now Lorraine was smiling tremulously.

Why didn't you want me here, Jenny wondered. Or did she imagine the way the girl had just looked at her?

Mrs. Ebsworth said, "There's a message from Mr. Morrison on your desk."

"Thank you." Paul turned toward the door that Jenny remembered as his office. "Would you bring me some coffee and sandwiches in?"

He went into the office, and Mrs. Ebsworth began to tell Timothy that she had made some gingerbread for him. If he came with her he could have a piece.

"Is Auntie Jen coming?" he wanted to know, and Jenny smiled and said she'd be along.

That seemed to do. He went, and none too soon because Lorraine's tears suddenly overflowed. She turned her face away. "I'm sorry, Jenny," she sobbed. "I know you feel as badly as I do, and it's worse for Paul, but I can't help it."

With her fragile physique and her translucent skin and the shadows like bruises around her eyes Jenny could believe that Lorraine's breaking point had been nearly reached. Lorraine had never been robust. On those holidays she had tired far sooner than Jenny, and now it was Jenny who did the comforting, so far as anyone could comfort.

Lorraine dried her tears, then went into the drawing room and swallowed a couple of pills from a pretty little jeweled pill box on the mantel. She said, "The doctor gave me these. They do help."

"Good," said Jenny. For how long, she wondered. And how many was Lorraine taking? She had to go after Timothy, because she had told him she was following and she must. But she could see why Paul had brought her here. Lorraine couldn't give Timothy a feeling of security again; Lorraine seemed lost herself.

Ebby was the solid one. Jenny remembered her with affection, and Alec Ebsworth her husband, "Eb" the gardener. They were both in the kitchen with Timothy and they turned to look approvingly at Jenny, counting Timothy's improvement her doing.

"This is more like our lad," said Eb.

Jenny's expression warned them the improvement could be temporary, and they knew it. But while Timothy ate his supper they pretended a mighty interest in everything he had done on his "holiday" and when the child's chatter ran out on that subject Ebby asked, "Where are you going to take Auntie Jenny tomorrow?"

"Down to the harbor first," said Jenny. "I want to see Tremain again."

Lorraine came into the kitchen as Jenny was taking Timothy off for his bath. She was calm now, and she said, "Bedtime, Timmy?"

"Yeah," said Timothy wistfully.

"See you tomorrow," said Lorraine. She ruffled his hair. "I'm glad you're back, and I'm glad you brought Jenny."

"She's having the room next to me." Timothy looked up at Jenny. "Not mom's room. Nobody's ever going to have mom's room, are they?"

"You must show me my room," Jenny said quickly. "I don't know which it is."

"I'll show you," said Timothy.

He had been a baby when Jenny was last here. In those days the nursery had had a frieze of flopsy bunnies and wall-eyed donkeys. Now it was a boy's room, three white walls, one navy; the nursery furniture exchanged for a sea chest, a bunk bed, fitted cupboards—one with a formica-topped working surface running the length of the wall under the windows.

There were posters of astronauts and dinosaurs. Timothy seemed to be covering quite a range of evolution, and although the room was tidy now Jenny knew that with Timothy around again the cupboard doors would burst open, their contents spilling everywhere, and the desk top would be piled high.

A connecting door led into Jenny's room. The bed was made up and turned back, and it was a pleasant room.

With Timothy in bed Jenny unpacked, putting her clothes in the chest of drawers that smelt of lavender, or hanging them in the deep clothes closet. She took her time unpacking, and then she brushed her hair, watching herself in the oval Victorian mirror that swung on its stand on top of the chest of drawers.

She looked pale and felt she looked plain. This had been the nanny's room in the old days when families were larger. There was a schoolroom too. Lorraine had been privately educated. Not Paul. Charterhouse and Oxford, for him.

I look like a Victorian governess, Jenny thought, *pale and plain and meek*. And she remembered Caterine with her tossing hair and glowing beauty and understood why their parents had loved Caterine best, why everyone loved Caterine best.

Timothy must have fallen asleep quickly. He was deep in slumber when she went to his bedside and looked down at him. She resisted the temptation to fuss, smoothing pillows or tucking in sheets, and went out of the room.

As she walked along the passage Lorraine called, "Jenny!" A bedroom door was open and Lorraine sat on the dressing-table stool, watching who passed the open door.

Jenny went in. They had giggled together as schoolgirls in here, but this room had changed as much as the nursery. The wall-to-wall carpeting was white and the walls shimmered with silk, the color of a summer sky. Jenny asked, "Whatever happened to the pop stars?"

Lorraine managed a smile. "I grew out of them." She looked around, as if she was trying to remember the way it used to be. "Do you like it?"

"Who wouldn't? It's beautiful."

"We had the rooms done about a couple of years ago."

"The rooms?"

"This and Caterine's."

Jenny remembered Caterine telling her about the topname interior decorator who had redesigned some of the house. Caterine and Paul's bedroom had been in another wing, overlooking the sea.

Lorraine picked up a perfume bottle from the dressing table, and dabbed pulse points lightly and nervously with a glass stopper. "Caterine never did like the sound of the sea. She never got used to it; she couldn't sleep because of it, so she had to have a room on this side of the house. She had the room right opposite the nursery."

She gestured helplessly. "Timothy keeps hiding in there, waiting for her, I suppose. Isn't that dreadful? The cupboards are full of her clothes and she chose the wallpaper and the curtains and the carpet, and it still feels like Caterine's room."

"Now Timmy's back something will have to be done,

won't it?" But Lorraine did not seem capable of doing anything, as she sat white-faced and stricken.

Locking the door or repapering the walls were short-term solutions, Jenny thought. Only time and love would get Timothy through this bewilderment of loss. He was very young and he was loved, and he would come through it as Jenny herself must.

Lorraine said huskily, "You weren't here, Jenny, you can't imagine how dreadful it was. I'll remember it all my life. When Timmy started screaming—"

Jenny didn't want to hear. She asked desperately, "How's the shop going?"

Lorraine ran a crafts shop down by the harbor where most of the artists displayed their wares, but now she looked blank. "The shop? Oh, the shop? I haven't been down since."

She sounded as though the accident had stopped the world. She said, "Someone's running it."

Paul Tremain had someone running everything around here, this was his kingdom, but surely Lorraine would have been better in the shop than in the house, reliving the tragedy, taking tranquilizers.

Jenny's saving had been getting out with Timothy, and she said, "Will you come down to the harbor with us in the morning?"

"I'll see how I feel." Lorraine was not promising.

"Has it changed much?" asked Jenny.

"Tremain? No."

"Still the same people?"

"There are some new faces among the artists, and some new men at the mine, but the families in Tremain are the same, and on the farms." She gave Jenny a side-wards glance. "Rolf Perrie brought Timmy up to you, didn't he?"

"Yes." Something in Lorraine's voice made Jenny return the look with raised eyebrows.

Caterine had spoken of young men who went out with Lorraine from time to time, but the affairs always seemed to peter out. Caterine would joke about them, "If I don't watch it I'll have two spinster sisters."

She hadn't talked of Rolf Perrie and Jenny asked casually, "Any particular man in your life right now?"

"No particular one."

"Not Rolf?"

Lorraine was jerked out of her lassitude. "Why on earth should you think that?"

"I don't really know," Jenny admitted.

"Rolf Perrie? Heavens, *no!*" Perhaps it was because up to now her voice had been hushed and husky that this sounded so shrill and Jenny was left wondering.

Jenny was tired. She had a hot bath and sank into bed, but was not surprised when she didn't fall asleep. She had brought up a book half expecting this, and stayed with it doggedly until her eyes began to blur and it was a relief to turn out the light.

You could hardly hear the sea at all in this room. Its sound was soothing and restful, and Jenny loved the sea. She remembered looking out from the other side of the house, thrilled by the magnificence of the view and Caterine beside her shuddering, saying, "They used to lure the ships onto the rocks down there, and if one man or one animal got ashore alive it wasn't legally a wreck, so no one ever did."

Caterine had not. Perhaps that was why she had always feared the sea. Jenny forced back the tears and made herself think of tomorrow while she waited for sleep. The time of weeping was over; life had to go on.

She woke to the faint rumble of thunder. It was some distance away, but it still sounded like storm, and storms terrified Timothy. She slipped out of bed and opened the dividing door between their rooms very quietly.

Moonlight shone on his bed, but there was no sign of Timothy, and Jenny ran out into the passage where light filtered opposite, edging the door of Caterine's room.

"Timmy goes in there, looking for Caterine," Lorraine had said, and Jenny bit her lip, angry with herself. She should have woken sooner. She should never have let this happen.

She opened the door and called softly, "Timmy," and saw Paul. He stood by the window. The curtains were wide and the window showed only darkness. Her eyes were dazzled by the light, but as he came toward her she saw grayness through the tan of his skin as though he was a dying man. He asked curtly, "What is it?"

"Timmy isn't in bed."

He went past her across the corridor into the nursery. Through the open doors she saw him pull back the counterpane, then stoop to lift the child higher. Timothy had slithered down in sleep, under the sheets.

Paul said a few quiet words of reassurance, but Timothy didn't wake. Then he came back and Jenny said wretchedly, "I should have looked closer, but I saw the light around the door and Lorraine told me he sometimes comes in here."

"Yes."

There were dustsheets on the furniture, but she could smell Caterine's perfume on the air. There was no other quite like it, floral but not sweet, a sharp scent that had been specially blended for her; persistent enough to make a child feel that the woman who always wore it was near. A child—or a man.

The cupboards were full of Caterine's clothes. To stir anything would be to stir fragrance.

Paul said, "You'd better get back to bed."

He closed the door after her and in her own room she picked up her watch and saw that it was past three o'clock. The night was almost over and Paul had been fully dressed, so he couldn't have slept at all. And he had driven down from the Midlands yesterday and he was presumably working today. Grieving in that shrouded room could do nothing, except help to break him.

She turned slowly, reluctant, but unable to switch off the light and go to sleep. She tapped the door and he opened it and she said, "Please don't stay here, please try to get some rest."

He exclaimed, "For God's sake!"

"I loved her too." That was her only excuse. "I know she wouldn't want—"

He said wearily, "You don't know what you're talking about," and shut the door in her face, but she had expected that. She went back to the child, the one she could help.

The thunder still faint and far away, Timothy still slept. She left the door ajar between her own room and the nursery and lay awake until she was sure the storm was coming no nearer tonight.

Lorraine did not go down to the harbor with them. She said, "Tomorrow, perhaps."

Timothy tugged at Jenny's hand and urged, "Come *on*, Auntie Jen."

The sea always cut off the cove below Moidores from the harbor of Tremain. Tremain was reached either by rounding the cliffs by boat, or by the cliff road, then down the cobbled way.

They had to pass where Caterine's car had crashed, Jenny knew it by the tightening of Timothy's fingers around her hand. The road curved slightly here, but Caterine must have been traveling fast to take her over the rough grasses and through the fencing. The prospect of a long journey ahead could have accounted for that, or simply that she was thinking of other things and misjudged.

Jenny talked all the way, about the people she used to know in Tremain. "The pink house? Who lives in the pink house now, Timmy, the house on the corner by the quay?"

"Dan," he said, "and Mrs. Blaskie."

"*Yes*," said Jenny. "He's a fisherman. Oh, I remember them. Start at the top of the hill and tell me all the way down."

Timothy did, although before he had catalogued halfway down the hill they had reached the signpost and were passing the houses. There was no pavement. Several of the houses clinging to the hillside did bed-and-breakfast and one was a guest house. There were shops, a pub called the Crow's Nest high on the hill, and another on the jetty called the Tremain Arms. At the bottom of the gorge narrow streets intersected, and around the little harbor were more houses, more shops.

It was picturesque and it was prosperous. Everything was brightly painted, some of the buildings colorwashed, some with white windows and doors contrasting with the gray of granite.

Today was a fine day, with visitors who had left their cars at the top walking down the steep and cobbled street, leaning over the harbor wall, spending their money and enjoying themselves.

All the locals knew Timothy, of course. They waved to him and called and looked to see who was with him. Even those who didn't remember Jenny saw her resemblance to Caterine and stopped smiling and looked sorry for her.

She bought ice cream from the sweet shop and Alice Pentreath, who had served behind this counter for twenty-five years, said, "Hello, Jenny, it's nice to see you again." As Timothy skipped ahead out of the shop licking his extra-large cone, she added, "I can't tell you how sorry everybody is. It's a wicked thing, she was a lovely girl." Alice's round face went haggard, her gaze following Timothy. "Poor little motherless soul. He's got a good father, of course, but it's not the same, is it? And Mr. Tremain's a busy man, and—well, it's never the same."

The harbor was full of boats, some bobbing on the water, some drawn up on the shingle. Timothy pointed to one, lying at anchor near the mouth of the harbor. "That's ours, the *Mylor*."

When Jenny had come here before the Tremain craft had been a gleaming white yacht. This didn't look so new, schooner-rigged, a little over thirty feet, she reckoned. She said, "I'd love to go sailing. I wonder if we might some time."

Timothy watched a seagull, squinting at it with a concentration that camouflaged his troubled frown. "I dunno," he said reluctantly. "Father doesn't always take anybody. He goes on his own most times."

"Never mind, there are lots of other things to do."

Timothy was not eager to sail and she wondered whether he was not sure Paul wanted him aboard until he said, "That's the Witch's Rock," and his voice shook.

The rock covered a small area but jutted high. It was over two miles out, but on a clear day you could see it from Tremain, even make out the pattern of it. It rose sheer above the waves facing the western seas, and sloping backwards toward the mainland until it curved in horseshoe shape, the inlet flattening to a tiny sandy cove.

According to the old story it was where the Tremain had caught the sea witch, and Jenny recalled it as a place of delight with its secret silver beach and its caves. At fifteen the caves had seemed to her pure magic, but Timothy didn't want to go to the Witch's Rock.

He turned his back on it now, and on the sea, and asked, "Want to see Auntie Lorraine's shop?"

"Mmm, of *course*!" Jenny pretended great enthusiasm and she did want to see the shop, which was in a good spot toward the end of the harbor, next to an archway leading to what had once been a boat builders' yard and a row of cottages, but was now the artists' colony.

It was a double-fronted shop, displaying some saleable stuff: one or two pieces of stone sculpture, some pottery, a bone carved and polished until it looked like ivory, piskies in pottery and metal and wood; and pictures, a lot of pictures.

There were several people inside, looking around, and a woman in blue jeans and a scarlet shirt was sitting at a table toward the back of the shop, sketching with charcoal on a large white pad. She seemed intent on her work, but as Jenny and Timothy neared her she said, "Hello, Timmy," without looking up.

Timothy said, "This is my Auntie Jenny," and she looked up then.

She had short graying hair and a tanned skin that made her teeth very white when she smiled. She said, "Grace Norbrook, I'm minding the store."

She took the money for a piskie and popped him into a bag, said "Thank you, do come again," then turned back to Timothy. "Leah and John are around somewhere. Have you come to play?"

Play would be fine, but Jenny was in charge of Timothy and a little apprehensive about letting him out of her sight. On the other hand he could surely come to no harm down here where everyone was his friend. Grace said with a smile, "They're in the same gang. They go to school together."

Timothy was going to boarding school next year. Jenny had thought that was a pity, but Caterine had said his name had been down practically from birth and boarding schools didn't come any better.

Now he looked longingly at the door and Jenny said, "Shall we go and find them?"

"If you'll mind the shop," Grace offered, "I will."

Jenny had never been a salesgirl, but she said, "Fine," and Grace went out through the side door that led to the courtyard.

Everything was priced, which made it simpler, and Jenny was completing the sale of a watercolor when Grace came back with two youngsters of Timothy's age: a little girl, fair and stolid, and a boy, gipsy brown and thin.

Timothy introduced her again, "This is my Auntie Jenny," and the two children grinned at her.

Grace Norbrook said, "They know they mustn't go away. They're to stay down in the harbor, and how long can Timmy stay?"

"Oh, an hour," said Jenny. Longer if they were having fun, because this was what Timothy needed. "I'll sit on the harbor wall," she said, "and get a sun tan." And watch Timothy. She mustn't be overprotective, but she would be happier keeping an eye on him.

The three children ran out together into the sunshine, going through the door in a squirming jumble, and Grace said, "You don't mind, do you?"

"Of course not."

"They get on well together, even when they're scrapping. And the roads are safe down here, no cars."

She remembered and bit her lip and said, "It was a terrible thing to happen."

A whole town mourned for Caterine, wherever you turned. And there was nothing you could say, except, "Yes, it was terrible."

Grace asked, "How's Lorraine?"

"Not too good yet," Jenny admitted.

Someone bought a shell from a huge basket of shells and went out listening to it. Standing near to a window

Jenny could see Timothy and his friends on the beach, walking with heads down, obviously searching. As Grace joined her again Jenny asked, "What are they looking for?"

"This sort of thing." Grace pointed towards a shelf of flotsam ware, root and branch sculptures. "These were all found on the shore—John's father specializes in them. And Leah's mother does these." She touched a paperweight of pearl pink shells and shining pebbles.

"Pretty," said Jenny.

"For the tourists," Grace smiled, and whispered, "They sell better than the pictures."

The shop seemed busy this morning, but it was brighter weather than for some time. Jenny asked, "What sort of season have you had?"

"Fair," said Grace. "Tremain cottage industries get around. Everything pays its way around here."

"That's good," said Jenny.

Grace said, "Yes, it is," as though there were those who thought otherwise. "Tell Lorraine we're coping, will you, although we'd like to see her back."

"Does she run this place on her own?" Grace Norbrook could probably cope with half a dozen jobs and keep her cool, but Jenny would have expected Lorraine to dither under any sort of pressure.

"More or less," said Grace. "If there's a rush someone gives a hand, and if there's a special exhibition of course."

"That surprises me," said Jenny.

"Does it?" Grace sounded reflective. "But perhaps you've only seen her up at Moidores."

"I haven't seen her at all for a long time. Is she different at Moidores?"

The house overlooking the next cove also dominated the harbor. Even when the sun was shining, as it was now, the sea face of Moidores looked dark.

Grace laughed. "I think everyone is. Paul Tremain isn't the man to approve of a girl having her say, or doing her thing, is he?"

He had dictated Caterine's way of life, and Lorraine had less spirit and less strength than Caterine.

Jenny asked, "What is Lorraine like down here?"

Grace said quickly, "Don't get me wrong, I'm not saying she's a brilliant business woman. She can be put on and she can be cheated, but she does know a good picture when she sees it, and she works hard. Down here she makes her own decisions."

She added dryly, "Mind you, if her brother thinks differently she soon changes them again."

"You mean he has the final word?"

"In Tremain," said Grace, "Paul Tremain *is* the final word."

"He sounds a thorough-going dictator." Some of the resentment Jenny had always felt on Caterine's behalf came through.

Grace said, "More benevolent feudal really. The maddening thing is he's usually right." She laughed again and asked, "How long are you staying?"

"I don't know." Jenny moved around the side of the window display, almost pressing her cheek to the pane to watch Timothy, still with his friends, talking to someone by the harbor wall. "As long as Timothy needs me."

"He seems better than we'd heard."

"The sun's shining," said Jenny. "It's storms that frighten him."

Timothy spotted her behind the glass of the window and pointed, and the man with the children turned and stared. Jenny saw his face stiffen and knew that it was her resemblance to Caterine that disturbed him.

Grace was saying, "Come down any time you need company. My house is the yellow door, third along, and the neighbors would be glad to see you."

"Thank you," Jenny murmured.

The man came into the shop. He was wiry, with black curly hair, wearing rope sandals, dingy slacks and a pink shirt open to the waist. He looked grave, but it was a face that would be attractive when he smiled.

"You're Jenny?" he said.

"Yes."

"I'm Jack Bastaple." Nobody had spoken of him to her, and he went on introducing himself as though he didn't expect the name to ring bells. "I live here. That's mine." "That" was a painting, and Jenny looked as he indicated. Probably it was good, a dramatic study of sea and sky. He went on, "Fancy a coffee or a drink?"

She hesitated. "Thank you, but I came down with Timothy and I know he's all right, but . . . ." She couldn't resist glancing back toward the window.

Jack Bastaple said reassuringly, "Of course he's all right. Anyhow, the pub has the sunshades out today, so we could sit there and watch the kids."

They were all being kind to Caterine's sister. Jenny said, "That sounds pleasant," and to Grace, "I'll see you later?"

The Tremain Arms was central, where the road joined the quay. There were little tables outside and Jenny sat down while Jack Bastaple brought out two iced lagers.

He hadn't mentioned Caterine until he said, "There is a likeness."

"A slight one."

He nodded, agreeing it was slight. "I shouldn't think you were really alike, were you?"

The glasses were so cold they were misted. Caterine had been confident and cherished and beautiful and beloved. Jenny took a sip of cold amber liquid and said, "No."

He said quietly, "She was enchanting."

There we were not alike, thought Jenny wryly; *I have never enchanted anyone in my life*.

"It was such a waste," he said. Then, with an obvious effort, he changed the subject. "Tell me about yourself. What do you do for a living?"

"Shorthand and typing," she said. "What could be duller?" She hadn't found it dull, it depended on where and what, but he was looking at her and remembering Caterine and she had no illusions that he really wanted the story of her life. She turned the talk back to him. "Have you lived here long?"

"I was born here." So he must have been around when Jenny came four years ago. "My father was a painter."

"Was?"

"My parents died before the changeover."

"What changeover?"

His voice was grim. "When Paul Tremain took over."

Jenny said without thinking, "But I thought Tremain was always his," and he laughed, the grimness dissolving.

"He's not *that* old." Paul had been five years older than Caterine, of course that wasn't what she'd meant. "The changeover after his father died. His father was a grand fellow. He'd have given you the coat off his back."

"And Paul wouldn't?"

Jack Bastaple looked as though the lager had turned sour. "I wouldn't care to be needing his coat unless I could offer a good price for it."

"I gather you don't like him?"

"I liked his father." He spoke with regret and affection. He looked at the little harbor. "And I liked this place before the tourists came swarming, when the only boats out there were fishermen's boats."

Some of the boats were probably fishing boats still,

but there were launches now, luggers, ketches, yawls, a couple of yachts. "My folk were poor," he told her, "but we were happy. If you couldn't raise the rent you knew it could wait. It didn't often have to wait because it wasn't much of a rent in those days."

He sounded like an old man recalling old times, although he couldn't be out of his twenties. "They were good days," he said, mourning them.

Jenny had never seen Tremain as the sleepy village of Jack Bastaple's boyhood, but she could understand his feeling that the visitors were intruders. As an intruder herself she was defensive. "But they are customers. They do buy your paintings."

"Sometimes," he admitted grudgingly.

He glowered at a plump lady who was demanding shrilly and nasally of a plump gentleman taking a movie, "Hon, isn't this just the sweetest, quaintest little old place you have ever seen?"

Jenny held back a giggle. "I think it's the sweetest too."

"You do?" He frowned at her, and to him it was no laughing matter.

Of course sweet was not the word. Down in the harbor now, in sunshine, with people in colorful holiday clothes, Tremain had a picture-postcard charm. But this was wrecker country, dangerous as the rocks under the shining water.

Out of season, in winter, it would be a very different place.

Jenny said, "I've never been here in the winter."

She picked out Timothy's bright blue T-shirt near the end of the jetty where one of the pleasure boats was moored. His friends were still with him. The stolid-looking little girl was skipping up and down, the boys were talking to the man who was helping passengers into the boat.

Jack asked, "Are you going to be here in winter?"

"I don't think so." This was the first week of August. "I think I'll be gone long before then."

"If you escape."

She turned to stare at him. *"What?"*

His eyes took her gaze out to the Witch's Rock. He said, "This Tremain would never have let the sea witch get away."

"What does that mean?"

"Moidores was a golden prison to Caterine. If you have any talents they'll die in that house. Tremain will see to that. Caterine wasted her gifts."

"I know." It seemed everyone knew, and to a dedicated artist wasting your gifts would be a betrayal. "But it was Caterine's choice and she *was* happy."

"She might have been happier."

Of course she might, if she could have had the best of both worlds. But she had counted her career well lost for love and she hadn't regretted it.

Jenny said, "What's the use of talking like this now?" What could be more futile? "And it was never any use talking. It was Caterine's choice."

"You've never tried fighting Tremain, have you?"

"No."

"The rocks out there are easier to move than him." Some of this bitterness could be for Caterine, but some was surely for himself.

Jenny heard herself say, "You hate him, don't you?"

That checked him. He sat silent for a morose moment, then he denied it. "No, I don't hate him." A few more seconds and he smiled, "It's just that I would like to see someone stand up to him for once and get away with it."

Behind that statement she sensed years of frustration. "In Tremain Paul Tremain *is* the final word," Grace had said.

Jenny smiled too, "You don't mean me," and he laughed with her and patted her hand on the table.

"Oh no, not you."

He meant she would stand no chance, she was no use for moving rocks, and he could well be right. But she could leave Moidores whenever she chose, and while she stayed Paul Tremain was making no rules for her.

The children were coming from the jetty, running along by the harbor wall, heading for the Tremain Arms, and Jenny leaned forward anxiously because they weren't smiling.

As they reached her Leah said firmly, "Timothy can go around the bay, can't he?"

John explained, "In the *White Wave*. It isn't full and Jim says we can go, only Tim says you mightn't let him."

Timothy hadn't spoken. Now he said jerkily, "I said I think we've got to go home." He was not breathless, he was holding his breath. A pleasure trip with his friends on a lovely day could have been the ideal way of dispelling his fears of the sea. But if there was any risk of panic his friends mustn't see it, for his pride was precious to him.

Jenny glanced at her watch and said, "I'm afraid we must. We have to look in the shop again, and then we do have to go home."

Leah and John scowled at her, the villain of the piece, the spoilsport. They were sorry for Timothy being lumbered with her.

Jack Bastaple got up and said, "I'll walk back with you." The children followed. Jenny heard Timothy say in answer to Leah's mutter, "She is *not*! She's all right."

Just outside the crafts shop Leah and John scampered away, back toward the jetty, and Timothy stood by the window looking through the glass into the shop.

He wasn't seeing the goods for sale, Jenny knew. He

was scared, and he was scared that his friends would guess. Her heart ached for him because at seven years of age, after what had happened, anyone—including stolid little Leah—would understand why he feared the sea. He shouldn't need pride at seven.

Grace was serving. Jack joined a couple who were viewing the paintings and told them that the artist they fancied but considered pricey had exhibited in last year's Academy. They looked as though that might tip the balance.

Jenny examined the shells in the basket by the door. She could see Timothy without looking at him directly, and as she poked carefully around he came inside and looked down with her.

He said, "You don't want to buy them. You can pick them up on the beach."

Jenny smiled. If Jack Bastaple heard that he would certainly think Timothy spoke as his father's son, although in Jenny's experience Paul Tremain was far from tight-fisted and Timothy loved giving.

"All right," she said. "You show me where to find them."

Grace went to the door with her customers, who now wanted to see a Cornish tin mine. She was giving them directions how to get there, and she stepped outside to finish. She came back, smiling. "We're having a busy morning. Jenny, you've brought the sunshine. And the trade."

"I only hope I can keep it up," said Jenny. "We're off home now. Is there anything you want me to tell Lorraine, anything I can take up for you?" While Grace was considering she added, "It might be a good idea," and Grace nodded, understanding.

"Ah yes—well, there's some correspondence here I'd set aside for Mr. Morrison."

Joseph Morrison, Paul's personal assistant. Jenny remembered him as a gray man: gray hair, gray suit, gray eyes. He had been middle-aged. He would still be middle-aged, very quiet and efficient.

Grace brought a large envelope out of a room at the back of the shop and said, "If Lorraine isn't up to it, give them to Mr. Morrison, would you?"

Jack Bastaple walked with them to the gates of Moidores and watched them down the drive and into the house. On his way back to Tremain he came again to the curve in the road where Caterine's car had skidded. With Jenny and Timothy he had passed it without a glance, but now he left the road and crossed the rough turf to the cliff's edge. He stood there for a long time. . . .

Ebby was in the kitchen and Jenny left Timothy with her to find Lorraine. Lorraine was in the drawing room, sitting at the little Georgian writing bureau with an open diary. As Jenny walked in she said, "It's Caterine's. There would have been a dinner party on Saturday."

Caterine had loved entertaining, Jenny knew. She was a wonderful hostess and had had so many friends. Lorraine said desolately, "It's so quiet without her. I keep expecting her to walk in, or I find myself listening for her." She tilted her head as though she was listening now and Jenny put down the envelope on top of the desk diary.

"Grace asked me to bring you that. Grace Norwood."

"You met Grace?" Lorraine looked at the envelope, making no attempt to open it.

"In the shop. And Jack Bastaple." As Lorraine said nothing Jenny went on, "I don't remember either of them, but Jack was born here, wasn't he? I don't think I met him before. Was Grace here then?"

"No. She and her husband came just after you stopped coming."

"I liked the shop," said Jenny. She talked about the customers she had seen this morning and asked about the artists, and from brief replies Lorraine gradually became more expansive. Jenny said, "Grace said if you didn't want to bother with these I was to give them to Mr. Morrison."

Lorraine tipped the contents of the envelope onto the desk and said, "I'd better see what they are."

Lunch was a light meal, eaten around the kitchen table with Eb and Ebby and Dolly the daily who lived in Tremain. Paul was rarely in to lunch, Jenny was told, and when she was down at the shop often as not neither was Lorraine.

Lorraine said that tommorrow she would be going down to Tremain, and after lunch she went back to the papers Jenny had brought for her.

Jenny and Timothy spent the afternoon in the cove below Moidores. The only way down was the iron steps fixed in the cliff face, and for that you needed fitness and a head for heights. Jenny was fit enough, but she closed her eyes while she was on the steps, finally feeling rock under her feet with remembered relief.

Once down it was worth the effort. The tide was going out, leaving behind wet shingle and cool rocks and little pools, each a tiny watery world. They clambered over the rocks and peered into the pools and Jenny felt as young as Timothy. He knew more about the seashore than she did. This having been his playground all his life, he knew the names of the weeds and the creatures.

The sun shone as they ran and splashed at the water's edge. Timothy was a good swimmer, but he didn't swim this afternoon, so Jenny said, "You'll have to teach me some time because I don't swim as well as you do."

"All right," said Timothy. "Do you like being here?" He spoke smugly, for it was his cove, and Jenny's delight in it was immense. She felt a content that glowed warmer than the sun on her skin, and when they had to leave, and Timothy scrambled ahead up the cliff face, she was relaxed and refreshed. Sea air suited her. It made her a new woman.

Paul didn't join them that evening. After dinner, with Timothy in bed, Jenny and Lorraine sat watching television and talking. Lorraine seemed more relaxed too, although whether that was tranquilizers or the work Grace had sent her Jenny couldn't know. She talked about the shop. She was proud of it, she enjoyed it, and she was going down tomorrow for a little while. But she still looked very pale and her eyes were full of shadows.

She went to bed quite early, before Jenny, and Jenny spent the next hour with Ebby and Eb in the big old-fashioned kitchen. She liked this room, always had. She was more at home in the kitchen, and that was a fact, just as Caterine's natural setting had always been the elegant rooms. But the Ebsworths kept early hours too, and when their bedtime came Jenny was still wakeful. She said good night to them, then went upstairs and looked in on Timothy, before coming downstairs again to watch the end of the television programs.

This room faced the sea and when she turned off the TV set Jenny drew back the curtains and looked out. There was a moon tonight, silhouetting the dark outline of the land, silvering the water, and to a girl used to shut-in city streets it was breathtaking. She turned an armchair to face the window and sat and watched the stars, motionless in the sky, dancing in the sea. She thought—and smiled at herself—no wonder the sea witch swam away; because this was enchantment. It turned the softness of the armchair into a cloud that floated along a silver road, out to the rock maybe. You couldn't see the rock, but it was there, and it was terrifyingly beautiful.

She could have stayed for hours and did stay longer

than she thought. Perhaps she fell asleep. She was startled when a clock on a side table struck one. After putting the chair back in place again, she made her way out of the room. The quiet house was such a vast place that it was eerie when there was no sound but the roll of the sea.

From the gallery she looked down into the hall, and saw diffused lighting from the closed door of the office. Sighing, she went on toward her bedroom. Paul couldn't be working this late, and he shouldn't be up still, particularly after last night. But Jenny couldn't intrude again. It was no business of hers. She was the last one in this house with the right to concern herself. Eb or Ebby, who had been here since Paul was a boy, might have opened that door and said, "This is doing no good. You'll only make yourself ill." Lorraine could have taken in a cup of coffee. She was her sister, he was her concern. He might be tough, but he couldn't go on like this.

As she reached Lorraine's door Jenny hesitated then tapped very lightly. It wouldn't have woken anyone, but Lorraine was awake, she called at once, "Yes?"

"It's Jenny."

"What is it?"

Jenny went in. "I fell asleep downstairs. It's after one o'clock and Paul's still in the office."

Lorraine wriggled herself into a hunched shape, her pale face turned to Jenny. "Is he?"

Jenny said, "He can't be working, can he?"

"I don't know. He's often up late."

One o'clock was nothing, but Jenny said, "I don't think he went to bed at all last night. I woke and I thought it was Timmy in Caterine's room, but it was Paul and that was after three o'clock. He was just standing there. You're his sister. Couldn't you go in to him?"

"No!" She sounded as though she cowered as she

spoke. Lorraine must know Paul and realize no one must offer him compassion.

Jenny said, "I'm sorry, I didn't mean to interfere, I just felt sorry."

"He loved Caterine," said Lorraine.

"I know."

Lorraine said in a whisper in the darkness, "He loved her, but in a way I suppose he killed her."

CHAPTER THREE

"KILLED HER?" Jenny echoed shrilly.

Lorraine said, "I didn't mean it like that."

She was biting her lip and Jenny demanded, "What did you mean?"

"I shouldn't have said that."

But she had said it and it had to be explained. Jenny pressed the button on the tiny bedside lamp and Lorraine put a hand over her eyes and turned her head, and Jenny felt like a bullying interrogator, but she had to know. She pleaded, "Please tell me."

"There'd been a quarrel." Lorraine's voice was muffled. "Caterine was terribly upset."

"She seemed all right when I spoke to her."

"She was an actress, wasn't she?" Of course she could have hidden her distress for those few moments on the telephone. Lorraine said dully, "She'd had a row with Paul, that was why she decided to visit you; it was all on the spur of the moment."

That explained why Caterine wouldn't wait till morning, and why she had driven with too little care.

Lorraine said, "I'd never seen her cry before." Nor had Jenny, even when their parents died. "I suppose this time she'd thought it would be different, with Timmy getting older. She really had thought Paul would let her do some acting again, but he wouldn't even discuss it."

So sacrificing her career had mattered to Caterine. She had tried to fight for the chance to use her talents, and Paul wouldn't even discuss it. Jack Bastaple had said—like the rocks, as unmoving and uncaring.

Now he cared. But it was too late. He had loved her in his fashion, but she had driven that car along the cliff road, weeping for the first time in her life because of him.

It was still an accident, but it should never have happened.

Jenny said bitterly, "So it isn't just grief that won't let him sleep, it's conscience."

"I think it is," Lorraine whispered. "And for me too. I wish I'd at least tried to say something to Paul, or tried to stop Caterine driving that night." She was almost wringing her hands. "Oh, I do wish I'd *tried*!"

"It wasn't your fault. Anybody can be wise afterwards." And neither Paul nor Caterine would have listened to anything Lorraine had tried to say. She seemed grateful that Jenny wasn't blaming her.

"I didn't really have a chance. She phoned you and she threw a few things into a case, kissed Timmy good-bye and told Ebby she'd decided to have a few days' holiday. She was laughing again then."

A grim thought struck Jenny. "Timmy didn't know about the quarrel?"

"No, he was with Ebby."

"Thank goodness for that!" Jenny wished she hadn't known herself. Bitterness choked her.

"I don't think he'll ever forgive himself," Lorraine said.

Jenny whispered savagely, "I hope he never can."

"Please don't," Lorraine implored. "You make things hard enough as it is."

"Why?"

Lorraine sat aureoled in the soft spotlight of the table lamp, looking at Jenny in the shadows. "You're much more like Caterine than you used to be. When I saw you first I thought—Jenny's like Caterine's ghost. We'll be living with Caterine's ghost."

There was more than a touch of hysteria in that and Jenny said flatly, "I'm no ghost, I promise you."

She turned to go and Lorraine called beseechingly after her, "You won't say anything about what I've told you will you?"

"Of course I won't. Who would I tell it to?"

She went through the nursery into her own room. Timothy was sleeping, but the faint click of the connecting door disturbed him and he murmured, not quite awake, "Auntie Jen?"

"Hush, Timmy, I've just come to bed."

He didn't look at her and see Caterine now. She was no ghost for Timmy. She was the security that comforted him and sent him back to sleep.

She wished Lorraine had not told her about the quarrel. She didn't want to feel revengeful. Paul was hating himself, allowing himself no peace. He had had to identify Caterine and live with the fact that he was partly responsible, and remembering that Jenny could almost pity him.

Almost but not quite. Not yet . . . .

She came down to breakfast next morning with Timothy running ahead. They were early, but Paul was finishing his meal as they went into the dining room.

He looked the same as usual. He said good morning to Jenny and hello to Timothy. Jenny took a seat. Timothy stayed by Paul to tell him about going down to Tremain yesterday, and to the cove in the afternoon, and that he was "going to teach Auntie Jen to swim because she doesn't swim as good as me."

"That sounds an excellent idea," said Paul. He drained his cup while the child chattered on.

Then Timothy said, "I'll tell Ebby," and skipped away toward the kitchen.

"More coffee?" asked Jenny.

"No, thank you."

She poured herself a cup and as Paul got up she heard herself say, "You worked late last night." The dark eyebrows raised a fraction. "There was a light on in the office, very late."

She looked back at him steadily. She hoped he was lonely. His possessiveness had helped to kill Caterine.

He said quietly, "You don't appear to be keeping early hours yourself. Excuse me." And left her feeling ashamed of that urge to put hurt on hurt. . . .

Eb was going over to Blades, the home farm, this morning, and Timothy was going with him. "Want to come?" asked Timmy, and Jenny almost said, "I'd like to," but there was no real need for her to go along. Eb would look after Timmy, and if Jenny went it would only be for her own pleasure.

She was not on holiday here. She was taking no salary, but she was living under Paul's roof at his expense, and after last night that was distasteful to her. Being with Timmy was not earning her keep, that was for love. She didn't count that, but there must always be scope for another pair of hands in a house the size of Moidores.

She asked Ebby, "Can I help you this morning?"

"If you like," said Ebby cheerfully, "if you've nothing better to do."

Jenny started with the washing up and Dolly, arriving on the dot of nine, was surprised to find her at the sink. Dolly, a plump and pretty little widow in her late thirties, hadn't said much at lunch yesterday, but sharing a sink seemed to bring out her friendliness and as she dried the dishes she told Jenny about her son, who was starting as a medical student at Exeter in September.

She was fetching the snapshots when Ebby came back into the kitchen and said, "Bedrooms this morning, Dolly," so Dolly replaced the snaps in her handbag and went to the broom cupboard to collect the vacuum cleaner.

Jenny asked, "Can I help with the bedrooms?"

"No," said Ebby, and Dolly went off on her own, humming to herself. "Get that one talking about young Andrew," said Ebby when the door had closed, "and there'll be no work done."

"He sounds like a nice boy. No wonder she's proud of him."

"He's all right," Ebby conceded. "He turned out all right."

"Good," said Jenny. "Now what do I do?"

Ebby thought about it. "Well, lunch will be cold meat. Probably no Mr. Paul again, and we won't know what milady's doing until she turns up or she doesn't turn up."

She meant Lorraine, who had gone down to Tremain. Jenny said, "I hope she stays at the shop."

"Let's hope she does," Ebby agreed emphatically. "She needs to be getting about again. You could do the vegetables for tonight."

While Jenny scraped potatoes and sliced runner beans Ebby set out the baking ingredients on the kitchen table and creamed away in the big mixing bowl.

Sunlight streamed through the windows and Ebby said suddenly, "Why don't you go down to the beach? We haven't had that much sunshine this summer. It's a shame to waste it."

It was a temptation and Jenny smiled, "I can't treat Moidores like a free hotel."

Ebby looked shocked. "I should hope not. Hotel indeed! You're part of the family."

"Not really," said Jenny. She didn't really belong, either in Moidores or Tremain. She said quietly, "From what I heard yesterday Paul expects most things to pay their way around here, so perhaps I'd better work for my supper."

"Please yourself." Ebby gave the already smooth mixture another bout of fast beating. Then she said sharply,

"Talking of working, some of them think it's easy for him because he's Tremain. If anyone starts on that tack you can tell them he works very hard."

Jenny was being scolded for sounding priggish, and because Ebby suspected she had listened to criticism of Paul Tremain without leaping to his defense. Ebby was completely satisfied with the way Paul managed his affairs, and it would have been useless for Jenny to say, "He works hard because he enjoys it. Being a tycoon is his life. So why couldn't he agree that Caterine's work should be a tiny part of her life?"

It would have been useless and cruel, and wrong. . . . No one had the right to sit in judgment, and Caterine had been happy. Paul had been kind to her, he had given her almost everything. He had loved her, but his last sight of the living Caterine had been of tears, and his last words to her had been harsh. That was enough for a man to bear.

Pity finally overwhelmed Jenny's bitterness. Paul wouldn't take pity, but someone in his household should make him see sense. She said, "He was still in the office last night after one o'clock. I fell asleep watching television, and I saw the office light still on."

Ebby sieved flour, salt and spices very carefully into the bowl. Jenny said, "I think someone should have suggested it was time he stopped working."

"Do you?" Ebby's mouth went down at the corners. "Why?"

"I asked Lorraine to go in to him." Ebby shook her head: she knew Lorraine. Jenny said, "She wouldn't. Would you have done?"

"Why didn't you?" said Ebby. "He can't sack you." That was a wry joke, for Jenny couldn't imagine the Ebsworths ever losing their jobs.

What Ebby meant was that she wasn't interfering and Jenny asked bluntly, "How much grieving does he think he can take? I don't believe he slept at all the night before, because he was walking around the house at three o'clock in the morning, and if he does crack up what happens to Timothy?"

"He won't let Timmy down," said Ebby. She went on with her cake mixing. "Nor any of us," she said firmly. "He'll bear the load."

She meant that Paul was a rock. As Jack Bastaple had said, but not in the way Jack had meant it. A man seen by two who were dependent on him, one accepting, one resenting.

But no man was rock. Paul Tremain was flesh and blood and he could break. Lorraine hadn't the strength to stand up against him even for his good; and Ebby believed he was still in control. To Ebby this was simply natural grief; but she didn't know about the quarrel. The load was heavier than she suspected.

For Timothy's sake he had to carry on. He wouldn't turn Jenny out of Moidores, because of Timothy. He certainly wouldn't listen to her advice, but if she had taken coffee to the office last night she would at least have disturbed his vigil, and next time she might do that.

She dusted and vacuumed the living room, drawn again and again to the windows that overlooked the bay and sea. It was another fine day, and with any luck the tourists would be trooping into Tremain, and customers in the shop might tempt Lorraine to go down to work again.

There were boats on the water, but the cove below Moidores was deserted, and this afternoon when Timmy was back Jenny hoped he would choose the lonely cove.

They might start their swimming lessons. That would get him into the sea again; she knew he had loved it before the accident. They had never been to swimming

pools when Timothy and Caterine had come on holiday
to Jenny's home, and he was too young to remember
Jenny's visits here. That was as well, for it meant he
didn't know that Jenny swam far better than he did.

In mid-morning, Dolly and Ebby stopped for a ten-
minute cup of tea, and Jenny took in Mr. Morrison's
tray: one cup of almost black coffee and two arrowroot
biscuits.

He was standing by an open drawer of a filing cabinet
going through a file, and he looked around with a faint
fleeting surprise.

Joseph Morrison had not changed. His hair had always been gray in Jenny's memory. The lines were not
marked in his face because he never allowed himself
more than minimal movement of facial muscles. She
could never recall hearing him laugh or his voice raised,
or seeing him scowl deeply or smile widely.

Caterine had not liked him. But she had admitted he
was a wizard with figures and accounts. He knew more
about Paul Tremain's affairs than anyone else. And he
had given Caterine the creeps.

"He's so gray," she had said to Jenny more than
once. "Like a shadow. I don't think there's any blood in
him. When he looks at you with those cold eyes of his
you feel he can read your mind and I wouldn't put that
past him."

Joseph Morrison had been the only person in Moidores and Tremain for whom Caterine had had an active antipathy. She had made fun of most of them, but
never of him. It was almost as though she was a little
afraid of him.

Once when Jenny had said, "If he worked for Paul's
father he must be getting on, isn't he due to retire?"
Caterine had snorted, "Paul wouldn't let him retire, he'll
be there forever. Paul likes the wretched man so much
he won't hear a word against him."

Now he took the tray from Jenny. "Good morning, Miss Douglas."

"Good morning," said Jenny.

She might have been in this room years ago, but she couldn't remember it, and she took in quickly the impression of office cabinets and wall graphs, in and out trays, a couple of phones, two desks—one very slightly the larger.

Mr. Morrison had a typewriter on his desk, the same make that Jenny had used in her last temporary job. She gave it a light pat. "They're good, aren't they?"

"We have always found it satisfactory," he told her.

There was nothing in the machine, and presumably he was going to drink his coffee and eat his biscuits, so it would be standing idle for a few minutes and Jenny asked, "May I try it?"

"Certainly."

She typed a few lines, and looked up to see what was surely the glimmer of a smile. She couldn't think what was amusing him. He was the last man in whom she would have expected humor.

He coughed at her inquiring expression. "Forgive me, but it seems a most unlikely thing that a sister of Mrs. Tremain should be typing so efficiently."

Jenny's lips curved. They did have that surface semblance, and the idea of Caterine tapping away at a typewriter was ridiculous. It was the spotlight for Caterine and the applause, in everyday life as well. Caterine was born to dazzle.

Jenny said ruefully, "I suppose I am an unlikely kind of sister."

She could see what Caterine had meant about Mr. Morrison's scrutiny, but she didn't go along with Caterine's opinion all the way. She would not have said that the gray eyes were cold. Piercing, yes, and very clear, but to Jenny it was not a chilling gaze. She said, on impulse, "You know that Paul asked me to come down to be with Timothy?"

"Yes." His voice conveyed regret for the circumstances, but he didn't add anything.

"I would very much like to earn my keep while I'm here. I suppose you have a secretary already?"

"At the mine."

The tin mine was only part of the Tremain estate, so there must be plenty of paper work connected with other property and industries. "Who does the typing here?" Jenny asked.

"Some we take over to the general office; some I do myself. It's a simple matter to recruit staff during the summer, but in the winter they usually decide to go inland."

She could believe that Mr. Morrison would prefer to do the work himself rather than face a constant change-over of staff. She said, "I'll only be here for a month or so, but if you could find me something to do I would be grateful. It would help me keep up my speeds, and I am used to office work. Anything."

"Have you discussed this with Mr. Tremain?"

"I didn't think about it until now."

"Then I suggest that you do." But he sounded as though he would raise no objections.

Encouraged, she asked, "Is there anything I could do now, so that I could show Paul something? Unless it's all top secret."

Again that faint smile. "This is not MI$_5$ headquarters," said Mr. Morrison, and Jenny giggled, realizing incredulously—he's nice.

"Can you understand this?" He pushed across some pages in a crabbed handwriting, referring to repairs on property, that had been lying on his desk. Jenny glanced through them.

"I think so."

She looked into the kitchen to tell Ebby, who said, "If

you're going to work in the office the next night Mr. Paul stays up too late you'll be able to go in and tell him won't you?"

"I might at that," said Jenny with a small grimace, and Ebby laughed.

She made a workmanlike job of the typing. The writing, which she guessed was Mr. Morrison's, was so small and closely packed it was almost illegible at times. And he had his own abbreviations that required guessing, but she worked her way through without asking for help.

She was on the last page when he said, "I'll be in the library for the next five minutes if there are any phone calls."

"Right," said Jenny. She was reaching the trickiest paragraph of all, overwritten in places, where a magnifying glass would have come in handy.

She sat frowning down, unwilling to give up here, as though she had come to the last pieces in a complicated jigsaw puzzle. It had become a challenge to decipher the darn thing to the end, but whether these words or those went first nobody but the man who had written them could say, and when he came back she was still undecided.

She tried it out again in her mind and Paul asked pleasantly, "Going through the accounts?"

"Oh!" She jerked up, surprise making her idiotic. "What are you doing here?"

He didn't bother to answer that and she explained, "Mr. Morrison's in the library. I was typing this out—I asked him if he could find me some work."

"Are you bored already?"

"*No.*"

"Where's Timothy?"

"He went with Eb to Blades. He'll be all right with Eb."

"I'm sure he will." There was irony in Paul's voice,

since he had hardly needed Jenny to reassure him about Alec Ebsworth.

She said, "I mean, Timothy doesn't need me as well this morning. I don't think he needs me to be around all the time so long as I'm near for a while."

The words were becoming tangled. She went on, "He's an independent little boy—very proud. He's been taking care of me, right from the beginning when Rolf Perrie brought him to me."

She was proud of Timothy. To hide his own fear and to feel for others was a marvelous thing in a child so young. She said, "He is a super kid."

"You could be prejudiced," said Paul. He smiled at her.

"I could," she agreed. "But he's still a super kid."

Mr. Morrison came back, carrying a thick book that looked like a directory, and Paul said, "I see we're increasing the staff."

Mr. Morrison picked up a typewritten page, gave it a brief glance and handed it to Paul.

Paul exclaimed "Good lord!" He was obviously surprised, and Jenny's voice had a tinge of huffiness. It was no compliment he should have expected her to produce second-rate work.

She said coolly, "I have had training, and some experience."

He picked up a second page. "So had the others," he said. "But you're the first in six years who could read Joe's writing."

She smiled. Mr. Morrison said, "A slight exaggeration, but I think we should avail ourselves of Miss Douglas's offer of help while she is here."

Somehow, instinctively, she knew that Paul did not want her working with him and she said, "I wouldn't neglect Timothy, but I am going to have time on my hands."

"There are pleasanter ways of passing your time. Why do you want to spend it cooped up in here?"

She explained, "Because when I go home I'll have to look around for a job again. I was very out of touch. I'm not so bad now, but I still need practice."

Paul's expression was not encouraging, and she turned to Mr. Morrison, who met her pleading eyes with a look of blank noncommittal. No further support seemed to be coming from him and she demanded of both of them, "Why not? I could do a couple of hours in the morning while Timothy's still on holiday, and maybe help with the mail."

A very small nod from Mr. Morrison, nothing from Paul, and she wailed at Paul, "Well, you could give me a try. If I'm no use you won't have lost anything, and if I am I wouldn't need paying. I just want to feel I'm earning my keep."

He said flatly, "If you worked for me you'd certainly be paid."

Jenny didn't want his money. Her mouth set and she began, "I don't—" He spoke quietly, cutting across her words.

"I wouldn't care to be in your debt any more than you want to be in mine." She realized then how petty she was being, considering she had lived for years on the allowance he had paid her mother. Making amends with a spark of mischief she smiled, "All right, it's a deal," and after a moment he laughed.

She consolidated her advantage, turning businesslike. "Just this line, Mr. Morrison, I'm not quite sure." He told her what came first, and she typed it, not looking at Paul again, hoping the laugh meant he was relenting.

Morrison watched her typing and asked, "Do you take shorthand, Miss Douglas?"

"Yes."

"Capital." He dictated another paragraph, completing the report, and she took it easily; he was not a fast talker. She was starting to type it when Timothy walked in.

He looked for Jenny first, and seeing her behind the typewriter grinned. Then he looked at Paul. "Hello, Father. Auntie Jen, do you want me to teach you to ride?"

"Not very much," said Jenny. "I'd rather you taught me to swim."

"Oh, I'll do that." That was settled and needed no further discussion. "But Snowy's a quiet horse."

"Good," said Jenny, "but is Snowy a little horse? Because when Auntie Lorraine tried to teach me I kept falling off."

Timmy blew out his cheeks while he thought about it, then decided, "A bit little."

"Near to the ground and very wide," said Paul, his deep voice not quite steady.

Jenny said gaily, "Made to measure. O.K., Timmy, I'll learn to ride. I'm doing some typing now, but I'll be finished in a few minutes."

"Oright," said Timmy, adding nonchalantly, "I'll teach you to swim this afternoon if you like."

"He expects a quick pupil," said Paul when the door closed. Then he spoke without laughter. "I am in your debt."

Jenny said quickly, "No. I'm getting more than I'm giving for the—" She bit her lip; she had been going to say, "for the first time in my life." The unspoken words hung in the air and both men heard them.

She began to type again, and Paul said to Mr. Morrison, "Perrie will be along this afternoon about Branch Three. I've brought the papers with me."

He took files out of a briefcase and they were deep in discussion when Jenny paper-clipped her report together and placed it beside the typewriter, then stood up.

Mr. Morrison looked up, and Jenny said softly, "Nine o'clock in the morning?" He gave his faint smile and she got out of the room quickly. Paul hadn't said "No" and that was good enough.

After lunch Jenny and Timmy went down to the cove below Moidores.

This time Jenny ran for the water's edge. She hadn't swum in the sea for years, but if she had been alone she would have struck off for one of the distant rocks, perhaps even the Witch's Rock.

She could swim without tiring almost indefinitely. Water seemed her natural element. She delighted in the cool caress of it against her skin, the feel of it lifting her hair; and in the shallows now she longed to slip into deeper waters and swim away.

She was a very quick pupil. They swam a short distance from the shore with Timothy circling and splashing around her like a protective porpoise. Then they picked their way back over the stones—Jenny needed sandals but the soles of Timothy's feet were leather tough—and climbed the cliffside steps back to the house.

Jenny said, "That was lovely; I had a wonderful swim."

Timothy said, "You're not bad, Auntie Jen, but you'd better get dressed now because you're not used to it and you'll catch cold."

She wasn't cold. She was hot beneath her bathing suit and Lorraine's towel jacket. She had borrowed the jacket this morning. Lorraine had said, "Timmy's teaching *you* to swim?" When Jenny explained she had agreed it was a good idea to get him playing in the sea again. "The children around here live in it all summer long."

Timmy had swum well out of his depth today, watching Jenny who reached for him sometimes, pretending she needed help but always smiling so that he laughed too.

The sea with the sun on it had had no fears for him, but the sun had not shone when Caterine died. When the storms came again the terror might seize him, but today Jenny felt they had taken a little hurdle.

Rolf Perrie was in the kitchen when she came down from bathing and changing. She had left Timothy in his room, setting up a train set that he had unearthed from one of the cupboards, and that seemed to have enough track to cover the entire floor of his room and probably of hers as well.

Rolf was sitting by the kitchen range and Ebby had a trayful of brasses on the table. She had reached the polishing stage and most of them gleamed.

Jenny said to Ebby, "Timmy's putting out his train set." Ebby rolled her eyes in mock resignation as Jenny commented, "There seems to be a lot of it."

"There is a lot of it," said Ebby dolefully.

Jenny's hair was still damp, plastered to her head, and she told Rolf unnecessarily, "We've been swimming, Timmy and me."

"It's all right for some," said Rolf. The tension that had aged him the night he brought Timmy to her had gone now. He looked his right age, and he was a good-looking young man with a sensitive face.

Jenny asked Ebby, "By the way, has Lorraine come back?"

"No." Ebby admired a candlestick at arm's length, breathed on one spot and gave it another rub. It was almost six, the time the shop would be shutting, so Lorraine had seen the day through, which was good.

Rolf Perrie got up. "I'd better be getting along." He still lived on his parents' farm, although he was now the manager of the tin mine.

Jenny said, "Remember me to your folk."

"I will."

"And tell your mother Timmy's determined I'm going to learn to ride, but if I come past your farm I'll try not to fall off into the pigsties again."

Rolf laughed, "I'll tell her, but she'd be pleased to see you."

A bell rang in the glass-fronted case of bells high on the wall, making Jenny jump. "Shall I go?" she offered. "Which room is it?"

"The office. It's all right." Ebby gave her hands a quick swill under the tap and dried them fast.

The moment he and Jenny were alone Rolf asked, "How is Lorraine?"

The query seemed casual, but why hadn't he asked the people better able to tell him than Jenny? Ebby or Paul. "She went down to the shop this morning," said Jenny. "She must have stayed there. At least I suppose she must."

"How did she seem to you?"

"Very upset. But that's to be expected, isn't it?"

"Of course."

If he wanted to know how Lorraine was there was a surer way than asking questions. "If you wait a little she'll be back," Jenny suggested. "Or you could go and meet her."

Rolf said, "No, I'd better be on my way."

"Any message?"

"No. Thank you." He looked up at the bells. "That's Tremain," he said. "Press a bell and somebody jumps. You did, didn't you, like Ebby and me? Caterine wouldn't have done. Nor Lorraine."

Jenny resisted an impulse to say "So what?" and said instead, "No message for Lorraine?"

"No," said Rolf for the third time.

All the same when Lorraine came back to Moidores half an hour later Jenny said, "Rolf Perrie was asking after you."

"Was he?" said Lorraine. "That was nice of him."

Then she began to tell Jenny about a couple who had come into the shop today and bought every flattish shell in stock to set in white cement on a patio wall.

They had had lunch at the Tremain Arms while Grace and Lorraine sent out all the local children on a shell hunt. After lunch they returned for the spoils, nearly three hundred shells in all.

Lorraine was more animated than Jenny had seen her. She told the tale amusingly and she seemed to have had a busy day.

Jenny had a full day too. Paul was home for dinner tonight. They ate in the dining room, and Jenny remembered Caterine at this table. They must all be remembering Caterine, recalling the candle flames dancing and the faces of guests, and Caterine holding court. And family meals like this, with Caterine here.

Paul was silent. Timothy chattered and Lorraine talked a little, and Jenny sat between them keeping the talk going with a façade of normality.

After dinner it was bedtime for Timmy, but they played with the train set for a while, Timmy in pyjamas showing Jenny how to work the controls. And when he snuggled down in bed she stayed in her own room, moving quietly around so that he knew she was near. He was sound asleep quite soon.

As she passed the door of Caterine's room she tried the knob. The door was locked and she was glad of that.

Downstairs in the drawing room Lorraine sat with her feet up on a Louis Quinze sofa, her silver fair hair spilling over a dark red velvet cushion. As Jenny walked into the room she asked fearfully, "Did you have any trouble?"

"Trouble?"

"With Timmy."

"No, he's asleep."

Lorraine was looking strained again, and she closed

her eyes letting out a soft breath of relief. "He hardly slept at all before Paul sent him up to you, and when he did he'd wake up and run into Caterine's room."

Since he had had Jenny near he had not run. Jenny said, "I think he'll sleep, he's tired. And Caterine's door's locked—that's as well, isn't it?"

Lorraine's eyes opened wide. "So Paul locked it?" She took the cushion from behind her head and held it in both hands. "Caterine's perfume," she said. It reached Jenny faintly. "She always used it. Paul can lock that door, but Caterine's everywhere still. Don't you feel that?"

She looked at Jenny with dark intent eyes. Jenny had not lived with Caterine for the last eight years, seeing her daily as Lorraine had done. Of course, while their mother lived no day had passed without Caterine's name being spoken. Jenny had always lived in Caterine's shadow, and she knew what Lorraine meant.

"She loved this house," said Lorraine. "When we were entertaining you could look around in here sometimes and everybody would be watching her, *everybody*. She glittered. Not just her clothes or jewels. Just—Caterine. And she's here still. She must still be here."

Jenny sighed. She missed Caterine too, her beautiful glittering sister. Lorraine's little pillbox was on a table beside her and Lorraine opened it, tipped out a couple and swallowed them.

"I've got to get a good night's sleep," she said as though Jenny had protested. "Lying awake is dreadful. But I do feel better today, I really do, and I'm glad I went down to the shop."

"Are you going again tomorrow?"

"Yes."

Jenny said, "I'm doing a couple of hours' office work in the morning."

She explained how that had come about and Lorraine

said, "Yes, of course, you were a secretary, weren't you? Somehow I've always thought of you as being at home, looking after your mother."

"So I was, for years."

"Yes." Lorraine was apprehensive, anticipating further trouble. "Jenny," she said slowly, "Paul isn't an easy man to work for. He doesn't make many allowances if things go wrong."

You only had to look at Paul Tremain to know that, but Jenny said, "Thanks for the warning, but I think I'll be working mostly for Mr. Morrison."

"Well, he won't shout at you," said Lorraine. "Caterine used to say he wouldn't raise his voice if the house was on fire."

Jenny laughed. She didn't point out, "I may have been the stay-at-home sister, but I was among the bright ones at school. Paul shouldn't have to make too many allowances for me." But that was what she was promising herself. . . .

Later, when Lorraine went to her room, Jenny walked along to the kitchen. Like last night Eb and Ebby were sitting there, but tonight Ebby said, "Here's your chance. He's still in the office."

Jenny's heart sank.

"So how about going in and telling him he's working too late?" said Ebby.

"Take no notice of her." Eb was shocked at the suggestion. His wife must have been telling him what Jenny was saying this morning, and Jenny was stuck with it.

She said, "He can sack me now, I'm on the payroll," and before Eb or her own common sense could stop her she turned and went back again down the corridor into the hall, then drew a deep breath before tapping lightly on the office door.

Paul called, "Yes?"

She opened the door. He was working, pen in hand,

and papers littered the desk. She began nervously, "Er . . . could I . . . ?"

"You could fetch me some coffee."

She sped to the kitchen and was back with a tray as fast as Ebby could perk it. Paul said absently, "Thank you." He drank his coffee still reading papers, making alterations and additions, while Jenny sat at Mr. Morrison's desk, cleared of everything but the typewriter, and sipped from the cup she had poured for herself.

Any minute Paul was going to ask, "Why are you still here?" and she would say, "It's half past ten, don't you ever stop working?" No, perhaps not. But she could say what time it was, and she could point out that it was late.

Paul said, "There are pencils and a pad in the top right-and drawer. Take a memo for Joe, will you?"

He rattled it off, but she got it down. "Now read it back."

On her mettle, she read it back, with a growing little glow of achievement, typed it out very carefully and took it across to him.

Then he said, "It's time you called it a day, Jenny."

"I came in here to tell you that."

"Did you?" He smiled. "And you're right. Good night."

She said good night to him and wondered if he would go to bed now. As she passed Lorraine's door she hoped that Lorraine slept peacefully. Timmy slept. Jenny stepped with care over the model railway lines, silver in the moonlight like a spider's web, and looked down on him with love.

Through Caterine she was involved with them all. With Timmy . . . with Lorraine . . . with Paul, who carried Tremain and who must not break. . . .

CHAPTER FOUR

AUGUST SLIPPED BY. With a few hours' office work most mornings, Jenny earned her keep and Mr. Morrison's approval. He never said much, but he had a weakness for perfect pages of typing, particularly figures, and when he murmured "Capital" Jenny always felt absurdly gratified.

Paul took perfect typing for granted, although he never missed a detail. Whether it was a cottage roof needing repair, or a mass of complicated data about farm or mining machinery, he needed no prompting; and when he came across thick-headedness or inefficiency he wasted no words.

He could be a swine, and Jenny spent a fair amount of time disliking him heartily. The rest of the time she veered between grudging respect and growing admiration, because he did the work of half a dozen men and he did it formidably well. He could be tough to callousness, but just when she was glowering with disapproval she would hear something like the story of Dolly's Andrew.

She was smarting on behalf of a maintenance man, who had not reported a piece of faulty equipment, when she went into the dining room, which Dolly was giving its weekly polish.

Andrew's A-level results had arrived recently and they were still a subject of rejoicing for Dolly. She told Jenny about them all over again—A's, no less, and three of them honors—and Jenny said how lucky Dolly was in her son.

"It would have been a very different tale if Mr. Tremain hadn't stood by him," Dolly said softly.

It seemed Andrew had run wild at fourteen after his

father died, ending up a young delinquent in a Birmingham magistrates' court. Paul had found him a lawyer, stood bail, and made himself responsible for Andrew's future conduct, and Andrew had been given a second chance.

His mother chuckled, polishing the table until her smile showed in it. "The magistrates didn't scare him," she told Jenny, "but by golly, Mr. Tremain did.

"He went back to school, and he daren't not work because Mr. Tremain wanted reports. He's a clever boy and he'll make a good doctor. His heart's set on it now, but it could have been very different."

Jenny returned to the office after that, the memory of Paul blasting the maintenance engineer merging into the picture of Paul handling a teenager whose whole future was in the balance. Andrew came up to Moidores to say goodbye before he set off for college. He was a nice lad, with more than a glint of humor, and he openly hero-worshipped Paul Tremain.

There was an Indian summer this year. Jenny and Timothy swam most days while the school holidays lasted. After the first week they were joined by a swarm of Timmy's friends, and his sea fears seemed allayed. Perhaps for as long as the summer lasted.

Jenny tried riding again. The horses were stabled at Blades, the home farm, and they were beautiful without exception. But Snowy, who was aging and putting on weight, although hardly as short or as wide as Jenny would have liked, was the steadiest of the lot.

She found them all endearing. She would have preferred petting and feeding them to sitting on them, but Timothy and Lorraine were patient with her and only took her across easy ground.

Lorraine was back at the shop now, but she usually rode once or twice a week. She was an accomplished horsewoman and Timothy rode well. Sometimes they would gallop ahead with the wind streaming through Lorraine's long fair hair and tousling Timmy's thick dark mop, while Jenny plodded on feeling like part of the herd heading for the old corral, knowing that at any sign of stampede they would be back to round her up in no time.

Fortunately Snowy was content to amble, and Jenny refused to urge him on to anything else. Mastering the rhythm of the amble and the trot was enough for her.

During their rides she renewed old acquaintances at the farms on the Tremain estate. The same families were still there, but a grandmother had died at Blades, and at another farm the daughter had married and moved away.

Rolf's father still farmed his small holding. It adjoined the home farm where the horses were stabled, they usually rode past it, but when Jenny asked, "Shall we call on the Perries?" Lorraine hesitated as Timmy turned his chestnut pony through the open five-barred gate, galloping down the rough track that led to the gray-stone farmhouse and buildings.

The girls followed. Timmy had ridden around to the back of the house and when they caught up Mrs. Perrie was with him. Jenny remembered Rolf's mother laughing over the misadventure of the pigsty that produced a hot bath followed by a hot drink, and the whole thing being a riotous joke. But she looked much older now. Pale and very composed. It was hard to imagine her giggling.

She welcomed Jenny and said how pleased she was to see them all, and they must come in for a cup of tea. She brought out eggshell china and served the tea in the parlor, and they talked about the weather and the changes since Jenny was last here. Jenny hadn't noticed many, but Mrs. Perrie could think of a few.

They stayed for about half an hour, by which time Timothy was fretting to get on with their ride and Jenny was running out of small talk. Lorraine hadn't contributed much, although she didn't make the first move to go.

It was Jenny who arose from her chair and said how nice it had been seeing Mrs. Perrie again.

"Call any time," said Rolf's mother.

"Thank you," said Jenny. "Remember us to Mr. Perrie and Rolf. I'm sorry we missed them."

"I will," said Mrs. Perrie.

Lorraine said, "Thank you," too.

Mrs. Perrie said graciously: "You are more than welcome, Miss Tremain."

Timothy held Snowy's head while Jenny mounted and Jenny grinned and said: "Do you remember the pigsty? I'm not much better now," and Mrs. Perrie laughed for a moment.

She wasn't looking much older, Jenny realized. It was her manner that gave that impression. There was a reserve about her now, a withdrawal. When she had just laughed that was the Mrs. Perrie Jenny remembered. Now she was grave again, waving them goodbye, turning to go back into the house before they had quite rounded the corner.

Timmy trotted ahead and when she was out of earshot Jenny said, "She's changed."

"Yes."

"What's the matter with her?"

"Paul bosses Rolf about, I suppose, and his mother doesn't like it."

"I shouldn't have thought Rolf would have whined at home about what happened at work."

Lorraine shrugged. Jenny went on, "And Paul doesn't pull rank unless things are going wrong."

"Doesn't he?" Lorraine laughed harshly. "He laid down the law for Caterine. And Rolf may be manager of that mine, but I don't suppose Paul lets him forget who owns it."

She dug her heels into her horse's sides and galloped away, beyond Timothy, who thought she was racing and tried to keep up with her, then when she outstripped him, he came back to Jenny to ask, "Where's Auntie Lorraine gone?"

"I don't know," said Jenny. "I think she felt like a ride on her own."

No further mention was made of the Perries, but they didn't call again. . . .

BY THE TIME Timothy and the other children went back to school after the holidays Jenny had a way of life going for her in Tremain. It had to be temporary, she knew that, but she was enjoying it while it lasted, working longer and well-paid hours in the office, giving Lorraine a hand in the shop sometimes.

Trade in the shop would drop during the winter months, of course, and the artists stockpiled for next season or sent their work to the agents and the galleries. Jack Bastaple was working for an exhibition in London in the spring.

Jenny was seeing rather a lot of Jack. Not dates exactly, but when she went down to Tremain he usually materialized before long. He always looked into the shop when she was helping there, and she had had several bread and cheese lunches with him at the Tremain Arms.

Jenny was making more friends than she had ever had in her life. She found the artists congenial company, Grace Norbrook in particular. Her husband Ben, a sculptor who worked in basaltic rock and the greenish granite of Cornwall, fashioned rugged heads and powerful neolithiclike figures. And she had always liked the fishermen and the shopkeepers and the folk who ran the two pubs.

Sometimes she and Lorraine would stay down in Tremain for their evening meal. Usually they ate with Grace, but it was always Jack who walked back with them to Moidores.

Timothy had had no more nightmares. With Ebby keeping a watchful guard Jenny felt fairly safe in being away from the house for a few hours. She would not have risked being away all night, nor away from him any time if there had been a threat of storm.

In the two months since she came, no storms had occurred, although now the Indian summer was drawing to a close.

This Saturday customers had been few, and Jenny stood at the window looking out. Timmy was at home, the quayside was almost deserted, and the boats bobbing on the water were regulars, natives. Paul Tremain's *Mylor* was at its usual anchorage in the mouth of the harbor.

Jenny had never been aboard. None of the family had so far as she knew, although Paul sailed most weekends.

Not today, though, it seemed. She had asked Mr. Morrison if he went along and he had said, "I find sailing a very overrated pastime. I never go sailing."

"Who does Paul take with him?" she'd asked and expected to be told to ask Paul, because it was certainly no business of hers, but he'd said, "Dan Blaskie occasionally."

Dan was one of the few remaining fishermen in Tremain. The shoals were getting sparser, the fishing less profitable. "Usually he sails alone," said Mr. Morrison.

Timmy had told her that the first day she came here. It looked like a beautiful boat, and it seemed a shame Paul wouldn't share it. Jenny would have given her eye-teeth—well, nearly—to sail in it, but she knew she would never find the courage to ask outright.

She often looked at it wistfully. She did now, and

Jack who was wandering around the shop asked, "What's the sigh for?"

"The sun," said Jenny promptly. "The weather's breaking." Clouds were sculling across the sky, and the sea looked dull and sullen. There was no one in the shop now, but Jenny and Jack, and Lorraine in the small office at the back going through some order books.

"Pity," said Jack.

"You should be pleased," Jenny teased. "There'll be no one left in Tremain but the people who live here."

Jack had come to stand beside her.

"It's a different place then. Are you staying to see?"

Did Timothy still need her here? There had been no talk of her going, and although she was hardly irreplaceable in the office she knew that Mr. Morrison at least would prefer not to replace her.

Jack said, "You might not like it in the winter, Jenny."

"No?"

He looked out with her across the gray waters. "When the people have gone," he said, "you'd find it very lonely."

She almost gasped. It seemed crazy that the man who was her closest male friend in Tremain should know so little about her that he thought she would be lonely without the press of people around. It could be lonely in cities, didn't he know that?

"I'll miss you," he said, as though it was certain she would go soon, and she supposed it was. . . .

"Will you come to Tremain for a month or so?" Paul had asked at the beginning of August. They were into October now. Soon she must go home.

She must go home. She went out of the shop, crossing to the harbor wall. No one played on the shingle today; a man was caulking an upturned dinghy, while seagulls wheeled overhead, and beyond the harbor low clouds smudged the outline of the Witch's Rock.

She saw every detail with singing joy and knew that if she left here she would be sick with longing for it. The house in which she had lived all her life held no part of her. She was alive here, and strong, and no one was going to send her away. She was home.

Jack was holding her arm and saying, "Don't go too soon, Jenny. We'll all miss you."

Moidores was big enough for a regiment, and no one needed Jenny's room. Paul would never ask her to go, Ebby had said she was part of the family. She couldn't announce, "I've decided to stay forever," but she had, and she felt light-headed with happiness.

If Paul should turn me out of Moidores, she thought, I'll live in the cave in the Witch's Rock. And Jack believed she was smiling because he had told her he would miss her.

He said, "You're very sweet, and you will come to my exhibition, won't you?"

Some of his pictures were stored in the shop, some in the studio. Jack lived in one of the cottages in the side streets, but he did most of his indoor work in the vast studio, with its high-beamed ceiling, over what had been the boatbuilder's shed. This room had plenty of light, and several of the artists used it. Jenny had been up there. The place was a bit like a clubroom, and she thought she had seen all the pictures Jack had ready for the exhibition so far.

He was working hard. They all said the exhibition should be a success, in a first-class gallery, owned by a friend of Paul's who had a high reputation as an art critic. Jack Bastaple would be getting an international store window for his work for a couple of weeks, and of course Jenny would go along to see the pictures on display.

"Of course," she said.

As they went back into the shop she picked up a shell from the basket by the door and put it to her ear. The old trick of "listening to the sea" never failed to fascinate her.

Lorraine had come out of the office and was tidying a shelf. Jack went to help her, and Jenny stayed where she was. There was really nothing to do; there would probably be no more customers today. The clouds seemed to thicken while she watched them and she thought, *We could be in for a storm. Perhaps I should be getting back to the house.*

The shell was cool against her cheek, so perfectly shaded and patterned that if it had been man-made it would have been worth more than any of the sculptures they were producing. She turned it, wonderingly, and Jack queried, "What's so marvelous about that one?"

"Look at it."

She held it in scooped hands, and he looked at her and said suddenly, "Come and see a picture."

"What picture?"

"One of mine, of course."

"All right?" she asked Lorraine.

"You don't have to ask me," Lorraine answered, and went on with her shelf dressing.

They went out through the side door into the courtyard and Jenny headed for the steps up to the studio when Jack said, "It isn't there. It's in the cottage."

She followed as he strode along. His cottage was about three minutes away, in the narrow streets at the bottom of the hill, a little back from the sea. She stepped right into a small cosy room, with a table and dresser, a couple of comfortably sagging armchairs, and three saddleback chairs. One door was closed, while another opened into a kitchen.

Jack said, "Not much of a place."

"I like it," said Jenny. She would have liked it. It was untidy, but a little caring could have made it charming.

"Compared with Moidores," said Jack.

"Who's comparing it with Moidores?"

He laughed. "Nobody, so far as I know. One of these days when I'm rich I'll buy my own castle. Sit down."

She sat. He said, "I want this hanging where it hits everyone who walks into that gallery, and no one has seen it yet."

She should have been flattered, but somehow she was uneasy. "Why should I be the first?"

He reached to touch her cheek. "Because I don't want you shocked."

"Shocked?"

This time he laughed at her. "You don't need to blush. It isn't pornography. I couldn't be more restrained."

"I'm not blushing." She knew he would not produce a gimmicky shocker for his exhibition, so she asked intuitively, "Is it Caterine?"

He sometimes did portraits. He had sketched Jenny once, over lunch at the Tremain Arms.

"Yes."

"But why hide it?"

He opened the second door and she heard him going up the stairs, his footsteps overhead. He brought the painting down with him.

The window in this room was small, with net curtains drawn across and short blue-sprigged curtains each side. They were a woman's curtains. Perhaps his mother or a girlfriend had chosen them. Jenny looked at them, although she knew she must turn her head now and look at the picture.

The room was too dark to see a painting clearly, but she didn't want the light switched on. When she saw Caterine she might weep, and shadows would hide tears.

He put the canvas on the dresser, beside the bread board with a cut cottage loaf and a bread knife, drew the sprigged curtains across the window and flicked down the light switch, and Caterine looked at Jenny.

Jenny sat very still.

Caterine's hair fell loose. She wore a green scarf like foam on her shoulders, and ropes of pearls circled her throat and her hair. She held a shell, as Jenny had held that shell minutes ago, golden rings on every finger, and heavy gold bracelets that fettered her wrists. She was the sea witch, a prisoner, chained with jeweled fetters, and Jenny demanded hoarsely, "What are you trying to do?"

She got up and went closer. It was Caterine. Everyone who had ever seen her would recognize her. The picture would be a talking point, and a savage indictment, because there was an anguish in the beautiful eyes as piercing as though the painting screamed.

Jack said heavily, "Remind some of them that she didn't escape."

"You can't do this! That's my sister, that's Timothy's mother. Caterine was not a prisoner."

It was well painted. It would probably sell. It might even be printed. Caterine's death and the legend of the sea witch would be enough to get this into the popular press where even Timothy's small friends might see it. She said, "Sell it to me."

"I'm sorry."

"You want to sell it, don't you?"

He looked at her with narrow eyes. "That wasn't why I painted it."

She knew that well enough. This was revenge for everything about Paul that Jack Bastaple resented. It was because the cottage was not much of a place compared with Moidores, because there were tourists on the quayside, because Paul Tremain was Tremain.

He said, "After the exhibition I'll give it to you."

"You're not going to show it!"

"Klopper doesn't censor, even if he is Tremain's friend. This is a good painting; he'll hang it."

He must mean the man who owned the gallery. Jenny said shrilly, "You are not putting Timothy's mother on show, looking as though she had no hope in life!"

"Jenny." Jack Bastaple gestured appeal. "Don't get hysterical. That's why I'm showing it to you now so that you have time to see it alone and calmly. Jenny, she *was* a prisoner."

Jenny retorted, "Come to that, we're all prisoners."

"Sure, I know that. But Caterine was a special person. Tremain had no right—"

"You have no right to do this! I won't let this happen. It would be monstrous. It's a travesty!"

He almost laughed again then. "Tremain gave her those bracelets on her last birthday. They weren't chained like handcuffs, but they should have been. And the pearls. Have you seen the pearls? I remember the eyes too. This isn't a travesty."

"You loved her?"

The question seemed to surprise him, but he said, "I suppose I did."

It wasn't surprising. All men seemed to be attracted to Caterine, although Paul was the only one she had loved. Jack Bastaple's devotion must have counted for nothing, or she'd never mentioned him to Jenny. But it might have been the resemblance between the sisters that made him seek Jenny's company, and it explained his hate for Paul.

She said, "I'm sorry."

"For me? Because I must have loved her?"

"Because it's left you hating. Please, Jack, don't send this painting to London. Please let me have it."

"I'm sorry."

Nothing would change his mind. She saw in the stubborn set of his mouth that no matter who suffered—and the hurt would go further than Paul, certainly to Lorraine, almost certainly to Timothy—Jack Bastaple would have that picture of Caterine hanging in that London gallery.

Jack stood by the window. Jenny picked up the bread knife and slashed the picture. She had never in her life before wilfully destroyed anything. She had never held a knife like a dagger, and in tearing Caterine's face she felt physlcal pain in herself so that she moaned.

It was the last thing he had expected. He couldn't believe it, even while he was watching. He could neither move nor speak, and Jenny put down the knife and looked at her hands as though she expected to see blood on them.

Then he muttered, "You're mad!"

"I couldn't let you do that."

But she was a quiet girl, a gentle girl. It was hard to believe she was Caterine's sister, except for that family likeness. It was mind-blowing that she should destroy his painting and that she was not hysterical.

She was calm, not even trembling. He took a couple of steps toward her, and she looked steadily at him. She was not afraid, and he had a sudden insane conviction that she was stronger than he was. That if he struck her with all his strength she still would not flinch.

That was nonsense: he could have killed her with a blow. He wanted to kill her, and he crashed down on the table with clenched fists, and a paralyzing force that almost broke the bones in his hands, so that he stood with bowed head gasping, "Get out while you can!"

Jenny walked past him.

"I shall paint it again," he said.

She couldn't stop him. If he did that she could do nothing.

As she reached the door he said through clenched

teeth, "Who are you protecting at Moidores—the child or the man?"

She lifted the latch. "Caterine's child." If he had loved Caterine he might remember Timothy while he painted. Caterine would not want her son to see that anguish in her eyes.

"Caterine's man," said Jack Bastaple savagely. "Don't ever forget it."

Jenny opened the door, heard faint thunder and began to run. The storm was coming and she had to get to Timothy.

The storm came slowly but inexorably. As she hurried up the cobblestoned hillside the sky grew heavier, clouds massing together like a black blanket, making the air so oppressive that there seemed no oxygen in it.

Jenny had cramp in her side and was laboring painfully for breath by the time she reached the cliff road, racing against the storm. The first heavy drops of rain were falling now, the thunder was nearer, the lightning brighter. She turned toward Moidores, forcing herself to keep running. Past the spot where Caterine's car had skidded—the weather must have been like this, a storm just breaking—looking up at the house and the turret window where Timothy had stood that day.

He wouldn't be there now—Ebby would see to that—but wherever he was he could be panicking and Jenny had to reach him.

She ran for the kitchen door, always unlocked during daytime, and by now the rain was a deluge. She hadn't bothered to put on her coat when she'd left the shop to see Jack's painting. She was in a pink sweater and a navy pleated skirt, and both were sticking to her. As she dashed into the kitchen Dolly gave a little protesting squeak as though she had seen a mouse, "Goodness, you're *soaked*! Come to the fire."

"Hello." Jenny could hardly get the word out. "Where's Timmy?"

"With his father." Dolly was mending household linen. She sat at the table, stitching a pillowcase, and Jenny went across to the fire in the inglenook, realizing that she could hardly have been wetter if she had swum all the way back to Moidores.

Timmy would be all right if he was with Paul. As soon as Jenny had her breath back she'd go and change. For the moment she stood and steamed, and the rain literally dripped off her onto the red polished flagstones.

The storm was right overhead, the thunder rolling, the lightning flashing. Jenny said, awestruck. "Just listen to it!" but Dolly's expression had the tranquility of a woman born and bred in Tremain.

"Sea witch weather," said Jenny. Dolly nodded, busy with her small neat darning.

"So they say." She gave the windows a glance and through the driving rain saw the forked lightning and admitted that this was a fairish storm. "I don't know whether I'll be getting home tonight."

No one would turn out in this if they had any choice at all. Lorraine would have to stay down in the harbor until it passed.

Jenny wondered if she would call on Jack's cottage then to see if Jenny was still there . . . what Jack would say. . . . "I painted a picture of Caterine and Jenny destroyed it." He had said he would paint it again. He must have worked in secret, from memory, but it was no secret now because Jenny knew. And who could she tell, "He's painting Caterine so that anyone who sees it will feel she's happier dead and wonder if she wanted to die"?

Ebby came into the kitchen and did a double take. "Didn't expect to see you for a while." Then she smiled, "His father's with him." She knew why Jenny had run back and she had expected to see her. "Couldn't you have borrowed a mackintosh?" she said.

From Jack? Hardly. Jenny's toes squelched in her shoes and she looked down apologetically at the damp she was spreading. "Sorry, I'll get changed."

"Before you do," said Ebby, "look in the drawing room. Mr. Paul said when you came would you look in."

Dolly bit off a thread. "You ought to get out of those wet things."

"Timmy's a bit bothered," said Ebby. That fixed the priorities. Jenny took her dripping self straight to the drawing room.

A good fire was burning in here too, and in here the curtains were drawn. Paul sat on a settee, his arm around Timothy, and a book on the child's knee. As Jenny opened the door they both turned. Then Timothy scrambled down so that the book fell, and Jenny went toward him.

He said, "Father said you were all right."

"Of course I'm all right." He reached for her hand and she brought him back to the fire.

"Where's Auntie Lorraine?"

"Still in the shop. I got caught in the rain on my way home. She'll come home when it stops raining."

Jenny stooped to pick up the book and looked up at Paul and he knew that she had run through the storm to reach Timothy.

"You're awful wet," said Timothy.

"Mmmm." She smiled. "You should have seen the mess I made on the kitchen floor! Ebby's not very pleased with me. I'm just going to get changed."

Everything must be casual. Probably all his life Timothy would dislike storms; they would always have that link in his mind with Caterine's accident. But Jenny had just come along the cliff road in the storm and the sea had not reached for her. The rain had soaked her, but she was smiling and safe as his father had promised him.

Timmy said, "I'm glad you came home."

"I'll be back in five minutes," she promised. She didn't say, "I'll always come home," but she would, she would.

She left the man and the child and went to her little room, toweled herself dry and dressed quickly. As she passed Caterine's door anger burned in her again against Jack Bastaple, because Caterine had been happy. Everyone in this house had loved Caterine.

They loved her and mourned her. Lorraine still blamed herself for not taking Caterine's part against Paul. That painting of Caterine chained would be searing for Lorraine. She still talked about her own weakness and Jenny was still reassuring her that she was in no way to blame.

Paul carried his grief alone, for he talked of Caterine to no one. But nearly three months after her death he kept the door of her room locked.

Downstairs now Timmy was lying flat on his stomach in front of the fire, reading his book. Paul still sat on the settee, also with a book. A particularly heavy peal of thunder crashed overhead as Jenny opened the door, and Timmy looked up at his father.

Paul didn't seem to notice the child's wide eyes on him. He turned another page and Timmy turned back to his reading. Paul's presence was reassurance enough now, it seemed.

The thunder had drowned the lesser sound of the opening door, and Jenny stood watching them, holding the tray she had just brought from the kitchen. She would have been happier to see Timothy still held close. He wasn't really scared any more, but he was not beyond needing an arm.

She said, "I took my things into the kitchen to dry and I brought some bread back to make some toast." She had also brought plates, butter, strawberry jam, peanut butter and cheese.

"Smashing!" grinned Timothy.

They made toast while the storm raged on. Behind those heavy curtains the lightning in sky and sea would be as spectacular as a giant fireworks display. It didn't pass through the curtains, but the thunder rolled and rumbled.

While they were busying themselves Jenny talked to Timmy who was soon chattering away. He toasted the bread and she spread it thick with butter, and when they had a tottering pile Paul asked, "When do we eat it?"

"We have done a lot." Timmy turned a glowing face from the fire to survey their handiwork. "Good job we're hungry."

Jenny asked Paul gravely, "Plain or à la carte?"

"Jam and peanut butter's nice." Timothy spoke like a connoisseur.

Paul said hastily, "Cheese."

"Jam and peanut butter sounds delicious," said Jenny.

"Are you having it?" they both asked.

"Why not?"

"What it is to be young!" sighed Paul.

Jenny said gaily, "Don't be pompous!" then wondered if she had gone too far.

But Paul laughed and Timothy said, "Shall I spread it for you?"

"I'll spread my own," she said. "We all will."

By scraping hers very thin it wasn't too dreadful. They could sit quieter now, since there was no need to keep talking. The thunder was no longer overhead and Timmy was relaxed and a little sleepy from the warmth of the fire. He sat, leaning against Jenny, and they found pictures in the fire.

Paul went on reading his book, and half an hour later when Lorraine came in Jenny and Timmy were into an involved tale of outer space. The fire was the planet Mars and they had reached the stage where they were happily watching a cartoon show.

Timmy invited, "Come and look, Auntie Lorraine," while Lorraine knelt down beside them and swore she could see the three-headed monster who immediately dissolved into a shower of sparks.

"They keep doing that," Timmy confided. "It's their secret weapon."

"Wheee!" said Lorraine. She had been worried about Timothy, although she had known that Dolly and Ebby would do everything they could to keep him from panicking. She hadn't known where Paul was, and she had hoped that Jenny had got home.

A couple of customers had come in after Jenny went off with Jack, and by the time Lorraine finished serving them the rain was pouring down.

She grinned at Jenny over Timmy's head. "Did Jack bring you home?"

"No."

She deduced that Jenny had run like mad and loved her for it.

She asked, "What was the picture like?"

"A seascape," said Jenny.

"Good?"

"I don't know. I didn't like it much."

"I hope you didn't say you didn't like it. Jack Bastaple always takes criticism badly. He's touchy about his work."

"Hard luck!" snapped Jenny.

Lorraine let it go. But later, after dinner, when Lorraine and Jenny were back in this room alone, she took it up again and asked, "What did you say to Jack about his painting?"

Jenny almost told her. But there was something so vulnerable about Lorraine and this was an ugly thing. Lorraine wouldn't understand how Jack could have painted that picture, nor how Jenny could have destroyed it. Remembering brought an acrid taste to Jenny's mouth. She wasn't proud of what she had done; it would be hard to justify. Perhaps he wouldn't paint the picture again. When he did—if he did—would be time enough for Lorraine to know.

Jenny said quietly, "I said I didn't like it."

"Oh dear!" Lorraine winced. "I'd have thought you'd have had more sense than that. They're all touchy about their work, but Jack needs handling with kid gloves."

Jenny bit hard on her lip. If Lorraine only knew!

"You do like Jack, don't you?" Lorraine sounded concerned. "I know he likes you." Until today. Today he had bruised his hands to keep them from striking her. . . . "He always asks if you're coming down to the shop."

Jenny said, "I don't think he'll be asking again," and Lorraine, who had been in a mood of gentle raillery until now, caught a deadly serious note.

She stopped smiling. "Not over a painting? Oh, for goodness' sake make it up, you idiot! That's stupid!"

Jenny said nothing, but from her expression Lorraine knew she was on dangerous ground. There must have been far more than tactlessness on Jenny's part and huffiness on Jack's. Perhaps Jack had made a pass—although Lorraine would have thought Jenny could have cooled that situation if she'd wanted it cooled.

They had left the shop friends, and for weeks now Lorraine had been watching their friendship approvingly. She liked Jack. He was a good painter and he was nice, and he and Jenny had looked right together. But something had finished their friendship that Jenny was not going to talk about. "I don't think we'll make it up," said Jenny.

Lorraine picked at the brocaded arm of her chair with a fingernail, raising several threads of the pattern. As she tried to pat them down again she asked, "Jenny, have you ever been in love?"

"I haven't had much chance. Mind you, there was this fantastic chap at the swimming pool. Only it was my butterfly stroke that turned him on, not me. He was the swimming coach." Lorraine laughed, but almost at once Jenny regretted having answered flippantly. She hadn't been in love. She hadn't had much chance. But it had been a serious question and she asked, "Have you?"

Lorraine went on smoothing the brocade, her long hair veiling her face. "No. One or two false alarms, but no. Caterine said we would be two old maids, you and I, did you know that?"

"Yes." She had said it to Jenny too, teasing in loving fashion. "There's a long way to go before then," said Jenny.

"But how do you know when you're really in love?"

There hadn't even been any false alarms in Jenny's life. She was younger and less experienced than Lorraine and yet she felt immeasurably more mature. She thought, *I'll know.*

But she said nothing and after a moment or two Lorraine jumped up and crossed to the windows. She pulled the curtains apart and said, "The air's still heavy. The storm's still around."

It growled like a tiger in the distance, and Jenny went upstairs several times to check on Timmy, but he was always asleep.

It was almost too hot for comfort. When she went to bed Jenny had to leave the windows closed and the curtains drawn, but she kept the doors open between the rooms and into the corridor.

After one crash of thunder Timmy gave a faint cry and she was out of bed in a flash. He stirred and raised his head and she said, "It's all right, Timmy, go to sleep." He looked such a little boy, curled beneath the bedspread. "Hush, close your eyes now, shhh!"

She began to croon to him, humming very softly, hardly a tune, just something to lull him to sleep, and he snuggled down again and his eyes closed. She went back to her own bed, and when the next thunder crash came Timmy didn't whimper, he called sleepily, "Auntie Jen—sing a bit," so she went on with her tuneless tune until she sang both Timmy and herself to sleep. . . .

The summer was over the next day. The storm had left everything gray. The sky and the sea merged, and the moors were drab with mud. There was no riding today, and there would be few holidaymakers in Tremain.

After breakfast Jenny went into the office. Since it was Sunday she wasn't working. She was typing a letter of her own to Louie Sumner, back in the house that Jenny owned but that had never been her home.

When the phone from the mine rang she answered it. "Who's that?" said a man's voice.

"Jenny Douglas. You want Mr. Tremain? I'll get him for you."

The man said, "Tell him there's been a rock fall in Branch Three, and Rolf Perrie's trapped." Paul was reading newspapers. She ran to tell him, and he got up without a word and strode fast for the office.

"Not Rolf?" Jenny turned and it was Lorraine. She wouldn't have recognized the voice. She would hardly have recognized the chalk white face. "Oh, please, Jenny, not Rolf . . . ."

And Jenny knew then for sure that Rolf Perrie mattered a great deal to Lorraine.

CHAPTER FIVE

"WHAT DID THEY SAY? What's happened?" Lorraine clutched Jenny's arm so hard that it hurt.

"That there'd been a rock fall," Jenny repeated.

"And Rolf?"

The man on the phone from the mine had said, "Rolf Perrie's trapped." Trapped could mean anything; it could mean crushed and buried alive, and Jenny wished now that she hadn't mentioned Rolf's name. But she had given Paul the message parrot fashion.

She said, "Just that Rolf was there," and Lorraine swayed, face in her hands. Jenny eased her into a chair and remembered how she had felt herself when the news came about Caterine.

When Lorraine whispered "No," Jenny recalled that reaction that if you denied it hard enough it wouldn't have happened.

She stood useless, and after a few moments Lorraine took her hands from her face, then looked at Jenny and said, "He's got to be all right." Jenny nodded. "Where's Paul?" whispered Lorraine. Jenny gestured toward the door. The shock of hearing Rolf's name must have dazed Lorraine so that she hadn't seen Paul leave the room, but she jumped up now and ran into the hall as Paul was coming out of the office.

She half screamed, "Paul!" and he came across to them. "What's happening?"

Lorraine was ashen, but Paul looked calm and sounded calm. He said, "Perrie was in one of the branch tunnels examining the working face, and there's been a fall at the entrance to the tunnel. We'll soon have it cleared."

"How do you know it's only at the entrance? How do you know the whole tunnel hasn't caved in?"

He explained, "Because the phone link is still intact. They've spoken to him."

"He's alive?" She sounded as though she couldn't quite believe it.

Paul turned to go, saying "I'll phone you as soon as there's any more news."

"I'm coming."

"No." His tone was flatly final. "You stay here. Jenny," he looked at Jenny for the first time, "give her a couple of tranquilizers and then stay by the phone. There might be calls coming through."

Then he went, wasting no more time. Lorraine said huskily, "I've got to see for myself. Paul might have been lying to me."

"Why on earth should he lie?"

"You don't understand," said Lorraine darkly. "Will you come?" And Jenny thought, *Maybe I'm beginning to understand.*

Lorraine had a car. Jenny couldn't keep her here against her will if she was determined to drive to the mine, and this time she seemed to be making her own decision in defiance of Paul. She was going, and she was in no state to go alone.

"Wait while I ask Eb or Ebby to listen for the phone," said Jenny, and ran to find the Ebsworths. She found Ebby, bustling around in the kitchen, and asked, "Where's Timmy?"

"In the greenhouse with Eb. Do you want him?"

Jenny didn't want to say this in front of Timothy, that was all. She said breathlessly, "There's been a cave-in at the mine. Rolf Perrie's involved and Lorraine's determined to go and see what's happening.

"They've just phoned to tell Paul and he said Lorraine was to stay here and I was to sit by the phone. But she's not going to stay and somebody will have to go with her if she's driving, so would you or Eb listen for the phone?"

Ebby looked worried. "If Mr. Paul told you to wait you'd better."

"Tell Lorraine that," said Jenny.

"Bad, is it?" asked Ebby.

"I took the call. He said a cave-in and Rolf Perrie was trapped and tell Paul."

"Oh dear!" Ebby sighed, and they hurried.

Lorraine was standing in the open door of the office looking at the silent telephone as though she was hypnotized by it. She was obviously dreading hearing it ring, convinced there would be no good news, and Ebby said gently, "You can't do any good down there, chicken, only get in the way."

Jenny had never heard Lorraine called chicken before, and Lorraine half smiled. The endearment brought memories of long-ago reassurances and comfort: Ebby bathing a cut knee, fussing away a childish fear. "I won't get in the way," Lorraine spoke tremulously, "but I have to be there."

Ebby didn't argue. She gave Lorraine a quick hug. "And I'll say a little prayer."

"Yes, Ebby, pray for him," whispered Lorraine. "Are you coming, Jenny?"

Paul had left, of course. If he hadn't he would have stopped her because she shouldn't have been handling a car. She was shaking so that she could hardly turn the ignition key, and when she did Jenny stretched across and turned it off again.

This was brutal but necessary. "Listen to me," said Jenny, "Caterine drove too fast when she shouldn't have been driving at all. If we're going to the mine we're going slowly."

"Caterine, now Rolf!" Lorraine wasn't weeping, but the black horror was back in her eyes.

Jenny said with deliberate calm, "Paul told you that Rolf was talking on the phone and that they'd soon get him out."

"I'll believe that when I see him."

"Does Paul lie?"

"No," Lorraine admitted.

"All right, then. Now drive sensibly or I'll stop the car—I do know which is the handbrake; and if you want to get there you'll have to walk."

Jenny would have preferred to walk, although it was some distance and a miserably gray day, but Lorraine pulled herself together with an obvious effort. The bullying seemed to be working, although if it came to a tussle there was no guarantee at all that Jenny would be able to stop the car.

They turned left from Moidores heading along the cliff road away from Tremain, then turning right for nearly two miles over the old road that had been cleared and resurfaced when Paul Tremain opened the mine again ten years ago.

Lorraine drove steadily. Other cars passed them, but she kept her own speed doggedly down. The wide track, lined most of the way with spiky bushes, ran through rocky gorse-covered heathland over which sheep roamed. They had to brake a couple of times to avoid the moronic creatures, but neither girl spoke until, without warning, tears began to roll down Lorraine's cheeks and Jenny said softly, "Pull in, love."

Then Lorraine stopped the car and put her head on folded arms on the steering wheel, and Jenny slipped an arm around her promising, "It will be all right," hoping and praying that it would.

Lorraine hiccuped, "It's Purdie's Beck. I'm sorry, I'm making a fool of myself."

The beck was a stream some distance from the track, bubbling between high boulders, and Lorraine looked across at the boulders, her lips quivering and her voice unsteady. "We used to meet there. We used to ride and meet each other there."

So it wasn't that Lorraine had suddenly realized how

fond she was of Rolf. There had been a time when they had had a meeting place.

She was talking to herself rather than to Jenny. "The way I feel now I must have been in love with him."

But when Jenny had asked if Rolf was in any way special in her life Lorraine had said, "Rolf Perrie? Good heavens, no!" Jenny had thought then that the denial was overemphatic. Things were making more sense now.

Lorraine said, "Paul said it was infatuation," and that made Jenny gasp.

"What had it got to do with Paul?"

"He'd have dismissed Rolf if we had married." Jenny sagged back in her seat in appalled astonishment.

"Paul threatened to *sack* him?"

"More or less. And Rolf had just been made manager and there aren't that many mines, are there? He'd have had to emigrate."

"Why?"

Lorraine's face was still wet with tears. She mouthed the words in bitter mockery. "Because he didn't consider it would be a suitable match. He didn't think that Rolf would be able to keep me in the standard to which I am accustomed."

That was very likely. Although who did the Tremains think they were? Why shouldn't Lorraine be a working man's wife?

Jenny's expression must have mirrored her thoughts, because Lorraine flushed and looked down at her own white hands on the steering wheel and said, "I couldn't see Rolf victimized, could I? And I wasn't really sure then."

She looked out of the window again at Purdie's Beck and said sadly, "But if Paul had left us alone I know now that it would have been Rolf. I never wanted anyone else."

Jenny said tartly, "The others were eligible, I suppose? They came up to Paul's standards?"

The flush was fading from Lorraine's cheeks, now she looked pale and lonely. "Oh yes, very eligible. Except that I didn't want them."

Jenny was sorry for her. Although whether her feelings for Rolf were very deep, or whether hearing he was in danger had exaggerated them, there was no telling. She seemed to have accepted the breakup equably enough until now. But she hadn't replaced Rolf, and when Jenny asked, "Has Rolf found anyone else?" she denied it with such certainty that she must have kept tabs on him.

"Do you want to go on?" said Jenny.

"Yes, I'm all right now."

They drove past the old mine entrance. They had ridden this way before, and to Purdie's Beck, circling the buildings of the present-day minehead before they turned for home. And Lorraine had never said one single word about Rolf Perrie.

The old entrance was almost hidden by boulders. A thick beam of wood blocked the way in and a danger notice marked it. Except for the beam and the warning it would have been possible to walk straight into the woodlined mouth of the shaft. The wood was rotten and crumbling, some of it hundreds of years old. Attempts had been made over a century ago to replace the edging with cut stone, but the work had not been completed. The mine had fallen into disuse, and for generations of Tremains it had been simply a ruin, a bit of history.

But Paul Tremain had nothing unproductive on his estate. The price of metals was rising again, sky-high this time. The old tin mine, with rich untapped lodes awaiting excavation, was next best thing to a goldmine; and with all that going for the Tremains Paul could surely have afforded to let Lorraine choose a man who had intelligence and kindness, without acting as though a bank balance was the be-all and end-all.

A dank moist smell hung over the old mine entrance, but after another quarter mile of new road the picture was very different. Here the buildings were modern stores and offices. Narrow gauge rail tracks for the iron trucks wound out of the mine and curved around the site huts to a huge mound of gleaming clay and stone deposit, and cables led from the generator hut into the entrance of the mine.

Usually, even above ground, the place hummed with activity, but there would have been no mining here today. The workers would have been maintenance men. And Rolf. There had been no mention of anyone trapped but Rolf. There was a small crowd of men. An ambulance and a fire service truck stood at the side, and a truck was drawn up near to the entrance.

Cars half filled the parking lot, and Lorraine turned in her car to join them, parking it as far as she could from Paul's. As Jenny began to get out she said, "Don't let Paul see you."

Jenny swung round. "See me? What about you?"

Lorraine didn't move. "Jenny," she hesitated, then said in a little rush, "Please, Jenny, go and ask for me. I can't."

Oh lor', thought Jenny, *I wish I could drive. I wish I could have given Lorraine those tranquilizers.* She said, "All right," and left Lorraine holding the steering wheel very tight and watching Jenny's retreating figure with wide frightened eyes. Jenny picked her way to the approach to the mine, over a morass of muddy clay, well trampled and wet with the leaking of water pipes and hoses leading to the mine. When she heard her name she looked around and spotted Mr. Morrison in the doorway of the office block.

She crossed to him. He wore a faint expression of disapproval, and as an extra mark of no welcome said nothing whatever to her but went into the office, presuming, quite rightly, that she would follow.

The general office had a lot of clerical equipment and a man sitting at a switchboard. There was no one else about. A door to a glass-partitioned section read, "A. Rogan, Assistant Manager," and an open door into another room, "R. Perrie, Manager."

Mr. Morrison had just gone through Rolf Perrie's door, and Jenny continued to follow. He closed the door as soon as she was in the room and said severely, "Why did you not stay at Moidores? I presume you have Miss Tremain in the car?"

"Yes, she's in the car. What's happening?"

"There's been a cave-in."

"I know, I took the message. What about Rolf?"

"He sounds in good spirits. Mr. Tremain told me to phone and tell you that all was under control. I spoke to Mrs. Ebsworth who was glad to hear it. And now perhaps you'll both go home again."

Jenny pleaded, "Will you come and tell Lorraine that it's all right?" He nodded and she led the way back to the car park and the car. She climbed into the seat by Lorraine as Mr. Morrison was getting into the back seat, and she had to reassure Lorraine right away. From the looks of Lorraine every second counted, so Jenny said at once, "Rolf isn't hurt. He's been talking to them."

Lorraine turned to face Mr. Morrison, her voice a croak. "How did it happen?"

He gave a crisp summary. "Mr. Perrie was inspecting a working face when a truck came adrift on the slope, dislodging a bit prop. Some of the roof came down. They're clearing it now."

He sounded as though this was no more than a tidying-up operation, but a runaway iron truck and a roof crashing down on you in an underground mine was horrific. And when part of a roof fell could there be a chain reaction? Lorraine echoed Jenny's fears. "What if there's another fall?"

"What would happen to Mr. Perrie, you mean?" His tone was dry. "He has been instructed over the phone to get back. As the rubble is being removed the roof is being shored up, but the men who could be hurt are the team who are doing the clearing, not Mr. Perrie."

"Oh." Lorraine sighed with relief. Right now she only had thoughts for Rolf.

Mr. Morrison went on in the same dry voice, "As it will be several hours before the rubble is cleared I do advise you both to go home."

"Soon," said Lorraine. "I think I'd better wait a little. If Jenny doesn't mind."

Jenny was still turned toward Mr. Morrison. She asked suddenly, "Where's Paul?"

"Down there."

Lorraine jerked around again. "You mean getting the rubble out?"

"Of course that's what he means." Jenny surprised herself, she sounded so snappish, but Lorraine didn't seem to notice.

Lorraine said, "Yes, that's where Paul would be," and almost smiled. "He'll be all right, he's indestructible."

"Is he?" Now Jenny sounded savage. "You could bury him alive and come back for him in six months' time, I suppose," and Lorraine stared at her as Mr. Morrison chuckled.

"I would not advise it," said Mr. Morrison. "He might well dig himself out, and he would come up in a very ugly frame of mind."

Jenny grinned, "He would, wouldn't he?"

"If you stay near the car," Mr. Morrison offered, "I'll keep you posted on progress."

"Thank you," said Jenny.

They watched him go. Lorraine said, "I didn't mean I'm not worried about Paul, but he will be taking care, won't he? They do know the risks. They'll be watching for trouble."

"I certainly hope so," said Jenny.

The time was half past ten. It took six hours to get Rolf Perrie out of the mine. A dozen men worked at clearing, another eight at shoring up the roof and loading the rubble onto the trucks, which were hauled to the surface by the winch attached to the back of the truck at the mine entrance.

Some of the time the girls sat in the car; sometimes they walked around, getting in no one's way, staying in the background, and Mr. Morrison kept his promise to keep them posted.

He reported the first small hole made through the barrier. Lack of air had been a hazard, he said—they hadn't thought of that—but it was all right now. And he came across to the car park to tell them when the stretcher was taken in.

"Stretcher?" Lorraine shrilled. "Why can't he walk?" She was out of the car, past Mr. Morrison, making for the group at the mine entrance, and Jenny squirmed out of the passenger seat and ran to stop her.

"Wait a bit," Jenny begged, so Lorraine waited until Mr. Morrison reached them, sounding testy.

"Miss Tremain, I beg of you, don't make a scene." Lorraine did look capable of flinging herself down beside the stretcher. That, Jenny reflected, would not please Paul, and it might not please Rolf either. Rolf might find it very embarrassing.

Lorraine snapped, "Of course I'm not going to make a scene!" and when Jenny loosened her arm she still walked fast, but she wasn't running now and she did hold back from the group.

Rolf didn't look too bad as they carried him out, and when he saw Lorraine he gave her a reassuring wave. She smiled and waved back, and while the stretcher was being lifted into the ambulance they went on smiling at each other.

There were a lot of men milling around, most of them wearing protective helmets and looking filthy, and when a hand fell on her shoulder for a split second Jenny didn't recognize Paul. Then he demanded, "What are you doing here?"

She gulped and said, "Just going."

The ambulance was away. She grabbed Lorraine again and they went back to the parking lot.

They drove in silence. Whatever Lorraine's thoughts were now she wasn't sharing them. But when the car was in the garage and switched off she said, "Thank you."

"What for?"

"For coming with me. For listening to me."

"What happens now?"

Lorraine's lips curved as they had done when she smiled at Rolf. "He looked for me," she said.

"I think he did." Jenny grimaced. "Paul did too."

"Yes, I know." And Jenny was dismayed to see how completely the happiness drained from Lorraine's face, and the look of apprehension that replaced it. . . .

Paul, Mr. Morrison and Anthony Rogan, the assistant manager of the mine, arrived at Moidores a couple of hours after the girls. Rolf had escaped with several broken bones in his foot. He had been X-rayed, put in a cast and, on his own insistence taken back to his parents' farmhouse. He had been lucky.

Mr. Morrison gave this information to the household, who were all sitting in the kitchen where Ebby had put on a huge tea. Paul had not looked in the kitchen. He had gone to change and would then be in the office.

"Sandwiches and coffee?" said Ebby.

"Capital," said Mr. Morrison. "We'll be working for most of the evening on reallocation of shift quotas."

"That sounds like fun." Lorraine's eyes danced mischievously; the good news about Rolf had put stars in them. The assistant manager grinned, but no one else did.

"Do you need a secretary?" Jenny asked.

Mr. Morrison said, "Tomorrow morning, probably, but tonight I don't think so," his meaning clear to everyone but Timmy and the assistant manager. Tonight Jenny would do well to keep out of Paul's way.

Later, when Timothy was in bed, and Lorraine said, "I'm going down to the harbor," that seemed a good idea. It would have been pleasant to spend the rest of the evening with Grace and the others, except for the prospect of facing Jack Bastaple again.

Keep out of Paul's way up in the house; keep out of Jack's way down in the harbor. . . . If Jenny went on like this the only safe place left for her soon would be the Witch's Rock.

"Coming?" said Lorraine.

"No."

"Why not?"

"Because I don't want to see Jack again for a day or two."

"You needn't," said Lorraine gaily. "We'll dodge him."

There was room enough in Tremain to avoid a meeting, and putting it off wouldn't really help. What guarantee was there that Jack would feel any better in a day or two about having had his picture ruined? He'd have had more time to brood about it. He could well be angrier, if that was possible, and she couldn't dodge him forever.

She said, "I'll tell Ebby. She'll listen for Timmy."

It was dark and damp outside although the lights of Tremain glowed warmly in the sky over the next cove. Lorraine's flashlight guided their footsteps until their eyes were accustomed to the night, by which time they were nearing the turning for Tremain. The track leading over the moors to the home farm was almost opposite and Lorraine stopped and said, "Don't be mad at me, Jenny."

Jenny knew what was coming, and she stormed, "Why couldn't you say we were going to see Rolf? Why tell me all that nonsense about going down to the harbor?"

Lorraine said in a small voice, "If you'd told Ebby she'd have told Paul."

Jenny was exasperated. "Stop acting like a child! If you want Rolf and he wants you it has nothing to do with anyone else, and I do not believe for one moment that Paul would sack him."

"It isn't that easy." Lorraine's long fair hair and pale face shimmered in the darkness, making her look waiflike, ghostlike. "Rolf works for Paul and Mr. Perrie farms Paul's land, and Paul made it very clear that he didn't want our friendship to go beyond friendship.

"You might not believe that Paul would hurt the Perries. Well, I'm not so sure, and I've known my brother a great deal longer than you have.

"But Rolf could have been killed today, and he's my friend and I want to talk to him. Are you coming with me or going down to the harbor or going back home?"

Jenny sighed, feeling trapped. The Perries' small holding was next to the home farm, a twenty-minute walk by this lonely track across the moors. Not an inviting prospect, but Jenny was Lorraine's alibi. Jenny had told Ebby—and because she believed it she had been convincing—that they were going down to Tremain. So long as they returned together, and unless they were spotted in the wrong place, no one was going to question that. If they didn't return together the truth would out.

"Why can't you wait till tomorrow?" Jenny demanded.

"I want to see him now," said Lorraine, mild but stubborn.

"But he almost certainly has to rest. He's had a grim day. Do you think he'll want to entertain visitors?"

"I think he'll want to see me," said Lorraine softly. She began to walk away down the track and Jenny stood for a moment. It was lonely and dark and not a walk for a girl alone. Jenny had to follow and when she caught up Lorraine said, "Thank you."

"Don't thank me," said Jenny huffily. "I feel an absolute fool playing cloak and dagger like this. What do we do if the house is full of his workmates?"

"I don't go in." Lorraine slipped a hand through Jenny's arm. "Jenny dear, don't be angry, I never had anyone to talk about Rolf with before. I am grateful."

"Didn't you talk to Caterine?"

"Caterine laughed at me."

Caterine laughed at most folk, but Lorraine was a sensitive girl, unsure of herself in spite of her looks and her position.

Jenny said, "She laughed at me too."

"She called him my ploughboy." But Rolf wasn't even a farmer, he was a highly qualified mining engineer.

"I'm sure she didn't mean it unkindly," said Jenny.

Lorraine agreed quickly. "No, she didn't, it was just her joke, she never took it seriously at all. Not many people knew, although it wasn't a secret. We'd known each other all our lives, of course, and when he came back from college and started work at the mine we went out together a few times, and we used to ride together.

"Then the manager retired and Paul made Rolf manager. Rolf was going to ask me to marry him, I know."

The track beneath their feet was damp and clogging from the storm, and a bleak wind blew. Jenny pulled her coat tighter around her, holding it together at her throat.

"Only Paul stopped him," said Lorraine. "It's c-cold, isn't it?" and her teeth were chattering.

"Yes," said Jenny. "Very cold. Let's try to walk faster."

There were no cars in front of the Perries' farmhouse nor in the yard. All the same Lorraine hung back and said, "Will you knock?"

Mr. Perrie answered the door. Jenny hadn't seen him since she came to Tremain this time, although she recognized him at once.

He still looked like an older edition of Rolf, but broader, perhaps more rugged. He knew her. "Jenny Douglas."

"Yes."

He saw Lorraine behind her and said, "Come in, then," so they stepped inside and he led the way into a room where Mrs. Perrie was sitting in a chair by the fire. Her face still showed the strain of the day, and she looked at Jenny and Lorraine for a moment as though they were enemies.

Then she said, "You were at the mine," as if that was in their favor. "Bill saw you."

They hadn't noticed Mr. Perrie. Until Rolf was brought out they had been some distance from the entrance and the groups of men around it. But two girls would have been conspicuous. "They wouldn't let me go," said Mrs. Perrie.

Her husband patted her shoulder. "You were better here, I know you." He smiled at the girls. "As it was she'd turned out all the cupboards and washed all the china and dropped half a dinner set before we got home."

Jenny smiled too—any joke was welcome—but Lorraine was in no mood for smiling. "How is Rolf?"

She was nearly in tears, and Rolf's mother said, "It's just his foot," her voice trembling like Lorraine's, "but he could have been killed."

Lorraine went to Mrs. Perrie. "How badly is he hurt?"

"They've set the bones." His father sounded cheerful. "There shouldn't be any complications. He has to stay in bed for a week, and after that he can start getting about again."

"It could have been . . . ." Lorraine shuddered.

"It could," echoed Rolf's mother, and the two women gripped each other's hands, reliving their ordeal of waiting.

"But it wasn't," Mr. Perrie reminded them.

"Can I see him?" Lorraine asked.

His mother said, "He's supposed to be resting, but a minute or two can't hurt, can it? Can it, Bill?"

Now Mr. Perrie looked serious. "If Rolf's asleep," he said, "I don't think we ought to disturb him again tonight. I'll see if he is."

"I will," said Mrs. Perrie promptly. Lorraine went with her and Jenny felt that Mr. Perrie would rather she hadn't. He said slowly, "Go on up, Miss Douglas."

"I'll come again," she said. If Rolf and Lorraine did have anything to say to each other they wouldn't want Jenny around.

"Take a chair, then." Mr. Perrie's cheerfulness had quite gone.

He sounded as though his thoughts were heavy and when Mrs. Perrie came back into the room she said, "She's only staying a minute, Bill," and looked at Jenny. "He doesn't know she's here, I suppose?"

"Paul? No."

"You've heard all about it, then?"

Mr. Perrie protested, "I'm sure Miss Douglas—"

"Who told you?" asked Mrs. Perrie. "Not Tremain, I'll be bound."

"Lorraine," said Jenny.

Mrs. Perrie went back to her chair by the fire. "Our boy's not good enough for his sister." She poked the fire, clattering the poker between the bars so energetically that her husband's protests were almost drowned. Then she looked up at him challengingly. "That was what he said, wasn't it?"

Bill Perrie was not a young man. Waiting at the mine had been as harrowing for him as it had for his wife, here with friends and neighbors around her. He had watched the rescue operation, so far as a man could who was above ground, and he knew what part Paul Tremain had played. Right now he did not feel like disparaging Tremain or listening to his wife's tirade.

In the pocket of his tweed jacket he felt the reassuring shape of his pipe and said wearily, "That's all in the past, all forgotten. Let's drop it, shall we?" Then he went out and lit his pipe and walked for a while around his farm buildings, getting some solace from a quiet smoke. That business with Lorraine Tremain had been a strange affair. Rolf had never talked much about it and his father had never worked out the rights and the wrongs of it. But Bill Perrie would have been happier tonight if he could honestly have believed it was all in the past and forgotten. Sarah Perrie had no doubts who was in the wrong. When her husband had declined to discuss it she had turned back to Jenny, who sat uncomfortably unsure whether she was about to be confided in, or abused as a near-Tremain.

"His father was a very different sort," said Mrs. Perrie nostalgically. Paul's father? Jack Bastaple had said that once. Mrs. Perrie pointed at Jenny. "He'd sit in that chair you're in and take a glass of ale. Always had all the time in the world for a joke and a chat."

That didn't sound much like Paul.

"He wouldn't have told Rolf he wasn't good enough," said Sarah Perrie, and her hurt was for her son. She spoke with dignity, and the anguish of someone who would never forget.

That didn't sound like Paul either. It must have happened, but Jenny couldn't believe it. To Jenny it didn't ring true.

"It's not Lorraine's fault." Lorraine was back in Mrs. Perrie's favor. "She's a good girl, but she's no match for Tremain."

Jenny wondered, "Why didn't Rolf walk out? How could he go on working for Paul after that?"

His mother bridled, "Why should he walk out? He has no quarrel with the job. He does it well, Tremain knows that." She reached for her empty teacup. "He nearly got himself killed doing it today."

Her face crumpled and Jenny jumped up. "Let me pour you some tea."

"Thank you, my dear." The cup clattered in the saucer as Sarah Perrie held it. As Jenny took it from her she said shakily, "That seems to be all I've done today, drink tea and drop dishes."

"All's well that ends well," said Jenny.

"Thank God it did," said Rolf's mother, and Lorraine came in and echoed that after her.

"But he's going to be all right," said Lorraine. "He really is." She was half laughing, half crying, and Jenny, pondering whether to pour tea for Lorraine too, decided it might be better to get her home.

Jenny was beginning to feel the strain herself. She would not be sorry to put her head on her own pillow and call it a day. She said, "We should be getting back."

"Yes, of course," Lorraine was amenable now. She flung her arms around Mrs. Perrie, and was hugged in return, and when Mr. Perrie came in she said, "We're off now," giving him a dewy-eyed smile.

He asked, "Did you walk here? I can't see your car."

"Yes," said Jenny.

Mrs. Perrie nodded meaningly at her husband. So Lorraine had had to sneak out like a thief in the night to see Rolf.

"I'll drive you back," said Mr. Perrie.

They climbed into his car and soon he had them at the gates of Moidores. There he stopped the car and asked Lorraine, "Would you like to get out here?"

She said quickly, "Yes, please."

"Right then," he said. "Out with you." They got out and thanked him, and he turned the car and drove home again, reflecting that she was a pretty lass and a nice lass, but she still didn't seem to have a spark of spirit.

Once in the house, having slipped in by a side door, Lorraine announced, "I'm going up to my room, my head's starting to ache. I'll see you in the morning."

She looked all in. Jenny could see she would need time before she could face any sort of questions, even from Ebby or Eb. And if Paul should loom up the pretense of having gone down to Tremain wouldn't last a minute.

"Sleep well," said Jenny, nearing exhaustion herself.

She looked in on Timothy, who had kicked off the bedclothes but appeared none the worse for it and tucked him in again. Then she went down into the kitchen. No one seemed to suspect them there. The only thing puzzling Ebby was why they were back so soon, and Jenny explained that Lorraine had a headache so she had come back for a reasonably early night.

Ebby sympathized and went up with headache pills

and a drink, so Lorraine could still find herself either fibbing or confessing.

The whole thing had been rather idiotic and Jenny was tired. *Bed for me too*, she thought. She said goodnight to Eb, then remembered a magazine left in the drawing room and went to collect it.

There she parted the curtains a little to look at the sea. There wasn't much light from the room; the clouds were still low, but the sound of the sea reached her like a singing in her own blood. She opened the window and listened to it and she was at the window when Paul came into the room.

"Do you need air?" he asked.

"No. I was listening to the sea." She closed the window and pulled the curtains back into place.

"How was the patient?"

She shrugged. "As comfortable as you can be with a smashed foot." She hadn't seen Rolf herself, but Paul obviously knew where they had been and splitting hairs wouldn't help.

"I gather she's reassured he's not on the danger list?"

"Yes," said Jenny.

Paul sat down, in the leather armchair. "I don't want that affair starting up again."

"*You* don't?"

"It wouldn't be in Lorraine's interests."

"Her happiness or her social position?"

"Her happiness, of course."

"And you'd know about that better than she would?"

"Yes." The arrogance of that shocked her deeply.

She came from the window and stood looking at him. "Did you threaten to sack Rolf Perrie?"

"Let's say I told them I wasn't prepared to subsidize them. Either through Perrie's career or through Lorraine's allowance."

"Lorraine's allowance?"

"She has nothing of her own."

"She doesn't own the shop? She doesn't own anything?"

"That's right."

"And you don't think Rolf Perrie is good enough for her?"

"She didn't think so herself until today. Now there's a risk that she'll sentimentalize the situation out of control."

Jenny protested, "She was very distressed today—she's very fond of Rolf. She says if you'd left them alone she'd have realized before that she loved him." Paul stayed impassive. "But she believes you'd victimize him and his family if she went against your wishes."

"Does she?"

"Would you?"

"That remains to be seen." He looked grim enough. "Don't encourage her."

"What do you mean 'encourage her'?"

She knew the signs of irascibility. He thought she was being deliberately dull-witted, and if he lost his temper she couldn't guarantee hers.

He said very slowly, "Don't listen to her; don't let her make a confidante of you."

"And what am I supposed to do if she wants to talk about Rolf? Snap her head off?"

"I'm sure you can deal with the situation."

She remembered yesterday and thought, *I'm less equipped for dealing with emotional situations than you imagine. Jack Bastaple will tell you I can run amok. Although why he should think anyone needs to protect you I can't imagine.*

"And don't let yourself get talked into playing the go-between," said Paul wearily. "You've acted like a couple of silly schoolgirls today."

How dared he? What did he think she had been

doing—getting a vicarious kick out of Lorraine's thwarted romance? Lorraine had said, "Paul laid down the law for Caterine." And for Rolf and Lorraine. Now for Jenny.

She said, "Those are my orders?"

"Call them what you like."

"No," she blazed, "oh no! You may be the last word here but not for me. You don't rule me, I'm not Lorraine and I am not Caterine!"

As she said it she froze. She saw the impatience leave him and he was calm and deadly cold. He said, "Indeed you are not Caterine," and she knew she had said the one thing that was unforgivable.

CHAPTER SIX

NEXT MORNING Jenny went alone to Lorraine's room as soon as she woke, before Timmy was up. It was daylight, but only just. She leaned over the silent figure and hissed, "Lorraine!"

Lorraine yawned into the pillow and asked, "What is it?"

"Paul knows where we were last night."

Lorraine made a groaning noise that ended up, "Wouldn't you know? How did he find out?"

"Worked it out, I think," said Jenny. "He gave me a lecture that made me feel about two inches high and said we'd been behaving like silly schoolgirls."

If he had phrased it differently Jenny might have agreed. It had been silly, pretending to go down to the harbor while they scurried over the heath to the Perrie's farm.

Lorraine said nothing.

Jenny said, "You are listening? You haven't gone to sleep again?"

"I'm listening."

"Well, this is your business, of course, but can I tell you what I'd do if I were you?"

"Yes?"

"I think Paul expects you to make a great fuss, so I'd play it as cool as I could. You and Rolf are friends, no one's trying to stop that, so take it from there until you're a hundred percent sure."

Lorraine laughed ruefully, "That was what Rolf said." Lorraine was impulsive and yesterday she had been prepared to promise anything. "They were almost his words—don't make a drama out of it."

That didn't sound like a man in love, although perhaps it did sound like a man who was not going to be hurt again.

"Could you come down to the shop this afternoon?" Lorraine asked.

"I don't know. You're going to see Rolf?"

"It's all above board, I won't pretend I'm going riding."

Jenny said, "I'll try."

As she turned to go Lorraine called after her, "Jenny, I'm ninety-nine per cent sure."

Jenny laughed, "That's a pretty good start!" She padded barefoot back along the carpeted corridor to the nursery and her own room. Lorraine could smile this morning, she and Rolf were starting again. This time the friendship might grow, or it might not, but they did have a second chance to make up their minds and Jenny wished them well.

She didn't feel much like smiling herself. She felt wretched and she knew why—that scene with Paul. She would have given months of her life not to have been in the drawing room last night when he'd passed the open door. She had woken this morning with a knot of misery where her heart ought to be, and for the first time since she came to Moidores she had woken feeling lonely.

Timmy was sitting up now, more asleep than awake, and she went over and hugged him. There was plenty of time and the child was warm in her arms and she needed warmth. He liked being hugged, when he was sleepy and not conscious of his male dignity, so he snuggled against her now and fell asleep again.

She stayed with an arm around him until it really was time he was up, then she said, "Hey, lazybones, you'll be missing the bus!"

She pulled the bedspread off him and he glared up at her, awake now, doing one of their morning routines. "Auntie Jen, I hate you!"

"I hate you." She gave back a ferocious scowl, and they both dissolved into giggles.

As Timmy rolled out of bed Jenny knew she wasn't lonely; she had a child for whom she would have given anything. But she went down to breakfast still wishing she hadn't gone to collect the magazine from the drawing room last night. Paul was at the breakfast table. He looked up from his newspaper and said "Good morning," then went back to his reading, and Jenny sat down with Timmy and tipped cornflakes into his bowl and poured milk and sprinkled sugar.

There was no mention of last night. Paul was immersed in a slab of small print, no more aware of Jenny than if he had been alone. She didn't exist for him. Caterine would have talked, no one ever ignored Caterine. She would have asked, "What's in the papers, darling? Not that dreary old political editorial you're reading, what are the headlines?"

Whether she cared or not what was happening in the world she wouldn't have sat quietly by Timmy. She would have had Paul reading the newspaper to her.

"Indeed you are not Caterine," he had said and then "Good night," so curtly that Jenny had almost run from the room, horrified at her own clumsiness.

Why hadn't she stopped to think before she'd said, "You don't rule me . . . I am not Caterine." She had been tired and indignant, and there were excuses for losing her temper. But not for losing her head so that she had not considered how her words would wound. Because Paul had overruled Caterine she had driven that car to her death. He had lost her forever.

In her own room Jenny had looked at her reflection in the little swinging mirror on top of the chest of drawers. She was not Caterine, in any way at all. She could hear Caterine laughing at the thought, head thrown back, as she must have laughed at Lorraine and her "ploughboy." "Caterine will always be here," Lorraine had said.

But now Jenny sat with Timmy, facing Paul over the breakfast table. When Paul got up he ruffled Timmy's hair and gave Jenny a brief nod. Usually he said, "See you later," to Jenny. That meant some time during the morning in the office, but this morning he said nothing to her.

Timmy had been chattering about the mine accident all through breakfast. It was going to be the big thing on the school bus this morning. Several of his schoolmates had fathers who worked in the mine and who had helped in the rescue operation.

The bus stopped to collect the children at the top of the turning for the harbor. When school had started again after the holiday Jenny had walked along with Timmy each morning, but most of the children came up the hillside unaccompanied and Timmy had said after a few days, "I can go on my own, you know." Now he did, unless Lorraine was going down to Tremain at the same time.

He was passing the spot of the accident, but habit and a child's resilience seemed to have taken the terror from it. The mended fencing had matured now, the grass and bushes no longer showed signs of a car out of control.

Timmy set off for school, and Lorraine—who decided she didn't want any breakfast—set off for the shop, and Jenny went into the office.

Both Mr. Morrison and Paul were there. It wasn't quite nine o'clock and the morning mail had just arrived.

They were going through it as Jenny sat down at the smallest desk, which had been brought in for her when she went on the payroll, and waited.

As soon as all the mail was opened and Paul had

glanced through it he said, "Right then, I'll see you."

"Where's he gone?" Jenny asked Mr. Morrison.

"To the mine."

There was plenty to be done here. Morrison dictated letters and produced papers for filing. Then while Jenny went to collect his mid-morning coffee and arrowroot biscuits he gathered his notes for an interview with the Inland Revenue, and she typed those out for him too.

At lunchtime she said, "Are you both out this afternoon?"

"Yes."

"If I'm through here can I go and help in the shop?"

"Of course." He had been nodding happily over his neatly typed pages; now he looked up to say, "Miss Tremain will be visiting the invalid, I presume?"

Both he and Paul seemed to have Lorraine's plan of campaign summed up. Jenny said nothing, and Mr. Morrison went on, "I advise you not to get yourself involved in that affair."

"I've been advised," said Jenny. "I've been ordered."

Mr. Morrison made a silent "Oh!" and Jenny demanded, "Why should Paul dictate who Lorraine marries? He pleased himself, didn't he? Caterine didn't have a bean, but they were happy."

In the months of working for Joe Morrison Jenny had learned to interpret the merest change of expression. To most he seemed to have no change of expression, but to Jenny now he looked sceptical.

She said quietly, "You didn't like my sister, did you?"

"What gives you that idea?"

Caterine had not liked him, and dislike is usually mutual. Jenny said, "She thought you didn't."

He said briskly, "Mrs. Tremain was a charming young lady, everybody liked her," and went back to the notes she had typed for him.

He would hardly be likely to admit it now, and there

was no point saying, "Everyone did like Caterine. And she seemed to like everyone here but you. Why didn't she like you?"

Mr. Morrison had always been kind to Jenny and Jenny liked him. Caterine did not trust him, but Jenny did. Jenny would have said he had complete integrity.

He put his notes in his briefcase and said goodbye.

Grace was in the shop with Lorraine and they were starting to stocktake. During the winter months the place would be redecorated, and most of the time a notice would advise anyone interested in seeing anything to apply to Number Three, The Close—Grace's house. Only the most hardy of tourists came down into Tremain in the winter months.

Lorraine beamed as Jenny walked in. "Good, you got away."

"Yes." She dumped her handbag and took off her coat, carrying it into the little back office to hang behind the door. "Paul's over at the mine. I asked Mr. Morrison and he said he presumed you were visiting." She mimicked Joe Morrison's caustic comment, and Lorraine and Grace smiled.

"That's right," said Lorraine gaily. "Im taking grapes and goodies." Looking very pretty, there was a glow on her, and she couldn't get away quick enough. She went off, almost running along the quayside, her coat flying wide.

Jenny said, "She's used up more energy yesterday and today than in all the weeks since I came here. She doesn't seem to have stopped rushing since that phone call about the accident."

"I noticed," said Grace. "We've brought the stocktaking forward three weeks, although I wouldn't say it won't have to be done again." She picked up the clipboard on which Lorraine had been making her list and drew a heart-with-arrow in the top right-hand corner.

"Love suits her," said Jenny.

"Love?" Grace made the word a question.

"What else?"

"If it's the same as last time," said Grace, "they like each other, but not quite enough."

"You knew about the last time?"

"Not till the balloon went up." Grace had been counting rings, slotted into velvet trays, six trays to a drawer. Jenny let her get through the tray she was on now and put down the numbers in the columns.

Then she asked, "Was there much fuss?"

Grace shook her head. "Surprisingly little. I suppose I know Lorraine as well as anybody, since I've worked in here on and off almost as long as she's been running the shop. I knew she went out with Rolf Perrie sometimes, but it seems they'd known each other since they were kids, and no one made anything of that. Not until Caterine started teasing her about him."

Grace sounded accusing and Jenny said, "Caterine always teased. She wouldn't mean to hurt Lorraine or cause trouble."

Grace snorted, "Well, she managed to do both." She took out another tray of rings and said, "After that we heard no more about Rolf Perrie from Lorraine. He stopped coming down to the harbor and Lorraine started dating in the higher income bracket, the Tremain circuit, Caterine's friends."

"Weren't you Caterine's friends?"

"Of course," said Grace. "But in the lower income bracket." She took out a ring that looked like a great gold nugget, except that it was brighter than gold. "What happened to all Caterine's jewelry? She had a ring like this, but the real thing. She had some fantastic stuff."

Bracelets and pearls, Jenny had seen them in the painting. She knew about Caterine's jewelry. Caterine usually brought some of it along with her when she visited her old home.

"Paul always bought her jewelry," Jenny said. "Birthdays and Christmases and anniversaries. Always. I suppose jewelry is an investment that never loses its value, but sometimes I should think she'd have liked a change, a surprise."

Grace looked at her quickly. "You're joking! Caterine never wanted anything except a bigger bracelet." Then, as though that had to be softened a little, "And why not? So would I if I had the chance. You know what Ben bought me for my last birthday?"

"What?"

"An electric range, with a box of chocolates on the top shelf. And I turned on the oven without spotting the chocolates. We got them out before the wrappings set on fire, but not before they'd all melted into each other. So then we put them in the fridge, and they made a very unusual dessert."

Jenny laughed, her thoughts grave. Everybody was Caterine's friend.

But not Mr. Morrison, and neither, without reservations, was Grace Norwood. Grace would not have spoken like that immediately after the accident, but the charisma of death was fading.

Of course Caterine would have been envied. She was outstandingly beautiful and rich. It was a wonder she had any friends at all, outside those she was on close and intimate terms with. The rest would just envy her and not know how warm and generous she was, how loving.

Jenny had adored Caterine all her life. It saddened her hearing anyone blaming Caterine for anything, but defending a memory would only remind her how much she herself had lost.

Grace had just told the joke about the chocolates to

change the subject, and Grace was not the only one who could be tactless and then wish that she hadn't.

So Jenny smiled and asked, "How do you take stock?" She listened carefully while Grace explained and gave her Lorraine's list to recheck.

They had the place almost to themselves for the next hour or two. They talked about the excitement at the mine yesterday. Grace knew what Jenny didn't know, that Paul had been the one to climb through the clearing in the rubble and find Rolf Perrie.

Most of the men working at the mine lived in Tremain. Yesterday everyone had waited: not only the miner's families, but artists, tradesmen, fishermen. And when it was all over every detail had been avidly discussed.

Grace knew much more than Jenny. That a single bolt in the coupling of a truck had given way causing the truck to crash down, uncontrolled, leaving the track and smashing into the timber supports. Just one bolt.

While the men worked, clearing a way, there had been other falls, and when there was a passage through somehow there had been no question that Paul Tremain was going into the darkness to find Rolf Perrie.

He had gone through before it was safe. No one had been certain what state Rolf was in. He had spoken on the phone hours earlier and been told to get back, well away from the fall. He had understood and said he would, but he had sounded groggy and finished, "Make it as soon as you can."

As soon as there was room to get through Paul Tremain had gone. The assistant manager had protested, "What do we do if it comes down again and you're both in there?"

Paul had grinned and said, "Carry on digging, for God's sake." That, said Grace, had struck them all as very funny. They were still laughing at that when Paul came back practically carrying Rolf, and the miners hadn't finished grinning over it yet.

"Do you think it's funny?" Grace asked.

"No," said Jenny. She went on, without quite knowing why, "Paul wasn't joking when I saw him last night. He was very short-tempered."

"He'd had a tiring day," said Grace, and with that Jenny had to agree.

Grace was counting things in the window when Jack Bastaple walked by. She tapped the window and called to Jenny, "Here's Jack!" and Jenny retreated farther into the shop, ending up by the door to the office with a hand on the knob.

But Jack didn't even glance at the shop and Grace queried in surprise, "What's got into him?"

"He thinks I might be in here." Jenny moved forward again. "We had a disagreement on Saturday about one of his pictures."

Grace grinned with cheerful malice, "Well, if you didn't like it he'll sulk until you say you've changed your mind and you're sorry."

But an apology wouldn't put the canvas back together, and Jenny had as little to say to Jack as he had to say to her. It would suit Jenny if they both kept their distance.

Grace may have thought she was being diplomatic, or it could just have been coincidence an hour or so later. There were customers in, and Grace was showing them jewelry, but she suddenly said in an aside to Jenny, "Ask Ben to turn the casserole on, there's a dear. He's in the studio."

"Shall I turn it on?" Jenny suggested.

"No," said Grace, "he understands the oven."

If it was a new range it should do what the dials said, but Grace was giving an animated sales talk about pendants, swinging one with a multicolored stone to catch the light; so Jenny went to the studio, although she had a sinking feeling that was where Jack Bastaple had been going.

There was very much the clubhouse atmosphere this afternoon. There were paintings around, unfinished models and sculptures on the benches, but most of the artists were sitting down drinking coffee. There was no hurry any more, with the heaviest season over.

Jenny knew them all, so they greeted her as she went in, and one girl waved a mug at her. "Cup of coffee, Jen?"

"No, thanks," said Jenny. She called, "Ben, message from Grace."

Ben Norwood was at the far end from the door, in his usual spot, sitting on the edge of a working bench, with a block of basalt beside him. Jack was there too, painting, and Jenny needed to pass Jack to reach Ben.

She hesitated briefly, but it would have been ridiculous to yell, and she began to walk the length of the barny old room. What was Jack painting? If it was Caterine again it would lose its impact if his colleagues watched him paint it. Jenny wouldn't look unless she had to; she would just walk down to Ben and ask him to go home and turn on the oven.

But as she passed Jack he growled, "You're not curious?"

So she stopped. It was not Caterine. It was an abstract of slashing colours. She could imagine it as a therapy for anger. He gave her no chance to speak, and what could she have said if he had? But he looked at her much as he had done on Saturday and walked past her, out of the studio, the steel tips on his heels clattering on the iron staircase outside.

The girl who had offered her coffee, the mother of Leah—one of Timmy's friends—said, "So it was you."

"What was?"

"Our Jack's foul mood. What have you done to him?"

Jenny said again, "I didn't like a picture he'd painted. We had a row." And they all smiled; Jack Bastaple's touchiness about his work was well-known.

"Which was it?" someone else asked.

Jenny said, "A sea picture." Reaching Ben Norwood, she added, "Please, Grace said would you turn on the casserole?"

"This very minute," said Ben Norwood cheerfully. He was a man of medium height, gray-haired, thick-set, with bright kind eyes in a round face. He went out with Jenny, and at the bottom of the steps he asked, "Was that why Grace sent you in, to patch up the quarrel?"

"I suspect it was," said Jenny. "But it wasn't so much a quarrel as a long farewell."

Ben laughed and clapped her on the shoulder and said, "Tell Grace that or she'll be getting you both around to supper."

"If she did it would probably choke Jack."

"Would you care?"

"Of course," said Jenny. "Well, perhaps not much," and she went back into the shop while Ben was still laughing.

Grace was finishing her sale. When the customers had gone she turned an inquiring look on Jenny. Jenny said, "Ben's switching on the oven right now," and without any pretence of gaiety, "Jack was there. He walked out of the studio as I walked in."

And then she told Grace about the painting of Caterine as the chained sea witch. "He wouldn't sell it to me, because he'd painted it for his exhibition. He was determined it was getting the biggest audience going, and it was terrifying. I think it would have given Timmy nightmares again if he'd ever seen it."

"Jack's a young fool," said Grace, her tolerance strained. "What's his idea?"

"He said Paul kept Caterine prisoner. Jack wanted to remind everybody that she didn't escape." She swallowed and it hurt. "She died, but she didn't escape."

"Prisoner my eye!" Grace exploded. "Caterine Tremain had a marvelous life!"

"I know, but Jack thinks that Paul shouldn't have stopped her acting. She did have tremendous talent, so I suppose she should have used it."

"Then she shouldn't have married a possessive man," said Grace, "and I think she was flattered that he wanted to keep her with him. She'd talk about the offers she'd had, but I'm sure she enjoyed saying, 'Paul would never let me.'"

That had been Jenny's impression over all the years of Caterine's marriage. Until just before the accident she was certain that Caterine had never really tried to make Paul change his mind. Jenny said huskily, "It looked like someone peering through bars."

"Did it?" Grace pulled a wry face. "I have to see this."

"You haven't heard it all." What Jenny had to say now would probably sound like murder to an artist. "I destroyed it."

Someone screeched suddenly outside the shop. The children were home from school, and Jenny and Grace both jumped. Then Grace gulped, "You *did*?"

"With the bread knife."

Grace groped for the chair behind her and backed into it. "That must have been a lulu of a scene!"

"I wouldn't like it to happen again," admitted Jenny bleakly. "Not that it will; he's not likely to let me near it a second time, but he said he'd paint it again."

"Silly lad!" Grace sighed. "He's always had this chip on his shoulder about Paul Tremain. He still hankers for the old days when this was a fishing village and nothing else. To hear him talk you'd think it was heaven on earth before Paul Tremain turned it into big business."

Perhaps it was, thought Jenny. When Jack Bastaple was a boy and it was peaceful all year round, except for the sea and the seabirds. She said quietly, "Perhaps Paul has spoiled Tremain," but Grace, innately practical, was not having that.

"How has he spoiled it?" she demanded. "The harbor's the same, the houses are the same. The only difference is that the mine's being worked again, and in the summer the tourists come. And while Jack's being snide about the tourists he's quick enough to take their money." She warmed to her argument, with a flourishing gesture for the layout of the shop. "There wouldn't be much point in a place like this, would there, unless somebody was going to look and buy?"

There were three of Jack's pictures displayed for sale, and several more stacked in the office. Jenny knew them all, but she went across now and looked again at the one of the old mine entrance.

The old mine was always a popular subject, and Jack's painting brought out the gold of gorse and the purple of heather, made the grass greener and emphasized the texture of the crumbling stonework.

She asked Grace, who was a professional and ought to know, "He is good, isn't he?"

"Much better than average," said Grace. She leaned back in her chair, casting a critical eye at the picture Jenny was viewing. "But he's no Van Gogh, so I shouldn't worry about having deprived the world of a masterpiece. By the way, can I tell Ben?"

She would anyway, but if Jenny asked it would go no further than that. Jenny said, "Yes, but please don't tell anyone else. If everyone knows Jack will have to paint Caterine again, out of bravado. But if no one says anything he might decide not to bother."

"Don't rely on it." Grace had known Jack a long time. "This could be the best chance he's ever had for knocking Tremain."

"It would be unpleasant for Paul," Jenny agreed, "but it would be so bad for Timmy."

"Yes, I see that." Grace rose and shoved the little gilt-cane chair back against the counter irritably, as though she was shaking Jack. "The man's a menace!" She grinned, her white uneven teeth flashing against the tan of her skin. "We could always pretend it was a painting of you, not Caterine."

"Me?" Jenny smiled too. "Oh no, it wasn't me. It was very much Caterine, and it was good of her, except that Caterine was nobody's prisoner."

"If it was good of her it was like you," said Grace. She gave Jenny the same impersonal appraisal she had just given the painting of the old mine. "One tends to forget how much you do look like her. You don't talk like her, nor act like her, but feature for feature you certainly look like her."

"*No*," said Jenny.

"Especially now your hair's longer." It hadn't been cut since Jenny came here. It touched her shoulders now, dark and softly waving.

From deep inside Jenny something said with longing, "I wish I was like Caterine."

Grace's lips parted to say, "You—" then she bit her lip and smiled, "What for? All that jewelry?"

"I wouldn't bother about the stones," said Jenny gaily. "I'm a junk jewelry girl." She picked up one of the pendants left on the counter from the selection Grace had been showing the last customers and admired it. "This is my idea of a super piece."

What would she want that had been Caterine's? She wouldn't let herself think.

She said, "School's out."

"You want to get back?" Grace suggested. "It's all right if you do."

"I think I will." Jenny got her coat from the office, and Ben came in through the side door from the courtyard and asked, "How many for supper?"

"Just us," said Grace. She looked across at Jenny.

Jenny said, "Do explain to Ben that I don't make a habit of it."

She meant, destroying paintings, and Grace said, "Oh, I will, I will."

"A habit of what?" asked Ben, intrigued. He came over to his wife, a comfortable not particularly ambitious man, doing work he enjoyed among people he liked, sharing everything with Grace.

Tremain suits them, thought Jenny, or is it that they suit each other?

She said goodbye and walked out onto the dock, looking across the water and waving at Dan Blaskie rowing in from the *Mylor*.

Beyond the *Mylor* loomed the Witch's Rock. Jenny hadn't been out to the Rock since she came to Tremain this time, but she believed she remembered everything about it: the tiny cove, secure and hidden from wind and wave, the honeycomb of caves.

Reaching it required masterly seamanship, because of tide-race and submerged rocks. Most ships kept clear, but she had been taken there for a picnic once when she and Lorraine were schoolgirls, and the caves had been a magic land to Jenny.

She wondered now whether the years between had broken the spell. One day she might find out. No one had changed the Witch's Rock as Paul Tremain had changed the world of Jack Bastaple's boyhood. In Jack's eyes that would always be a lost Shangri-La.

As she passed the side street where Jack lived Jenny was filled with exasperated pity for him. Because if he was in the cottage painting that portrait again he was hurting himself more than he could ever hurt Paul.

"I remember the eyes," Jack had said, but the eyes he had painted had been agonized. From time to time Caterine had yearned a little for a career she might have had. When she'd talked about it of course she had portrayed her emotions vividly: she was a born actress. But there had been no agony.

Jack had exaggerated, like painting grass greener than it grew and the shadowy entrance to the old mine black as pitch.

Jenny knew what Caterine's reaction would have been to that painting. She would have stared at it, and at the man who had painted it, and then she would have laughed. . . .

Lorraine came home looking happy. Not deliriously, but bathed in a quiet content. She had been at the Perries all afternoon, had helped Rolf's mother prepare the tea, and she had fetched and carried trays for the invalid.

Paul had been there in the morning, and so had the doctor, and Rolf was fine.

She told them all this in the kitchen, and meeting Ebby's worried frown she teased, "Don't fuss, Ebby, we're not going to elope. We wouldn't get far unless I wheeled him in a wheelbarrow."

"What's 'elope'?" Timmy tugged Jenny's sleeve and Ebby said dourly, "A passel of trouble."

"Run away," said Lorraine, smiling, and Jenny felt Timmy's fingers tighten around the stuff of her sleeve.

That night when he was in bed he said, "Auntie Jen, you wouldn't ever elope, would you?" and she had to explain that elope did not mean disappearance, desertion; it meant getting married.

"Oh, is that all?" He seemed reassured, and as she turned to leave the room and go downstairs again he said, "And if you did get married you'd marry someone from here wouldn't you?"

"Would I?"

"Oh yes." She hid a smile when he followed that with, "You don't want to get married yet, but you'll find somebody before you're old, and if you don't I'll look after you."

Downstairs she said to Lorraine, "Do you see any gray hairs? Timmy's planning my old age, but not to worry because if I can't get anyone to marry me he's going to look after me."

Within a fortnight Rolf Perrie was hobbling around the farmhouse with the aid of a stick. Branch Three of the tin mine, which he had been inspecting because it was almost worked out, had been sealed and another seam opened up. The excitement was over: routine was reestablished at the mine, and the patient was recovering at a gratifying rate.

Lorraine and Rolf had not eloped, and Jenny saw no sign that they were likely to when Rolf was mobile again, although Lorraine went over to the Perries' farm most evenings.

She went openly now. Paul knew she was a constant visitor. Everyone knew, but he didn't seem to object. He even gave her a folder of papers once to deliver to Rolf, as though there was no longer any risk or danger in the relationship. Jenny, who saw them together from time to time, would have described it all as cosy as an old slipper.

Rolf had plenty of callers, for he was well liked, but when Lorraine was the only visitor they did crosswords and played chess and listened to records. So Lorraine told Jenny, and when Jenny went along there was the chessboard, and Jenny could believe it.

Mrs. Perrie was nicer these days, much friendlier, and an evening at the Perries' was pleasant, but there was nothing electric in the air. Rolf's welcome for Lorraine was hardly a lover's. A good friend's, yes, someone very glad to see her; and Lorraine enjoyed fussing around Rolf, helping to look after him.

He humored her, and their affection for each other seemed genuine enough, but it was not a passion. Jenny couldn't imagine them defying Paul and risking Rolf's job or anything else to be together. They seemed a pair who might have drifted into marriage and been happy enough, so long as no difficulties were put in their way.

So Paul need not have read the riot act the night of the accident, because Lorraine was not going to need a go-between nor a confidante. And if Paul hadn't bullied her Jenny would not have said what she did—and many times she had regretted that, because ever since that night Paul had been unapproachable.

She worked with him in the office, ate meals with him sometimes—not often—sat in the evenings, reading, watching television, and beneath the surface there was no point of contact at all.

No one else realized that, not even Mr. Morrison. Paul talked to Jenny—he was never verbose with anyone—but he did address remarks to her. He spoke kindly, sharply, sometimes with humor, and Jenny answered, followed instructions, joined discussions, and all the time there was this great invisible wall.

She could do nothing about it. Seized with a strangling shyness at the thought of wording an apology, she was so ill at ease in his company that she avoided him as much as she could.

She took care not to make it conspicuous. She was around office hours of course, but when Paul worked late at nights now she didn't go into the office. If he'd asked her to work she would have done, but he never did.

She spent some of her evenings with Eb and Ebby,

and some with Lorraine, or with Grace and her neighbors. Down in Tremain Jack was still acting as though she was a plague-carrier, to the amusement of his colleagues. "What is this picture all the fuss is about?" one rather spiteful soul had inquired, and been thunderously asked what the hell he was talking about.

"Whether Jack is painting it again I wouldn't know," Grace said to Jenny. "If he is he's painting it at home, not in the studio."

Grace and Ben were still the only ones who knew that the painting had been of Caterine. Lorraine had no idea, and she still thought the breach between Jenny and Jack was a pity. As Jack walked past them on the dock one Friday afternoon, staring rigidly ahead, Lorraine said with smothered laughter, "You certainly turned him off, and you could have done with some company this weekend."

Next day Lorraine was taking Timmy to a birthday party and they were staying overnight. "It looks as if I'll have to manage without Jack," said Jenny. "Hi, Dan!"

Dan Blaskie was making for the jetty, carrying a cardboard box full of provisions. He was brown and tough as old leather, and when he reached the two girls he grinned, jaws clamped on a short dirty-looking clay pipe. He always had a smile for Lorraine and a joke for Jenny. Today he put down the cardboard box, took his pipe out of his mouth, and inquired, "Do ee fancy a trip around the bay, m'dear?"

"You're on," said Jenny. "Where are we going?"

She looked at the *Mylor* that was Dan's pride and joy, and he said smugly, "She's a good ole sea-boat, is that. You could go around the Cape in ur."

"When?" said Jenny.

She laughed and Dan said, "Have to see the skipper, but he don't belong to have passengers messin' around. He goes to get away from 'em."

"Get away from what?" Jenny joked. "Not the Tremain estates, surely. I wonder he can bear to leave them."

"Do ee, m'dear?" The sailor's keen eyes were hooded. "And he wonders how he can stomach comin' back to 'em." He chuckled as he spoke. Lorraine was smiling a sweet vague smile, paying only slight attention, but Jenny looked hard at him, and he picked up his box again and said, "Young Perrie still comin' on all right, then?"

Another few days and Rolf would be taking over his desk duties again at the mine. He had been doing some work from home, but he was a restless invalid, intolerant of his disability.

Last night Jenny had been at the Perries', sitting in the parlor with Rolf and Lorraine, when the phone rang in the hall and Mr. Perrie had shouted, "Rolf!"

Rolf had reached for his stick, and Lorraine, jumping up and holding out a hand, had said, "Come on, lean on me."

"I can manage."

She watched him with a crooked smile, then she said quietly, "Scared I'll let you down?" Rolf had smiled, too, and walked with the aid of his stick slowly and carefully out of the room to answer the phone. . . .

In the office this morning Jenny had said to Mr. Morrison, "I can't think why anyone worried about that affair setting light. Rolf's more like Lorraine's brother than her brother is." Paul had always seemed more like his sister's guardian to Jenny.

Mr. Morrison shrugged slightly, and Jenny went on, "Paul knows that, of course. Does he have his spies?"

That shocked Mr. Morrison, although how else would Paul know? Jenny couldn't resist teasing, "Because if he does he'll hear that I'm carrying the love letters this weekend." Then she relented, "It's all right, I'm only taking a book. Lorraine doesn't think Rolf can exist till Monday night without another thriller."

Jenny thought he could. He had said he had books he hadn't finished reading, but this was a new one by a favorite author, and Lorraine had said, "Jenny, would you bring it on Saturday?"

"Of course," Jenny had said. But she was sure that Rolf would have survived the weekend without the book, and she was equally sure he would survive the weekend without Lorraine. . . .

Jenny rarely worked Saturday mornings, although Paul and Mr. Morrison did. After breakfast Lorraine and Timmy drove away for the birthday party, and Jenny enjoyed her walk over the heathland to the Perries' farm. She was having lunch and spending the rest of the weekend with Grace and Ben, and the weather was frosty and exhilarating. She walked fast, bringing color into her cheeks.

Mrs. Perrie, aproned for housework, answered the door, and Jenny would have handed in the book with a few words, but Mrs. Perrie insisted on her coming in for a cup of tea. The cup of tea was in the kitchen with Rolf; his mother was busy with upstairs chores. He had working papers on the table and he put down the book beside them, and said, "Thank you, but you shouldn't have bothered."

"I promised Lorraine. She was very anxious you should have it."

"She was, wasn't she?" He picked the book up again and frowned. He was looking at the picture on the dust jacket, but Jenny felt he was not seeing it. He asked, "Where has she gone, Jenny?"

"She told you. She's taken Timmy to a birthday party. The Lawrences, their little girl Susan is ten."

"Oh yes," said Rolf mockingly, "the Lawrences."

When Caterine had given parties at Moidores the

Lawrences were always on the guest list. Since Caterine's death there had been no entertaining, but the Lawrences had called and Jenny had met them, and they had seemed an amiable pair of upper-middle-class intellectuals. She asked, "What's the matter with the Lawrences?"

Rolf laughed, "There's nothing the matter with the Lawrences." But there was something the matter with him that was putting an edge on his voice and a bleakness in his eyes. "They're rolling in money," he said. "She'll come to no harm there."

Jenny said levelly, "That doesn't make much sense." Although she knew what he meant.

"Oh, but it does," he said.

"Lorraine would rather be here with you than taking Timmy to a party."

Neither was drinking the cups of tea that Mrs. Perrie had poured for them. Jenny held hers untasted, and Rolf's had been untouched since his mother set it down. He said cynically, "She might at that, she's enjoyed playing Florence Nightingale."

Jenny tried to protest, "You make it sound as though it's been a game to her."

He demanded, "Well, hasn't it?"

She challenged him, "Is it a game for you? How much do you really care for Lorraine?"

For an unguarded moment he looked lost and hopeless. He cared deeply, and it was plainer than words. Then he said, "Too much to persuade her to give up the life she has for the life I could give her. She'd have to be tough, wouldn't she, to go with me to the kind of places I could find a job?"

She would have to be a hundred percent sure, ninety-nine percent wasn't enough. Jenny said, "Did Paul threaten to sack you?" and Rolf managed a grin.

"He didn't give us his blessing."

"Would you risk it?"

"For myself? Sure I would."

"Does Lorraine know that?"

"I told her once, and nothing's changed. It's up to Lorraine."

She asked, "Can I tell her that?"

He said quietly, "Why bother? She's always known it."

CHAPTER SEVEN

JENNY WALKED BACK to Tremain slowly, hands deep in her coat pockets, thinking, remembering Rolf's words just now and Lorraine's expression when she heard that Rolf was trapped in the mine.

There had been no pretense then. Lorraine had been racked with fear for him. But now there was no danger, and maybe Lorraine was enjoying playing Florence Nightingale.

There didn't seem to be much Jenny could do. Suppose she told Lorraine what Rolf had just said and added her own mite of persuasion, and they did stand up to Paul and Paul did chuck Rolf out of his job?

Emigration could be an exciting challenge for some folk. Rolf could cope with it, although he'd obviously rather stay where he was. Lorraine was physically delicate; should anyone be urging her to give up a comfortable sheltered life unless her own heart dictated it overwhelmingly?

By the time Jenny crossed the cliff road and started down the cobblestoned track to the harbor the only resolve Jenny had reached was to leave well alone. This was between Rolf and Lorraine; no one else should interfere. Except Paul, and the only way he should interfere was by stopping the blackmail.

Think of the devil, she thought, as she reached the dock. Although it was fine and bright, there were no tourists around today because it was November and cold. Tremain must be near enough now to what it was when Jack Bastaple was a boy. No gay umbrellas outside the Tremain Arms, and locals sitting on the benches, all men, and children playing around.

One of the men standing talking was Paul Tremain,

wearing a thick black sweater and reefing jacket, oil-stained trousers and gumboots. The wind made his dark thatch of hair look like Timmy's. Jenny smiled and waved—they all knew her. All nodded at her as she rounded the Tremain Arms and came into view.

She was surprised what a change of clothing could do. That morning at breakfast he was Tremain of Tremain. Now he was a Cornish seaman, and his empire was that boat out there.

She said, "Hello," here and there as she walked along by the harbor wall. It was midday and she was having lunch with Grace and Ben. But first she walked out onto the jetty to where the dinghy for the *Mylor* was moored.

Her exasperation at Lorraine—who didn't seem to know what she did want—had transferred to herself. She knew she wanted to go sailing. Paul didn't take passengers and he would say so, but she'd be no worse off than before and she was going to ask.

The freshness of the wind blowing across the sea from the north-west brought with it a zest and a sweetness that made her a little high when she breathed deeply, and the sun glittered dazzlingly on the sea and the boats and the seagulls flying; and when Paul and Dan Blaskie came along the jetty she was in such a state of euphoria that she managed to say easily and gaily, "Dan says you don't take passengers. What are the chances for a stowaway?"

They both smiled. It was a quip, a joke, only it wasn't. Her hair blew across her face blinding her, and she held it back and pleaded, "I'm not joking. Please will you take me with you?"

That wasn't so easy, and Paul stopped smiling and said, "The weather forecast isn't too good."

"Foreboding ole weather, I do call it," Dan backed him up. But he hadn't said no.

"I wouldn't be seasick."

Of course she wouldn't, although Paul was looking at her quizzically and asking, "How much sailing have you done?"

Hugging the coastline and back for tea, and he knew it. She said desperately, "If I am I'll hide. I'll hide all the time if you like, I'll keep right out of your way."

"It isn't that big a boat."

He was smiling and he hadn't said no, and she said, "I'll find somewhere. *Please!*"

"All right," he said. "Ask someone to phone the house and let Ebby know where you've gone."

"I was staying with Grace Norwood, I'll tell her—won't be a minute." She didn't waste a second. She sped back along the jetty, through the archway and through the bright yellow front door of Grace's cottage. In the tiny hall she shouted, "Grace!" and Grace caroled back from the kitchen.

"In here!"

"I'm going sailing with Paul and Dan—you don't mind, do you?"

Grace almost dropped the frying pan. She put it on the stove, turned down the heat and gave all her attention to Jenny.

"How did that happen?"

"I just asked Paul and he said all right."

Grace was speechless for all of five seconds. Then she said. "You can't sail in those shoes."

They were stout walking shoes with smooth rubber soles for the trek over the heathlands to the Perries' farm. "I've got another pair in my bag," Jenny said.

She had brought down an overnight bag yesterday afternoon. It was now in Grace's spare bedroom, containing pyjamas, sponge bag, and with a dress hanging in the wardrobe.

As Jenny ran up the stairs Grace stood at the bottom calling up after her, "What did you *say*?"

"Could I come, and I wouldn't be seasick and if I was I'd keep out of sight."

She wouldn't need the dress. She was in sweater and skirt under a tweed coat. She yelled, "Grace, can you lend me some jeans?"

Grace was taller than Jenny, but narrow-hipped, and she seemed to live in jeans and trousers. She went into the other bedroom and came out with a pair of blue dungarees. "If you roll them up they should do. Have you got time to try them on?"

"No, they'll fit. Thanks." Jenny shoved them into the bag. "See you tomorrow."

"Where are you going?"

"I don't know. But they always come back on Sunday, don't they?"

Grace chortled behind her, "A night under the stars with old Dan Blaskie!"

"Don't worry about my reputation," Jenny laughed. "There's always Paul for chaperone."

"Yes," said Grace, "there is, isn't there?"

She walked to the archway with Jenny, and Jenny gave a little cry because they hadn't waited for her. The dinghy had left the jetty and was almost at the *Mylor*, and she felt a stinging disappointment that emptied her of joy and left her hollow and sick.

It wasn't fair! She wanted to shout that after them, like an ill-treated child.

And then the void in her filled with churning anger. She dropped her bag and ran again, and Grace scooped it up and hurried after her. At the end of the jetty Grace caught up as Jenny stooped to fiddle with the buckle of her shoe. "What are you doing?" Grace asked.

"I'm swimming out," said Jenny.

"You are *not*!" yelped Grace as Jenny yanked off first one shoe and then the other. "Don't be daft—it's cold. You'll get pneumonia if you don't drown."

"I won't drown," said Jenny. "He'll have to pick me up, he can hardly leave me swimming out to sea."

"He'll just bring you back. If he's changed his mind there's nothing you can do about it."

"I can make a nuisance of myself." Jenny unbuttoned her coat with furious fumbling fingers. "I feel like making a nuisance of myself!"

The dinghy reached the *Mylor* and one man got aboard. The other stayed at the oars and began to row back. Grace began to laugh, almost hysterically.

Tears rolled down her cheeks until she clung to a capstan, weak with laughter, gasping, "Oh, I wish they'd taken a minute longer. You'd have been in the water. It would have been the funniest thing."

Jenny began to laugh, too. Another couple of minutes and she would have dived in from the end of the jetty. It was idiotic that it hadn't occurred to her that they could have decided there was no point both of them waiting. She had been so sure Paul had changed his mind and was going without her.

She begged, "Stop laughing, for heaven's sake, he'll think I'm crazy."

Grace sobbed, "You are crazy. Get your coat and your shoes back on, they think it's a striptease."

Jenny was getting a fair amount of attention. Several of the children had followed to see why she and Grace were running. If she had taken off her skirt and started swimming out they would have loved that, and Paul would have had every good reason for doubting her sanity. She donned shoes and coat quickly, but each time she looked at Grace the giggles took over, and when Paul—it would be him rowing back, not Dan—drew up alongside the jetty they were still struggling to regain their composure.

He greeted Grace and helped Jenny across into the dinghy, and Grace handed over Jenny's bag and said,

"Don't—forget this," hiccuping as she tried to hold down laughter.

She sounded so odd that Paul asked, "What's the matter?"

"Not a thing," gasped Grace. "Goodbye." She waved briefly, and turned away with shaking shoulders, and Jenny sat facing Paul.

"What's the matter?" he asked again, pushing off from the jetty.

She looked beyond him at the *Mylor* and the Witch's Rock and admitted, "I thought you'd changed your mind and gone without me."

"Was that what Mrs. Norwood found amusing?"

"No. I nearly dived in and swam out."

He didn't believe her. He said, "If I had changed my mind I'd have stayed to tell you, and I hope you weren't considering swimming."

"I'm a strong swimmer."

"I thought Timothy was teaching you to swim."

"That was to get Timmy playing in the water again." She added quietly, "He was afraid of the sea."

Paul knew why. She watched a seagull perched on a bobbing red buoy, and they were almost at the *Mylor* before he spoke again.

"You're not?" he asked.

"I love the sea."

"Let's hope you feel the same way tomorrow. And when you do go swimming remember there are tides and currents here as well as rocks. You may think you're a good swimmer, but this is not a swimming pool."

He thought she was talking boastful nonsense, and perhaps she was. It must sound like nonsense from a girl who had never been farther out to sea than the Witch's Rock, on one picnic in high summer, years ago.

She promised herself, I'll be quiet from now on, you

won't know I'm aboard. But when they came alongside the *Mylor* she looked at it with dazzled eyes and whispered, "She's beautiful."

Paul said, "You should have seen her when I found her."

"Wasn't she beautiful then?"

"I thought so."

She wanted to say, "Where? When? Tell me how you found her."

But Dan was there and Paul was saying, "Take her down to her cabin," and she went meekly and silently, thanking her lucky stars that she hadn't dived into the harbor. Because if she had she knew she would have been promptly landed back on the jetty and never allowed to set foot on the mellowed teak deck of the *Mylor*.

She followed Dan through a two-door hatch on the forepeak of the boat, into a small cabin with sail lockers and stores, then down a couple of steps into another cabin containing fishing gear, scuba-suit, oxygen bottles, a trunk and a hard wooden bunk.

Dan chuckled as she looked at the bunk, wondering if she would be sleeping on bare boards. "Weren't expectin' ee, m'dear. 'Tes a snug li'l berth when it's made right. Doan't ee worry 'bout that."

"That's a relief," Jenny admitted.

Dan produced a seaman's waterproof coat from one of the lockers, satisfied himself that she had a pair of non-skid shoes and left her to it. She changed into Grace's jeans, rolling them up at the ankles and the coat up at the sleeves. The effect was not glamorous, but it was warm and practical, and that was all that mattered right now.

She wanted to explore. The memory of her visit to the Witch's Rock was stirred again, because she had gone into the caves with just this feeling of awe and excitement, this tingling delight. Ever since she came back tc Tremain the schooner, usually anchored at the mouth of the harbor, had been like a mirage, something wonderful and unattainable, and now she was aboard she wanted to see every nook and cranny.

Another door from this cabin led past the foot of the main mast, which came down through the decking, into the main cabin. The engine had started up now, and they were moving out of the harbor. She peered through the porthole for a while, then turned back to admire the cosy comfort of the cabin.

The walls were mahogany panelled, and when the paraffin lamps were lit the grain of the wood would glow warm. There were two wide cushioned settees and a narrow table, and a small galley and toilet leading off.

Jenny touched nothing and she went back the way she had come. She had promised not to get underfoot and she kept out of the way of both men.

Paul came looking for her once as she stood at the rail that rose in a curve around the bow of the *Mylor*. The coastline was already a blur astern, and Jenny noticed that it was warmer out at sea than back on land and the sun still shone.

"All right?" Paul asked.

She nodded, smiling.

"Good," he said. He didn't tell her that when she first came up on deck he had said to Dan, "Keep an eye on her. Get her to tie herself to the rails if she looks as if she might lose her footing."

It was calm weather yet, but there was a suggestion of a swell and he felt responsible. But Dan had announced approvingly afterwards, "Sure-footed as a cat. Moves about a boat like one reared to it."

Jenny was moving with the boat. It was like floating, like flying. The engine had served its purpose taking them out of harbor. Now the sails billowed and although the wind was not strong Paul was using every possible combination of sail and technique to scoop in sufficient wind to make four knots against the tide and swell.

Jenny snuggled behind the large collar of her seaman's jacket, her eyes sparkling and her skin glowing. When Dan came forward checking the rigging she asked, "Where are we going?"

They were following a looping course that would take them about thirty-five miles offshore, out of the shipping lanes. There they would ride at anchor overnight if the weather held fair and then loop back, stopping at the Witch's Rock.

Jenny almost clapped her hands. "The Rock?"

"The skipper allus looks in there if it's only for an hour. Though this ain't no time o' year for sailing in to Witch's Rock."

But he didn't seem particularly perturbed by the prospect and Jenny was delighted. As Dan stuffed his short clay pipe with tobacco she said, "Of course we'll make it. *Mylor*'s a good ship."

His weathered wrinkled face with its dark tan cracked in a smile. "You're right there, m'dear. No malice in ur." Jenny understood what he meant. The *Mylor* would obey the helm and return loving care, and would ride the sea without harshness as if she was part of it.

"And the skipper's a good seaman," said Dan. "He respects the sea. He could take a boat through the eye of a needle."

The short daylight hours passed as *Mylor* dipped and curtseyed on the waves, and Jenny leaned over the bows, secured by a rope, looking for fish and hoping to see a dolphin. Once she thought she had, just ahead of the bows, but it turned out to be a school of smaller fish.

With the coming of darkness came an appreciable chill and she moved aft as the light failed and stood for a while on the afterdeck behind the partly covered wheelhouse where Paul was still at the wheel.

She saw the first stars come out, and in a short time the whole sky was ablaze. Jenny could only stare. She had never known how wonderful a clear night at sea could be on a crisp cloudless November night.

She stood enraptured, watching a shooting star, trying to make out the pattern of the planets. She found the Plough and the North Star. She thought she found Orion, the hunter.

The only sounds were the creak of the mast, an occasional flap of the sails and the slap of the waves against the bows. Then Paul said, "Get below. It's chilly."

She hadn't noticed him turn before; nor did he now, but he must have known she was here all this while, just behind him.

She almost protested, "I'm all right, I don't want to go below," but it was cold, her breath was frosted and he was the skipper. Refusing to obey orders could be mutiny.

She looked once more at the stars, at the lights on the swaying mastheads, then she bent down under the hatch coaming and went down the companionway to the main cabin.

The lamps were lit now, and in the galley a coffee pot and a saucepan stood on the hanging gas stove. In spite of the movement of the boat the stove stayed level, and the table top was fixed in the same way.

Dan was drinking coffee, and plates on the table showed that he had just finished his meal. He said, "Ready for a bite to eat, then?"

"Oh, please!" She was suddenly ravenous, and he brought her a bowl of thick stew, which she ate with a spoon and a hunk of bread. The dishes all fitted into rimmed depressions in the table top. "Marvellous," said Jenny.

"My missus makes a lovely drop of broth," said Dan.

"She certainly does," Jenny agreed. "Does Mrs. Blaskie always do the cooking?"

"Bless ee, no. I bring a drop of broth along sometimes, but most times I cook, or the skipper does."

"I could get the meals," Jenny offered, but Dan looked doubtful about that and she realized she had been pushing. She said fervently, "Thank you for letting me come," and Dan admitted she had been no trouble at all up to now.

When Dan went up to take over the steering Paul came down for his supper. Paul Tremain was a big man. The spacious rooms of Moidores had always seemed about the right size for him, but he moved around the small cabin and the smaller galley with a coordinated economy. Jenny watched as he brought his meal to the table. She said, "I've had the best day of my life."

That was the simple truth. She had never been so carefree or so happy. The self-consciousness she had always felt when she was with Paul, particularly since the accident at the mine, had gone.

He said, "I'm glad you've enjoyed it."

More than enjoyment, it was deeper and more satisfying. She said, "You are so lucky to have this boat."

"I know that."

"Where did you find her?"

"Lying at anchor off St. Ives. She's old, her paint had flaked, but her timbers were sound." As he ate his meal he explained the work that had been done to make *Mylor* seaworthy again, and Jenny listened, spellbound. It was as though she had found and fallen in love with the boat herself and helped to bring her back to life.

As well as making her hungry, the strong sea air in the warm little cabin had made her tired; and when the meal was over and Paul had gone back on deck she found her eyelids getting heavy.

She would have liked to have gone up again herself, but Paul said goodnight and told her that Dan had fixed her cabin. He did not want her on deck in darkness, leaning over the side, and very soon when she was left alone she was yawning.

She went to her cabin through the access doors, and the wooden bunk was now a comfortable bed, with a foam rubber mattress and sleeping bag and a couple of spare blankets folded on the tin trunk.

There was a pressure lamp fitted to a bracket at the side of the bunk. She'd never used one of those before, but she wasn't calling to ask how to turn it off if she could work it out for herself. She studied it for a while before deciding which screw to turn, and then the light died away, the faint hot paraffin smell dissipating quickly in the fresh sea air. She lay in the darkness. In spite of the confined space and the rolling of the ship she was completely relaxed and comfortable. With Paul Tremain at the helm, or indeed with Paul Tremain anywhere, nothing much would go wrong. He had that kind of competence and it was always reassuring.

Everything felt right. She listened to the slap of the waves and the hiss of water creaming past the knife-edged bows. She saw the distorted images of stars through the tiny porthole glass, wet with spray, when the ship rolled sufficiently to show the sky.

Vaguely, later, she recognized the rumble of the anchors going down, but there was no apparent change in movement and she did not realize that the *Mylor* was anchored for the night.

Nor did she realize that she had been asleep. She blinked a little, and there were no stars in the sky, just a gray light showing through the little porthole.

She was awake then, instantly fully alive, and it wasn't sea air she could smell. Someone was cooking, for she could smell bacon, and she got up and dressed quickly and went up through the hatch onto the deck. The kitchen and the washroom both led off the main cabin below the wheelhouse, but the main cabin converted into a bunk room overnight, and no matter how hungry she was she couldn't barge in there without warning. The ship was still anchored. Wisps of mist blew over the sea. The light was pearly gray and the clouds seemed low. It was like being the only living soul in another world. No voices, just the wind and the sounds of the sea blending with the creaking of the ship.

There was no one in the wheelhouse, and the wheel moved gently, slightly, to and fro, anchored in place with straps. The mast, bare of sails, seemed to gyrate.

She stepped carefully to the bows, holding the rail, and stared down the double chain of the anchors into the depths. *How deep*, she wondered. And what lived down there in those dark green waters?

"Sleep well?" asked Paul, suddenly from behind her.

She jumped. "You startled me! Yes, thank you, I slept marvelously."

He joined her at the rail. "What were you looking at?"

"Just staring down. Hoping for dolphins, or sea witches."

He smiled. "I can't hold out much hope of either, but in the meantime breakfast's nearly ready."

Jenny washed in the little bathroom area; she needed no makeup today, for her skin was glowing and her hair crackled like mad when she combed it. She began to sing to herself from the sheer joy of being alive and when she stepped out into the main cabin she went on humming, under her breath, until she realized that Paul was looking at her. Then she stopped.

"What is that you're humming?" he asked. She flushed and laughed.

"I don't know, I think I heard it in a shell. It isn't

really a song at all, I can't sing. Although I suppose it's Timmy's song. It sends him to sleep when there are storms around."

Dan came out of the galley carrying a plate of bacon and eggs and sausages. "Aye," he said, "that could be where you heard it," and he put down the dish on the little table.

The three of them ate breakfast together, no one doing much talking, not because there was any restraint but as though they knew each other so well they didn't need words.

Jenny could hardly believe that this was her first trip. *Mylor* seemed an old friend, as though Jenny had been beside Paul when he first saw the boat riding at anchor. When he'd turned from that first sight Jenny's had been the eyes he had met and he had asked, "Well?" and she had said yes.

Now Paul was listening. "The wind's changing," he announced, and he and Dan disappeared up the companionway ladder to the deck.

She heard the anchors being taken in and the sound of the engine. There was movement as the ship turned, and she did the washing up, enjoying herself finding the places for the crockery and cutlery. All the time she could hear shouts and footsteps above as the sails were hoisted and the engines stopped: then the motion of the ship changed again as they heeled to the wind.

Dan clattered down briefly, saw that Jenny was putting things where they should be and grunted, "Good lass, put your jacket on when you come up." Then he was gone.

When she finished she went on deck and the wind was fresher now, with an occasional thin spurt of rain lashing across. Paul was at the wheel and Dan was busy among the rigging. Jenny went over to Dan and asked. "What are you doing?"

"Checkin' the lashin' on the cleats," said Dan.

"What's a cleat?" It was a strange tongue, but Dan pointed out and explained, and Jenny asked, "Do you mind if I watch you?"

"Bless ee, m'dear, I don't mind," so she trotted along behind Dan and got her first lesson in seamanship from an expert.

Paul stayed at the wheel. Later she brought him hot coffee from the galley in a brown enamel jug. Dan had said, "Take this to the skipper," and she smiled as she handed it over.

"Tomorrow when I fetch your coffee in the office I'm not going to believe this."

He agreed, "It is another life."

In Tremain he was unapproachable, but here and now she could say, "Dan says you never really want to go back."

"I don't."

She didn't ask, "Then why do you?" Paul Tremain was Tremain—he had to be in charge or the empire would crumble. She held her own mug of coffee in both hands, letting it warm her fingers, she said, "Why did you change Tremain? Why didn't you leave it a sleepy little fishing village?"

"Because it wasn't sleeping, it was dying."

"Dying?"

"Another year or two and it would have been derelict. There isn't enough fish left to provide a livelihood for more than a handful of men. The mine hadn't been worked in generations, and the farms weren't being run economically."

"But why?"

He smiled wryly. "Because my father was a man who couldn't say no. Everybody liked him. He lived the easy life and it wasn't until he died that I found out Tremain was bankrupt."

"When it became your responsibility?"

"Yes."

"What did you want to do with your life?" Although he did the job superbly he had not wanted to be Tremain of Tremain.

"I was going into the Navy, but I came down from university for his funeral and I never went back again."

"*Why?*" Of course she knew why. Being the man he was he could have made no other choice.

He said, mocking himself, "Because I couldn't leave it to die."

What had Ebby said when Jenny first came? "He won't let any of us down, he'll bear the load."

Jenny said, "But you have *Mylor*." He renewed his strength from the lonely hours of sailing, and she was only now realizing the extent of her intrusion.

She said, "Thank you for letting me come."

He smiled and drank his coffee, set the mug down and then said, "You wanted to come."

"So very much."

"Look." He seized her arm. "Just off the port bow."

A faint gray shape was rising out of the sea ahead of them and she whispered, "The Witch's Rock?"

"Yes."

She had never seen it before from the seaward side. The low mist around it made it look unreal, something from a ghost story, but as they drew nearer she saw that it rose sheer and high, surrounded by jagged rocks and crashing waves. On the day Jenny had picnicked here, coming out from Tremain, the sea had been calm as a millpond, but now the roar of the waves on the rocks was terrifying. She wailed. "We can't anchor!" and *Mylor* heeled hard over, speeding around the rock.

Everything happened so quickly. The sails came down as if by magic as the engine started up. Paul swung the wheel violently, first one way and then the

other, and the ship passed between two rows of project-
ing rocks and they were dropping anchor in the tiny bay
facing Tremain. The shelving beach was only a few
yards of deep water away, and here was protection from
the wind. Jenny was still speechless as Paul picked up a
haversack, and the men unlashed the dinghy and threw
it overboard.

"I be tellin' av ee, ee'll do this once too often," said
Dan, grinning broadly. Paul grinned too, and Jenny
looked at the rise of rock from the little beach and the
entrance to the caves.

It was how she remembered. The only difference that
between July and November. She was the first to scram-
ble ashore and she helped the men pull the dinghy up
on to the beach.

At first the air was full of beating wings, because the
rock was a bird sanctuary and they were rarely disturbed, but they settled again, and Dan lit his pipe and
sat down on a flat rock puffing contentedly as Paul
stood looking out across the water.

Jenny asked, "Would you have a flashlight in that
haversack?"

"Yes," said Paul, and she held out a hand for it, explaining, "I want to look around the caves."

"Not alone." As Paul turned to walk over the shingle
toward the cave entrance she fell into step beside him.

"I went alone last time."

"When was the last time?"

"The only time. The first year I came here. We came
out for a picnic." Jenny and her mother, Caterine and
Lorraine, and one or two others. Not Paul. She only
vaguely remembered the others—they were Caterine's
friends, it was their yacht. She said, "It was a blazing
hot day, and everyone sunbathed and I went to explore
the caves."

She had stepped into the entrance then as she did

now. It was a cool gloom, not entirely dark, with a greenish tinge. Light came in from several fissures and water cascaded down inside from crevices in the rock. Then, as Paul had just done, she had switched on her flashlight and the smooth colored pebbles underfoot had shone like jewels and the shells had gleamed pearl-like.

She walked ahead through a string of similar caves with linking passages, straight on, although sometime she would like to explore the narrower passages that ran off this one.

It was all as she remembered, the veined colors of the rock, the natural bridge that took them over running water, and then at last the cavern where everything seemed silver.

The moss was so luminous here, it could be seen without the flashlight. There were shining white pillars and water dripping with a sound of tinkling bells. And in the middle the smooth deep pool.

It was just the same. She knelt down to look at her reflection, as she had done as a younger girl. It had been the only mirror that made her beautiful, and again her face swam palely with a secret smile. But this time of course there was another reflection, Paul's dark face, dark hair, dark eyes.

It was strange. Of course she knew he was standing behind her, but her first reaction was shock; followed by a turmoil of emotions as though this was the reflection of a stranger and at the same time the one of whom she knew everything.

When she raised her head to turn and look up at him Paul was not smiling. Their eyes met and locked as he held out a hand. She heard the sea and saw the glittering walls of the silver cave and looked up silently at the man, and it was like something half-recalled from a dream.

Then she took his hand, but she still held back resisting. For seconds, no longer, but time was suddenly unsure. She trembled as she stood against him and his arms tightened around her. They stood utterly still, searching each other's faces in the pale silver light, and to Jenny recognition came.

She saw her own dark lover. No other woman's, as she could be no other man's. Deep calling deep, as though they had been together through ages past and nothing could ever part them for more than a moment.

Paul still held her and looked at her, and someone was shouting from somewhere.

The shout broke the spell. It was Dan hollering "Skipper!" sounding as though he called through cupped hands through the echoing caverns.

"What is it?" Paul shouted back. He picked up the kit bag and torch, slung the bag over his shoulder and kept a guiding arm around Jenny.

Dan was easy to find. He was in the central passage and he came toward the gleam of their torch. He said as he neared them, "I'm not over fond of the looks of this ole sky. Unless we belong to stay here for the night we best be casting off."

"Right," said Paul. "Come on, Jenny."

They went quickly and the sky was overcast. Jenny blinked as they came out onto the shingle; it looked later than she had expected. They must have been in the caves an hour or more, though it hadn't seemed so long. Dan, a little ahead, had already begun to drag the dinghy into the water.

As the engines of *Mylor* started up the seagulls flew again, wildly for a few minutes. Paul was at the wheel and Jenny stood at the rail, watching the lights coming on in Tremain.

It might have been the atmosphere of the rock and remembering the old legend that had stirred Jenny so strangely, but that didn't change the fact that as surely as the sea was in her blood so was Paul Tremain. The wind and the spray stung against her skin, and there was nothing dreamlike about it. It was stinging sharp and bitter cold.

She was awake and thinking clearly, and she knew that she wanted Paul to make love to her, to love her, to need her as lover and friend and companion and sharer in everything forever.

That was how he had looked at her in the caves, but who had he seen in that brief moment? Jenny or Caterine?

She must have looked like Caterine, hair loose in the faint silver light; they all said she looked like Caterine. And when the spell broke Paul had turned back at once into skipper, intent on getting his boat safely back into harbor, a hundred percent practical and competent, as though for him that moment had been for a memory, not for the flesh-and-blood girl who was still beside him.

The waves were high, threatening to break over the decks, and he called now, "Get below, Jenny!"

"We're nearly in Tremain." She came to the comparative shelter of the wheelhouse. It was a turbulent sea, but there had been no thunder or lightning and she hoped that Timmy was safely home. Out at sea she had forgotten the problems in Tremain for a while, but now she remembered Lorraine and Rolf and said, "You see things clearer from here."

"I've found that," said Paul.

"You wouldn't dismiss Rolf and cut Lorraine off if they married." She knew that for certain now.

"No," said Paul, "but if the risk stops them they're not very involved."

"Rolf would chance it."

Paul's voice was dry. "I'm more concerned about Lorraine."

The storm didn't develop, although the winds continued to lash the sea and were something to battle against on the way along the clifftop road back to Moidores.

Paul took the brunt, with Jenny hanging on to his arm, with no breath for words or laughter, although it was a little comic, and they smiled at each other more than once when Jenny almost spun off her feet, or when a particularly strong and steady gust demanded all their weight be used to stay where they were.

Once in the house Paul went into the study, checking if anything untoward had happened in his absence, and Jenny went seeking Timmy and Lorraine.

They were in the drawing room in front of a blazing fire. "You went *sailing*?" Lorraine squeaked.

"It was wonderful." Jenny described the trip mainly for Timmy, whose eyes widened fearfully when she said they had moored a while at the Witch's Rock.

But Jenny's own delight was contagious. She described the little bridge, the silver cave that played music . . . the strange cave, although she didn't say that, where she had known that she belonged to Paul Tremain. . . .

Timmy had been to the rock in summertime. "Yeah," he said now, remembering pleasant hours, "it's a smashing place."

It had also been a smashing party. He had won a trumpet, and brought home a piece of cake for Jenny, and when he went up to bed he played his trumpet all the way. He seemed in high spirits, but when he put down his trumpet on the ledge under the window he said thoughtfully, "Auntie Jen, I know mom had a car smash, I know that's what happened. It wasn't the sea, or anything's fault."

"No, love," said Jenny gently.

"She has gone, hasn't she?"

"Yes, Timmy."

"She isn't in her room." He watched Jenny closely. "The door's always locked, but she isn't in there, is she?"

"No," said Jenny, "there's nothing in there but furniture and clothes. It's just an empty room."

The door had to be opened so that Timmy could see that, and Ebby promised, "I'll have a word with Mr. Paul," when Jenny told her.

Lorraine said fiercely, "I think Caterine's things should be left where they are."

"We'll see what Mr. Paul says," said Ebby.

Next morning Paul handed over the key to the housekeeper and Ebby went in to take off the dust sheets and give the room an airing and a cleaning.

It was an ordinary Monday morning in the office, but not for Jenny. When she brought in mid-morning coffee she knew Paul was reminded of yesterday, and she could taste salt spray on her own lips. There was a complicity between them.

At midday Paul went off to the home farm. He and the manager were going somewhere to buy a tractor. Mr. Morrison was spending the afternoon working on the accounts, and over lunch Ebby suggested that Jenny and Lorraine might look through Caterine's clothes.

"Mr. Paul said to give them away, or send them to a charity. It's a wicked waste to leave them hanging in the cupboards and filling the drawers."

That was a task neither girl wanted. Caterine's perfume was everywhere when they stirred the silks of lingerie drawers and opened the wardrobe again. But it was wasteful to leave such beautiful and expensive clothes to the moths.

Jenny could have worn most of them, but they would have given her no pleasure. They were gorgeous but they were still poignantly Caterine's, and Lorraine was too tall and too pale.

Ebby would know how to dispose of them, and Jenny and Lorraine emptied the drawers, making tidy heart-breaking piles of Caterine's things.

They took the dresses and the suits and the coats with the couture name-tabs from the hangers, and Lorraine would say, "She only bought this the week before," or, "She looked lovely in this."

They were taking out shoes, dozens of pairs, when Lorraine picked up a slip of paper from the back of the closet. They had emptied drawers and cupboards of trivia as they had gone along, putting most of it into the wastepaper basket.

Lorraine read this, and gasped as she read.

"What is it?" Jenny took it from her nerveless fingers, and her own eyes raced over the lines in outraged disbe-lief. "This isn't *true*! It *can't* be!"

It was a page of a letter. Passionate and pleading. Begging "Caterina" to leave Paul Tremain.

CHAPTER EIGHT

LORRAINE SAID in a small stunned voice, "It's from Rolf." It was typewritten and there seemed no indication who had typed it.

Jenny was stunned herself. Her own voice was a whisper. "It isn't true, Caterine couldn't—"

"Oh, but she could. Because he was mine. She would think that was the joke."

"Of course it's not Rolf."

"That was our meeting place." It mentioned Purdie's Beck, and Lorraine's smooth face was white and lined as though she was in pain.

"Rolf loves you," Jenny insisted. "On Saturday he said it's always been up to you," but Lorraine was listening to nothing but her own thoughts.

"I knew she could have anyone she wanted but I never thought she'd dare cheat on Paul. He could give her more than anyone else, and that was what counted with Caterine: money, position. It *was*!" She sounded as though she expected Jenny to deny it, and Jenny crumpled the letter fiercely.

"Paul mustn't know," Jenny said.

"How *could* Rolf?"

Rolf was Lorraine's problem; Jenny was protecting her own. She caught Lorraine's arm, making her listen. "You're not to tell Paul. Caterine's dead. No one's going to spoil her memory."

"*Tell Paul?*" Lorraine echoed shrilly. "Can you see me?"

Jenny couldn't, but she could see that jealousy had gone deep. Perhaps that was where Rolf had made his mistake; he had been too available, and Lorraine had believed she could turn to him anytime. "No," she had told Jenny, "Rolf hasn't found anyone else." Now she would never be so smugly confident again.

Jenny did not believe for a moment that it was Rolf Perrie, but she said, "If you're jealous ask him. Although you've no grounds for complaining, since you opted out. And why should he wait forever? He's an attractive man."

But not to Jenny, and how could Paul's wife want any other man? She opened her hand on the crushed letter and the enormity of it overwhelmed her again. This . . . isn't Caterine."

"How do you know?" Lorraine sounded bitter. "You haven't lived with her for the last eight years. She could charm the birds off the trees, but she wanted everything."

They had gone through pockets, but casually, not as searchers, and now Jenny turned again to the piles of clothes. Paul mustn't know. There must be nothing left to start a wildfire of scandal when Caterine's possessions were handed around in Tremain, or wherever Ebby was sending them. Jenny was going through everything again with a fine-tooth comb, looking for any scrap of evidence.

Not that she cared who had sent the letter. She didn't want to find any more evidence—the prospect horrified her. She went through the pockets of the first jacket and checked in the lining while Lorraine said quite calmly, "I can't. I've seen enough."

"I must," said Jenny.

Lorraine pressed her fingertips to her temples. "I think I'm going to have the migraine of my life, and when it's over I'll go and see Rolf. I'm sorry I can't help you anymore."

"There's no need," said Jenny, remembering Caterine's little writing bureau downstairs, her diary, wondering was there anywhere else that secrets might hide. She was sure there was no local gossip, for she would have heard a whisper of it if there had been.

Lorraine went slowly to the door. She began. "If you find anything else—"

"I'll burn it," said Jenny.

"That would be the best thing," said Lorraine.

Jenny searched like a crime-squad member for clues. She went with quick deft fingers through everything in that room. Even the junk in the wastepaper basket was now suspect: theater tickets, meal checks, hotel receipts. She burned them on the open fires downstairs, some in this room, some in that. The mass of papers in the bureau seemed innocuous and the desk diary had always been open for anyone to see, full of social engagements but nothing that looked like code or incrimination.

Caterine had covered her wandering tracks well. The only betrayal was that single sheet.

Lorraine had gone to bed and Ebby was blaming herself for the migraine. "A bit too much for her, going though the mistress's things." She looked with concern at Jenny. "Not a nice job for either of you, but it had to be done. Come and have a cup of tea now."

Jenny was looking strained too, and Ebby resolved to get the contents of that room out tomorrow.

The curtains in Lorraine's room were closed and Jenny opened the door silently and came to the bedside, making no sound on the thick carpet. She would have left again without speaking if Lorraine hadn't asked, "Did you find anything?"

"No. How's the head?"

"Horrible," said Lorraine weakly.

"I'm sorry." The migraine was real enough, but it was also an escape, as Lorraine's not-too-robust physique always seemed to provide an escape from harsh reality. Jenny said, "Try to rest."

"I will. A night's sleep should settle it."

"What about tomorrow?" Jenny couldn't help asking, and Lorraine's pain-filled eyes looked at her steadily.

"Tomorrow I grow up," said Lorraine.

THERE WAS JUST Paul and Timmy and Jenny for dinner that evening, and Timmy had been thinking during the day about Jenny having gone sailing on the *Mylor*. She had enjoyed herself so much and he believed what she told him so implicitly that his nameless fears had disappeared.

Sometimes he thought he would like to go sailing again himself. He would be safe with his father, he always knew that, but if Auntie Jen was going they would have a lot of fun. Timothy worshipped his father, but his father was never scared, so you couldn't tell him that storms made you feel sick unless Auntie Jen sang to you. Not as badly as they used to, but out at sea they might.

There was nothing you could teach father or show him that he didn't know already, but you had to take care of Auntie Jen sometimes, and she tucked you in better at night and she had soft hands.

Timothy asked over the soup, "Auntie Jen will be coming, won't she?"

Timothy's presence seemed conditional on that and Jenny was relieved when Paul smiled and said, "I hope she will, but you'd better ask her."

Jenny and Timothy began to plan long journeys, taking in all sorts of impossible places, and ending almost seriously with a globe of the world and a huge atlas, brought into the drawing room from the library and plonked on the floor.

Paul sat in a leather wing-backed chair, but Jenny and Timothy knelt beside the globe. Whether they would ever sail to the Greek Islands Jenny couldn't know, but the thought of it filled her with delight. Paul

seemed to consider it possible; he described the wonders, answering Timmy's questions, and Jenny found
that she was listening to him as saucer-eyed as Timothy.
She grimaced to herself ruefully. She didn't want to pass
as another child, least of all with Paul.

Lorraine didn't come down that evening, and she was
sleeping when Jenny peeped in again after she had put
Timmy to bed.

Downstairs Paul was turning the globe reflectively,
and Jenny went back to her patch on the carpet, the
other side of the globe, and asked, "Was that make-
believe for Timmy, about taking the *Mylor* to Greece?"

"Not entirely. It's a trip I've thought about for when I
can find the time."

"Why don't you make the time?"

He smiled, "It might come to that." He didn't take
many holidays. Caterine had always been going on a jet
to somewhere. She had had fabulous holidays with
friends, with Lorraine and Timmy, but Paul had usually
been too busy to join them.

Perhaps he had neglected her, not materially, heaven
knows, but perhaps that explained the note they had
found this afternoon. It was burnt now, gone, and Paul
was never going to know if Jenny could help it. If his
pride wouldn't let Caterine take the small TV parts she
had been offered from time to time how would he react
to learning she had taken a lover?

"Who are you protecting at Moidores, the child or
the man?" Jack Bastaple had sneered. Right now, the
man. Strong though he was, Jenny was his shield in this.

She touched the globe. "So tell me again where we're
going," and they went over the route again, and then
over countless seas to numberless countries. They
twirled the world on its axis, and Jenny asked, "You'll
take me with you?"

"Of course."

"If you don't I'll swim after you."

He smiled, "I'm beginning to believe that!"

"I was going to. I had my shoes off and my coat and I was nearly out of my skirt. It was as well you were rowing and had your back to the jetty and I had time to get into them again. The children were fascinated and Grace Norwood was in hysterics."

He was laughing when Ebby tapped the slightly open door and stepped in to say Mr. Morrison was on the phone. She stayed to look wonderingly after him. "I haven't heard Mr. Paul laugh like that since I don't know when."

"Since . . . Caterine died?"

But Ebby shook her head, "Since his father died, more like."

"What was his father like, Ebby? Everybody seems to have been very fond of him."

Ebby's smile was fond too. "Ah, you'd have liked him. He was a real gentleman."

"So they all say," Jenny teased. "Meaning that Paul isn't," and Ebby turned on her indignantly.

"I mean nothing of the sort—of course Mr. Paul's a gentleman. And he's twice the man his father was, which is as well for all of us if not for him. He works too hard."

"He is thinking about a holiday some time," Jenny ventured. "Sailing to the Greek Islands, taking Timmy and me."

She wondered how Ebby would take that. She hadn't said much about Jenny's last brief trip, and she was somewhat straitlaced. Setting off for a month or two in the *Mylor* might bring out her strong disapproval.

But Ebby showed no surprise at all. She said, "Dan Blaskie was telling his wife the skipper wouldn't be sailing alone again," and while Jenny was assimilating that she smiled. . . .

Lorraine was over the worst of her migraine by morning. She was pale at breakfast and she told them she was going over to the Perries'. Paul took no particular notice, but he caught Jenny's questioning glance, quickly though she tried to mask it.

Before she went into the office Jenny managed a few moments alone with Lorraine and warned her, "If the letter wasn't from Rolf you realize you could be starting up a scandal?"

"I can't help that."

"Mrs. Perrie dislikes Paul. If she gets to hear everyone else will."

"Rolf wouldn't tell her."

"Maybe not, if he was the man. If he wasn't he very well might, or at any rate discuss it with his father."

"I must know," insisted Lorraine.

They were still at the breakfast table. Lorraine had eaten nothing and only drunk half a cup of coffee. "Why?" said Jenny levelly. "What right have you?"

"You don't understand." That was a snub to shut Jenny up, and Lorraine pushed back her chair, but Jenny was at the door first.

"Please," Jenny begged, "ask him if you must, but please don't say we found a letter. Just say you're jealous, you're scared there might have been someone."

Lorraine smiled bleakly. "That's what it comes down to, doesn't it? I'm jealous and I'm scared—and how can I start to tell him that?"

"You could start by telling him you love him," said Jenny.

"Yes," Lorraine sounded as though that had occurred to her, "I could, couldn't I?"

LORRAINE WAS BACK at Moidores for lunch, but Jenny had lunch in the office. Paul had a full list of appointments and Mr. Morrison was working like a beaver.

Most of the exterior property repairs and painting in
Tremain was done during the winter months, and it
seemed that every building had a list of "musts." It was
after six o'clock before Jenny could get to Lorraine.

She was desperately anxious to know what had happened and for once in her life she could have done without Timmy's chatter. Lorraine wasn't going out of her
way to tell. There always seemed to be someone else
within earshot, Ebby, Dolly and Timothy at first, and
then Paul. As though Lorraine was deliberately avoid-
ing being alone with Jenny.

That wasn't encouraging; Jenny had to read what she
could without being told. Lorraine was quiet and appeared thoughtful. Thoughtful or depressed, it was hard
to tell which.

When Paul asked after Rolf she said, "He's fine—he's
back at work on Monday, isn't he?"

Paul said that he was and that was all that was said
about Rolf, but Jenny noticed that Lorraine didn't look
at Paul when she spoke to him. She kept her eyes downcast, and then perhaps Jenny's anxiety communicated
itself, because she gave Jenny a half smile.

After saying good night to Timmy Jenny went back
again into Caterine's room. Taking the clothes from the
cupboards had raised the scent again. It could still bring
back the memory of Caterine so vividly that Jenny
could almost see her.

It was hard for Jenny to believe in that letter even
now, but Lorraine had believed it. "Caterine wanted
everything. . . . You haven't lived with her for the past
eight years," Lorraine had said. Nor for the three years
before her marriage either. Caterine had been Jenny's
dream sister and of course there were things Jenny
didn't know, but she loved her and mourned her and
felt older than Caterine now, as though Caterine had
been a beautiful willful child who must be protected. If

Jenny had found that letter when she was alone she would have burned it and no one would have seen it.

"That was what counted with Caterine, money, position . . . ." "Caterine never wanted anything except a bigger bracelet . . . ." Jenny stroked the silk dress on top of the pile of dresses. She hadn't realized that she could feel sorry for Caterine. Not the searing sorrow that had come with Caterine's death, but a quiet regret that Caterine should have cared so much for the things that hardly mattered at all.

Lorraine held the bracelet. She was sitting in the drawing room, where Jenny had left her to go upstairs with Timmy, and she was holding the bracelet from the painting. Jack Bastaple had painted two bracelets as golden chains, and the other bracelet was on the table.

There was a large white leather jewelry box and several flat boxes, and one of the paintings was down, revealing the wall safe behind.

All Caterine's belongings had come to Paul. They had made wills when they married, his providing for a host of dependants—Caterine's share would have made her a wealthy widow—she willing her nothing to him. Eight years later she had left a sizeable bank account and some enviable jewelry. Today he had collected the jewelry from the bank vaults and taken out the pieces that had been left in the wall safe.

He said, "I think Caterine would have wanted you to share this."

Lorraine and Jenny, her sisters. Lorraine held the bracelet on the flat of her hand and said in an unnaturally high voice, "I think she would rather have been buried with it." And then, "Oh no! Oh, I'm *sorry*," looking wildly and piteously from Paul to Jenny.

Paul said harshly, "Perhaps you'll decide what you want. I'll leave you to it."

He went and Lorraine dropped her hands into her

lap, the heavy bracelet falling to the floor. She whispered, "Why did I say that?"

"Because you think Caterine could have taken Rolf, I suppose," said Jenny with anger.

"I don't think it was Rolf."

"You told him about the letter?"

"No." Because of that Jenny would forgive her most things. "I had no right, like you said. But that doesn't stop me being scared when I realize I could have lost him. He still loves me." That seemed to surprise her. "Caterine called him a ploughboy and said I'd be a fool to marry him." She picked up Caterine's bracelet and put it on the table. "I think he'll be a fool to marry me because I am such a coward, but I do love him."

"I'm glad," said Jenny. "Why didn't you tell me?"

"I wanted to run away." Lorraine was shamefaced although she was smiling. "That was my idea. Paul could still have sacked Rolf and thrown his folk off their farm, but he couldn't have unmarried us and that was what I wanted to do, only Rolf wasn't having it."

She was regretful as though she would still have preferred that way. "Rolf says we have to tell Paul what we're doing."

You face Paul and you face reality, thought Jenny. The price would spelled out. She could have told Lorraine there would be no backlash, but she mustn't.

She asked again, "Why didn't you tell me this before?" and Lorraine got up and hugged her.

"Because you're not a coward. You're going to say—all right, tell Paul, what are you waiting for? And I'm waiting for Thursday."

"Thursday?" Jenny echoed. "What's special about Thursday?"

"Rolf said take another day or two to be sure. He'll come here on Thursday and ask me again. And then we'll tell Paul."

"Are you sure?"

"Oh yes." For the first time there was ringing sincerity in Lorraine's voice. "But I'd give my right hand to know that Paul won't make it hard on the Perries and won't sack Rolf."

"I've never thought he would," said Jenny, and Lorraine grabbed that as though it was eighteen-carat reassurance.

"You haven't, have you, and you're pretty close to Paul, aren't you?"

To change the subject, with the risk that she wouldn't be able to resist saying, "I know it will be all right because Paul told me," Jenny turned to the jewelry and said wryly, "You've got a dowry here, whatever happens, and you're welcome to the lot. I don't want any."

"Because of what I just said? Oh, Jenny, I'm sorry, of course Caterine would have wanted us to have them. That was sheer bitchiness."

Caterine had been generous. She had always brought presents when she came home. Of course none of the gifts had meant any sacrifice. She had given away nothing she wanted herself, and Lorraine probably knew more than Jenny how possessive she was over her jewelry. But Caterine didn't want it now, and no woman could have been unmoved by the beauty of stones and workmanship. These were exquisite pieces, every one. Caterine had always had good taste, and these were heirlooms for the future.

"Please," said Lorraine. "The bracelets, you should have those—they're heavy, they'll suit you better." She looked around, anxious to involve Jenny. "There's a silver and pearl filigree set here that I've always liked." She found the box and opened it. "You know, I've never had much fun wearing jewelery before because Caterine always looked so much better than I did in everything."

She took out the necklace, which was fine as a frozen spider's web, and held it against Jenny's throat and the scarlet sweater she was wearing. A red jumper was hardly right, but Lorraine said, "So do you. You could stand here if this room was full and almost everyone would be watching you, but it wouldn't hurt."

She was looking at the jewels, remembering Caterine wearing them and the years of living as Caterine's shadow. "Because you wouldn't be laughing at me, would you?"

Jenny protested, "I don't believe that Caterine was laughing at you," and Lorraine tried to laugh at herself.

"She laughed at most things."

"Yes, she did." Life had been gay and good for Caterine, what did she know of bruised egos? Lorraine was easier bruised than most.

Lorraine was a baby when her mother died, only a child when she lost her father. From then on her brother had been an autocratic father-figure, less approachable than her real father had been. She still held him in awe. Caterine had dazzled her and outshone her in everything.

After Thursday when she knew that Paul would put no obstacles in the way of her marrying Rolf, and when she had proved her own courage to herself by defying Paul, she could well bloom wonderfully.

Jenny, although her heart was hardly in it, sat down with her and chose some pieces of Caterine's jewelery, and helped Lorraine choose. Trying them on, they compared and admired, as though they were dipping into the junk jewelery in the little shop down in the harbor rather than sharing out a small fortune.

When they finished Jenny rose. "Where are you going?" Lorraine asked.

"To find Paul."

"You wouldn't tell him, would you? I promised Rolf I wouldn't get you to tell him."

"I'm glad about that," said Jenny.

"You promise?"

"Like a flash."

"I think I'll take mine to my room."

Lorraine gathered them together in the larger jewel box, and Jenny said doubtfully, "Do you think it's safe? If you mislay any of that there's going to be trouble."

"If Paul puts them in the wall safe he might not let me have them back again. They are a gift, aren't they? He has given them to me."

"Yes," Jenny agreed. "And he couldn't have timed it better."

Lorraine smiled impishly. "I don't know whether I'm so happy I could cry, or so scared I could cry."

"But you and Rolf are getting married?"

"Yes." Her eyes shone like sapphires. "I'm scared of facing Paul, but oh, Jenny, I am happy!"

Jenny found Paul in the office, sitting at his desk, with the documents Mr. Morrison had left for him. She said, "Please would you come and put this back in the safe?"

"Have you shared it?"

"Yes."

He walked with her to the drawing room and asked, "Where's Lorraine?"

"She's gone to her room."

Obviously taking her share with her. Paul looked quizzically at Jenny and she found herself blushing as though she had a guilty secret. It was remembering what she had said about a dowry. Because she knew why Lorraine feared that Paul might regret and possibly revoke his generosity.

He picked up the jewel cases left on the table. "You want it all put away?" She nodded. "Then you'd better learn the combination."

She tried to explain, "I would be happier with just one piece, I don't really want—" but he overrode that impatiently.

"This is Caterine's gift to you, not mine. This puts you under no obligation to me."

She bit her lip on a smile. "You mean I can put them into a suitcase and ring for a taxi?"

"If you like." With his back to her he began to open the safe and she laughed. "Is that amusing?"

"Yes." Ridiculous and impossible. She said, "I don't ever want to leave here, unless I can come right back."

He turned then and smiled and said, "Come and see how this works."

She watched and memorized, and when he put back the portrait of a fair-haired girl who looked a little like Lorraine, painted in the year Victoria became queen, she said, "Don't work any more tonight. I can tell you what's in that pile on your desk. Mr. Morrison dictated it to me and I typed it. Twenty-two roofs need repairing for a start and they won't get repaired tonight, so that can wait till morning."

"How bad are the roofs?"

"A tile off here and there."

"That can wait till morning." He took her hand and drew her down beside him on the settee in front of the fire. He said, "When you leave I'll take you, to make sure you come back."

"Do you want me to tell you about the work on your desk?"

"No, I want you to stay here with me, and be quiet."

She slid inside his arms and laid her head on his chest, and she felt him relax. After a while she said quietly, "Was it a grim day?"

"Like most of them."

"Nothing you couldn't handle?"

"That's the size of it."

He could handle all the emergencies, all the strains and the stresses. He had the strength and the self-discipline and the brains and the guts, but last night and tonight he had come home to her. And if she had felt relaxed and safe in her berth on the *Mylor* with Paul at the wheel she was infinitely more content now, half asleep in his arms, watching the fire flare and flicker, listening to the sea.

They talked lazily when they talked at all, easy as old friends, and when a clock chimed midnight Jenny said, "I'd better get to my bed," and moved her head to touch Paul's cheek with her lips.

His skin was not quite smooth and he turned so that their mouths brushed, and kissed her briefly but with a purpose and feeling that every nerve in her answered. Then he said huskily, "I think you had. Good night, Jenny. Bless you."

She said good night. Timmy was sleeping. Jenny slept too, and Paul stayed with her in her dreams.

Next afternoon Jenny was out of the office, down in Tremain with Mr. Morrison still dealing with repairs and renovations. The shop was closed and there was no sign of Lorraine, and when they finished, and Mr. Morrison went home to his rooms in the Crow's Nest pub halfway up the hill, Jenny looked in on Grace Norwood.

She hadn't seen Grace since Saturday, when she had left her laughing on the dock, and Grace's first words were, "You're staying to eat, aren't you?"

"Thanks," said Jenny.

She went to phone from the shop to tell Ebby she wouldn't be very late and had a word with Timmy. Then she took Grace the spare key back and helped to set the table.

Ben's latest masterpiece was set in the center of the table; he had brought it over from the studio that afternoon. It was a hideously scowling head in gray granite, and as she laid the plates around it Jenny patted the head and said, "Hello."

"Like him?" asked Grace.

"I don't know that I'd care to live with him," said Jenny.

"I hope somebody will," laughed Grace. "We need the money." Ben's powerful studies sold well. The uglier they were the quicker they sold.

He looked up from his armchair and his newspaper now and asked, "Don't you recognize Paul Tremain?"

"You've got to be joking!" Jenny exploded. "This is one of your cold Cornish giants."

"Isn't Paul Tremain?" Ben grinned at her.

"Well, he doesn't look like that," said Jenny. "You look more like that than he does. Go on, frown and twist your mouth to one side." As he obliged she pointed a fork at him. "That's it! It's a self-portrait. They've all been self-portraits. Grace, you're married to a Cornish monster."

"I've suspected it for a long time," chuckled Grace.

The Norwoods ate heartily, enjoying their food, and tonight's meal was a steak-and-kidney pie, cauliflower au gratin, and a bottle of red wine in Jenny's honor. Eating and talking passed a pleasant hour or so.

There were two subjects intriguing Grace: Jenny's trip in the *Mylor* and Caterine's jewelry.

Jenny described the route the *Mylor* had taken and said she had had a marvelous time, and Grace seemed almost as pleased to hear about the sharing of the jewelry as though she had been included herself.

Lorraine had told them about that this morning. "I suppose it was the obvious thing for him to do," said Grace. "You are Caterine's family, after all. Which is your favorite?"

"I don't know," Jenny admitted, and Grace began enthusing about the piece she coveted most, the silver filigree that had been Lorraine's first choice.

Lorraine had told them about the jewelry, but she

hadn't told them she and Rolf were planning to get married. If she had Grace would have had some questions to ask about that. Jenny said nothing, although when Grace did hear she was going to be indignant. "You *knew*, Jenny, and you never breathed a word?" But Jenny had promised and it wouldn't be long before everyone knew.

She helped with the washing-up and refused to let either Ben or both of them walk to Moidores with her. The offers were kindly, but of course they would rather stay by their cosy fireside, and Jenny would walk fast and fearlessly.

When she had gone Grace looked at the carved head again and asked her husband, "That isn't really meant to be Tremain, is it?"

"Good lord, no!" Ben chuckled at his joke. "But didn't Jenny rise to it?"

The harbor was deserted except for one man, leaning on the sea wall, looking out across the dark waters, and Jenny recognized Jack Bastaple. He said, "Good evening," as though he was expecting her.

"Hello."

"Did you get the bracelet?" He had heard about the jewelry. Lorraine had been down in the shop, so it would have been news for all the artists' colony.

Jenny said, "Yes," and Jack walked along beside her.

"And do they feel like chains?"

She turned on him angrily but kept walking. "They were never chains."

The night was clear, with the usual wind from the sea whipping her hair, and he said raggedly, "You look more like Caterine every time I see you."

She was angry, but she pitied him. She asked almost gently, "Have you painted the picture again?"

"I've tried." He shrugged heavily. "But I don't think it's going to work a second time." He looked out again to sea. The *Mylor* in the mouth of the harbor had a light on its masthead like a star. He said, "You went sailing. Are you falling for it too?"

"For what?"

"The *Mylor*. Moidores. All of it. Do you want to be Queen of Tremain?"

There was nothing to say to that. She walked on and he still walked beside her, taunting her, "After Queen Caterina Queen Jenny doesn't sound right, does it?"

Caterina . . . the name in the letter . . . and Purdie's Beck when he was painting the old mine entrance. Jack Bastaple had always been much more likely than Rolf Perrie. She asked, "Is that what you called Caterine—Caterina?"

"Sometimes." His voice was husky.

"And you tried to get her to leave Paul."

That wasn't a question, but he answered, "Yes."

"I see," she said.

"You don't."

But she did, and she could have said, "You had an affair with Caterine, but it was never serious for her. It would be a joke, because Caterine laughed at everything. A secret joke and no more." But she said nothing.

He went on, "She wasted her talents, she wasted her life here. He made her afraid to risk living poor. She couldn't get away."

"Couldn't or wouldn't?" That Jenny had to say.

"Couldn't," he said. "*Couldn't*. Tremain would never have let her go. He keeps what he has, and he was born to it. Everything handed to him on a plate." Bitterness choked him. He was overwhelmed by envy so that he sounded as though he tasted bile on his tongue, and almost spat out, "He just sits back and the money rolls in."

"Nonsense," said Jenny briskly. "He works a darn sight harder than you've ever done, my lad." She realized that she sounded like Ebby. She said, "Good night," and left him at the corner of the road that led to his cottage and went up the hill so fast that she was out of breath before she reached the Crow's Nest and had to slow down and take the rest at a reasonable rate.

Jenny went into Moidores by the kitchen door and Ebby greeted her with, "You picked the wrong night to stay out. We've been having some real excitement here."

"What?"

Both Eb and Ebby were smiling, but almost guiltily. "Seems we're having a wedding," said Ebby.

Why had they brought the announcement forward? And had they told Paul yet or only Eb and Ebby? Jenny asked, "Where are they?"

"Gone to tell his folks," said Eb. "Even they didn't know." He fixed Jenny with a shrewd eye. "You did, though."

She nodded, then swallowed to ask, "How did Paul take it?"

"He's eating his dinner," said Ebby, "so it hasn't taken his appetite."

"Good. Are you pleased?"

Eb said firmly, "Rolf Perrie's a nice young fellow. I never could understand what the master had against him," and Ebby went on smiling.

"Of course we're pleased. She looked so happy. She said to tell you she'd see you later."

Paul and Timothy were alone in the dining room and the meal was almost finished. Timothy was eating the last crumb of chocolate sponge pudding and Paul had cheese and biscuits on his plate. They both looked toward the door, since they had heard Jenny coming, but only Timothy was smiling.

Timmy burst out as she walked in, "Auntie Jen, did you know Auntie Lorraine's getting married?"

"Ebby's just told me," she said, and Paul's expression conveyed such a grasp of the situation that Jenny couldn't meet his eyes.

Timmy babbled on, "She's marrying Rolf. Isn't that super?"

"Super," echoed Jenny weakly.

"I like Rolf," Timmy confided. "I think that's a good idea."

He scraped his dish and Jenny said, "Finished? Come on, then."

Timmy had expected more chat, but Jenny was turning toward the door again, so he said good night to his father and went with her.

Paul did not think it was super. No one had expected he would. But he had looked at Jenny just now as though it was at least partly her fault, and she was not looking forward to being questioned.

"John's coming to tea tomorrow," Timmy, in pyjamas and ready for bed, reminded her.

"That's nice." She knew. Children were always coming to tea. Timothy had a sociable little gang of playmates.

"Can we play with the train set?"

"Why not?"

"Can we get them out now?" he suggested cunningly. The play was to delay bedtime and Jenny was tempted to agree and stretch out another half hour or so before she went down to Paul again. But Paul had to be faced, and Lorraine was happy, and happiness was surely what Paul really wanted for his sister.

"Get the trains out when John comes tomorrow," said Jenny. "You can set them up between you."

Timmy hadn't thought the ploy would work, although it had been worth trying. He grinned, "I hate you."

"I hate you." Jenny tickled him briefly, and he squirmed and spluttered.

He asked when she let him go, "Will Auntie Lorraine go away?"

"Not far." Rolf would still be working at the mine.

"But she won't live in this house any more?"

So far as space went there would be plenty of room for a flat. But space might not be the problem.

"I don't know. Into bed with you." Timmy clambered into his bunk and she said, "Good night, love."

She didn't have to stay around until he fell asleep now. He was well through the stage of utter dependence on her. He was a healthy happy small boy again, the nightmares fading.

Paul was still sitting at the dining room table, and Jenny went back into the room. The sooner this was over the better. He looked weary, but he looked grim too, and although she had intended to say, "Please don't be angry," she sat down before she tried to start explaining and he spoke first.

"You knew they planned to get married?"

"Yes."

"Why didn't you tell me?"

"I—promised not to say anything."

"It seems I should have asked for your promise instead of relying on your discretion."

He thought she had told them that Rolf's career was not in jeopardy, and that Paul was not going to finish with Lorraine if she married against his wishes. Well, she had always said she believed that.

She demanded, "What does it matter? What have you got against Rolf?"

"Nothing," said Paul, "but I would like to have been sure that Lorraine's attraction for him wasn't the mine and the money."

Put starkly like that it was horrifying. Jenny was so shaken that she was almost incoherent. "Why should it be? Rolf is in love with her. How can you think he only wants her because . . . ." Words failed her. It was degrading to say them.

But Paul said quietly, "Why not? That was why Caterine married me."

Power was overwhelmingly attractive to some women, and Paul Tremain's empire would have made him outstandingly eligible, but Jenny stammered, "Caterine loved you."

"Less than she loved what I could buy for her. I realized that very soon." He spoke calmly and his smile was self-mocking. "It didn't affect me too deeply, but Lorraine is a different proposition." He stopped smiling and said harshly, "It could destroy her."

"Not Rolf." He had to believe that. "I'm sure, I'm *sure*."

He said flatly, "We'll never be sure now."

But Jenny knew that Rolf had always been prepared to risk everything for Lorraine. He would have loved her if she had been a salesgirl in the little shop in the harbor, instead of Tremain's sister, the golden girl. She had to make Paul understand. She said, "Rolf told me last week, 'It's up to Lorraine. It's always been up to Lorraine.' "

He believed her so far. He said cynically, "Then you told Lorraine I was bluffing and she told Rolf?"

"I *didn't*!" She was vehement, but he almost laughed.

"It was just coincidence that they immediately called my bluff? If you didn't make up Lorraine's mind for her, who did?"

Jack Bastaple did. His letter to Caterine had made Lorraine afraid of losing Rolf. And Jenny couldn't tell Paul about that. Better let him believe Jenny had betrayed a confidence, a little thing, than tell him how Caterine had betrayed him.

She made a small helpless gesture, and Paul said, "Don't let me detain you. I'm sure you and Ebby and

Lorraine are wanting to plan the wedding." He didn't sound angry, but he sounded tired. He said, "Although as a bridesmaid you'll probably outshine the bride."

. . . As Caterine would have done, but I am Jenny. . . . "Paul." She stretched a hand across the table to touch his hand.

Last night he had drawn her into his arms; now he said, "Run along," as though she wearied him. And he was untouchable.

It was no use arguing or trying to explain, and she had a growing and desolate conviction that she might never get near to him again.

Timothy was still awake. She went into her room and he heard her and called, "Auntie Jen?"

"What is it?"

She opened the communicating door and looked in on him. He sounded pleased with himself, as though he had come up with a bright solution to a knotty problem.

"Auntie Jen, why don't you marry father? Then you'll always stay here and he'll look after you."

She heard her own voice, gay and teasing. "Don't you think one wedding at a time's enough?"

Then she closed the door again and sat on the side of her bed, face in her hands, knowing that she mustn't begin to cry.

CHAPTER NINE

JENNY STAYED IN HER ROOM that evening, and no one looked for her until Lorraine came back from the Perries'. Then, just after ten o'clock, Lorraine peeped in, all smiles.

Jenny had gone to bed with a magazine. She wasn't reading, but she certainly wouldn't be sleeping, so she was lying, propped up with an extra pillow, leafing through a glossy monthly.

Lorraine ran across to fling arms around her. "Oh, Jenny, isn't it wonderful? I can't believe it, I just can't!" She did look quite radiant, and Jenny had to rejoice with her; she would have been a poor friend if she hadn't, although she was feeling sick at heart herself.

She said, "I'm so glad. I do like Rolf, I know you're going to be happy."

"Oh yes!" Lorraine was confident of happiness. "I thought this morning—why put off telling Paul till tomorrow, I'll feel the same tomorrow as I do now. So I drove over to the farm and I told Rolf, and Jenny, it wasn't so hard. You were right. Of course Paul isn't going to dismiss Rolf."

"I'm glad," said Jenny again. "When are you getting married?"

Lorraine laughed softly, "We thought Christmas Eve." That didn't leave much time, but one way or another they had already had a long engagement.

"Paul didn't seem all that surprised," Lorraine elaborated. "Almost as though he'd expected it. He said he appreciated our telling him first." She giggled slightly, mimicking her brother's deep voice: 'I am the first to be told,' he said, and I said 'Well—Jenny,' and that didn't surprise him either. He said, 'After Jenny, of course.'"

She looked at Jenny fondly. "You knew it would be all right, didn't you?"

"Yes." For Lorraine and Rolf.

"There isn't anything the matter?"

Jenny's pretense at gaiety must be slipping, because Lorraine sounded suddenly concerned, and Jenny explained, "Paul thinks I did the persuading."

Lorraine was indignant for a moment. "He doesn't think I'm capable of making up my own mind?" Then she had to admit, "It was the letter. I needed that. It wasn't Rolf, I'm sure, but one day it might have been, with some other girl, and like you said I had no right to complain."

She grinned, "I have now, though, and so has he, and I couldn't be more grateful to Caterine and whoever the man was." Her grin faded. "But we can't tell Paul that, can we?"

"Hardly," said Jenny. It wasn't fair to spoil Lorraine's happiness tonight; she shrugged as though it didn't matter much and asked, "What did Rolf's parents say?"

"They kept asking how Paul was taking it. His mother couldn't believe Rolf hadn't been thrown out of the house."

She was joking, but Mrs. Perrie had needed reassuring, and she had kissed Lorraine, welcoming her as a daughter-in-law, with some defiance as though the vengeance of Tremain might strike at any moment.

"You will be my bridesmaid, won't you?" Lorraine asked.

"I'd love to!"

There wasn't much risk of her outshining anyone. Lorraine would be a dazzling bride, and Jenny felt a hundred years old.

Next day the news was all over. The phone was already ringing at breakfast time, friends offering congratulations, wanting to know when the wedding was. Lorraine was jumping up and down to answer the phone all through breakfast and Timmy was hard to get off to school, suspecting that he would be missing some excitement.

In the end Jenny had to run with him to catch the school bus. As they ran he panted, "Don't forget John's coming to tea. Don't let Ebby forget she promised to make gingerbread men."

"I'll remind her," Jenny promised and did as soon as she got back before she forgot herself.

Lorraine was spending the day with Rolf. They were buying the ring. Any one of the three rings that had fallen to Lorraine from Caterine's jewelry was probably grander than the best Rolf could afford, but Lorraine wanted Rolf's ring, even if he did have to hobble into the shop to buy it for her. Lorraine anticipated a lovely day, but Jenny did not.

Jenny was right, Paul was at his most irascible. Mr. Morrison made no mention at all of the engagement and Paul was halfway through the morning mail when the phone on his desk rang and it was a reporter.

Yes, said Paul, he was delighted at his sister's choice. Lorraine and Rolf Perrie had been friends from childhood and no, he had not saved Rolf Perrie's life recently. That rescue operation had entailed a score or more men.

Paul didn't answer the phone again. Each time it rang Mr. Morrison took it, and when he said that Mr. Tremain was not in the office Jenny presumed that was because somebody wanted to discuss Miss Tremain and Mr. Perrie.

Maddeningly none of this seemed to impair Paul's efficiency. His dictation was crisper than ever, and when Jenny's pencil snapped he glared at her as though that was her fault too.

She had Mr. Morrison's sympathy. Once he almost winked at her. Perhaps it was hardly a wink, but his eyelids drooped in fellow-feeling when Paul asked if something was ready for signature and it wasn't.

It might have been if nothing had disturbed her, but she had brought them in coffee at eleven, and she had spoiled a couple of pages that had to be retyped. So it wasn't ready, and Paul snapped, "I hope it will be when I get back. It has to go today."

She shrilled, "Well of course it will. It isn't going to take me all day!"

"I'm glad to hear that," he said.

She flopped in her chair when he went out and Mr. Morrison said, "Don't take it personally."

"It is personal."

"No." He shook his head at her. "You know better than that. This marriage is not altogether to his liking, and you are drawing the fire because your mind is not altogether on your work."

She typed another line, then she said, "I never thought that Paul would do any of the things that Lorraine worried about, sacking Rolf, taking away the farm from his parents, telling her never to darken his doors again—all that melodrama. Did you?"

"It seemed unlikely," Mr. Morrison conceded.

"I knew he wouldn't. I asked him and he said he wouldn't but he thinks I told them what he said."

"You didn't?"

"No!"

Mr. Morrison made his silent "Oh . . . ."

"So this is personal," Jenny smiled, but her lips were unsteady.

Mr. Morrison said quietly, "Mr. Tremain almost invariably keeps his own counsel. If he feels that you betrayed a confidence I suggest you tell him, forcibly, that you did not."

This time Jenny did smile. "He isn't the easiest man to use force on." Mr. Morrison chuckled with her. Then he went back to his work and she went on with her typing. It was good advice. She wished she could follow it, but Paul wasn't going to listen to her, so what chance had she of telling him anything?

Moidores was full of activity that evening. Paul was not around, but Rolf was, and Lorraine had her engagement ring and plans for the wedding were going ahead. Half the population of Tremain seemed to be in the drawing room, although in fact there was only Grace and Ben and four others, artists who were Lorraine's closest friends. Not Jack, for which Jenny was thankful.

Lorraine had gone down to the harbor earlier to ask them up to a little party with a lot of talk and laughter. Jenny joined in for a while, then went along to see how Timmy and his guest were faring. They were setting up and dismantling the train set, and arguing every inch of the way. Then she slipped out of the house for a breath of fresh air, because she wanted to be alone.

She went across the springy turf of the clifftop gardens at the back of the house. The coastline and the sea spread out below her, and she neared the edge of the cliff where the gnarled old trees, planted a hundred years ago, made dark grotesque silhouettes against the skyline.

Paul stood by one of the trees, and when Jenny saw him he had already seen her and was turning, facing her. Her step quickened instinctively, she took a couple of paces almost running toward him. Then she caught herself and steadied herself and went quietly.

He asked, "What are you doing out here?"

"I came for some air. What are you?"

"I do sometimes walk in my garden. You're too near the cliff edge for nighttime."

The moon was out, so she could see clearly and was

as safe as he was. "And it's cold," he said. "You'd better go in."

He didn't want her staying or walking with him. She said, "Lorraine's very happy and she could be penniless and Rolf would still love her."

"Very romantic," he said cynically, and she went on with what she was trying to tell him.

"And I told Lorraine all along that I didn't believe you'd sack Rolf, but I never told either of them that I'd asked you."

"Just a coincidence?"

"Coincidences do happen."

"Of course." But there was irony in his voice. "And now you'd better go back to the party, unless you want them all out here looking for you."

He left her and walked away, along the cliff's edge overlooking the cove of Moidores. What could she do? How could she force him to believe her? She went back into the house, and gave a reasonable imitation of a girl without a care in the world.

Paul was in the office next morning and Jenny concentrated fervently on her work so that he could find no fault with that. The atmosphere was calm enough but hardly relaxing, and after lunch when she was alone with Mr. Morrison it was easier to type without making mistakes.

"Where is Paul?" she asked. It was easier without him, but empty.

"He's gone to St. Agnes," said Mr. Morrison, "to see the Frearsons." Paul owned a crafts shop they ran.

Jenny frowned. "But I thought that was tomorrow." The appointment was down under Saturday morning.

"He changed it." Mr. Morrison looked up at her. "He's not in tomorrow. You didn't know that?"

"No."

"You haven't straightened out that little matter?"

"I tried to. He wouldn't listen. He just walked away."

"Going sailing. Leaving tonight, I believe."

Without her, of course. Her eyes brimmed with sudden tears, and she looked down hastily and said brightly, "He can always get away from it all for a while. He's lucky."

"Not always," said Mr. Morrison.

"I can't believe that."

A few moments passed during which Mr. Morrison made a decision.

He said, "You once suggested that I did not like your sister." Jenny remembered. "I didn't dislike her," Mr. Morrison insisted, "but I didn't admire her." Knowing what she knew now Jenny couldn't leap to Caterine's defence, and he went on. "Now, Mr. Tremain is a man for whom I have a great respect and a great deal of affection." The expressionless face softened briefly, then set in severe lines. "I'd be distressed to see him make a second mistake."

He looked hard at Jenny and she faltered, "A second mistake?" Not sure if he was meaning her until he smiled.

"You," he told her, "have many attractive qualities, Miss Douglas. Certainly you have initiative." She sat wondering what this was leading to. "I hear that your trip on the *Mylor* was a success. Dan Blaskie expects you to be sailing with them again."

"Not today," she said ruefully, and Mr. Morrison who had sat with pen in hand during all this made a little squiggle of notes in the margin of the paper before him.

As he wrote he said, "A pity. Mr. Tremain could hardly walk away if he was at the wheel of a boat."

On the *Mylor* she could have talked to Paul, or on the Witch's Rock. You saw things clearer out there, without interruptions or pretense. "That's true," she said.

"I'd like you to take a message down to the Tremain Arms." He could have phoned that, whatever it was.

"Yes?" Jenny waited.

"About the alterations in the saloon bar. Would you tell the Trevarricks that I'll be along this evening to discuss them?"

"Yes, I will. What about this?" She touched the typewriter.

"That can wait till Monday."

"Thank you." If she managed to get herself aboard the *Mylor* she could have the sack by Monday. She could be well and truly out of Moidores, or everything could be right again. It all depended. She was taking a gambler's risk, and at the door she looked back to say, "Wish me luck."

"With all my heart, Miss Douglas," said Mr. Morrison.

Jenny changed her shoes and put on a thick coat, then rammed a few things into a large handbag and hurried. If Paul was already aboard she was a loser right away, for he wouldn't take her along if he knew about it.

But the *Mylor* dinghy was moored by the jetty, and she crossed her fingers and touched the studded black oak door of the Tremain Arms. She wouldn't have admitted being superstitious, but she needed all the luck she could get.

Mrs. Trevarrick took the message and smiled at Jenny, who had always seemed a nice girl to her, and from what they were saying could well be Mrs. Tremain before long.

It seemed romance was in the air. Miss Lorraine and Rolf Perrie coming together after all. Mrs. Trevarrick was a sentimental soul. She tried to get Jenny to stay, to have a drink, a cup of tea or coffee, and Jenny thanked her, said she would have loved to, but she was in a hurry; and Mrs. Trevarrick followed her out into the street still talking about what a nice young man Rolf Perrie was and what a lovely bride Miss Lorraine would make.

Dan Blaskie's pink-washed cottage was on the corner, the other side of the road from the Tremain Arms. Jenny knocked on the door with Mrs. Trevarrick still smiling at her.

Suppose Paul opened the door? He might have called for Dan. Then she could only ask, "Will you take me with you?" and he would say, "No." Or she could be a coward and pretend she'd come to see Dan.

Dan answered. Maybe touching wood worked. He grinned at her and she asked, "Are you going out to the *Mylor*?"

"No. Everything's ready, all shipshape. Want to get aboard early, do ee?"

He was taking it for granted she was going. Luck *was* with her. "Yes, please," she said.

"Oright, m'dear." He called back into the house to his wife, "Back in no time," and they walked together along the dock and climbed into the dinghy.

It couldn't be this easy. Jenny was nervous as a cat on hot bricks, and not at all surprised when Dan asked what was troubling her.

He was bound to tell Paul that she had gone on ahead. She pleaded, "Will you do something for me?"

"Name it."

She twisted her hands together in her lap. "Paul hasn't asked me to go sailing this time."

That brought Dan's head up from between his shoulders, his leathery neck stretched like a tortoise coming out of its shell. "Please don't tell him I'm on board," she implored.

Dan faltered in his rowing. "What's this, then? What's the skulking for?"

"He hasn't said I can't go. You could say you took it

for granted I'd got permission. Well, you did, didn't you?"

He growled, "Sure of it I was," looking at Jenny beneath beetling brows as if she had taken advantage of him. The dinghy was making no progress now, while Dan considered whether to go on or back. He demanded, "Why didn't you ask him, then?"

"He wasn't in a good mood this morning."

"Reckon he'll be better tempered out there?"

"He usually is, isn't he?"

"Aye, as a rule."

"So please don't say anything."

Dan brooded for a while longer; then he dipped the oars once more, and the dinghy skimmed on toward the *Mylor*. "Not unless I'm asked." He yielded that much, and she accepted it gratefully.

It would give her a chance. Someone who had seen her being rowed across the bay might tell Paul, and then he would certainly ask Dan. But there was a chance of her getting out to sea before she was discovered. Paul might let her stay aboard if he found her in harbor, but she would rather stay hidden until they had passed the point where he hadn't much option.

She would admit she had hoodwinked Dan so no blame was attached to him.

Dan wasted no time. He rowed off as soon as she scrambled aboard, and she went at once through the forward two-door hatch into the small room with the sails and stores lockers, down the steps into the cabin where she had slept last Saturday.

The bed was not made up. She found blankets and sheets in the tin trunk, and three foam mattresses, one of which she presumed was hers, in a cupboard under the settee in the main cabin.

It was cold. No lamps or stoves were lit, and Dan's last words had been a warning that she could be in for a longish wait. "I'll wait," she'd said. She had to, now. She made up her bed, and then went back through the access doors past the foot of the mainmast and into the main cabin again.

She was apprehensive, but glad to be here. It would have been unbearable tonight, in her own quiet room in Moidores, knowing that Paul had left her behind. Mr. Morrison would cover for her with Ebby and Timmy, and Paul too until Paul left. Then he would explain where she had gone.

That had been a surprising thing he had done. Putting this idea into her head, and putting himself in a very awkward position when the *Mylor* sailed back into Tremain.

She couldn't even light a lamp, although it was almost bound to be dark before they left harbor. She watched Tremain through the porthole, seeing the lights come on trying to distinguish tiny figures on the dock and when dusk fell rain came, spattering on the porthole. The chill was beginning to reach her bones and she went to her own cabin and got into bed, fully dressed except for shoes, and huddled under the blankets.

She could see nothing through the porthole. There were no stars or moon tonight to silver the sea. She could hear the wind and the slapping water and it sounded like a bleak night, so that she wondered if Paul might change his mind.

She would look a right idiot if he did, and she was stuck out here until Dan rowed over for her in the morning.

She giggled weakly at the thought. She was warm under the blankets now, lulled by the movement and creakings of the boat, and Paul would come, she knew he would. She closed her eyes, remembering the blissful sanctuary of his arms around her.

The sound of engines woke her. *Mylor* was leaving

harbor and she stayed where she was, curled snug and quiet in her bunk.

There was no sound of footsteps on deck. Dan was probably in the main cabin, but she daren't even go along there until they were well out to sea. The wheelhouse was directly overhead and Paul would overhear voices.

She was a stowaway and he was likely to blow his top when he saw her, but she could take that, although now that the prospect was near she had butterflies in her stomach and an uncomfortable tightening in her throat. He couldn't throw her overboard, but he could make her feel like jumping.

It was too late to change her mind now, unless she stayed a stowaway and starved till Sunday.

She looked for the Witch's Rock, but rain masked the porthole. It wouldn't be pleasant up there in the wheelhouse, although it would be cosy in the cabin. Dan would probably come looking for her. He'd have to, for his own alibi. He'd brought her aboard, and he'd have to say something about that before long, or Paul would know he had an uneasy conscience.

But Dan didn't come. The engines were quiet now. They were well out of harbor and the *Mylor* was powered by sail.

Jenny stayed where she was for an hour or more, then she crept very quietly through the main cabin. It was a choppy night, and the boat was pitching. She had to take care, and there were no lamps on in here either.

No sign of life at all, so both men must be up on deck. She went to her cabin to get the waterproof coat from one of the lockers that Dan had found for her last time. Then she went up on deck herself.

She was prepared for rain, but it was teeming down and seemed dark as pitch around. The decks looked slippery and hazardous, and she held on to the rail, looking back at the wheelhouse. As she stood in a patch of light she heard Paul roar over the sound of wind and slapping sails, "Get below!"

Well, he'd seen her. He knew she was here. Perhaps Dan had already told him. The reckoning was to come, but he might be less annoyed if she made herself useful.

She lit the lamps, thankful that she had followed Dan around last time, learning all she could. Then she lit the gas stove and looked for food. The galley was well stocked and there were a couple of flasks. She unscrewed and checked them: coffee and soup.

The cabin was warm in no time, and Jenny alternated between guilt and high delight. She had gatecrashed, but that wasn't so dreadful. There was room, and she was doing no harm. She was so enchanted with the *Mylor* that she couldn't keep her fingers from stroking the wooden panelling on the walls, moving the cushions around, poking around the store cupboard.

The ship moved and breathed like a living thing, and Jenny told it. "You are so beautiful," and although she laughed at herself the words didn't sound ridiculous.

Then she put on her waterproof again and went up the companionway into the wheelhouse. Paul was in glistening black oilskins, large and looming and dripping wet.

"Where did you come from?" he demanded.

"You wouldn't believe I swam out?" But he was probably in no mood for jokes and she admitted, "Dan brought me, but he thought you'd said I could come."

"Why didn't you ask me?"

"You might have said no, and I wanted to talk to you, and you can't walk away from the wheel, can you?"

"Not on a night like this in a shipping lane."

"Where's Dan?"

"At home."

So he had intended to make this trip alone and he

would have said no and she was an intruder. She should have said, "Sorry," but she wasn't sorry. She asked, "Where are we going?"

"We should be going back to Tremain."

"No!" she wailed.

Then as the deck sloped she slithered, and Paul grabbed her and ordered, "Get below, for God's sake, you'll be overboard!" He shoved her toward the companionway and she climbed down a few steps so that she was sheltered but could still look up at him.

"Please don't turn back," she pleaded. "*Please.* I'll be no trouble, I promise. I'll stay in my own cabin. It's a big boat."

"Not that big."

"This is ridiculous!" she cried desperately. "Going all the way back just to get rid of me. What am I supposed to be, a jinx aboard? Do you think I whistled up the storm?"

He laughed suddenly, "I wouldn't put it past you," and she laughed too, because he wasn't angry, he wasn't turning back.

"Then you'd better maroon me on Witch's Rock with the sea witch."

"No," he said. "Oh no."

The rain and spray blew in gusts so that in spite of the protective shield of hatch-coaming it was wet and cold in the wheelhouse. She wanted him in, out of the storm. "I've lit the lamps," she said. "And the food's ready any time. How long before we can anchor?"

"Another hour before we reach harbor."

"Not Tremain?"

"No."

"I'll bring the coffee up."

She brought the flask and half filled the brown enamel mugs, but even so they slopped over with the rise and fall of the boat. This time she was prepared and kept her footing, and stayed beside him under the awning and drank some of her coffee.

Then she said, "I came to tell you again that I didn't tell Lorraine what you said. Rolf was prepared to lose his job and Lorraine was ready to go with him anywhere."

"I'm glad to hear that."

"You believe me?"

"Yes."

A hooter signaled mournfully as the lights of a passing ship showed in the distance. Paul answered with the *Mylor*'s siren and the echoes seemed to linger. It was a larger ship than this, probably carrying cargo. Jenny watched it pass and vanish into the darkness. Then she said, "I think they'll be happy."

"I hope so."

He was cynical because he thought Caterine had married him for his money, and perhaps she had, but she had made sacrifices too. She had given as well as taken. Jenny said, "Maybe Caterine did enjoy being the wife of a rich man, but she gave up her career for you."

He sounded amused. "Not for me. That was her choice."

"But . . . ." Jenny gulped and was silent. Caterine had always said it was Paul who insisted she gave up acting. "Paul won't hear of me acting again," Jenny remembered her telling them before she married, and since, lots of times since.

"But," Jenny faltered, "the work she was offered you made her turn down. Didn't you?"

"Acting's an overcrowded profession." He was watching the compass as he spoke. "Can you see someone who wasn't an established name getting genuine offers years after they'd left the business?"

"She didn't?"

"She had theatrical friends. There was talk about productions, but anyone who suggested Caterine for a role knew there was no risk of the offer being taken up. She never considered going back to work."

"You didn't stop her?"

"Why should I?"

"But I thought that—Caterine *told* me, she told everyone you wouldn't let her."

"That was one of Caterine's fantasies."

Hadn't Grace said that Caterine enjoyed saying, "Paul wouldn't let me." Jenny had often thought that herself, although she had believed that Caterine had sacrificed her career for love. Caterine had had talent and promise, but it was no real surprise to hear that she had preferred the pampered life. Acting was hard work; Queen Caterina of Tremain was a cushier role.

That left one thing unexplained. Jenny said suddenly, "But, the quarrel?"

"What quarrel?"

Hands on the wheel, he turned to look at her, and she blurted, "The night Caterine died, she'd asked you, hadn't she, if she could go back to the stage, and you'd said no? Wasn't that why she suddenly decided to visit me? She was upset, crying. Wasn't she?"

He said heavily, "Who told you this?"

"Lorraine. She was there."

"She was not there."

But Lorraine had told her why Caterine was weeping, why she had driven that car erratically and too fast.

Paul said, "Lorraine may have heard Caterine's version, but take my word there were no witnesses to that scene."

Then what was Paul's version? Jenny whispered, "What happened?"

He said wryly, "Nothing that matters now. Nothing that really mattered then. My wife was welcome to a career, but not to a lover."

"You *knew*?" Did he know who? How did he know? "How?"

"More to the point—how did you?"

"There was part of a letter. Lorraine and I found it while we were clearing the cupboards. That was what made up Lorraine's mind. She thought at first it might be Rolf and she was jealous, and she knew then how much Rolf meant to her." She added quickly, "It wasn't Rolf."

"No," said Paul. He knew who it was. "Why didn't you tell me this?"

"I didn't want you hurt—I didn't think you knew. I don't think it was really anything, just a flirtation."

"Thank you," he said dryly, "no one ever tried to protect me before. I know what it was and I suspect you do. Caterine was a good actress, and if I hadn't been sure of my facts I might have believed her."

Jenny could imagine Caterine protesting her innocence, claiming that she was wounded to the heart, that she was going to her sister's . . . getting away from Paul because she was guilty and afraid.

She would never have considered that she might lose Paul Tremain and the rich life, for a stupid little infidelity that didn't really count. She had kept her head when she met Lorraine, with tears still on her face, and sobbed out the old story, Paul wouldn't let her go back to acting, only this time, for the first time, there had been this horrible quarrel.

Lorraine wouldn't ask Paul about that. No one would dare ask Paul, and Caterine would get to Jenny's and it would all blow over, because it wasn't really true that she had been unfaithful. Jack Bastaple didn't count, Jack Bastaple was nothing. . . .

The things that counted for Caterine were the things that Paul Tremain could give her. Her jewelry in the bank vault and in the wall safe. Oh, she would have planned on coming back, poor silly Caterine, running scared for the first time in her life.

Jenny said huskily, "She paid."

"Too high a price," said Paul. "I should never have let her drive that car."

"Would you have taken her back?"

"Probably."

There were a few lights a long way away, little clusters interspersed by darkness. They were heading for a lonely coastline.

Paul said, "When I first saw Caterine it was like a blow between the eyes. I seemed to recognize her. I'd never seen her before, I'd never even seen a photograph of her, but I felt that she was part of me, that she'd shared everything that had ever happened to me.

"It sounds insane."

He looked at Jenny and she said, "Go on."

"I knew her," he said, "but she wasn't the woman I knew. I stopped looking for that woman in her a long time ago, but she was beautiful and talented and she amused me. Even her greed was tolerable, it was so obvious.

"Yes, I'd have taken her back. I had an affection for her that I thought was as deep as love would go for me."

But he was in no way a shallow man. He was deep as the sea and enduring as the rocks. In his arms she could live forever.

Her lips tasted salt with spray and she went closer to him. He put an arm around her and they stood at the wheel of the *Mylor* and he said quietly, "My ancestors have been here for a thousand years. Do you believe there's such a thing as a race memory?"

They said so, those who should know. That we remembered sometimes, fleetingly, things that had happened to the men and women from whom we came. An echo from the past, a whisper in the blood.

She said, "In the Witch's Cave?"

"What I thought I saw in Caterine," said Paul, "was you."

"Was there a sea witch?"

"There's no record. It's just one of the old Cornish legends."

"If there was," said Jenny, "I think she came back."

"She has," said Paul. He kissed her slow and hard, and there were no lights on the cliffs ahead as the sails folded and the engines purred and the *Mylor* came to a quiet harborage.